This is Volume One of

FOREVER AMBER

This magnificent novel has, in the twenty years of its life, been an enormous bestseller throughout the world: in America, Great Britain, France, Germany, Denmark, Czechoslovakia, Holland, Finland, Bulgaria, Italy, Norway, Portugal, Spain, Sweden, Hungary, and Poland. More than 20,000,000 people saw the 20th Century-Fox film, which was one of the great box-office attractions of its day.

The most striking thing about the book is its obviously authentic background; and its unforgettable heroine, Amber St. Clare, is surely one of the best-known characters in fiction. Abandoned on the streets of London and soon to have a child, sixteen-year-old Amber managed, by her wits, beauty, and courage, to climb to the highest position in the land: the favourite mistress of Charles II.

This is a brilliant, teeming novel, which for sheer excitement and tremendous readability must rank with the most famous books of all time.

Also by KATHLEEN WINSOR

THE LOVERS
STAR MONEY

and published by CORGI BOOKS

KATHLEEN WINSOR

FOREVER AMBER

Volume One

CORGI BOOKS
A DIVISION OF TRANSWORLD PUBLISHERS

FOREVER AMBER Volume One

A CORGI BOOK

Originally published in Great Britain
by Macdonald & Co. (Publishers), Ltd.

PRINTING HISTORY
Macdonald Edition published 1945
Corgi Edition published 1957
Corgi Edition reprinted 1958
Corgi Edition reprinted 1959
Corgi Edition reprinted 1959
Corgi Edition reprinted 1960
Corgi Edition reprinted 1961
Corgi Edition reprinted 1961
Corgi Edition reprinted 1962
Corgi Edition reprinted 1963
Corgi Edition reissued 1965
Corgi Edition reprinted 1965
Corgi Edition reprinted 1966
Corgi Edition reprinted 1967
Corgi Edition reprinted 1967
Corgi Edition reprinted 1968

552 07116 1

Corgi Books are published by Transworld Publishers, Ltd.,
Bashley Road, London, N.W.10

Made and printed in Great Britain by
Richard Clay (The Chaucer Press), Ltd., Bungay, Suffolk

"But, good God! What an age is this, and what a world is this! that a man cannot live without playing the knave and dissimulation."

—Samuel Pepys

1644

PROLOGUE

THE SMALL ROOM was warm and moist. Furious blasts of thunder made the window-panes rattle and lightning seemed to streak through the room itself. No one had dared say what each was thinking—that this storm, violent even for mid-March, must be an evil omen.

As was customary for a lying-in chamber, the room had been largely cleared of its furniture. Now there remained only the bed with its tall head and footboards and linen side curtains, half a dozen low stools, and the midwife's birth-stool, which had arm rests and a slanting back and cut-out seat. Beside the fireplace was a table with a pewter water-basin on it, brown cord and a knife, bottles and ointment-jars, and a pile of soft white cloths. Near the head of the bed was a very old hooded cradle, still empty.

The village women, all perfectly silent, stood close about the bed, watching what was happening there with tense, anxious faces. Sympathetic anguish, pity, apprehension, were the expressions they showed as their eyes shifted from the tiny red baby lying beside the woman who had just given it birth to the sweating midwife bending down and working with her hands beneath the spread blankets. One of the women, pregnant herself, leant over the child, her eyes frightened and troubled—and then all at once the baby gasped, gave a sneeze, and opening its mouth began to yell. The women sighed, relieved.

"Sarah—" the midwife said softly.

The pregnant woman looked up. They exchanged some words in low murmuring voices and then—as the midwife went to the fireplace and sat down to bathe the child from a basinful of warm red wine—the other slid her hands beneath the blankets and with firm gentle movements began to knead the mother's abdomen. There was a look of strained anxiety on her face that amounted almost to horror, but it vanished swiftly as the woman on the bed slowly opened her eyes and looked at her.

Her face was drawn and haggard, with the strange new gauntness of prolonged suffering, and her eyes lay sunk in dark sockets. Only her light blonde hair, flung in a rumpled mass about her head, seemed still alive. As she spoke her voice, too, was thin and flat, scarcely above a whisper.

"Sarah—Sarah, is that my baby crying?"

Sarah did not stop working but nodded her head, forcing a quick bright smile. "Yes, Judith. That's your baby—your daughter." The baby's angry-sounding squalls filled the room.

"My—daughter?" Even exhausted as she was, her disappointment was unmistakable. "A girl—" she said again, in a resentful tired little whisper. "But I wanted a boy. John would have wanted a boy." Tears filled her eyes and ran from the corners, streaking across her temples; her head turned away, wearily, as if to escape the sound of the baby's cries.

But she was too exhausted to care very much. A kind of dreamy relaxation was beginning to steal over her. It was something almost pleasant and as it took hold of her more and more insistently, dragging at her mind and body, she surrendered herself willingly, for it seemed to offer release from the agony of the past two days. She could feel the quick light beating of her heart. Now she was being sucked down into a whirlpool, then swirled up and up at an ever-increasing speed, and as she spun she seemed lifted out of herself and out of the room—swept along in time and space . . .

Of course John won't care if it's a girl. He'll love her just as much—and there will be boys later—boys, and more girls, too. For now the first baby had been born it would be easier next time. That was what her mother had often said, and her mother had had nine children.

She saw John's face, the shock of surprise when she told him that he was a father, and then the sudden breaking of happiness and pride. His smile was broad and his white teeth glistened in his tanned face and his eyes looked down at her with adoration, just as they had looked the last time she had seen him. It was always his eyes she remembered best, for they were amber-coloured, like a glass of ale with the sun coming through it, and about the black centers were flecks of green and brown. They were strangely compelling eyes, as though all his being had come to focus in them.

Throughout her pregnancy she had hoped that this baby would have eyes like John's, hoped with such passionate intensity she never doubted her wish would come true.

From the time she had been a very little girl Judith had known that one day she was to marry John Mainwaring, who would, when his father died, succeed to the earldom of Rosswood. Her own family was a very old one in England—their name had been de Marisco when they had first arrived with the Norman Conqueror, but during the centuries it had changed to Marsh. The Mainwarings, on the other hand, had sprung to their greatest power in the last century, sharing the spoils from the break-up of the Catholic Church. Their lands adjoined and there had been friendship between them for three generations—nothing could be more natural than that the eldest Mainwaring son should marry the eldest Marsh daughter.

John was eight years older than she and for many years he paid her scant attention, though he took it for granted that eventually they would marry; the betrothal papers had been signed while he was yet a child and Judith no more than a baby. All during the years that they were growing up she saw him frequently, for he came often to Rose Lawn to ride and shoot and fence with her four older brothers—but he was no more interested in her than in his own sisters and merely tolerated, with good-natured indifference, her awe-struck admiration. He went away to school—first to Oxford, then to the Inner Temple for a year or so, and finally off to Europe for his Tour. When he returned he found her a young lady, sixteen years old and beautiful, and he fell in love. Since Judith had always been in love with him and the families were so well agreed, there seemed no reason to wait. The wedding was planned for August: the August that war began.

Judith's father, Lord William Marsh, immediately declared for the King, but the Earl of Rosswood—like many others—spent some weeks of indecision before joining the Parliamentarians. Judith had heard the two of them arguing, time and again, for the past year or more, and though they had often grown so angry that they began to shout and brandish their fists, at the end they had always agreed to drink a glass of wine and talk about something else. She never guessed that the quarrels might change her life.

The Earl of Rosswood had said a hundred times that he could stand Charles I's absolutism, but not Laud's church policy—while Lord Marsh was convinced that should the crucial moment come his friend would gather his wits and go with the King. When Rosswood did not he was shocked and then filled with bitterness and hate. Judith had not actually realized that England was at civil war until her mother coolly told her that she must think no more of John Mainwaring—the wedding would never take place.

Stunned, Judith nodded her head in agreement—but she did not really believe it. The war would be over in three months, her father said so, and when it was they would make up the quarrel again and all be friends. The war would be merely a brief unpleasant interval in their lives—it would change nothing of importance, undo no serious plans, destroy no old familiar customs. It would not really affect her or anyone she knew.

But when John came to tell her goodbye before he left for the army, Lord William rode out to meet him in a threatening rage and ordered him off the grounds. Judith cried for hours when she heard about it, for now he was gone away to war with never so much as a kiss between them.

A few days later Lord William and her four brothers went to join the King and with them went most of the able-bodied men on the estate and from the village. The war began to seem real to her now and she hated it, resented the intrusion into her life which had been so secure, so gracious and happy.

As Lord William had predicted, success ran with the Royalists. His Majesty's nephew, gigantic, handsome Prince Rupert, won victory after victory, until almost all England but the southeast corner was in the King's hands. But the rebels did not give up, and the months began to drag on.

Judith was busy, for there was a great deal to do now that the men were gone. She had no time to practice her dancing or singing, to embroider or to play the spinet. But no matter how much work she did she continued to think of John Mainwaring, wondering when he would come back to her, still planning for a future untouched by civil war. Her mother, who guessed easily enough at the reason for Judith's thoughtful quietness, impatiently ordered her to put him out of her mind. She hinted that she and Lord William were planning another and more suitable marriage, to a man whose loyalty was unquestioned.

But Judith did not want or intend to forget John. She could no more have considered marrying another man than she could have accepted some strange new God thrust suddenly upon her.

When John had been gone five months he managed to send her a note, telling her that he was well and that he loved her. "We'll be married, Judith, when the war's over—no matter what our parents have to say." And he added that as soon as he could he would come, somehow, to see her again.

It was mid-June before he was able to keep his promise. Then, making up some story to tell her mother, she rode out to meet him by the little stream which ran between the two properties. It was the first time in all the years they had known each other that they had been perfectly alone, free, and unwatched; and though Judith had felt apprehensive and nervously embarrassed—now she was off her horse and into his arms without hesitation or misgiving. Never before had she felt so sure of herself, so right and content.

"I haven't long, Judith," he said swiftly, kissing her. "I shouldn't be here at all— But I had to see you! Here—let me look at you. Oh, how pretty you are—prettier even than I remembered!"

She clung to him desperately, thinking that she could never let him go again. "Oh, John! John, darling—how I've missed you!"

"It's *wonderful* to hear you say that! I've been afraid— But it doesn't matter, does it—that our parents are quarreling? We love each other just the same—"

"Just the same?" she cried, her throat choking with tears of happiness and dread. "Oh, John! We love each other more! I never knew how much I loved you till you were gone and I was afraid that— Oh, this terrible, terrible war! I hate it!

When will it end, John? Will it end soon?" She looked up at him like a little girl begging a favour, and her blue eyes were large and wistful and frightened.

"Soon, Judith?"

His face darkened and for several moments he was quiet while she watched him anxiously, fear creeping through her.

"*Won't* it be soon, John?"

He slipped one arm about her waist and they started to walk, slowly, toward the river. The sky was blue with great puffs of fleecy clouds, as though a shower had just cleared; the air was full of moisture and the smell of damp earth. Along the banks grew delicate alder and willow trees and white dogwood was in bloom.

"I don't think it will be over soon, Judith," he said finally. "It may last a great while longer—perhaps for years."

Judith stopped, and looked up at him incredulously. At seventeen, six months was an age, one year eternity. She could not and would not face the prospect of years going by in this way, separated.

"For years, John!" she cried. "But it can't! What will we do? We'll be old before we even begin to live! John—" Suddenly she grabbed him by the forearms. "Take me with you! We can be married now. Oh, I don't care how I have to live—" she said quickly as she saw him begin to interrupt. "Other women go with the camp, I know they do, and I can go too! I'm not afraid of anything—I can—"

"Judith, darling—" His voice was pleading, his eyes tender and full of anguish. "We can't get married now. I wouldn't do that to you for anything in the world. Of course there are women following the camp—but not women like you, Judith. No, darling—there's nothing for us to do but wait— It'll end some day— It can't go on forever—"

Suddenly everything that had happened this past year seemed real to her and sharp and with permanent meaning. He was going away, soon, this very day—and when would she see him again? Perhaps not for years—perhaps never— Suppose he was killed— She checked herself swiftly at that, not daring even to admit the possibility. There was no use pretending any longer. The War *was* real. It *was* going to affect their lives. It had already changed everything she had ever hoped for or believed in—it could still take away her future, deny her the simplest wants and needs—

"But, John!" she cried now, bitter and protesting. "What will happen to us then? What will you do if the King wins? And what will become of me if Parliament wins? Oh, John, I'm scared! How is it going to end?"

John turned his head, his jaw setting. "God, Judith, I don't know. What do people do with their lives when a war ends? We'll work it out someway, I suppose."

Suddenly Judith covered her face with her hands and began

to cry, all the loneliness that was past and still to come flooding up within her, bursting out of her control. And John took her into his arms again, trying to soothe and comfort her.

"Don't cry, Judith darling. I'll come back to you. Someday we'll have our home and our family. Someday we'll have each other—"

"Someday, John!" Her arms caught at him desperately, her face was frightened and her eyes reckless. "Someday! But what if someday never comes!"

An hour later he was gone and Judith rode back to the house, happy and at peace, content as never before in her life. For now—no matter what happened, no matter who won or lost the war—they were sure of each other. Sometimes they might have to be apart, but they could never be really separated again. Life seemed simpler to her, and more complete.

At first the thought of seeing her mother again, of looking her squarely in the face, confused and frightened her. She felt as she had when she was a little girl and Lady Anne had always known—even without seeing her at it—whether she had been into mischief. But after the first few uncomfortable days were safely past Judith let herself settle into the luxury of remembering. Every smile, every kiss and touch, each phrase of love, she brought forth again and again like precious keepsakes, to solace her empty hours, comfort her doubts, banish the dark enclosing fears.

Only a month later news came of a great Royalist victory at Roundway Down and Lord William wrote his wife to expect peace at any time. Judith's hopes soared with wild optimism, heedless of Lady Anne's stern warning that neither John Mainwaring nor any member of his family would ever set foot on Rose Lawn again. If only the war would end, no matter *how* it ended, they would work out their problems someway. John had said so.

And then she realized that she was pregnant.

For some time she had been noticing strange symptoms, and though she believed at first that it was only some slight indisposition, finally she knew. The shock sent her to bed for several days. She could not eat and grew pale and thinner, and whenever her mother was in the room she lay watching her with sick apprehension, dreading each glance, each sentence, sure that she saw suspicion in her eyes and heard contempt in her voice. She did not dare think what would happen if they should ever find out. For her father's temper and prejudices were so violent he would surely seek John out and try to kill him. Somehow, before it became noticeable, she must get away—go to John, no matter where he was. She could not give birth to an illegitimate child; it would be a stain upon the honour of her family which nothing could ever erase.

Lord William came back in September, jubilant with tales of Royalist success. "They won't be able to hold against us another month," he insisted. And Judith, who had had not a word from John, listened to her father eagerly—hoping to hear at least the mention of his name, some hint that he was alive and unhurt. But if Lord William knew anything about him he did not speak of it before Judith, and her mother was equally uncommunicative. Both of them pretended to be unaware that John Mainwaring existed or had ever existed.

Then she was told that they had selected a husband for her.

He was Edmund Mortimer, Earl of Radclyffe. Judith had met him a year and a half before, when he had paid a visit to Rose Lawn. He was thirty-five years old, not long widowed, and the father of a baby son. She remembered little except that she had not liked him. He was no more than five feet six or seven inches tall, with delicate bones and head too large for his narrow shoulders and thin body. His features were aristocratic, narrow-nosed and tight-lipped, and though his eyes were hard and cold they reflected a trained, austere intelligence. These were not qualities to recommend him to a girl of seventeen whose heart was full of a handsome, virile, gallant young man. And something about the Earl, she did not know what, repelled her. She would not have wanted him for a husband even if she had never seen John Mainwaring.

"I don't want to get married," she said, half surprised at her own audacity.

Her father stared at her, his eyes beginning to glitter dangerously, but just as he opened his mouth to speak Lady Anne told her to leave the room, adding that she would talk to her later. Judith's sulky stubbornness angered and surprised her parents. Nevertheless they went briskly ahead with plans for the wedding, and did not consult her again, for they were convinced that the sooner she was married and began to get John Mainwaring out of her head the better it would be for everyone concerned.

Her wedding-gown, made a year and a half ago for her marriage to John, was taken out of its trunk, brushed and pressed and hung up in her room. It was heavy white satin, embroidered all over with seed pearls. The deep collar and cuffs were cream-coloured lace, and the slit skirt draped up in back over a petticoat of luminous, crusty silver-cloth. Handmade in France, it was a beautiful and very expensive gown, and at first she had loved it. Now she could not even bring herself to try it on, and passionately told her nurse that she would as soon be fitted for her own shroud.

Some time later the Earl arrived and Judith, though she had been warned repeatedly to show him all respect and affection, refused to do either. She avoided him whenever she could, spoke to him coldly, and cried in her own room for hours without end. The fourth month of her pregnancy had passed and she was in constant terror of being discovered, though her full skirts would certainly give no hint for several weeks longer. Worry and anxiety had made her thin; she jumped nervously at the slightest unexpected sound and was quiet and moody and easily irritated.

What's going to happen to me? she would think wildly as she stood by the windows, hoping, praying to see John or some messenger sent by him come riding up over the hill to save her. But no one came. Since June she had not heard from him. She did not even know whether he was alive or dead.

Her relief was intense, if guilty, when—less than a fortnight before the day set for the wedding—news arrived that the Parliamentarians had attacked a great house twenty miles to the southeast, and the Earl rode off with her father.

Rose Lawn lay on the boundary which separated Royalist territory from that held by Parliament, and news of an attack so near had ominous significance. The house had been kept in readiness for any possible emergency since the beginning of the war and now, following her husband's instructions, Lady Anne began to make preparations for a siege. It was not unusual for a few women and old men to stave off an attacking force for weeks or months, and no one who knew Lady Anne could doubt that if Rose Lawn were to be besieged she would hold it until every last child and dog was dead of starvation.

The following night there was a sudden alarm from the watch. The women began to scream with terror, thinking that the moment had come; children bawled and dogs barked; somewhere a musket went off. Judith leaped from the bed, flung on a dressing-gown, and rushed out to find her mother. She discovered her downstairs in conversation with a farmer, and as she appeared Lady Anne turned and handed her a sealed letter. Judith gave a little gasp and her face turned white, but even under her mother's cold and accusing eyes she could not mask the passionate gratitude and relief she felt. It must be from John. While she tore open the seal and began to read, Lady Anne dismissed the farmer.

"In a few days we will attack Rose Lawn. I cannot prevent the attack but I can carry you and her Ladyship to a place of safety. Bring nothing with you that will make travelling difficult and wait at the mouth of the river beneath the house as soon as it is dark tomorrow night. I won't be able to see you, but I have a servant I can trust and I have made arrangements for you to be cared for until I can come to you."

Judith raised her eyes to her mother's and then slowly, as if by compulsion, she handed her the letter. Lady Anne gave it a quick glance, crossed the room and threw it into the fire. She turned back to face her daughter.

"Well?" she said at last.

Impulsively Judith ran toward her. "Oh, madame, we've got to go! If we stay here we may be killed! He'll take us where we'll both be safe!"

"I do not intend to leave my home at such a time as this.

And certainly I will not accept the protection of an enemy." Her eyes watched Judith coldly. She looked proud, indestructible, and a little cruel. "Make your own choice, Judith, but make it carefully. For if you do I shall tell your father that you were captured. We will never see you again."

Judith had a moment of intense longing to tell her mother what had happened. If only she could explain it to her somehow, could make her understand how truly they loved each other—how impossible it was to stifle that love merely because England was at war— But looking into Lady Anne's eyes she knew that her mother would never understand, that she would only despise and condemn her. The decision was hers to make, and there could be no explanation once she had made it.

With only one extra gown and her few jewels, she left Rose Lawn. All that night she and the servant travelled and by mid-morning of the following day had come to a farmhouse in Essex which was well within the borders of Parliamentary domination. There she was introduced to Sarah and Matthew Goodegroome as Judith St. Claire, wife of John St. Claire, who had left her home because of a quarrel between her family and her husband's. Sarah knew that she was a lady of quality but did not know her rank; and Judith, according to John's instructions, told her nothing more. When the War was over and John came for her they would explain everything. Meanwhile Sarah introduced her to the village women as her own sister, come to live with her because the armies were fighting about her husband's farm.

There was something sure and free and vibrantly contented about Sarah Goodegroome that gave Judith a sense of security and brought back her optimism. They became close friends, and Judith was happier than she had been for a long while.

Whenever he could, John sent her a message, always saying that he would join her as soon as possible. Once he mentioned, briefly, that Rose Lawn still held. But her home, her parents, the Earl of Radclyffe, seemed almost unreal to her now. Her life was absorbed in the farmhouse, in her new friends and the little village of Marygreen, in her thoughts and dreams of John—and most of all in the tiny creature her body carried. Now that her worries and apprehensions were over, now that she was thought to be—and almost thought herself—as respectable a married woman as any of them, she grew happier and prettier by the day. Pregnancy became her well. But she was eager for the day when she would bear John his first son; never once did it occur to her that the child might be a girl.

She was beginning to move restlessly, conscious of painful cramps in the muscles of her arms and legs. She could see only dimly now, as if she had her eyes opened under water. And though she could not tell how much time had gone by, Sarah was still working, kneading her belly with capable strong fingers, her face strained and wet.

I must tell her to stop, thought Judith drowsily. She looks so tired.

She heard the baby squalling and remembered again that it was a girl. I've never even thought of a name for her. What shall I call her? Judith—or Anne—or perhaps it should be Sarah—

And then she said softly, "Sarah—I think I'll name her Amber—for the colour of her father's eyes—"

She became aware of the other women nearby, of a bustle and stir in the room, and now one of them leaned down to lay a warm cloth across her forehead, at the same time removing another which had grown cool. Blankets had been piled on her, but still her face was cold and wet and she could feel moisture on her fingers. Her ears were ringing and the feeling of dizziness came again, swooping down and whirling her up and away until she saw nothing but a hazy blur, heard only a confused murmurous babble.

And then as she moved slightly, trying to ease the cramps that knotted again and again in her legs, Sarah suddenly put her face in her hands and began to sob. Without an instant's hesitation another woman bent, began to work, firmly kneading and massaging.

"Sarah— Please, Sarah—" whispered Judith, full of pity for her.

Very slowly and with great effort she drew her hand from where it lay at her side under the blankets and raised it toward her. As she did so she saw that the palm and fingers were smeared with wet blood. For a moment she stared at it dreamily, without comprehension, and then all at once she understood why she had had such a strange sense of comfort, as though she lay in a warm bath. Her eyes widened with horror and she gave a sharp cry or pleading and protest.

"Sarah!"

Sarah dropped to her knees, her face contorted with grief.

"Sarah! Sarah, help me! I don't want to die!"

The other women were sobbing wildly but Sarah, gaining control of herself again, forced a smile. "It's nothing, Judith. You mustn't be frightened. A little blood is nothing—" But the next moment her features twisted with unbearable anguish and she was crying, unable to control herself any longer.

For several seconds Judith stared at her bowed head and shaking shoulders, full of wild, angry, helpless resentment, terrified. I *can't* be dying! she thought. I can't! I don't want to die! I want to live!

And then slowly she began to drift, floating back into some warm pleasant world where there was no fear of death, where she and John would meet again. She could see nothing at all now, and she let her eyes close—the ringing in her ears had shut out every other sound. She was no longer struggling; she drifted willingly, suffused with so intolerable a tiredness that she welcomed this promise of relief. And then all at once she could hear again, loud and clear, the sound of her daughter's cries. They were repeated over and over, but grew steadily fainter, fading away, until at last she heard them no more.

She tried to speak to Sarah again, to beg for help—to demand it—Sarah! Sarah—don't let me die— But she heard no words, she could not even tell if her lips formed them.

1660

PART I

Chapter One

MARYGREEN DID NOT change in sixteen years. It had changed little enough in the past two hundred.

The church of St. Catherine stood at the northern end of the road, like a benevolent godfather, and from it the houses ran down either side—half-timbered cottages, with overhanging upper stories, and thatched with heather or with straw that had been golden when new, then had turned slowly to a rich brown, and now was emerald green with moss and lichen. Tiny dormer windows looked out, wreathed with honeysuckle and ivy. Thick untrimmed hedges fenced the houses off from the road and there were small wooden gates, some of them spanned by arches of climbing roses. Above the hedges could be seen the confusion of blooming flowers, delphinium and lilacs, both purple and white, hollyhocks that reached almost to the eaves, an apple or plum or cherry tree in full blossom.

At the far end from the church was the green, where on festive occasions the young men played football and held wrestling matches and all the village danced.

There was an inn built of soft red brick and showing the aged silver-grey oaken timbers of its frame; a great sign painted with a crude golden lion swung out over the street on an elaborate wrought-iron arm. Nearby was the blacksmith's cottage with his adjoining shop and the homes and places of business of the apothecary, the carpenter, and another tradesman or two. The rest of the cottages were occupied by husbandmen who divided their time between working on their own small holdings and on the large neighbouring farms. For there was no manor or squire's estate near Marygreen, and the economic existence of the village depended upon the well-to-do yeomen farmers.

The day was quiet and warm, the sky blue with long streaks of white clouds, which seemed to have been put there by a paintbrush drawn across wet water-colour; the air was full of spring moisture and a rich loamy smell of damp earth. Chickens and geese and tiny sparrows had taken possession of the road. A little girl stood before one of the gates, holding a pet rabbit in her arms.

There were few people in sight, for it was late afternoon and each person had his own work to do, so that the only idlers were dogs, a playful kitten or two, and children too young to have learned a useful task. A woman with a basket on her arm walked along the street, pausing for a few moments to talk to another housewife, who threw open an upstairs casement window and leaned out, surrounded as though in a frame with wandering clematis and morning glories. Grouped about the village cross, which had somehow escaped Cromwell's soldiers, were eight or ten young girls—cottagers' daughters who were sent every day to watch their parents' cattle on the common and make sure that no single goat, cow, or sheep should stray or be stolen.

Some of the younger ones were playing "How many miles to Babylon?"—but the three oldest girls talked among themselves, full of indignation and bad humour. With hands on their hips they glared across the common to where two young men, thumbs hooked awkwardly in their breeches, shifting their weight from one foot to another, stood deep in conversation with someone who apparently upset their not too well established poise. But their combined bulk hid whoever it was from view.

"That Amber St. Clare!" muttered the eldest girl with a furious toss of her long blonde hair. "If ever there's a man about, you may be sure *she'll* come along! I think she can smell 'em out!"

"She should 've been married and bedded a year ago—that's what my mother says."

The third girl smiled slyly and said in a knowing sing-song: "Well, maybe she an't married yet, but she's already been—"

"Hush!" interrupted the first, nodding toward the younger children.

"Just the same," she insisted, though she had lowered her voice to a hiss, "my brother says Bob Starling told him he had his way with her on Mothering Sunday!"

But Lisbeth, who had started the conversation, gave a contemptuous snap of her fingers. "Uds Lud, Gartrude! Jack Clarke said the same thing six months ago—and she's no bigger now than she was then."

Gartrude had an answer. "And d'ye want to know why, Lisbeth Morton? B'cause she can spit three times in a frog's mouth, that's why. Maggie Littlejohn seen her do it!"

"Pooh! My mother says *nobody* can spit three times in a frog's mouth."

But the argument was cut short. For suddenly a sound of galloping hoofs echoed through the quiet little valley and a body of men on horseback rounded the turn of the road above St. Catherine's and came rushing headlong up the narrow street toward them. One of the six-year-olds gave a scream of terror and ran to hide behind Lisbeth's skirts.

"It's Old Noll! Come back from the Devil to get us!" Even

dead, Oliver Cromwell had not lost his salutary effect on disobedient youngsters.

The men reined in their horses, bringing them to a prancing nervous halt not more than ten yards from where the girls stood in a close group, their earlier fright and apprehension giving way now to frank admiring interest. There were perhaps fourteen men in all but more than half of them were either serving-men or guides, for they wore plain clothes and kept at a discreet distance from the others. The half-dozen in the lead were obviously gentlemen.

They wore their hair in the shoulder-length cut of the Cavaliers, and their dress was magnificent. Their suits were black velvet, dark red velvet, green satin, with broad white linen collars and white linen shirts. On their heads were wide-brimmed hats with swirling plumes, and long riding capes hung from their shoulders. Their high leather boots were silver-spurred and each man wore a sword at his hip. They had evidently been riding hard for some considerable distance for their clothes were dusty and their faces streaked with dirt and sweat, but in the girls' eyes they had an almost terrifying grandeur.

Now one of the men took off his hat and spoke to Lisbeth, presumably because she was the prettiest. "My services, madame," he said, his voice and eyes lazily good-humoured, and as he looked her over slowly from head to foot, Lisbeth blushed crimson and found it difficult to breathe. "We're looking for a place to eat. Have you a good tavern in these parts?"

Lisbeth stared at him, temporarily speechless, while he continued to smile down at her, his hands resting easily on the saddle before him. His suit was black velvet with a short doublet and wide knee-length breeches, finished with golden braid. He had dark hair and green-grey eyes and a narrow black mustache lined his upper lip. His good looks were spectacular —but they were not the most important thing about him. For his face had an uncompromising ruthlessness and strength which marked him, in spite of his obvious aristocracy, as an adventurer and gambler, a man free from bonds and ties.

Lisbeth, swallowed and made a little curtsy. "Ye mun like the Three Cups in Heathstone, m'lord." She was afraid to recommend her own poor little village to these splendid strangers.

"Where's Heathstone from here?"

"Heathstone be damned!" protested one of the men. "What's wrong with your own ordinary? I'll fall off this jade if I go another mile without food!" He was a handsome blond red-faced young man and in spite of his scowl he was obviously happy and good-natured. As he spoke the others laughed and one of them leaned over to clap him on the shoulder.

"By God, we're a set of rascals! Almsbury hasn't had a mouthful since he ate that side of mutton this morning!"

They laughed again at this for apparently Almsbury's appetite was a well-established joke among them. The girls giggled too, more at ease now, and the six-year-old who had mistaken them for Puritan ghosts came out boldly from behind Lisbeth's skirts and edged a step or two nearer. At that instant something happened to create an abrupt change in the relationship between the men and girls.

"There's nothing wrong with our inn, your Lordship!" cried a low-pitched feminine voice, and the girl who had been talking to the two young farmers came running across the green toward them. The girls had stiffened like wary cats but the men looked about with surprise and sudden interest. "The hostess there brews the finest ale in Essex!"

She made a quick little curtsy to Almsbury and then her eyes turned to meet those of the man who had spoken first and who was now watching her with a new expression on his face, speculative, admiring, alert. While the others watched, it seemed that time stopped for a moment and then, reluctantly, went on again.

Amber St. Clare raised her arm and pointed back down the street to the great sign with its weather-beaten gilt lion shimmering faintly as the falling sun struck it. "Next the blacksmith's shop, m'lord."

Her honey-coloured hair fell in heavy waves below her shoulders and as she stared up at him her eyes, clear, speckled amber, seemed to tilt at the corners; her brows were black and swept up in arcs, and she had thick black lashes. There was about her a kind of warm luxuriance, something immediately suggestive to the men of pleasurable fulfillment—something for which she was not responsible but of which she was acutely conscious. It was that, more than her beauty, which the other girls resented.

She was dressed, very much as they were, in a rust wool skirt tucked up over a green petticoat, a white blouse and yellow apron and tight-laced black stomacher; her ankles were bare and she wore a pair of neat black shoes. And yet she was no more like them than a field flower is like a cultivated one or a sparrow is like a golden pheasant.

Almsbury leaned forward, crossing his arms on his saddle bow. "What in the name of Jesus," he said slowly, "are *you* doing out here in God's forgotten country?"

The girl looked at him, dragging her eyes away from the other man, and now she smiled, showing teeth that were white and even and beautifully shaped. "I live here, m'lord."

"The deuce you do! Then how the devil did you get here? What are you? Some nobleman's bastard put out to suck with a cottager's wife and forgotten these fifteen years?" It was no uncommon occurrence, but she looked suddenly angry, her brows drawing in an indignant scowl.

"I am *not,* sir! I'm as much my father's child as you are—or more!"

The men, including Almsbury, laughed heartily at this and he gave her a grin. "No offense, sweetheart. Lord, I only meant you haven't the look of a farmer's daughter."

She smiled at him quickly then, as though in apology for her show of temper, but her eyes went back immediately to the other man. He was still watching her with a look that warmed all her body and brought a swift-rising sense of excitement. The men were wheeling their horses around and as his turned, its forelegs lifted high, he smiled and nodded his head. Almsbury thanked her and lifted his hat and then they rode off, clattering back up the street to the inn. For a moment longer the girls stood silently, watching them dismount and go through the doorway while the inn-keeper's young sons came to take care of their horses.

When they were out of sight Lisbeth suddenly stuck out her tongue and gave Amber a shove. "There!" she cried triumphantly, and made a sound like a bleating female goat. "Much good it did you, Mrs. Minx!"

Swiftly Amber returned the shove, almost knocking the girl off balance, crying, "Mind your knitting, chatterbox!"

For a moment they stood and glared at each other, but finally Lisbeth turned and went off across the green, where the other girls were rounding up their charges, running and shouting, racing with one another, eager to get home to their evening suppers. The sun had set, leaving the sky bright red along the horizon but turning to delicate blue above. Here and there a star had come out; the air was full of the magic of twilight.

Her heart still beating heavily, Amber crossed back to where she had left her basket lying in the grass. The two young farmers had gone, and now she picked it up again and continued on her way, walking toward the inn.

She had never seen anyone like him before in her life. The clothes he wore, the sound of his voice, the expression in his eyes, all made her feel that she had had a momentary glimpse into another world—and she longed passionately to see it again, if only for a brief while. Everything else, her own world of Marygreen and Uncle Matt's farm, all the young men she knew, now seemed to her intolerably dull, even contemptible.

From her conversations with the village cobbler she knew that they must be noblemen, but what they were doing here, in Marygreen, she could not imagine. For the Cavaliers these past several years had retired into what obscurity they could find or had gone abroad in the wake of the King's son, now Charles II, who lived in exile.

The cobbler, who had fought in the Civil Wars on his Majesty's side, had told her a great many tales of things he had seen and stories he had heard. He had told her of seeing

Charles I at Oxford, of being almost close enough to have touched him, of the gay and beautiful Royalist ladies, the gallant men—it was a life full of colour and spirit and high romance. But she had seen nothing of it, for it disappeared while she was yet a child, disappeared forever the morning his Majesty was beheaded in the yard of his own Palace. It was something of that atmosphere which the dark-haired stranger had brought with him—not the others, for she had scarcely noticed them—but it was something more as well, something intensely personal. It seemed as though, all at once, she was fully and completely alive.

Arriving at the inn she did not go in by the front entrance but, instead, walked around to the back where a little boy sat in the doorway, playing with his fox-eared puppy, and she patted him on the head as she went by. In the kitchen Mrs. Poterell was rushing about in a frenzy of preparation, excited and distraught. On the chopping-block lay a piece of raw beef into which one of the daughters was stuffing a moist mixture of bread-crumbs and onions and herbs. A little girl was cranking up water from the well that stood far in one corner of the kitchen. And the turnspit-dog in his cage above the fireplace gave an angry yowl as another boy applied a hot coal to his hind feet to make him move faster and turn the roasting-joint so it would brown evenly on all sides.

Amber managed to catch the attention of Mrs. Poterell, who was careening from one side of the room to the other, her apron full of eggs. "Here's a Dutch gingerbread Aunt Sarah sent you, Mrs. Poterell!" It was not true, for Sarah had sent the delicacy to the blacksmith's wife, but Amber thought this the better cause.

"Oh, thank God, sweetheart! Oh, I never was in such a taking! Six gentlemen in my house at once! Oh, Lord! What shall I do!" But even as she talked she had begun breaking the eggs into a great bowl.

At that moment fifteen-year-old Meg emerged from the trapdoor which led down into the cellar, her arms full of dusty green bottles, and Amber rushed to her.

"Here, Meg! Let me help you!"

She took five of them from her and started for the other room, pushing the door open with her knee, but she kept her eyes down as she entered, and concentrated all her attention on the bottles. The men were standing about the room, cloaks off though they still wore their hats, and as she appeared Almsbury caught sight of her and came forward, smiling.

"Here—sweetheart. Let me help you with those. So they play that old game out here too?"

"What old game, m'lord?"

He took three of the bottles from her and she set the other two on the table, looking up then to smile at him. But instantly her eyes sought out the other man where he stood next the windows with two companions, throwing dice on a table-top. His back was half turned and he did not glance around but tossed down a coin as one of the others snapped his fingers at a lucky throw. Surprised and disappointed, for she had expected him to see her immediately—even to be looking for her—she turned again to Almsbury.

"Why, it's the oldest game in the world," he was saying. "Keeping a pretty bar-maid to lure in the customers till they've spent their last shilling—I'll warrant you've lured many a farmer's son to his ruin." He was grinning at her and now he picked up a bottle, jerked out the cork and put it to his lips. Amber gave him another smile, arch and flirtatious, wishing that the other man would look over and see her.

"Oh, I'm not the bar-maid here, sir. I brought Mrs. Poterell a cake and helped Meg to carry in the bottles."

Almsbury had taken several swallows, draining half the bottle at once. "Ah, by God!" he declared appreciatively. "Well, then, who are you? What's your name?"

"Amber St. Clare, sir."

"Amber! No farmer's wife ever thought of a name like that."

She laughed, her eyes stealing swiftly across the room and back again, but he was still intent on the dice. "That's what my Uncle Matt says. He says my name should be Mary or Anne or Elizabeth."

Almsbury took several more deep swallows and wiped his mouth with the back of his hand. "Your uncle's a man of no imagination." And then, as she glanced toward the table again, he threw back his head and laughed. "So that's what you want, is it? Well, come along—" And taking hold of her wrist he started across the room.

"Carlton," he said, when they had come up to the group, "here's a wench who has a mind to lay with you."

He turned then, gave Almsbury a glance that suggested some joke between them, and smiled at Amber. She was staring up at him with her eyes big and shining, and had not even heard the remark. She was no more than five-feet three, a height convenient for making even a moderate-sized man feel impressive, but he towered over her by at least a foot.

She caught only a part of Almsbury's introduction. "—a man for whom I have the highest regard even though the bastard does steal every pretty wench I set my eyes on—Bruce, Lord Carlton." She managed to curtsy and he bowed to her, sweeping off his hat with as much gallantry as though she were a princess royal. "We're all of us," he continued, "come back with the King."

"With the King! Is the King come back!"

"He's coming—very soon," said Carlton.

At this astonishing news Amber forgot her nervous embarrassment. For though the Goodegroomes had once been Parliamentarian in sympathy, they had gradually, as had most of the country, begun to long for monarchy and the old ways of life. Since the King's murder his people had grown to love him as they had never done during his lifetime, and that love had been transferred to his heir.

"Gemini!" she breathed. For it was too great an event to realize all at once—and under such distracting conditions.

Lord Carlton took up one of the bottles which Meg had set on the table, wiped the dust from its neck with the palm of his hand, and pulling out the stopper began to drink. Amber continued to stare at him, her self-consciousness now almost drowned in awe and admiration.

"We're on our way to London," he told her. "But one of our horses needs shoeing. What about your inn? Is it a good place to stay the night? The landlord won't rob us—there aren't any bed-bugs or lice?" He watched her face as he talked, and for some reason she did not understand there was a look of amusement in his eyes.

"Rob you?" she cried indignantly. "Mr. Poterell never robbed anybody! This is a mighty fine inn," she declared with staunch loyalty. "The one in Heathstone is *nothing* to it!"

Both men were grinning now. "Well," said Almsbury, "let the landlord steal our shoes and lice be thick as March crows in a fallow field, still it's an English inn and by God a good one!" With that he made her a solemn bow. "Your servant, madame," and went off to find another bottle of sack, leaving them alone.

Amber felt her bones and muscles turn to water. She stood and looked at him, cursing herself for her tongue-tied stupor. Why was it that she—who usually had a pert remark on her tongue for any man no matter what his age or condition—could think of nothing at all to say now? Now, when she longed with frantic desperation to impress him, to make him feel the same violent excitement and admiration that she did. At last she said the only thing she could think of:

"Tomorrow's the Heathstone May Fair."

"It is?"

His eyes went down to her breasts which were full and pointed, upward tilting; she was one of those women who reach complete physical maturity at an early age, and there had long since ceased to be anything of adolescence about her.

Amber felt the blood begin to rise in her neck and face. "It's the finest fair in all Essex," she assured him quickly. "The farmers go ten and twenty miles to it."

His eyes came back to meet hers and he smiled, lifting one eyebrow in apparent wonder at this gigantic local festival, then drank down the rest of his wine. She could smell the faint pungent odour of it as he breathed and she could smell too the heavy masculine sweat on his clothes and the scent of leather from his boots. The combination gave her a sense of dizziness, almost of intoxication, and a powerful longing swept through her. Almsbury's impertinent remark had been no very great exaggeration.

Now he glanced out the window. "It's growing dark. You should be getting home," and he walked to the door, opening it for her.

The evening had settled swiftly and many stars had come out; the highpitched moon was thin and transparent. A cool little breeze had sprung up. Out there they stood alone, surrounded by the talking and laughter from the inn, the quiet country sounds of crickets and a distant frog, the whir of tiny gnats. She turned and looked up at him, her face white and glistening as a moonflower.

"Can't you come to the Fair, my lord?" She was afraid that she would never see him again, and the idea was intolerable to her.

"Perhaps," he said. "If there's time."

"Oh, please! It's on the main road—you'll pass that way! You *will* stop, won't you?" Her voice and eyes pleaded with him, wistful, compelling.

"How fair you are," he said softly, and now for the first time his expression was wholly serious.

For a moment they stood looking at each other, and then Amber swayed involuntarily toward him, her eyes shut. His hands closed about her waist, drawing her to him, and she felt the powerful muscles in his legs. Her head fell back. Her mouth parted to receive his kiss. It was several moments before he released her, but when he did it seemed too soon—she felt almost cheated. Opening her eyes again she saw him looking at her with faint surprise, though whether at himself or her she did not know. The world seemed to have exploded. She was as stunned as though she had been given a heavy blow, and all the strength had gone out of her.

"You must go now, my dear," he said finally. "Your family will be troubled to have you out so late."

Quick impulsive words sprang to her lips. I don't care if they are! I don't care if I never go home again! I don't care about anything but you— Oh, let me stay here and go away with you tomorrow—

But something kept her from saying them. Perhaps the image—somewhere not too far back in her mind—of Aunt Sarah's troubled, cautioning frown, Uncle Matt's stern, lean, reproving face. It would never do to be so bold, for he would only hate her then. Aunt Sarah had often said men did not like a pert woman.

"I don't live far," she said. "Just down this road and over the fields a quarter-mile or so." She was hoping that he would offer to walk the distance with her but he did not, and though she waited a few seconds, at last she dropped him a curtsy. "I'll look for you tomorrow, m'lord."

"I may come. Good-night."

He made her a bow, sweeping off his hat again, and then with a smile and a glance that took her in from head to foot he turned and went inside. Amber stood there a moment like a bewildered child; then suddenly she whirled about and started off at a run and though she stopped once to look back he was gone.

She ran on then—up the narrow road and past the church, quickening her pace as she went by the graveyard where her mother lay buried, and soon she turned right down a tree-lined lane leading over the fields toward the Goodegroome farm. Ordinarily she would have been a little scared to be out alone when it was almost dark, but ghosts and witches and goblins held no terror for her now. Her mind was too full of other things.

She had never seen anyone like him before and had not realized that such a man could exist. He was every handsome, gallant gentleman the cobbler had ever described, and he was what her dreams had embroidered upon those descriptions. Bob Starling and Jack Clarke! A pair of dolts!

She wondered if he was thinking of her now, and felt sure that he must be. No man could kiss a woman like *that* and forget her the next moment! The kiss, if nothing else, she thought, would bring him to the Fair tomorrow—draw him there perhaps in spite of himself. She complimented herself that she understood men and their natures very well.

The night air was cool, as though it had blown over ice, and the meadows were thick with purple clover and white evening campion. Amber approached the farmhouse from the back. She crossed the creek on a bridge which was nothing but a couple of boards with a hand-rail, passed the plot where the cabbages and other vegetables grew, and made her way between the numerous outbuildings—barns and stables and cowsheds—all of them whitewashed, their roofs covered with moss and yellow stone-crop. Then, skirting the edge of the duck-pond, she entered the courtyard.

The house was two-storied, the oak frame ornately carved, and the soft red brick walls were spread with vines. Each chimney was muffled in ivy, and an arched lattice overgrown with honeysuckle framed the kitchen-door, above which had been nailed a horseshoe for protection against witches. In the brick-paved courtyard, over against the walls, grew Sarah's flowers, low clusters of white and purple violets, hollyhocks reaching up to the eaves, a thick clump of fragrant lavender to put between the sheets. Several fruit trees were in bloom, scenting the air with a light sweetness. A low wooden bench had two thatch-roofed beehives on it; attached to the wall beside the door was a tiny bird-house, lost in the pink roses; and a saucy green-eyed kitten sat on the door-sill cleaning its paws.

The house had beauty and peace and the suggestion of an active useful life. It was more than a hundred years old and five generations had lived in it, leaving behind them a comfortable aura of prosperity—not of wealth but of solid ease and plenty, of good food and warmth and comfort. It was a house to love.

As Amber went in she stooped and took the kitten up into her arms, caressing its smooth soft fur with her fingers, hearing it purr with a low, contented little rumble. Supper was over and only Sarah and fifteen-year-old Agnes remained in the kitchen—Sarah just drawing hot loaves of bread from the oven sunk into the wall beside the fireplace, Agnes mending a rushlight.

Agnes was talking, her voice petulant and resentful: "—and it's no wonder they talk about her! I vow and swear, Mother, I'm ashamed she's my cousin—"

Amber heard her but did not care just then. Agnes had said the same thing often enough before. She came into the room with a joyful little cry and ran to fling one arm about her aunt. "Aunt Sarah!" Sarah's head turned and she smiled, but there was a look of searching worry in her eyes. "The inn's full of noblemen! His Majesty's coming home!"

The troubled expression was gone. "Are you sure, child!"

"Aye," said Amber proudly. "They told me so!" She was full of the importance of her news and the wonderful thing that had just happened to her. She thought anyone must be able to tell by looking at her how greatly she had changed since leaving home two hours before.

Agnes looked frankly suspicious—and contemptuous—but Sarah turned and rushed out of the house toward the barns, where most of the men had gone to finish their evening tasks. Amber ran after her. And the moment the news was told, by both women at once, a general shout of rejoicing went up. Men came running out of the barns and cow-sheds, women rushed from their little cottages (there were several on the farm), and even the dogs barked with a loud gay sound as if they, too, would join in the hilarity.

Long live his Majesty, King Charles II!

At market the week before Matthew had heard rumours of a Restoration. They had been floating through the country since early March, carried by travellers, by itinerant pedlars, by all those who had commerce with the great world to the south. Tumbledown Dick, the Protector's son, had been thrown out of his office. General Monk had marched from Scotland, occupied London, and summoned a free Parliament. Civil war seemed on the verge of breaking out again between civilians and the great mobilized armies. These events had left in their wake a trail of weariness and hope—weariness with the interminable troubles of the past twenty years, hope that a restored monarchy might bring them peace again, and security. They yearned for the old familiar ways. And now, if the Cavaliers were returning, it *must* mean that King Charles was coming home—a Golden Age of prosperity, happiness, and peace was about to begin.

When at last the excitement had begun to die down and everyone went back to his work, Amber started for the house. They would get up early tomorrow morning to leave for the Fair and she wanted to sleep long enough to look and feel her best. But as she was going by the dairy on her way into the kitchen she heard her name spoken softly, insistently, and she stopped. There was Tom Andrews standing in the shadows, reaching out a hand to catch her wrist as she went by.

Tom was a young man of twenty-two who worked for her Uncle, and he was very much in love with Amber who liked him for that reason—though she knew that he was by no means a match for her. For she was aware that her mother had left her a dowry which would enable her to marry the richest farmer in the countryside. But she found a certain luxury in Tom's adoration and had encouraged him in it.

Now, with a quick glance around to make certain that neither Aunt Sarah nor Uncle Matt would see her, she went inside. The little room was cool, sweet and fresh, and perfectly dark. Tom caught hold of her roughly, one arm about her waist his hand immediately sliding down into her blouse as he sought for her lips. Obviously this was not new to either of them, and for a moment Amber submitted, letting him kiss and fondle her, and then all at once she broke away, pushing violently at him.

"Marry come up, Tom Andrews! Who gives you leave to be so bold with me!"

She was thinking that it was incredible the kiss of an ordinary man should be so different from that of a lord, but Tom was hurt and bewildered and his hands reached out for her again.

"What's the matter, Amber? What've I done? What's got into you?"

Angrily she wrenched her hand free and ran out. For she now felt herself above such trifling with men of Tom Andrews' station and was only eager to get upstairs and into bed where she could lie and think of Lord Carlton and dream of tomorrow.

The kitchen was deserted except for Sarah, sweeping the flag-stoned floor one last time before going to bed. There were three or four rushlights burning, a circle of tiny moths darting about each tenuous reaching flame, and only the bell-like song of the crickets invaded the evening stillness. Matt came in, scowling, and without a word went to the barrel of ale which stood in a far cool corner of the room, poured himself a pewter mugful and drank it off. He was a middle-sized serious man who worked hard and made a good living and loved his family. And he was conscientious and God-fearing, with strong beliefs as to what was right and what was wrong, what was good and what was bad.

Sarah gave him a glance. "What is it, Matt? Is the foal worse?"

"No, she'll live, I think. It's that girl."

His face was sour and now he went to stand before the great fireplace which was surrounded on all sides with blackened pots and pans, gleaming copper, pewter polished till it looked like silver. Bacon and hams, in great nets, hung from the overhead beams, and there were several thick tied-up bunches of dry herbs.

"Who?" asked Sarah. "Amber?"

"Who else? Not an hour since I saw her come out of the dairy and a minute later Tom Andrews followed her, looking like a whipped pup. She's got the boy half out of his noddle—he's all but useless to me. And what was she doing, pray, down at the inn with a pack of gentlemen?" His voice rose angrily.

Sarah went to stand the broom just outside the door and then closed it, throwing the bolt. "Hush, Matt! Some of the men are still in the parlour. I don't think she was doing anything she shouldn't have. She was just passing by and saw them—it's natural she should stop."

"And come home alone in the dark? Did it take her an hour to hear that the King's to return? I tell you, Sarah, she's got to get married! I won't have her disgracing my family! D'ye hear me?"

"Yes, Matt, I hear you." Sarah went to the cradle beside the fireplace where the baby had begun to stir and whimper, took him out and put him to her breast, then she went to sit down on the settle. She gave a weary little sigh. "Only she don't want to get married."

"Oh!" said Matt sarcastically. "So she don't want to get married! I suppose Jack Clarke or Bob Starling's not good enough for 'er—two of the finest young fellows in Essex."

Sarah smiled gently, her voice soft and tired. "After all, Matt, she is a lady."

"Lady! She's a strumpet! For four years now she's caused me nothing but trouble, and by the Lord Harry I'm fed up to the teeth! Her mother may have been a lady but she's—"

"Matt! Don't speak so of Judith's child. Oh, I know, Matt. It troubles me too. I try to warn her—but I don't know what heed she pays me. Agnes told me tonight— Oh, well, I don't think it means anything. She's pretty and the girls are jealous and I suppose they make up tales."

"I'm not so sure it's just tale-telling, Sarah You've always got a mind to think the best of folks—but they don't always deserve it. Bob Starling asked me for her again today, and I tell you if she an't married soon not even Tom Andrews 'll have her, dowry or no!"

"But suppose her father comes, and finds her married to a

farmer. Oh, Matt, sometimes I think we're not doing the right thing—not telling her who she is—"

"What else can we do, Sarah? Her mother's dead. Her father's dead, too, or we'd have heard some word of him—and we've never found trace of the other St. Clares. I tell you, Sarah, she's got no choice but to marry a farmer and for her to know she's of the quality—" He made a gesture with his hands. "God forbid! the fellow who gets her 's got my pity as 'tis. Why make it any the worse for 'im? Now, don't give me any more excuses, Sarah. It's Jack Clarke or Bob Starling, one or t'other, and the sooner the better—"

Chapter Two

In their painted blue and red wagons, on foot and on horseback, every farmer and cottager within a twenty-mile radius converged upon Heathstone. With him he brought his wife and children, the corn and wheat and livestock he had to sell and the linens or woollens woven by the women during the long winter evenings. But he came to buy also. Shoes and pewter-plates and implements for the farm, as well as many things he did not need but which it would please him to have: toys for the children, ribbons for his daughters' hair, pictures for the house, a beaver hat for himself.

Booths were set up on the green about the old Saxon cross, making lanes which swarmed with people in their holiday dress—full breeches and neckruffs and long-sleeved gowns—all many years out of the style but nevertheless kept carefully in wardrobes from one great occasion to the next. Drums beat and fiddles played. The owners of the booths bawled out their wares in voices which were already growing hoarse. Curious crowds stood and stared, each face contorted with sympathy, to watch a sweating man have his rotten tooth pulled, while the dentist loudly proclaimed that the extraction was absolutely painless. There was a fire-eater and a stilt-walker, trained fleas and a contortionist, jugglers and performing apes, and a Punch and Judy show. Over one great tent flew a flag to announce that a play was in progress—but the Puritan influence remained strong enough so that the audience inside was a thin one.

Amber, standing between Bob Starling and Jack Clarke, frowned and tapped her foot as her eyes ran swiftly and impatiently over the crowd.

Where is he!

She had been there since seven o'clock, it was now after nine, and still she had seen no sign of Lord Carlton or his friends. Her stomach churned with nervousness, her hands were wet and her mouth dry. Oh, but sure, if he was coming at all he'd be here by now. He's gone. He's forgot all about me and gone on—

Jack Clarke, a tall blunt-faced young man, gave her a nudge. "Look, Amber. How d'ye like this?"

"What? Oh. Oh, yes, it's mighty fine."

She turned her head and searched the gleefully yelling group about the jack-pudding who stood on a stand, covered from head to foot with a mess of custard which had been thrown at him, so many farthings a custard.

Oh, why doesn't he come!

"Amber—how d'ye like this ribbon—"

She gave them each a quick smile in turn, trying to drag her mind away from him, but she could not. He had been in her thoughts and heart every waking moment, and if she did not see him again today she knew she would never be able to survive the disappointment. No greater crisis had ever confronted her, and she thought she had met many.

She had dressed with extraordinary care and was sure that she had never looked prettier.

Her skirt, which did not quite reach her ankles, was made of bright green linsey-woolsey, caught up high in back to show a red-and-white-striped petticoat. She had pulled the laces of her black stomacher as tight as possible to display her little waist; and after leaving Sarah she had opened her white blouse down to the valley of her breasts. Wreathing the crown of her head was a garland of white daisies, their stems twisted together, and in one hand she carried a broad-brimmed straw bongrace.

Now, must all that trouble go to waste on a pair of dolts who stood hovering over her, jingling the coins in their pockets and glaring at each other?

"I think I like this—" She spoke absently, indicating a red satin ribbon which lay in the pile on the counter and then, frowning again, she turned her head—and saw him.

"Oh!"

For an instant she stood unmoving, and then suddenly she picked up her skirts and rushed off, leaving them to stare after her, bewildered and astonished. Lord Carlton, with Almsbury and one other young man, had just entered the fair grounds and were standing while an old vegetable woman knelt to wipe their boots according to the ancient custom. Amber got there out of breath but smiling and made them a curtsy to which they all replied by removing their hats and bowing gravely.

"Damn me, sweetheart!" cried Almsbury enthusiastically. "But you're as pretty a little baggage as I've seen in the devil's own time!"

"God-a-mercy, m'lord," she said, thanking him. But her eyes went back instantly to Lord Carlton whom she found watching her with a look that made her arms and back begin to tingle. "I was afraid—I was afraid you were gone."

Agnes and Lisbeth Morton and Gartrude Shakerly. All three of them were staring at her with their mouths wide open—amazed, indignant, shocked, furious with jealousy. Amber's eyes met her cousin's for one instant, she gave an involuntary gasp of horror, and then swiftly looked the other way and tried to pretend she had not seen them. Nervously her fingers began to pick at the brim of her bongrace.

"Uds Lud, your Lordship!" she muttered in an excited undertone. "There's my cousin! She's sure to run and tell my aunt! Let's go over this way—"

She did not see the smile on Carlton's face for already she had started off, making her way through the crowd, and without glancing around at the three girls he followed her. Amber looked back just once to make sure that Agnes was not at their heels and then she gave him the brightest smile she could muster. But she was scared now. Agnes would rush to find Sarah or Matt, and after that she would be sought out by some member of the family and summoned back to safety. They must get away, out of sight—for she was determined to have this hour or two, whatever discomfort it caused her later.

Now she said hastily: "Here's the churchyard—let's go in and make a wish at the well."

He stopped then and she stopped too, looking up at him with a kind of apprehensive defiance. "My dear," he said, "I think you're only going to get yourself into trouble. Evidently your uncle's a very moral gentleman and I'm sure he wouldn't care to have his niece in the company of a Cavalier. Perhaps you're too young to know it, but the Puritans and the Cavaliers don't trust each other—particularly where it concerns female relatives."

There was the same lazy sound in his voice, the same look of mild amusement on his face that had so strangely affected her the night before. For she was able to sense that this idle indifference but thinly concealed a temper at once relentless, fierce, and perhaps a little cruel. Without being able to recognize her own desires she was vaguely conscious of wanting to break through that veneer of urbanity, to experience herself something of the stormy power which was there just under the surface, not dormant but carefully leashed.

She answered him recklessly, for she was beginning to feel more sure of herself. "I don't care about my uncle— My aunt always believes me—Leave me alone for that, your Lordship. *Please,* sir, I want to make a wish."

He shrugged his shoulders and they started on, crossed the road and went through the ivy-grown lych-gate to where two small wells stood three feet or so apart. Amber dropped to her knees between them, plunging one hand in each until the cold water covered her wrists, and then closing her eyes she made a silent wish.

I wish for him to fall in love with me.

For a moment she remained still, concentrating intensely,

and then lifting each cupped hand she drank the water. He reached out one hand and raised her to her feet.

"I suppose you've wished for all the world," he said. "How long before you'll get it?"

"In a year—if I believe it—but never, if I don't."

"But of course you do?"

"All my other wishes came true. Don't you want to wish too?"

"A year isn't long enough for most of my wishes."

"Not long enough? Gemini! I'd thought a year must be long enough for anything!"

"When you're seventeen, it is."

She began looking around her then, partly because she could no longer meet the steady stare of his green-grey eyes, but also because she was searching for some place where they might go. The churchyard was too public. Other people were likely to wander that way at any time, and every man or woman or child seemed a threat to her happiness. She felt that they were all in league to call her away, to make her leave him and go back to the dry sterile protection of her uncle and aunt.

At the side of the church was a garden and beyond it the meadow which separated Heathstone from Bluebell Wood. Why, that was the place of course! In the wood it was cool and dark and there were many little nooks where no one would ever see them—she knew several, remembered from the Fairs of the past three or four years. Now she started off that way, hoping that he would think they had merely chanced upon it.

They went through the garden, climbed the stile, and set out across the meadow.

The grass there was sown thickly with buttercups and field daisies and wild yellow irises. Underfoot the ground was spongy with contained water and their feet sank a little at every step. Farther ahead near the river was an orange wash of colour where the marigolds grew, and as they came closer they could see the tall green reeds standing in the water. On the banks were pussywillow trees and across the stream at the edge of the forest was a cluster of aspen, their leaves glistening like sequins in the sun.

"I'd almost forgotten," he said, "how beautiful England is in the spring."

"How long since you left it?"

"Almost sixteen years. My mother and I went abroad after my father was killed at Marston Moor."

"Sixteen years abroad!" she cried incredulously. "Lud, how'd you shift?"

He looked down at her, smiling with a kind of tenderness. "It wasn't what any of us would have chosen, but the choice wasn't ours. And for my part I've got no complaint to make."

"You didn't like it over there?" she demanded, shocked and almost indignant at this blasphemy.

Now they were crossing the swift-flowing river on a narrow shaky footbridge built of logs; below them the fish darted and dragon-flies zoomed low over the water and among the lily-pads that grew in a quiet pool. On the other side they entered the forest and took a wandering faint little path which led among the trees and ferns and flowering wild hyacinth. It was cool in there and still, fragrant with the smell of flowers and rotting leaves.

"I suppose it's petty treason for an Englishman to admit he likes another country. But I liked several of them—Italy and France and Spain. But America most of all."

"America! Why, that's across the ocean!" That was, in fact, all she knew about America.

"A long way across," he admitted.

"Was the King there?"

"No. I sailed once on a privateering expedition with his Majesty's cousin, Prince Rupert, and another time on a merchant-fleet."

She was entranced. To have seen such faraway places—to have even sailed across the ocean! It was incredible as a fairy-tale. Heathstone was as far from home as she had ever been, and that just twice a year, for the spring and autumn fairs. While the only person in her acquaintance who had been to London, twenty-five miles south-west of Marygreen, was the cobbler.

"What a fine thing it must be to see the great world!" she heaved a sigh. "Have you been to London, too?"

"Just twice since I've been old enough to remember. I was there ten years ago and then a couple of months after Cromwell died. But I didn't stay long either time."

They had stopped now and he gave a glance up at the sky, through the trees, as though to see how much time was left. Amber, watching him, was suddenly struck with panic. Now he was going—out again into the great world with its bustle and noise and excitement—and she must stay here. She had a terrible new feeling of loneliness, as if she stood in some solitary corner at a party where she was the only stranger. Those places he had seen, she would never see; those fine things he had done, she would never do. But worst of all she would never see him again.

"It's not time to go yet!"

"No. I have a while longer."

Amber dropped onto her knees in the grass, her mouth pouting, eyes rebellious—and after a moment he sat down facing her. For several seconds she continued staring sulkily, mulling over her dismal future, and then swiftly her eyes went to his. He was watching her, steadily, carefully. She stared back at him, her heart pounding, and there began to steal over her a slow weakness and languor, so consuming that even her eyes felt heavy. Every part of her was tormented with longing for him. And yet she was half-scared, uncertain, and reticent, filled with a sense of dread almost greater than her desire.

At last his arm reached out, went around her waist, and drew her slowly toward him; Amber tipping her head to meet his mouth, slid both her arms about him.

The restraint he had shown thus far now vanished swiftly, giving way to a passion that was savage, violent, ruthlessly selfish. Amber, inexperienced but not innocent, returned his kisses eagerly. Spurred by the caressing of his mouth and hands, her desire mounted apace with his, and though at first she had heard, somewhere far back in her mind, Sarah calling out to her, warning her, the sound and the image grew fainter, dissolved, and was gone.

But when he forced her back onto the earth she gave a quick movement of protest and a little cry—this was as far as her knowledge went. Something mysterious, almost terrible, must lie beyond. Her hands pushed at his chest and she gave a frightened little sob, twisting her face away from his. Her fear now was irrational, intense, almost hysterical.

"No!" she cried. "Let me go!"

She saw his face above her, and his eyes had become pure glittering green. Amber, crying, half-mad with passion and terror, suddenly let herself relax.

With slow reluctance Amber became again conscious of the surrounding world, and of both of them as separate individuals. She drew a deep luxurious sigh, her eyes still closed—she felt that she could not have moved so much as a finger.

After a long while he drew away from her and sat up, forearms resting on his knees, a long blade of grass between his teeth, staring ahead. His tanned face was wet with sweat and he mopped across it with the black-velvet sleeve of his doublet. Amber lay perfectly still beside him, eyes closed and one arm flung over her forehead. She was warm and drowsy, marvellously content, and glad with every fibre of her being that it had happened.

It seemed that until this moment she had been only half alive.

Aware of his eyes on her she turned her head slightly and gave him a lazy smile. She wanted to say that she loved him but did not quite dare, even now. She wished he would say that he loved her, but he only bent and kissed her, very gently.

"I'm sorry," he said softly. "I didn't expect to find you a virgin."

"I'm glad I was."

Was that all he was going to say? She waited, watching him, beginning to feel uncertain and a little afraid. He looked again as he had when she first saw him—she could never tell now by his expression or manner how close they had been. She was surprised and hurt, for what had happened should have changed him as much as it had her. Nothing should ever be the same again, for either of them.

At last he got up, squinting overhead at the sun. "They'll be waiting for me. We want to get into London before nightfall." He reached down a hand to help her and she jumped up quickly, shaking out her hair, smoothing her blouse, touching her earrings to make sure she had not lost them.

"Lud, we mustn't be late!"

Knocking at the dust on his hat, he gave her a glance of quick astonishment, then set it back on his head. He scowled, as though he had got more than he had bargained for.

At his look, Amber's smile and excitement went suddenly dead. "Don't you *want* me to go?" She was almost ready to cry.

"My dear, your aunt and uncle would never approve."

"What do I care! I want to go with *you!* I hate Marygreen! I never want to see it again! Oh, please, your Lordship. *Let* me go with you." Marygreen and her life there had suddenly become intolerable. He had crystallized all the restlessness, the thirst and longing for a broader, brighter life which had been working within her, half unrealized, ever since she had first talked to the cobbler many years ago.

"London's no place for an unmarried girl without money or acquaintance," he said in a matter-of-fact tone, which even Amber knew meant that he did not care to be troubled with her. And then he added, perhaps because he was sorry to hurt her, "I won't be there long. And what would you do when I go? It wouldn't be easy to come back here—I know well enough what an English village thinks of such escapades. And in London there aren't many means of livelihood open to a woman. No, my dear, I think you'd better stay here."

All of a sudden, to his surprise as well as her own, she burst into tears. "I won't stay here! I *won't!* I can't stay here now! How d'ye think I'm to explain to my Uncle Matt where I've been these two hours—when a hundred people I know saw us leave the fair grounds!"

A look of annoyance crossed his face, but she did not see it. "I told you that would happen," he reminded her. "But even if he's angry it'll be better for you to go back and—"

She interrupted him. "I'm not going back! I won't live here any more, d'ye hear? And if you won't take me with you—then I'll go alone!" She stopped suddenly and stood looking up at him, angry and defiant, but pleading, too. "Oh, please—your Lordship. Take me along."

They stood and stared at each other, but at last his scowl faded away and he smiled. "Very well, you little minx, I'll take you. But I won't marry you when we get there—and don't forget, whatever happens, that I told you so."

She heard only the first part of what he said, for the last seemed of no immediate importance. "Oh, your Lordship! *Can* I go! I won't be any trouble to you, I swear it!"

"I don't know about that," he said slowly. "I think you'll be aplenty."

It was mid-afternoon when they rode into London over Whitechapel Road, passing the many small villages which hung on the edge of the city and which despite their nearness to the capital differed in no external aspect from Heathstone or Marygreen. In the open fields cattle grazed, wrenching lazily at the grass, and cottagers' wives had spread their wash to dry on the bushes. As they rode along they were recognized for returning Royalists and were cheered wildly. Little boys ran along beside them and tried to touch their boots, women leant from their windows, men stopped in the streets to take off their hats and shout.

"Welcome home!"

"Long live the King!"

"A health to his Majesty!"

The walled City was a pot-pourri of the centuries, old and ugly, stinking and full of rottenness, but full of colour too and picturesqueness and a decayed sort of beauty. On all sides it was surrounded with a wreath of laystalls, piled refuse carted that far and left, overgrown with stinking-orage. The streets were narrow, some of them paved with cobblestones but most of them not, and down the center or along the sides ran open sewage kennels. Posts strung out at intervals served to separate the carriage-way from the narrow space left to pedestrians. And across the streets leaned the houses, each story overhanging the one beneath so as to shut out light and air almost completely from the tightest of the alleys.

Church-spires dominated the skyline, for there were more than a hundred within the walls and the sound of their bells was the ceaseless passionately beautiful music of London. Creaking signs swung overhead painted with golden lambs, blue boars, red lions, and there were a number of bright new ones bearing the Stuart coat-of-arms or the profile of a swarthy black-haired man with a crown on his head. In the country it had been sunny and almost warm but here the fog hung heavily, thickened with the smoke from the fires of the soap-boilers and lime-burners, and there was a penetrating chill in the air.

The streets were crowded: Vendors strolled along crying their wares in an age-old sing-song which was not intended to be understood, and a housewife could make almost all necessary purchases at her own doorstep. Porters carried staggering loads on their backs and swore loudly at whoever interrupted their progress. Apprentices hung in the shop doorways bawling their recommendations, not hesitating to grab a customer by the sleeve and urge him inside.

There were ballad-singers and beggars and cripples, satin-suited young fops and ladies of quality in black-velvet masks, sober merchants and ragged waifs, an occasional liveried footman going ahead to make way for the sedan-chair of some baronet or countess. Most of the traffic was on foot but some travelled in hackney-coaches which plied for public hire, in chairs, or on horseback, but when the traffic snarled, as it often did, these were liable to be stalled for many minutes at a time.

It took no sharp eye to see at a glance that the Londoner was a different breed from the country Englishman. He was arrogant with the knowledge of his power, for he was the kingdom and he knew it. He was noisy and quarrelsome, ready to start a murderous battle over which man got the walk nearest the wall. He had supported Parliament eighteen years before but now he prepared joyously for the return of his legitimate sovereign, drinking his health in the streets, swearing that he had always loved the Stuarts. He hated a Frenchman for his speech and his manners, his dress and his religion, and would pelt him with refuse or blow the froth from a mug of ale into his face before proposing a toast to his damnation. But he hated a Dutchman or any other foreigner almost as fiercely, for to him London was the world, and a man worth less for living out of it.

London—stinking dirty noisy brawling colourful—was the heart of England, and its citizens ruled the nation.

Amber felt that she had come home and she fell in love with it, as she had with Lord Carlton, at first sight. The intense violent energy and aliveness found a response in her strongest and deepest emotions. This city was a challenge, a provocation, daring everything—promising even more, She felt instinctively, as a good Londoner should, that now she had seen all there was to see. No other place on earth could stand in comparison.

The group of horsemen parted company at Bishopsgate, each going his separate way, and Bruce and Amber went on alone with two of the servingmen. They rode down Gracious Street and, at the sign of the Royal Saracen, turned and went through a great archway into the courtyard of the inn. The building enclosed it on every side and galleries ran all the way around each of the four stories. Bruce helped her to dismount and they went in. The host was nowhere about and after a few moments Bruce asked her to wait while he went out to find him.

Amber watched him go, her eyes shining with pride and admiration and the almost breathless excitement she felt. I'm in London! It can't be true but it is. I *am* in London! It seemed incredible that her life could have changed so swiftly and so irrevocably in less than twenty-four hours. For she was determined that no matter what happened she would never return to Marygreen. Never as long as she lived.

Wearing Bruce's cloak she moved nearer to the fire, reaching out her hands to its warmth, and as she did so she became conscious that there were three or four men sitting over against the diamond-paned casement, drinking their ale and watching her. She had a quick sense of pleased surprise, for these men were Londoners, and she turned her head a little to give them a view of her profile with its delicate slightly tilted nose, full lips, and small round chin.

At that moment Bruce came back, looking down and grinning at the little man who walked beside him and who reached scarcely to his shoulder. Evidently he was the host, and he seemed to be in a state of great excitement.

"By God, your Lordship!" he was shouting. "But I swear I thought you were dead! They were here not a half-hour after you'd gone, those Roundhead rogues, and they tore my house apart to find you! And when they didn't they were in such a rage they carried me into the courtyard and flung me into the coalhole!" He made a noise and spat onto the floor. "Bah! Plague take 'em! I hope to see 'em all strung up like hams on Tyburn Hill!"

Bruce laughed. "I don't doubt you'll get your wish." By now they had come to where Amber was standing and the host gave a start, for he had not realized she was there; then he made her a jerky little bow. "Mrs. St. Clair," said Bruce, "may I introduce our host, Mr. Gumble!" She was relieved that he called her "Mrs." St. Clair, for only very little girls and professed whores were called Miss.

Amber nodded her head and smiled, feeling that she had now advanced too far in the world to curtsy to an innkeeper. But she did have an uncomfortable moment of wondering if the look he gave her meant that he disapproved of his Lordship travelling with a woman who was not his wife. Bruce, however, seemed as casual as if she were his sister, and Mr. Gumble immediately took up the conversation where he had been interrupted:

"It's mighty lucky you're not a day later, my lord. I vow and swear my house has never been so crowded—all England's come to London to welcome his Majesty home! By the end of the week there won't be a room to let between here and Temple Bar!"

"How is it you haven't set a crown on your Saracen to pass him for the King? Half the signs we've seen are King's Heads or King's Arms."

"Ho! They are, at that! And have you heard what they're saying now? If the King's Head is empty—the King's Arms are full!" He shouted with laughter at that, Bruce grinned, and even the men across the room gave out noisy guffaws. But Amber did not know enough of his Majesty's reputation to quite understand the jest.

The little man took out his handkerchief and mopped at his perspiring brow. "Ah, well, we'll be mighty glad to have him home, I warrant you. 'Sdeath, your Lordship! You'd never think what we've been through here! No cards, no dice, no plays. No drinking, no dancing. My God! They even wanted to make fornication a capital crime!"

Bruce laughed. "I'm glad I stayed abroad."

But again Amber missed the point because she did not know what "fornication" meant. Still, she smiled appreciatively and tried to look as though such witticisms were a commonplace to her.

"Well, enough of this. Your Lordship must be hungry, and perhaps tired. I have the Flower de Luce still vacant—"

"Good! It brought me luck last time— Perhaps it will again."

They started up the stairs and as they went they heard the men below begin to sing, their voices roaring out in jovial good humour, off key and untuned:

"The King he loves a bottle, my boys,
The King he loves a bowl!
He will fill a bumping glass
To every buxom lass
And make cuckolds of us all, my boys.
And make cuckolds of us all!"

At the top of the staircase Mr. Gumble unlocked a door and stepped back to let them go in. The room was of good size and, in Amber's opinion, very magnificent, for she had never seen anything like it before.

The walls were panelled oak, dark and rich, and the chimney piece was also oak, elaborately carved with patterns of fruit and flowers. The floor was bare and all the furniture was in the heavy florid style belonging to the early years of the century, though the chairs and stools had been covered with thick cushions of sage-green or ruby-coloured velvet, worn just enough to have acquired a look of mellowness.

In the bed chamber was an immense four-poster bed hung with red velvet curtains which could be pulled at night to enclose the occupants in privacy and suffocation. Two wardrobes stood against the wall for clothing. There were several stools and a couple of chairs, a small table with a mirror hung above it, and a writing-table. One side of the room was filled with long windows and had doors opening onto the gallery, from which a flight of stairs led down to the courtyard.

Amber stared about her, momentarily speechless, while Bruce said, "It looks like home. We'll take our supper up here— Send whatever you think is best."

After several assurances that he would furnish anything at all which either of them might require, Mr. Gumble left—and Amber burst suddenly out of her spell. Flinging off the cloak she ran to look out of the parlour windows, down two stories into the street. A group of boys had built a fire there and were roasting skewered chunks of meat in derision of the Rump

Parliament; the voices of the men still singing downstairs filtered up faintly through the solid walls.

"Oh! London! London!" she cried passionately. "I love you!"

Bruce smiled, tossing off his hat, and coming up behind her he slid one arm about her waist. "You fall in love easily." And then, as she turned about quickly to look up at him he added, "London eats up pretty girls, you know."

"Not me!" she assured him triumphantly. "I'm not afraid!"

Chapter Three

AND now at last, when it had seemed that nothing would ever change, he was coming home to England and to his people. Charles Stuart was Charles Lackland no longer.

Eleven years before, a little band of Puritan extremists had beheaded his father—and the groan that had gone up from the watching thousands echoed across Europe. It was a crime that would forever lie heavily upon English hearts. Exiled in France, the dead King's eldest son first knew that his efforts to save his father had failed when his chaplain knelt and addressed him as "your Majesty." He turned and went into his bedroom to mourn alone. He found himself a king with no kingdom, a ruler with no subjects.

And in England the mighty heel of Cromwell came down on the necks of the English people. It was now a crime to be a member of the aristocracy, and to have been loyal to the late King was an offense often punishable by confiscation of lands and money. Those who could followed Charles II abroad, hoping to return someday in a happier time. A gloomy piety settled over the land, discouraging much that was essentially English: the merry good humour, the boisterous delight in sports and feasts and holidays, the robust enjoyment of drinking and dancing and gambling and love-making.

May-poles were chopped down, theatres closed. Discreet women left off their gaily coloured satin and velvet gowns, put away their masks and fans and curls and false hair, covered in the low necklines of their dresses and no longer dared touch their lips with rouge or stick on a black patch for fear of falling under the suspicion of having Royalist sympathies. Even the furniture grew more sober.

For eleven years Cromwell ruled the land. But England found at least that he was mortal.

When the news of his illness began to get abroad an anxious crowd of soldiers and citizens gathered at the gates of the Palace. The country was in terror, remembering the chaotic years of the Civil Wars when bands of roving soldiers had pillaged through all the length and breadth of England, plundering the farms, breaking into and robbing houses, driving off the sheep and cattle, killing those who dared to resist. They did not want Cromwell to live, but they were afraid to have him die.

As night closed in, a great storm rose, gathering fury until the houses rocked on their foundations, trees were uprooted, and turrets and steeples crashed to the ground. Such a storm could have for them only one meaning. The Devil was coming to claim the soul of Oliver Cromwell. And Cromwell himself cried out in terror: "It's a fearful thing to fall into the hands of the living God!"

The storm swept all of Europe, raging through the night and on into the next day, and when Cromwell died at three o'clock in the afternoon it was still desolating the island. His body was immediately embalmed and buried with haste. But his followers clothed a waxen image of him in robes-of-state and set it up in Somerset House, as though he had been a king. In derision the people flung refuse at his funeral escutcheon.

But there was no one to take his place, and almost two years of semi-anarchy followed. His son, whom the Protector had designated to succeed him, had none of his father's ability, and at last the military autocrats got rid of him—much to his own relief. Immediately skirmishes began between the cavalry and the infantry, between veterans and new recruits, and another civil war between the army and the people seemed inevitable. Despair flooded the land. To go through with it all again—when nothing had been gained the first time. They began to think of a restored monarchy with longing, as their only salvation.

General Monk, who had served Charles I but who had finally gone into service for Cromwell when the King was dead, marched from Scotland and occupied the capital with his troops. Monk, though a soldier, believed that the military must be subordinate to the civil power, and it was his scope to liberate the country from its slavery to the army. He waited cautiously to determine the temper of the country and then at last, convinced that the royalist fervour which swept through all classes was an irresistible tide, he declared for Charles Stuart. A free Parliament was summoned, the King wrote them a letter from Breda declaring his good intentions, and England was to be, once more, a monarchy—as she preferred.

London was packed to overflowing with Royalists and their wives and families, and if a man existed in all the city who did not wholeheartedly long for his Majesty's return he was silent, or hidden. And the gradual return to laughter and pleasure which had been apparent since the end of the wars took a sudden violent spurt. Restraint was thrown off. A sober garment, a pious look were regarded as sure signs of a Puritan sympathy and were shunned by whoever would show his loyalty to the King. The world did a somersault and everything which had been vice was now, all at once, virtue.

But it was not merely a wish to appear loyal, a temporary exuberance at the returning monarchy, the joyousness of sudden relief from oppression. It was something which struck deeper, and which would be more permanent. The long years of war had broken families, undermined old social traditions, destroyed the barriers of convention. A new social pattern was in the making—a pattern brilliant but also gaudy, gay but also wanton, elegant but also vulgar.

On the 29th of May, 1660—his thirtieth birthday—Charles II rode into London.

It was for him the end of fifteen years of exile, of trailing over Europe from one country to another, unwanted anywhere because his presence was embarrassing to politicians trying to do business with his father's murderer. It was the end of poverty, of going always threadbare, of having to wheedle another day's food from some distrustful innkeeper. It was the end of the fruitless efforts to regain his kingdom which had occupied him incessantly for over ten years. Above all it was the end of humiliation and scorn, of being ridiculed and slighted by men who were his inferiors in rank and in everything else. It was at long last the end of being a man without a country and a king without a crown.

The day was clear and bright, brilliantly sunlit, perfectly cloudless, and people told one another that the weather was a good omen. From London Bridge to Whitehall, along his line of march, every street and balcony and window and rooftop was packed. And though the procession was not expected until after noon, by eight in the morning there was not a foot of space to be found. Trainbands to the number of 12,000 men lined the streets—they had fought against Charles I but were now detailed to keep the crowds in order for his son's return.

The signs were draped with May flowers; great arches of hawthorn spanned every st[illegible] and green oak boughs had been nailed over the fronts of many buildings. Garlands looped from window to window were decorated with ribbons and silver spoons, brightly polished, gleaming in the sun. From the homes of the well-to-do floated tapestries and gold and scarlet and green banners—flags whipped out gallantly on even the humblest rooftop. The fountains ran with wine and bells pealed incessantly from every church steeple in the city. At last the deep ponderous booming of cannon announced that the procession had reached London Bridge.

It began to wind slowly through the narrow streets, the horses' hoofs clopping rhythmically on the pavement, trumpets and clarinets shrilling, kettledrums rolling with a sound as of thunder echoing across the hills. The whole procession glittered and sparkled—fabulously, almost unbelievably splendid. It passed in a stream that seemed to have no end: troops of men in scarlet-and-silver cloaks, black velvet and gold, silver and green, with swords flashing, banners flying, the horses prancing and snorting, lifting their hoofs daintily and with pride. Hour after hour it went on until the eyes of the onlookers grew dazzled and began to ache, their throats were raw from shouting, and their ears roared with the incessant clamour.

The hundreds of loyal Cavaliers, men who had fought for the first Charles, who had sold their goods and their lands to help him and who had followed his son abroad, rode almost at the end. They were, without exception, handsomely dressed and mounted—though all this finery had been got on credit. After them came the Lord Mayor, carrying his naked sword of office. On one side of him was General Monk, a short stout ugly little man, who nevertheless sat his horse with dignity and commanded respect from soldiers and civilians alike. Next to the King he was perhaps the most popular man in England that day. And on the Lord Mayor's other side rode George Villiers, second Duke of Buckingham.

The Duke, a big, handsome, flagrantly virile man, with hair blond as a god's, smiled and nodded to the women in the balconies who flung him kisses and tossed flowers in his path. His rank was second only to that of the princes of the blood, and his private fortune was the greatest in England. For he had contrived to marry the daughter of the Parliamentarian general to whom his vast lands had been given, and so had saved himself. Many knew that for his numerous treacheries he was in disfavor amounting almost to disgrace, but the Duke looked as well pleased with himself as though he had personally engineered the Restoration.

Following them came several pages, many trumpeters whose banners bore the royal coat-of-arms, and drummers shining with sweat as they beat out a mighty roar. At their heels rode Charles II, hereditary King of England, Ireland, and France, Monarch of Great Britain, Defender of the Faith. A frenzy of adoration, hysterical and almost religious, swept through the people as he passed, and surged along before him. They fell to their knees, reaching out their hands toward him, sobbing, crying his name again and again.

"God bless your Majesty!"

"Long live the King!"

Charles rode slowly, smiling, raising one hand to them in greeting.

He was tall, more than six feet, with a look of robust good health and animal strength. His physique was magnificent and never showed to better advantage than on horseback. The product of many nationalities, he looked far more a Bourbon or a Medici than he did a Stuart. His skin was swarthy, his eyes black, and he had an abundance of black shining hair that fell heavily to his shoulders and rolled over on the ends into great natural rings; when he smiled his teeth gleamed white beneath a narrow moustache. His features were harsh and strongly marked, seared by disillusion and cynicism, and yet in spite of that he had a glowing charm that went out to each of them, warming their hearts.

They loved him on the instant.

On either side of him rode his two younger brothers. James, Duke of York, was likewise tall, likewise athletic, but his hair was blond and his eyes blue, and more than any of the other children had he resembled his dead father. He was a handsome man, three years younger than the King, with thick well-defined dark eyebrows, a slight cleft in his chin and a stubborn mouth. But it was his misfortune that he did not have his brother's instantly winning manner. And from the first they held in reserve their estimation of him, critical of certain coolness and hauteur they discovered in his expression which offended them. Henry, Duke of Gloucester, was only twenty, a happy vivacious young man who looked as though he was in love with all the world and did not doubt that in return it loved him.

It was late that night when at last the King begged off from further ceremonies and went to his own apartments in Whitehall Palace, thoroughly exhausted but happy. He entered his bedchamber still wearing his magnificent robes and carrying on one arm a little black-and-tan spaniel with a plume-like tail, long ears, and the petulant face of a cross old lady. Between his feet scampered half-a-dozen dogs, yapping shrilly—but at a sudden raucous screech they skidded to a startled halt and looked up. There was a green parrot, teetering in a ring hung from the ceiling, eyeing the dogs and squawking angrily.

"Damn the dogs! Here they come again!"

Recognizing an old enemy the spaniels quickly recovered their courage and ran to stand in a pack beneath him jumping and barking while the bird bawled down his curses. Charles and all the gentlemen who followed him laughed to see them, but finally the King gave a tired wave of his hand and the menagerie was removed to another room.

One of the courtiers thrust his fingers into his ears and shook his head vigorously. "Jesus! I swear I'll never be able to hear again! If there's a man left in London who can use his voice tomorrow—he's a traitor and deserves to be hanged."

Charles smiled. "To tell you the truth, gentlemen, I think I can blame only myself for having stayed so long abroad. I haven't met a man these past four days who hasn't told me he's always desired my return."

The others laughed. For now that they were home again, lords of creation once more and not unwanted paupers edged from one country to another, they found it easy to laugh. The years gone by had begun already to take on a kind of patina, and now they knew the story had a happy ending they could see that, after all, it had been a romantic adventure.

Charles, who was being helped out of his clothes, turned to one of the men and spoke to him in a low voice. "Did she come, Progers?"

"She's waiting belowstairs, Sire."

"Good."

Edward Progers was his Majesty's Page of the Backstairs. He handled private money transactions, secret correspondence, and served in an ex-officio capacity as the King's pimp. It was a position of no mean prestige, and of considerable activity.

At last they trooped out and left him alone, giving them a lazy wave of his arm as he stood there in riding-boots, knee-length breeches, and a full-sleeved white linen shirt. Progers went also, by another door, and Charles strolled over to stand by the open windows, snapping his fingers impatiently while he waited. The night air was cool and fresh, and just below ran the river, where several small barges floated at anchor, their lanterns pricking the water like so many fireflies. The Palace lay around the bend of the Thames, but the innumerable bonfires back in the city had cast a glow against the sky and he could see the flashing yellow trails of rockets as they shot up and then dropped hissing into the water. The booming of cannon came again and again, and faintly the sound of bells still ringing.

For several moments he stood at the windows, staring out, but the expression on his face was moody and almost sad. He looked like a tired, bitter, and disappointed man, far more than like a king returned in triumph to his people. And then, at the sound of a door opening behind him, he spun swiftly on his heel, and his face lighted with pleasure and admiration.

"Barbara!"

"Your Majesty!"

She bent her head, curtsying low, as Progers backed discreetly out of the room.

She was some inches smaller than he but still tall enough to be imposing. Her figure was magnificent, with swelling breasts and small waist, suggesting lovely hips and legs concealed by the full satin skirts of her gown. She wore a violet velvet cloak, the hood lined in black fox, and she carried a great black-fox muff with a spray of amethysts pinned to it. Her hair was dark red, her skin clear and white, and the reflection from her cloak changed her blue eyes to purple. She was strikingly, almost aggressively beautiful, creating an immediate impression of passion and a wild, lusty untamableness.

Instantly Charles crossed and took her into his arms, kissing her mouth, and when at last he released her she tossed aside her muff and dropped off her cloak, aware of his eyes upon her. She stretched out her hands and he took both of them in his.

"Oh! it was wonderful! How they love you!"

He smiled and gave a slight shrug. "How they'd have loved anyone who offered them release from the army."

She disengaged herself and walked a little from him toward the windows, consciously flirtatious. "Do you remember, Sire," she asked him softly, "when you said you'd love me till kingdom come?"

He smiled. "I thought it would be forever."

He came to stand behind her, his hands going to her breasts, and his head bent so that his mouth touched the nape of her neck. His voice was husky, deep, and there was a swift demanding impatience on his face. Barbara's hands had tight hold on the window ledge and her throat arched back, but she stared straight ahead, out into the night.

"Won't it be forever."

"Of course it will, Barbara. And I'll be here forever too. Come what may, there's one thing I know—I'll never set out on my travels again." Suddenly he put one arm under her knees and swung her up off the floor, holding her easily.

"Where does the Monsieur think you are?" "The Monsieur" was their name for her husband.

She put her lips to his smooth-shaven cheek. "I told him I was going to stay the night with my aunt—but I think he guesses I'm here." An expression of contempt crossed her face. "Roger's a fool!"

Chapter Four

AMBER sat looking at herself in the mirror that hung above the dressing table.

She was wearing a low-cut, lace-and-ribbon-trimmed smock made of sheer white linen, with belled, elbow-length sleeves and a long, full skirt. Laced over it was a busk—a short, tight little boned corset which forced her breasts high and squeezed two inches from the twenty-two her waist normally measured. With it on she had some difficulty both in breathing and in bending over, but it gave her such a luxurious sense of fashionableness that she would gladly have suffered twice the discomfort. Her skirt was pulled up over her knees so that she could see her crossed legs and the black silk stockings that covered them; there were lacy garters tied in bows just below her knees, and she wore high-heeled black-satin pumps.

Behind her hovered a dapper little man, Monsieur Baudelaire, newly arrived from Paris and having at his fingers' ends all the very latest tricks to make an Englishwoman's head look like a Parisienne's. He had been working over her for almost an hour, prattling in a half-French and half-English jargon about "heart-breakers" and "kiss-curls" and "favourites." Most of the time she did not understand what he said, but she had watched with breathless fascination the nimble manipulations of his combs and oils and brushes and pins.

Now, at last, he had her hair looking glossy as taffy-coloured satin, parted in the center and lying sleekly over the crown of her head in a pattern of shadowy waves. Fat shining curls hung to her shoulders, propped out a little by invisible combs to make them look even thicker. In back he had pulled all the hair up from her neck and braided and twisted it into a high scroll, securing it there with several gold-headed bodkins. It was the style, he told her, affected by all the great ladies and it quite transformed her features, giving her a piquant air at once provocative and alluring. Like a cook decorating his masterpiece he now fastened one pert black-satin bow at each temple and then stood back, clasping his hands, tipping his head to one side like a curious little bird.

"Ah, madame!" he cried, seeing not madame at all but only her hair and his own handiwork. "Oh, madame! C'est magnifique! C'est un triomphe! C'est la plus belle—" Words failing him, he rolled his eyes and spread his hands.

Amber quite agreed. "Gemini!" she turned her head from side to side, holding up a hand mirror so as to see both back and front. "Bruce won't know me!"

It had taken six weeks to get a gown made, for every good tailor and dressmaker in London had more orders than it was possible to fill. But Madame Darnier had promised to have her dress finished that afternoon and his Lordship had told her that he would take her wherever she wanted to go. She had been counting the days eagerly, for so far she had had little amusement but hanging out the windows to watch the crowds in the streets and running down to make some purchases from every vendor who passed. Lord Carlton was gone a great deal of the time—where, she did not know—and though he had bought a coach which was usually at her disposal she was ashamed to go out in her country clothes.

Now, everything would be different.

When she was alone she had occasional pangs of homesickness, thinking of Sarah, whom she had really loved, of the numerous young men who had run at her beck and call, of what a great person she had been in the village where everything she did was noticed and commented upon. But more often she thought of that bygone life with scornful contempt.

What would I be doing now? she would ask herself.

Helping Sarah in the still-room, spinning, dipping rushlights, cooking, setting out for the market or going to church. It seemed incredible that such dull occupations could once have engaged her from the time she got up, very early, until she went to bed, also very early.

Now she lay as long as she liked in the mornings, snuggled deep into a feather mattress, dreaming, lost in luxurious reverie. And her thoughts had just one theme: Lord Carlton. She was violently in love, completely dazzled, dejected when he was gone and wildly happy when they were together. And yet she knew very little about him and most of that little she had learned from Almsbury, who had come twice when Bruce was away.

She found out that Almsbury was not his name, as she had thought, but his title, the whole of which was John Randolph, Earl of Almsbury. He had told her that they had passed through Marygreen because they had landed at Ipswich and gone north from there a few miles to Carlton Hall where Bruce had got a boxful of jewels which his mother had not dared take when they fled the country—the territory having been at that time in Parliamentary hands and overrun with soldiers. Marygreen and Heathstone lay on the main road from there to London.

It seemed to her a miracle wrought by God Himself that she had chanced to be standing near the green at the moment they had come along. For Sarah had first told Agnes to take the gingerbread, but Amber had coaxed until she let her go instead—she was always eager to get away from the farm and out into the wider world of Marygreen. Agnes had been furious but Amber had sailed off, humming to herself and keeping a quick eye for whatever or whoever might be about. And then she had loitered so long with Tom Andrews coming across the meadow that another quarter-hour and she would never have seen them at all. By such thoughts she convinced herself that they had been fated since birth to meet on the Marygreen common, the fifth day of May, 1660.

He told her that Bruce was twenty-nine, that both his parents were dead and that he had one younger sister who had married a French count and lived now in Paris. She was very much interested in what he had done during the sixteen years he had been away from England, and Almsbury told her something of that also.

In 1647 both of them had served as officers in the French army, volunteer service being an expected part of every gentleman's training. Two years later Bruce had sailed with Prince Rupert's privateers, preying on the shipping of Parliament. There had followed another interval in the French army and then a buccaneering expedition to the West Indies and the Guinea Coast with Rupert. Almsbury himself had no taste for life at sea and preferred to remain with the Court, which had led a wandering hand-to-mouth existence in taverns and lodging-houses over half of Europe. With Bruce's return they had travelled together around the Continent, living by their wits; which meant, for the most part, by the proceeds from their gambling. And two years ago they had been in the Spanish army, fighting France and England. Both of them, he said, were the heirs of their own right hands.

It was the pattern of life which had been generally followed by the exiled nobility, with the difference that Carlton was more restless than most and grew quickly bored with the diversions of a court. To Amber it sounded the most lively and fascinating existence on earth and she always intended to ask Bruce to tell her more of what he had done.

To help her while away the days he had employed a French instructor, a dancing-master, a man to teach her to play the guitar, and another to teach her to sing; each one came twice a week. She practised industriously, for she wanted very much to seem a fine lady and thought that these accomplishments would make her more alluring to him. She had yet to hear Lord Carlton say that he loved her, and she would have learned to eat fire or walk a tightrope if she had thought it could call forth the magic words. Now she was counting heavily upon the effect of her new clothes and coiffure might have on his heart.

Just then there was a knock at the outer door and Amber leaped up to answer it. But before she had got far a buxom, middle-aged woman came hurrying into the room, her taffeta skirts whistling, out of breath and excited.

She was Madame Darnier, another Parisian come to London to take advantage of the rabid francophilia which raged there among the aristocracy. Her black hair was streaked with grey and her cheeks were bright pink, a great chou of green satin ribbon was pinned atop her head just behind a frontlet of false curls, and her stiff shiny black gown was cut to a precarious depth. But still she contrived, as a Frenchwoman should, to look elegant rather than absurd. In her wake scooted a young girl, plainly dressed, bearing in her arms a great gilded wooden box.

"Quick!" cried Amber, clasping her hands and giving an excited little jump. "Let me see it!"

Madame Darnier, chattering French, motioned at the girl to lay the box on a table, off which she grandly swept Amber's green wool skirt and striped cotton petticoat. And then, with a magnificent flourish, she flung up the lid and at one swoop snatched out her creation, holding it at arm's length for them to see. Both Amber and the hairdresser gasped, falling back a step or two, while the other girl beamed with pride, sharing Madame Darnier's triumph.

"Ohhh—" breathed Amber, and then, *"Oh!"* She had never seen anything so lovely in her life.

It was made of black and honey-coloured satin with a tight, pointed bodice, deep round neckline, full sleeves to the elbows, and a sweeping gathered skirt, over which was a second skirt of exquisite black lace. The cloak was honey-coloured velvet lined in black satin and the attached hood had a black fox border. There was a lace fan, long perfumed beige gloves, a great fox muff, and one of the black velvet vizard-masks which every fine lady wore when going abroad. In fact, all the trappings of high fashion.

"Oh, let me put it on!"

Madame Darnier was horrified. "Mais, non, madame! First we must paint the face!"

"Mais oui! First we must paint the face!" echoed Monsieur Baudelaire.

They went back to the table, all four of them, and there Madame Darnier untied a great red-velvet kerchief and spread out its contents: bottles and jars and small China pots, a rabbit's foot, an eyebrow brush, tiny booklets of red Spanish paper, pencils, beauty patches. Amber gave a surprised little shriek when the first eyebrow was pulled out, but after that she sat patiently, in a condition of ecstatic delight at the change she saw coming over herself. Arguing, chattering, shrieking among themselves, in half an hour they had made her into a creature of polish and sparkle and artifice—a worldly woman, at least in appearance.

And then at last she was ready to put on her gown, a major enterprise, for there must not be one wrinkle made in it, not a hair displaced, not a smear of lip-pomade or a smudge of powder. It took all three of them to accomplish that, with Madame Darnier scolding and clucking, screaming alternately at the girl and at Monsieur Baudelaire. But at last they had it settled upon her, Madame pulling the neckline down so that all of her shoulders and most of her breasts showed, and finally she put the fan into her hand and ordered her to walk slowly across the room and turn and face them.

"Mon Dieu!" she said then, with complacent satisfaction. "If you don't outdo Madame Palmer herself!"

"Who's Madame Palmer?" Amber wanted to know, looking down to examine herself.

"His Majesty's mistress." Madame Darnier rustled across the room to adjust a fold, twisting one sleeve a quarter of an inch, smoothing a tiny wrinkle from the bodice. "For today, at least," she muttered, frowning, absorbed in what she was doing. "Next week—" She shrugged. "Perhaps someone else."

Amber was pleased by the compliment—but now that she was finally ready she wished he would come. Outside she felt new and crisp as tissuepaper, but her stomach was fluttering with nervousness and her hands were moist. Maybe he won't like me this way! She was beginning to feel scared and almost sick. Oh! *why* doesn't he come!

And then she heard the door open and his voice called her name. "May I come in?"

"Oh!" Amber's hand flew to her mouth. "He's here! Quick!"

She began shooing them out and the three rushed everywhere at once, gathering up boxes and bottles and combs, flocking out the door of the bedroom just as he reached it. Bowing and curtsying as they went, they could not resist looking back gleefully over their shoulders to see what he would do. Amber stood in the middle of the room, lips parted, not even breathing, her eyes glistening with expectation. He walked through the doorway smiling and then suddenly stopped, surprise on his face, at the threshold.

"Holy Jesus!" he said softly. "How lovely you are!"

Amber relaxed. "Oh—*do* you like me this way?"

He came toward her and took the fingers of one hand to turn her slowly about, while she looked back at him over her shoulder—unwilling to miss the slightest expression of pleasure on his face. "You're all the dreams of fair women a man ever had." At last he picked up her cloak. "Now— Where shall we go?"

She knew exactly and was eager to set out. "I want to see a play!"

He grinned. "A play it is—but we'll have to hurry. It's almost four now."

It was after four-thirty when they arrived at the old Red Bull Playhouse in upper St. John Street, and the performance had been under way for more than an hour. The theatre was hot and stuffy, almost humid, and it smelt strongly of sweat and unwashed bodies and powerful perfumes. There was a bustle and stir over the house which never ceased, and dozens of heads turned curiously as they went to their seats in the fore of one of the boxes. Even the actors took time out to give them a glance.

Amber was completely intoxicated, trying to see everything at once, thrilled by the whole noisy, bad-smelling, ill-bred but strangely exciting conglomeration. She felt that the triumph was peculiarly her own—and did not realize they would have stared at any other pretty woman arriving late. Any diversion was a welcome one, for neither players nor audience seemed seriously interested in the performance.

All the bottom floor of the house was called the pit and its benches were crowded with about three hundred young men who buzzed eternally among themselves. A few women were seated there also, most of them rather well-dressed but boldly over-painted, and when Amber asked Bruce in a loud whisper who they were he replied that they were prostitutes. There had been no prostitutes in Marygreen and if there had they would have been set up in the stocks and pelted with refuse by every right-thinking farmer and housewife. And so she was amazed to see that here the young men used them with apparent respect, talked to them openly, and even occasionally kissed or embraced one of them. Nor did the ladies themselves seem in any wise self-conscious or remorseful. They laughed and chattered loudly, looked happy and quite at ease.

Ranged against the apron-shaped stage, which extended out into the pit, stood half-a-dozen girls with baskets over their arms, bawling out their wares—oranges and lemons and sweetmeats—which they sold at exorbitant prices.

Above the pit, but down close to the stage, was a balcony divided into boxes, and there sat the ladies of quality, gorgeously gowned and jewelled, with their husbands or lovers. Above that was another balcony filled with women and rowdies. And in one still higher were the apprentices who beat time to the music with their cudgels, gave a loud hum by way of disapproval and, when really indignant, sounded their catcalls—loud whistles that filled the theatre.

Essentially the audience was aristocratic—the harlots and 'prentices being almost the only outsiders—and the ladies and gentlemen came to see and to be seen, to gossip and to flirt. The play was a secondary consideration.

Amber found nothing to disappoint her. It was all she had expected, and more.

Taut with excitement and happiness, she sat very straight beside Bruce, her eyes round and sparkling and travelling from one side of the theatre to the other. So *this* was the great world! Yet she could not but be poignantly aware of her new gown, her elaborate coiffure, the scent of her perfume, and the unfamiliar but pleasurable feeling of cosmetics on her skin, the silken caress of her fur muff beneath her fingers, the voluptuous display of her breasts.

And then, as she looked around at the boxes near them, she encountered the eyes of two women who were leaning slightly forward, watching her—and the expression on their faces was a sudden rude shock.

They were both handsome, richly dressed, sparkling with jewels, and they had an indefinable hauteur and confidence which she already associated with quality. Bruce had bowed and spoken to them when they came in—as he had spoken to several other men and women nearby and had acknowledged waves of greeting from gentlemen in the pit. But now, as her eyes met theirs, they gave her a sweeping contemptuous glance, exchanged smiles with each other; one woman murmured something behind her fan—and with a concerted lift of the eyebrows they both looked away.

For an instant Amber continued to stare at them, surprised and hurt, almost sick with humiliation, and then she looked down at her fan and bit her lower lip to force back the sudden impulse of tears. Oh! she thought in passionate mortification, they think I'm a harlot! They despise me! All at once the glory was gone from her outing into the gay world and she wished she had never come, had never exposed herself to their scorn and disdain.

When Bruce, who had evidently seen the exchange of glances, gave her hand a warm reassuring pressure her spirits lifted a little and she flung him a look of gratitude. But though she returned her eyes to the stage then and tried to take an interest in what was going on she found it impossible. She only wished that the play would end so that she might get back to the comforting seclusion of their apartment. How ashamed Sarah would be, how furious Uncle Matt, to see to what a condition she had come!

At last the epilogue had been spoken and the audience began to rise. Bruce turned to her with a smile, putting her cloak over her shoulders. "Well, how did you like it?"

"I—I liked it." She did not look him in the eyes and dared not glance about for fear of confronting the two women again, or some other sneering face.

Below in the pit several of the men were clustering about the orange-girls, kissing them, handling them familiarly, while others indulged in horseplay among themselves, clapping one another on the back and pulling off hats. The actor who had impersonated Juliet, still in his long blond wig and a gown with padded chest, came out and stood talking to some of the beaus. Others were climbing up onto the stage and going back behind the scenes. Overhead they could hear tramping feet making for the exits, and the ladies and gentlemen about them were pausing in small groups—the women kissing one another and squealing while the men smiled with smug tolerance. But all the while Amber stood with a troubled frown on her face, her eyes fixed on Bruce's cravat, wishing they would all get out.

"Shall we go, my dear?" He offered her his arm.

Outside the theatre they made their way through the loiterers to his coach where it stood in line with several others, all jamming the streets until foot-traffic was almost at a standstill. Everyone was pushing to get through and vendors and porters were swearing angrily. All of a sudden a beggar thrust himself before them, making weird undistinguishable sounds, his mouth open, and he put his face up to Amber's to show her where his tongue bled from having been cut out. Sickened with pity and a little frightened she drew closer to Bruce, holding his arm.

Bruce tossed the man a coin. "Here. Out of the way."

"Oh—that poor man! Did you see him? Why did they do that to him?"

They had reached the coach and he handed her in. "There was nothing wrong with him. It's a trick they have of rolling their tongues out of sight and poking them with a stick until they bleed."

"But why doesn't he work instead of doing that?"

"He does work. Don't think begging's the easiest profession in the world."

She sat down while he turned to talk to two young men who had called his name, and she saw them both looking at her from over his shoulder, frank appraisal in their eyes. For one bold instant Amber returned their stares, lifting her brows and slanting the corners of her eyes—and then suddenly she blushed and looked the other way. Oh, Lord! they were most likely thinking the same thing about her that the women had!

But still she could not resist sneaking them another slow cautious glance—and her eyes met once more the full stare of the handsomer one. Swiftly she glanced away. And yet—there was no doubt it did not seem so insulting, coming from a man.

Bruce finally turned back, spoke to the driver and got in, sitting down beside her as the coach gave a jog and started to move. He took one of her hands in his. "You've set the town by its ears. That was my Lord Buckhurst and he says you're far more beautiful than Barbara Palmer."

"You mean the King's mistress?"

"Yes. How the devil do you manage to get all the current gossip?" He looked down at her, amused as though she were a pretty doll or a plaything.

"The dressmaker told me about her. Bruce—who were those two ladies? The ones in the next box that waved to you?"

"Wives of friends of mine. Why?"

She looked down at her fan, frowning, counting the sticks. "Did you see how they looked at me? Like this—" She pulled her face into a sudden grimace, a perfect though somewhat exaggerated and malicious imitation of the stares they had given her. "They think I'm a harlot—I know they do!"

Bruce gave her a look of surprise and then, to her astonishment, threw back his head and laughed.

"Well!" she cried, offended. "What the devil is there to laugh at, pray?"

She was beginning already to pick up some of his expressions, words and phrases Matt Goodegroome would never have allowed even his sons to use. It seemed to Amber that all fine persons swore and that it was a mark of good breeding.

"I'm sorry, Amber. I wasn't laughing at you. But to tell you the truth I think they glared at you for another reason—jealousy, no doubt. Certainly neither of them has any reason to have an ill opinion of another woman's character. Between 'em I think they've laid with most of the men who went to France."

"But you said they're married!"

"So they are. If they weren't they might have been more discreet."

She was relieved, but at the same time a quick suspicion entered her mind. Could *he* have been one of those men? But she promptly decided that if he had been he would never have mentioned the matter at all—and she thrust that thought aside. She began to feel happy again, and eager for the next adventure.

"Where are we going now?"

"I thought you might like to have supper at a tavern."

Back in the City they stopped in New Street before a building which bore the sign of a great golden eagle. When she stepped down Amber lifted her skirts high to show her black lace garters, just as she had seen several ladies do outside the theatre. Then, as they were about to go in the door, they heard a loud shout in a familiar masculine voice.

"Hey! Carlton!"

Curiously they looked around. It was Almsbury, riding by in a hackney jammed with several other men, and as the coach pulled up he jumped out, waved his companions goodbye and came toward them at a run. He blinked his eyes twice as he saw Amber and then swept off his hat in a deep bow.

"Holy Christ, sweetheart! Damn me if you aren't as beautiful as a Venetian whore!"

The delightful smile froze on Amber's face.

Well! So that was what *he* thought of her too! Her eyebrows drew together in a furious scowl, but at a glance from Bruce the Earl hastened to repair his breach. He shrugged his shoulders and made a comical face.

"Well—after all, you know, Venetian prostitutes are the prettiest women in Europe. But then, I suppose if you—"

He paused, watching her with an ingratiating grin and Amber slowly raised her eyes to his again. She could not resist his friendliness and all of a sudden she smiled. He took her arm. "Lord, sweetheart, you know I wouldn't offend you for anything on earth." The three of them went inside and, at Bruce's request, were shown upstairs to a private room.

After the men had ordered, the waiter brought them a small barrelful of oysters and they began cracking them open, eating them raw with a sprinkle of salt and a few drops of lemon juice, scattering the shells on the table and floor. Almsbury predicted that oysters would become the staple food at Court and when Amber looked puzzled Bruce told her what he meant. She laughed heartily, thinking it a very good joke.

By the time they had finished the oysters the rest of the meal appeared: a roast duck stuffed with oysters and onions, fried artichoke bottoms, and a rich cheesecake baked in a crust. After that there was Burgundy for the two men, white Rhenish for Amber, fruit, and some nuts to crack. For a long while they sat at the table talking, all of them warm and well-fed and content, and Amber quite forgot her earlier chagrin.

The wine was stronger than the ale to which she was accustomed and after a couple of glasses she became quiet and drowsy, and sat with her eyes half closed listening to the men talk. A sense of lightness pervaded her, as though her head had become detached and floated somewhere far above her. She watched Bruce admiringly, every expression that crossed his face, every gesture of his hands. And when he would turn to smile at her or, as he did once or twice, lean over to brush his lips across her cheek, her happiness soared dizzily.

At last she whispered in his ear and, when he answered, got up and crossed the room to a small closet. While she was in there she heard a knock at the outer door, another voice speaking, and then the sound of the door closing again.

When she came out, Almsbury was sitting at the table alone, pouring himself another glassful of wine. He glanced around over his shoulder. "He's been called out on business but he'll be back in a moment. Come here where I can look at you."

Ten minutes or more dragged slowly by with Amber watching the door, looking up with swift eager expectancy at each slight sound, nervous and unhappy. It seemed as though he had been gone an hour when the waiter came in. He bowed to Almsbury.

"Sir, his Lordship regrets that he has been called away on a matter of important business, and asks that you do him the kindness of carrying madame to her lodging."

Almsbury, who had been watching Amber while the man delivered his message, nodded his head. And now Amber looked at him with her face white, her eyes as hurt as if she had been struck.

"Business," she repeated softly. "Where can he go on business at this hour?"

Almsbury shrugged his shoulders. "I don't know, sweetheart. Here, have another drink."

But though Amber took the wineglass he proffered she merely sat and held it. For a month and a half she had looked forward to this night—and now he must go off somewhere on business. Every time she asked him where he had been or where he was going it was always the same answer—"business." But why tonight? Why this one night for which she had planned so long and from which she had hoped so much? She felt tired and discouraged and hung listlessly in her chair, scarcely speaking, so that after a few minutes Almsbury got up and suggested that they go.

During the ride back she did not trouble herself to make conversation with the Earl, but when they reached the Royal Saracen she asked him if he would care to come upstairs, half hoping that he would refuse. But he accepted readily and, while she went on ahead to take off her gown, stopped in the taproom for a couple of bottles of sack. Coming out of the bedroom in a pair of clopping mules and a gold satin dressing-gown—another recent acquirement—she found him stretched comfortably on a cushion-piled settle before the fire. He gave a wave of his arm, signalling her to come to him and, when she sat down beside him, took hold of one of her hands, looked at it reflectively for a moment and then touched it to his lips. Frowning, Amber stared off into space, scarcely conscious of him.

"Where d'you think he went?" she asked at last.

Almsbury shrugged, tilted the bottle again.

"What the devil is this 'business' he's always about? Do *you* know what it is?"

"Every Royalist in England has business nowadays. One wants his property back. Another wants a sinecure that'll pay a thousand a year for helping the King on and off with his drawers. The galleries are full of 'em—country squires and old soldiers and doting mamas who've heard the King has an eye for pretty women. They all want something—including me. I want Almsbury House back again and my lands in Herefordshire. His Majesty couldn't please all of us if he were King Midas and high Jupiter rolled into one."

"What does Bruce want? Carlton Hall?"

"No, I don't think so. It was sold, not confiscated, and I don't believe they'll give back property that was sold." He finished the bottle and leaned over to pick up another one.

The Earl could drink more with less effect to himself than any man she had ever seen, and Bruce had told her that it was because he had lived so long in taverns that his blood had turned to alcohol. She still was not sure whether he had meant it as a joke or the solemn truth.

"I don't see what he can want," she said. "As rich as *he* is."

"Rich?" Almsbury seemed surprised.

"Well—isn't he?"

Amber knew very little about money for she had never had in her possession more than a few shilling at a time and could scarcely tell the value of one coin from another. But it seemed to her that Lord Carlton must have fabulous wealth to own a coach-and-four, to wear the clothes he did, to buy such wonderful things for her.

"By no means. His family sold everything they had to help the King and what they didn't sell was taken from them in the decimations. That jewellery he found at Carlton Hall was just about everything that was left. No—he's not rich. In fact, he's damned near as poor as I am."

"But what about the coach—and my clothes—"

"Oh. Well—he has that much. A man who knows what he's about can sit down for a few hours at cards or dice and come away several hundred pounds to the good."

"Cheating?" She was rather shocked, almost inclined to think that Almsbury was lying.

But he smiled. "Well, perhaps he plays a little upon advantage. But then, we all do. Of course some of us are clever at it and some not so clever— Bruce can slur and knap with any man in Europe. He made his living for most of fifteen years with a pair of dice and a pack of cards—and he lived a damned sight better than most of us did. In fact, the other night I saw him win twenty-five hundred in four hours at the Groom Porter's Lodge."

"Is that what all this business is he goes upon—gambling?"

"Partly. He needs money."

"Then why doesn't he ask the King for it—since everyone else does?"

"My dear, you don't know Bruce."

At that moment she heard a coach come banging down the

street and left him to rush to the window—but to her disappointment it continued on by and rounded the next corner. She stayed there, looking out into the darkness, for there were no street lights of any sort but only the pale gleam from the new moon and the stars. The streets were deserted, not a person was in sight. London citizens stayed home at night unless they had a very good reason to go abroad, and then they took with them an escort of linkboys or footmen.

In the distance she saw the glow of the bellman's lantern and could hear his monotonous refrain: "Past ten o'clock of a fine warm summer's night and all's well. Past ten o'clock—"

Completely absorbed in her worries about Bruce, she had forgotten that Almsbury was there at all. But now she felt his arms go around her, one hand sliding into her dressing-gown, and with the other he turned her about and kissed her on the mouth. Astonished, she gave a little gasp and then suddenly shoved him away, slapping him resoundingly across the face.

"Marry come up, sir!" she cried. "A fine friend you are! When his Lordship hears about this he'll run you through!"

He stared at her for an instant in surprise, and then threw back his head and laughed. "Run me through! Jesus, sweetheart, but you've a droll wit! Come, now—surely you don't think Bruce would give a damn if I borrowed his whore for a night?"

Amber's eyes blazed in violent anger. Then in a fury she kicked out at his shins, beginning to pound his chest with her clenched fists. "I'm *not* a whore, you damned dog! Get out of here— Get out of here or I'll tear you to pieces!"

"Hey!" He grabbed her wrists, giving her a shake. "Stop it, you little vixen! What are you trying to do? I'm sorry. I apologize. I didn't—"

"Get out, you varlet!" she yelled.

"I'm going. I'm going— Hold your bawling."

Picking up his hat, which she had knocked off, he crossed to the door. There, with his hand on the knob, he turned to face her. She was still glaring at him, fists planted on her hips, but tears glistened in her eyes and it was all she could do to keep from crying. His flippancy vanished.

"Just one thing, sweetheart, before I go. Contrary to what your Aunt Sarah may have told you—a man's not insulting you when he invites you to bed. And if you'd be honest you'd admit yourself you're flattered that I did. For if there's one thing a woman will never forgive a man—it's not wanting to lie with her. Now I'll trouble you no more. Good-night." He made her a bow and opened the door.

Amber stood and looked at him like a little girl getting a lesson in etiquette from her grown-up uncle. She was beginning to find that her suit of country morals was as much out of fashion here in London as her cotton petticoat and green woolen skirt had been. Now she held out her hand in an impulsive but still uncertain gesture, and took two or three steps toward him.

"My lord—don't go. I'm sorry— Only—"

"Only you're in love with Bruce."

"Yes."

"And so you think you shouldn't lie with another man. Well, my dear, perhaps someday you'll discover that it doesn't make so very much difference after all. And if you do— Your servant, madame." He made her another bow.

She stood and looked at him, not knowing what to do next. For though she had to admit to herself that she really was, in a sense, flattered by his proposal, she could not agree with him that fidelity to the man you loved was of no importance. It seemed incredible she could ever so much as think of lying with another man. She never would, not as long as she lived.

And then there came again the sound of a coach rattling over the cobblestones; she whirled around and ran once more to the window. The coach came careening down the street, rocking from side to side, the driver hauled on the reins and it stopped just beneath. Nimbly as a monkey the footman got down from his perch and ran to open the door, and after a moment Lord Carlton got out, turning then to speak to someone inside. Another footman held a flaring torch which lighted one side of his Lordship's face and threw stark shadows up the street and upon the walls of the houses.

Amber was about to lean out and call a greeting when, to her horror, a woman thrust her head from the coach-window and she caught a glimpse of a beautiful white face, laughing, and a tumbling mass of red hair. Bruce's head bent above her and she heard their voices murmuring. After a moment he stepped back, bowing and removing his hat, the footman closed the door and the coach rolled away. He turned and disappeared through the arch below.

Amber stood clutching at the sill, almost sick enough to faint. And then, by a great physical effort, she straightened again and turned slowly about. The colour had washed out of her face and her heart was beating violently. For several moments she stood and stared before her—not even seeing Almsbury who was watching her with a kind of compassionate sympathy on his face. She let her eyes close and one hand went up slowly to her forehead.

At that moment the door opened and Bruce came in.

Chapter Five

He paused as if in surprise, glancing from one of them to the other, but before he had had time to say a word Amber burst into tears and ran into the bedroom, slamming the door behind her and flinging herself onto the bed.

The sobs wrenched and tore at her and she gave herself up to them with complete abandon. This was the most miserable moment in all her life and she had no wish to be brave and restrained. Suffering in silence was not her way. And, when he did not come in immediately, running after her as she had expected, she grew increasingly hysterical—until finally she began to retch.

But finally she heard the door open and then the sound of his footsteps crossing the floor. Her sobs became louder than ever. Oh! she thought vehemently, I wish I'd die! Right now! Then he'd be sorry!

The room began to glow as he lighted a couple of candles. She heard him toss his cloak and hat aside and unbuckle his sword, but still he said nothing. At last she lifted her head from her arms and looked at him; her face was streaked and her eyes red and swollen.

"Well!" she cried, challenging him.

"Good evening."

"Is *that* all you have to say?"

"What else should I say?"

"You might at least tell me where you've been—and who you've been with!"

He was untying his cravat now, and taking off his doublet. "Don't you think that that's my business?"

She gasped, as hurt as if he had struck her. She had given herself to him so wholeheartedly, with not a single reservation, that she had made herself believe he had done the same. Now she realized all at once that he had not. His life had not changed, his habits had not changed, she had scarcely touched him at all.

"Oh," she said softly, and looked away.

For a moment he stood watching her, and then he came suddenly and sat down on the bed. "I'm sorry, Amber, I didn't mean to be rude. And I'm sorry I had to leave you—spoil your evening that you've been counting on for so long. But it really was business that called me away—"

She looked at him skeptically, the tears brimming over her eyes again and falling in drops onto her satin gown. "Business indeed! What kind of business does a man do with a woman!"

He smiled, his eyes tender and yet amused. She always had the feeling, and it made her uncomfortable, that he did not quite take her seriously.

"More than you might imagine, darling, and I'll tell you why: The King can't possibly satisfy or repay everyone who was loyal to him—he's got to make a choice from among a thousand claims, one as good as another. I don't think his Majesty could ever be persuaded by a woman—or anyone else—to do something he didn't want to, but when it comes to choosing between several things he'd like to do—why then the right woman can be very useful in helping him to make up his mind. Just now there's no one who can do more to persuade the King than a young woman named Barbara Palmer—who's been kind enough to use her influence in my behalf—"

Barbara Palmer!

So that was the woman she had seen!

She had a sudden horrified sense of defeat, for certainly the woman who could charm a king must have some almost unearthly allure. Her confidence plunged, beaten and overwhelmed by her own superstitious belief that a King and everything which surrounded him was more than half divine. Her head dropped into her hands.

"Oh, Amber, my dear—please. It's not as serious as that. She happened to be driving by and saw my coach and sent up to ask if I was there. I'd have been a damned fool to refuse. She's helped me get what I wanted more than anything on earth—"

"What? Your lands?"

"No. Those were sold. I won't get them back again unless I can buy out the present owner, and I don't think I will. She helped me persuade the King and his brother to go into a privateering venture with me; they both contributed several thousand pounds. I got my letter-of-marque yesterday."

"What's that?"

"It's a letter from the King authorizing the bearer to seize the vessels and cargo of other nations. In this case I can take Spanish ships sailing off the Americas—"

Her fear and jealousy of Barbara Palmer vanished.

"*You're* not going to sea?"

"Yes, Amber, I am. I've bought two ships of my own, and with the money I'll get from the King and York I can buy three more. As soon as they're provisioned and the men are signed we'll sail."

"Oh, Bruce, you can't go away! You can't!"

A flicker of impatience crossed his face. "I told you that day in Heathstone I wouldn't stay long. It'll be two months yet, or perhaps a little longer, but as soon as I can, I'm going."

"But *why?* Why don't you get a—a—I forget what Almsbury called 'em—where you get money for helping his Majesty put on his drawers?"

He laughed, though her face was passionately serious. "As it happens I don't want a what-d'you-call-'em. I need money, but I'll get it my own way. Crawling on my belly for the rest of my days isn't the way I want to do it."

"Then take me with you! Oh, please, Bruce! I won't be any trouble—let me go along, please!"

"I can't, Amber. Life on ship-board is hard enough for a man—the food's rotten, it's cold and it's uncomfortable, and there's no getting off when you get tired of it. And if you think you wouldn't cause any trouble—" He smiled, running his eyes over her significantly. "No, my dear—it's no use talking about it."

"But what about me? What'll I do when you go? Oh, Bruce, I'll die without you!" She looked at him pitifully and reached over to put her hands on his arms, already forlorn as a lost puppy.

"That's what I asked you when you wanted to come to London with me. Or have you forgotten? Listen to me, Amber. There's only one thing for you to do—go back to Marygreen right now. I'll give you as much money as I can. We'll think of some tale or other to tell your aunt and uncle—I know it won't be easy for you, but even in a village a large sum of money doesn't go unrespected. After a while the gossip will run down, and you can get married— Wait a minute, let me finish. I know I'm to blame for having brought you here, and I won't pretend my motives were noble. I wasn't thinking about you or what would happen to you, and to tell the truth I didn't very much care. But I care now; I don't want to see you hurt any more than I can help. You're young and you're innocent and you're beautiful, and all that with your enthusiasm for living can easily ruin you. I wasn't joking when I said that London eats up pretty girls—the town's aswarm with rogues and adventurers of every conceivable breed. You'd be snapped up in a minute. Believe that I know what I'm saying and go back home, where you belong."

Amber's eyes sparkled angrily, and she lifted her chin as she answered him. "I a'nt so innocent, my lord! I warrant you I can look to my own interests as well as the next one! And don't think I can't see what you're about, either! You've grown tired of me now the King's mistress has caught your eye, and think to fob me off with some lame story that I should go back for my own good! Well, you don't know what you're talking about! My Uncle Matt wouldn't so much as let me in the house —money or no! And the constable would likely set me up in the stocks! Every man in the parish would laugh in his fist at me and—" She stopped suddenly and burst into tears again. "I won't do it! I *won't* go home!"

He reached over and took her into his arms. "Amber, my darling, don't cry. I swear it, I don't give a damn about Barbara Palmer. And I was telling the truth when I said I thought you should go back for your own sake. I still do. But it isn't because I've grown tired of you. You're lovely—you're more desirable than you can know. My God, no man could grow tired of you—"

Under his stroking fingers her sobs grew quieter, a warmth began to come over her and she purred like a kitten. "You aren't tired of me, Bruce? I can stay with you?"

"If you want— But I still think—"

"Oh, don't say it! I don't care! I don't care what happens to me—I'm going to stay with you!"

He gave her a light kiss and got up to finish undressing while she sat on her knees watching him, glowing admiration in her eyes. His body was magnificent—with a splendid breadth through chest and shoulders, sleek narrow hips, and handsome muscular legs. His flesh was hard-surfaced, the skin of his torso browned by exposure. Every movement he made had the easy gracefulness of an animal, seemingly unhurried, yet lithe and quick.

He crossed the room to snuff out the candles. And suddenly Amber could restrain herself no longer.

"Bruce! Did you make love to her?"

He did not answer but gave her a glance, half-scowling, that intimated he considered the question a superfluous one, and then his head bent and he blew out the last candle.

From the beginning Amber had both half-hoped and half-feared that she would become pregnant. She hoped because her love for him yearned to be fulfilled in every way. But she feared, too, because she knew that he would not marry her, and it was her vivid memory that a woman who gave birth to a bastard child had no very tender treatment at the hands of the community. Two years before in Marygreen a daughter of one of the cottagers had become pregnant and had either not known or refused to tell the father's name, so that sheer force of public antagonism drove her to leave the town. Amber remembered the circumstance well, for it had been the subject of chatter among the delighted and scandalized girls for weeks on end, and she had been as contemptuous, as jeering as any of them.

Now, that might happen to her.

She was well enough acquainted with the early symptoms of pregnancy for she had often discussed the subject with those of her friends who were married, and she had watched Sarah carry four children during the years since she had been old enough to notice such things. But by the end of June, when they had been in London almost two months, she still had no reason to think herself with child. And so, to settle her own suspense, she went to consult an astrologer.

It was no very diffcult matter to find one for they were all over the city, thick as flies in a cook-shop, and she set out one day in Bruce's coach-and-four to learn her fortune from a certain Mr. Chout. She watched as they rode along and when she saw a sign marked with a moon, six stars, and a hand, she called to the driver to stop and sent the footman to knock at the door. The astrologer, who had peeked out the window and seen her crested coach, came forth himself to invite her in.

He did not look to her like a mystic. He had a large red face, dirt-clogged pores covered his nose, and there was a rank odour about him. But he greeted her so obsequiously, bowing as though she were a duchess of the blood royal, that her confidence in him increased.

The footman followed her into the house and waited while she and Mr. Chout retired to a private parlour. The room was filthy and smelt no better than its owner, and Amber glanced dubiously at the chair before she sat down in it. He took a stool opposite her and began talking about the King's return and his own invincible loyalty to the Stuarts. While he talked he rubbed his dirty hands together and his eyes looked at her as though they could penetrate her cloak. Finally, like a doctor who has humoured his patient long enough by gossiping of other things, he asked her what she wanted to know.

"I want to know what's going to happen to me."

"Very well, madame. You've come to the right man. But first there are some things you must tell me."

Amber was afraid that he would ask her some embarrassingly personal questions, but all he wanted was the date and hour of her birth and where she was born. When she had told him he consulted several charts, gazed into a round crystal ball he had on the table, peered occasionally at both her palms—holding her hands in his own moist and grimy ones—and nodded his head gravely. All the while she watched him with anxious eagerness, now and then giving an absent-minded caress to the large grey cat that came and nudged against her skirts.

"Madame," he said finally, "your future is of singular interest. You were born with Venus in separating square aspect to Mars in the Fifth House." Amber solemnly absorbed that, too impressed at first even to wonder what it meant. Then, as she was about to ask, he continued, having reached his conclusions as much by looking at her as at his charts: "Hence you are inclined, madame, to over-ardent affections and to rash impulsive attractions to the opposite sex. This can cause you serious trouble, madame. You are also too much inclined to indulge yourself in pleasure—and hence must suffer the attendant difficulties."

Amber gave a wistful little sigh. "Don't you see something good, too?"

"Oh, indeed, madame, indeed. I was coming to that. I see you in possession of a great fortune." By the appearance of her clothes and smart coach he had surmised that she must already have access to a large amount of money.

"You do?" cried Amber, delighted. "What else do you see?"

"I see jealousy and discord. But also," he added hastily at a protesting frown from Amber, "I see that the sextiles of Venus to Neptune and Uranus give you considerable magnetism—no man may resist you."

"Ohhh—" breathed Amber. "Gemini! What else do you see? Will I have children?"

"Let me see your palm again, madame. Yes, indeed, a very

fair table—the line of riches well extended. The wheels of fortune are large. These intersparsings betoken children. You will have—let me see—several. Seven, I should say, more or less."

"When will I have the first one? Soon?"

"Yes, I think so. Very soon—" His eyes went down over her cloak, but nothing was revealed there. "That is, of course," he added cautiously, "within a reasonable time. You understand, madame."

"And when will I get married—soon, too?" Her voice and eyes were hopeful, almost pleading with him.

"Let me see. Hmmm—let me see. Now, what did you dream last night? I've found there's nothing to compare with a dream for telling a woman when she'll marry."

Amber frowned, trying to remember. She could recall nothing but that she had dreamed of pounding spices, which she had often done for Sarah—particularly after the two annual fairs, when they were purchased in bulk. That fragment, however, was enough for Mr. Chout's purpose.

"That's very important, madame. Very important. To dream of pounding spices always foretells matrimony."

"Will I marry the man I love?"

"Why, truly, madame, that I can't say for certain." But at Amber's stricken expression he again hastened to amend his statement. "Of course, madame, you will marry him one day—perhaps not today or tomorrow—but someday. These lines here betoken husbands. You will have, let me see, some half-a-dozen, more or less."

"Half-a-dozen! I don't want half-a-dozen! I just want one!" She pulled her hand away from him, for he seemed sticky and repulsive to her, and he had been holding on somewhat too tightly. But he was not done yet.

"And one thing more I see—if I may be frank with you?—I see that someday you will have, madame, a hundred lovers." His greedy eyes watched her with obscene calculation, taking vicarious pleasure from her look of surprise and the faint pink blush that spread over her face and neck. "More or less, that is."

Amber gave an excited little laugh. He was making her feel ill-at-ease and she wished that she was out of there; it was difficult to breathe, and though he had moved no nearer he seemed to be oppressively close. "A hundred lovers!" she cried, trying to sound city-bred and casual. "Marry come up! One's enough for me! Is that all, Mr. Chout?" She got to her feet.

"Isn't that enough, madame? I don't often discover as much, let me tell you. The fee is ten shillings."

Amber took a dozen or more coins from her muff and dropped them onto the table. His broad grin told her that most likely she had overpaid, again. But she did not care. Bruce always left a handful of coins for her to use and when one pile was gone another appeared in its place. Ten shillings as a sum of money meant nothing to her at all.

I'm going to have a baby and marry Bruce and be rich! she thought exultantly as she rode home.

That night she asked Bruce what the planet Venus was, though she did not tell him of her visit and did not intend to, until something more definite had come of it. But perhaps he guessed.

"It's a star called Venus after the Roman goddess of love. It's supposed to control the destinies of those who are born under it. I believe such people are thought to be beautiful and desirable and generally dominated by emotion—if you believe in that kind of nonsense." He was smiling at her, for Amber's face showed her shock at this heretical statement.

"Don't *you* believe in it?"

"No, darling, I don't believe in it."

"Well—" She put her hands on her hips and gave her curls a toss. "One day you will, I warrant you. Just wait and see."

But nothing which happened immediately seemed to indicate that any of Mr. Chout's predictions were coming true. And meanwhile her life continued very much as it had been.

Most of the time Bruce was away from home, either gambling at the Groom Porter's Lodge, where the nobles went to play cards and dice, or overseeing the supplying and loading of his ships. Often, too, she knew that he went to balls or suppers given at Court or the homes of his friends. And though she thought wistfully of how wonderful it would be to go with him he did not ask her and she never mentioned it. For she was still strongly conscious of the great gulf which separated his social position from hers—and yet when she lay waiting for him to come back she was lonely and sad, and jealous too. She was morbidly afraid of Barbara Palmer and other women like her.

Almsbury often came to call and, if Bruce was not there, took her out somewhere with him.

One day they went to see a bull-and-bear baiting across the river in Southwark. And Amber leaned out of the coach window to gape at the weatherbeaten heads, some twenty or thirty of them, exposed above London Bridge on poles that stuck up crazily, like toothpicks in a glass. Another time he took her to a fencing-match, and one of the antagonists lost an ear which flopped off into the lap of a woman sitting down in front.

They went to supper at various fashionable taverns and two or three times he took her to the theatre. She paid no more attention to the play than did the rest of the audience—for she was too much interested, though she pretended not to be, in the havoc she was creating down in the pit. Some of the young men came up to Almsbury in such a manner that he could not avoid presenting them, and two or three made her outrageous proposals beneath his very nose. Almsbury, however, always assumed his dignity at this and let them know she was no whore but a lady of quality and virtue. While Amber, ashamed of her country accent, hoped that they would indeed take her for a Royalist lady who had lived retired with her parents during the Protectorate and had only now come up to Court.

But the greatest adventure of all was her visit to Whitehall Palace.

Whitehall lay to the west, around the bend of the river from the City. It was a great sprawling mass of red brick buildings in the old Tudor style, honeycombed with hallways and having dozens of separate apartments opening one into another like some complex maze of huge rabbit-warren. Here lived the royal family and every court attendant or hanger-on who could wheedle official lodgings on the premises. It fronted directly on the river, so close that at high tide the kitchens were often flooded. And through the grounds ran the dirty unpaved narrow little thoroughfare of King Street, flanked on one side by that part of the Palace called the Cockpit and on the other by the wall of the Privy Garden.

Whitehall was open to all comers. Anyone who had once been presented at Court or who came with one who had could get in, and many total strangers filtered through the carelessly watched gateways. Hence, when Amber and Almsbury arrived in the Stone Gallery they found it so thronged as to be almost impassable.

The gallery was the central artery of the Court, a corridor almost four hundred feet long and fifteen feet wide, and on the walls were hung some of the splendid paintings which Charles I had collected and which his son was now trying to reassemble—paintings by Raphael, Titian, Guido. Scarlet-velvet drapes covered all doors opening into the royal apartments, and Yeomen of the Guard were posted before each one. The crowd was a motley assortment of satin-gowned ladies, languid sauntering young fops, brisk men-of-business hurrying along with an air of having weighty problems to solve, soldiers in uniform, country squires and their wives. Amber could easily recognize these latter for they all wore clothes hopelessly out of fashion—boots, when no gentleman would be seen off his horse in them; high-crowned hats like a Puritan's, though the new mode was for low ones; and knee-gartered breeches, although wide-bottom ones were now the style. Here and there was even a ruff to be seen. Amber was contemptuous of such provinciality and glad that her own clothes did not betray her origin.

She was less confident, however, about herself. "Gemini!" she whispered, round-eyed, to Almsbury. "How handsome all the ladies are!"

"There's not one of 'em," said the Earl, "half so pretty as you."

She gave him a grateful, sparkling smile and slipped her arm through his. She and Almsbury had become great friends and though he had not asked again to sleep with her he had told her that if she ever needed money or help he would be glad to give it. She thought that he had fallen in love with her.

And then all at once something happened. A ripple of excitement flowed along the Gallery, turning heads as it passed, catching the Earl and Amber in its wake.

"Here comes Mrs. Palmer!"

Amber's head turned with every other. And she saw advancing toward them, with people falling back on either side to make way for her, a magnificent red-haired white-skinned woman, trailing behind her a serving-woman, two pages, and a blackamoor. Haughty and arrogant, she walked with her head held high, seeing no one, though she could not but be well aware of the excitement she was creating. Amber's eyes began to burn with rage and jealousy and her heart set up a suffocating flutter. She was sickeningly afraid that Madame Palmer would see Almsbury—who she knew was acquainted with her—and stop. But she did not. She went past them without a glance.

"Oh! I hate her!" The words burst out as though driven by some pent-up violence.

"Sweetheart," said Almsbury, "someday you'll learn it's impossible to hate every woman a gentleman may make love to. It wears out your own guts, and that's all the good it does."

But Amber neither could nor wished to accept his Lordship's mellow philosophy. "I don't care if it does!" she insisted stubbornly. "I do hate her! And I hope she gets the pox!"

"No doubt she will."

After that they went to the Banqueting Hall to watch the King dine in state, which he usually did at one o'clock on Wednesday, Friday, and Sunday. The galleries were massed to see him but he did not come and at last they had to go away, disappointed. Amber had been much impressed when she had seen King Charles the day he returned to London; after Bruce she thought him the finest man in England.

About the first of August Amber became convinced that she was pregnant, partly because she had at least one symptom but mostly because it was forever on her mind. For a couple of weeks past she had waited and counted on her fingers and nothing had happened. Now her breasts began to feel stretched and sore and as though pricked by a thousand pins. She wanted to tell Bruce and yet she was half scared, for she guessed that he would not be pleased.

He got up early every morning—no matter how late he might have come in the night before—and Amber would put on her dressing-gown and talk to him until he left, after which she went back to sleep again. On this day she sat at the edge of the bed, swinging her bare feet and pulling a tortoise-shell comb through the tangled snarls of her hair. Bruce stood near her, wearing only his breeches and shoes, shaving with a long sharp-bladed razor.

For several minutes Amber watched him and neither of them spoke. Each time she tried to open her mouth her heart gave a leap and her courage failed her. Then all at once she said: "Bruce—what if I should get with child?"

He gave a slight involuntary start and cut himself, the bright blood showing in a little line on his chin, and then he turned to look at her. "Why do you say that? Do you think you are?"

"Well—haven't you noticed anything?" She felt strangely embarrassed.

"Noticed what? Oh—I hadn't thought about it." He scowled and even though it was not at her she felt a sudden frightened loneliness; then he turned back, took up a small bottle and put a drop of liquid styptic on the cut. "Jesus!" he muttered.

"Oh, Bruce!" She jumped off the bed and ran to him. "Please don't be mad at me!"

He had started shaving again. "Mad at you? It's my fault. I intended to be careful—but sometimes I forgot."

Amber looked at him, puzzled. What was he talking about? She'd heard in Marygreen that it was possible to avoid pregnancy by spitting three times into the mouth of a frog or drinkin sheep's urine, but Sarah had warned her often enough that such methods were unreliable.

"Sometimes you forgot what?"

"Nothing it will do any good to remember now." He wiped his face with a towel, tossed the towel onto the tabletop and then turned to put on the rest of his clothes. "Oh, Lord, Amber—I'm sorry. This is a devil of a mess."

She was quiet for a moment, but finally she said, "You don't like babies, do you?"

She asked the question so naïvely, looked up at him with so sad and wistful an expression that all at once he took her into his arms and held her head against his chest while one hand stroked tenderly over her hair. "Yes, my darling, of course I like them." His mouth was pressed against the top of her head, but his eyes were troubled and a little angry.

"What are we to do?" she asked him at last.

Held close in his arms with her body against his she felt warm and safe and happy—the problem had dissolved. For though he had told her he would not marry her and she had believed it at first, now she was almost convinced that he would. Why shouldn't he? They loved each other, they were happy together, and during the past several weeks of living with him she had almost forgotten that he was a lord and she the niece of a yeoman farmer. What might once have seemed impossible to the point of absurdity now seemed to her quite natural and logical.

He let her go and stood with his arms hanging at his sides while he talked, his green-grey eyes hard and uncompromising, watching her steadily. There was no doubt he meant every word he said.

"I'm not going to marry you, Amber. I told you that at the first and I've never once said anything to the contrary. I'm sorry this has happened—but you knew it probably would. And remember, it was your idea that you come to London—not mine. I won't just leave you to drift—I'll do everything I can to make it easier for you—everything that won't interfere with my own plans. I'll leave you money enough to take care of yourself and the baby. If you won't go back to Marygreen the best thing is for you to go to one of the women here in London who take care of pregnant women and arrange for their lying-in—some of those places are very comfortable and no one will inquire too closely for your husband. When you're well again you can do as you like. With a few hundred pounds in cash a woman as beautiful as you are should be able to marry a country-squire, at the least—or perhaps a knight, if you're clever enough—"

Amber stared at him. She was suddenly furious, all the pride and happiness she had felt at the prospect of bearing him a child was drowned now in pain and outraged pride. The sound of his voice enraged her—talking so coolly, as if falling in love with a man and having his baby was a matter to be settled with money and logic, like provisioning a ship! She almost hated him.

"Oh!" she cried. "So you'll give me money enough to catch a knight—if I'm clever! Well, I don't want to catch a knight! And I don't want your money, either! And as for the matter of that—I don't want your baby! I'm sorry I ever laid eyes on you! I hope you go away and I never see you again! I hate you! —Oh!—" She covered her face with her hands and began to cry.

Bruce stod watching her for a moment, but at last he put on his hat and started out of the room. Amber looked up. And when he had scarcely reached the bedroom door she ran after him.

"Where are you going?"

"Down to the wharf."

"Will you come back tonight? Please come back! Please don't leave me alone!"

"Yes—I'll try to get here early. Amber—" His voice was again warm and smooth, caressing, tender. "I know this is hard for you and I'm truly sorry it's happened. But it'll be over sooner than you expect and you'll be none the worse for it. It's really no great tragedy when a woman has a baby—"

"No great tragedy to a man! You'll go away and forget all about it—but *I* can't go away! *I* can't forget it! I'll never be able to forget it— Nothing will *ever* be the same for me again! Oh, damn men!"

As the days passed she became convinced beyond all doubt that she actually was pregnant.

Less than a week after she had told him, she began to retch the moment she lifted her head in the mornings. She was morose and unhappy and cried upon the slightest provocation, or with none at all. He began coming home even later at night and when he did they often quarrelled; she knew that her ill temper was keeping him from her, but she could not seem to control herself. But she knew also that nothing she had said or could say would make him change his mind. And when he was away once for an entire day and night and until late the next night, she realized that she must give over her haranguing and tantrums or lose him even before he sailed. She could not bear the thought of that, for she still loved him, and she made a tremendous effort to seem once more gay and charming when they were together.

But alone she was no more reconciled than she had been and the hours without him seemed endless, while she trailed idly about the house, steeped in pity for herself. This great world of London to which she had come with such brilliant expectations only four months ago now seemed a dismal place and full of woe. She had not the vaguest idea as to what she would do when he was gone and refused to discuss it with him, even pushing the thoughts out of her own mind when they began to creep in. When that day came she felt that the end of the world would also come, and did not care what happened afterward.

One hot mid-morning in late August Amber was down in the courtyard playing with some puppies that had been born at the inn a month or so before. She knelt on the flag-stones in the mottled shade of a fruit-heavy plum tree, laughing and holding two of the puppies in her arms while the proud mother lay nearby, wagging her tail and keeping a careful eye on her offspring. And then, unexpectedly, she glanced up and saw Bruce leaning on the rail of the gallery outside their bedroom, watching her.

He had left several hours before and she had not expected him back till evening, at the earliest. Her first reaction was one of delight that he had come home and surprised her and she gave him a wave as she got quickly to her feet, putting the puppies back into their box. But then immediately a slow stealthy fear began to sneak in. It grew ominously, and as she reached the stairs and started to mount them she raised her eyes and met his. She knew it then for sure. He was leaving today.

"What is it, Bruce?" she asked him, warily, as though she could ward off the answer.

"The wind's changed. We're sailing in an hour."

"Sailing! In an hour! But you said last night it wouldn't be for days!"

"I didn't think it would. But we're ready sooner than I expected and there's nothing to wait for."

While she stood there, helpless, he turned and went through the door, and then she followed him. There was a small leather-covered nail-studded trunk of his on the table already packed more than half full, while the wardrobe in which he kept his clothes was opened and empty. Now he took some shirts from a carved oak chest, piled them into the trunk, and as he did so he began to talk to her.

"I haven't much time, so listen to what I say. I'm leaving the coach and horses for your use. The coachman gets six pound a year with his livery and the footman gets three, but don't pay them until next May or they'll likely rub off. I've paid all the bills and the receipts are in the drawer of that table. So are the names and locations of a couple of women who can take care of you—ask them what the charge will be before you move into the house. It shouldn't be more than thirty or forty pound for everything."

While Amber stood staring at him, horrified at the brusque impersonal tone of his voice, he closed the lid of the trunk and walked swiftly to the door of the other room where he made a signal to someone evidently waiting out in the hall. The next moment he was back, followed by a great man with a patch over one eye, who shouldered the trunk and went out again. All the while Amber had been watching him, desperately trying to think of something she could say or do to stop him. But she felt stunned, paralyzed, and no words came to help her.

From the pocket of his doublet Bruce now drew a heavy leather wallet, closed by draw-strings and bulging with coins, and tossed it onto the table.

"There's five hundred pound. That should be enough to take care of you and the baby for several years, if necessary, but I'd advise you to put it with a goldsmith. I'd intended to do that for you, but now I haven't time. Shadrac Newbold is perfectly reliable and he'll allow you six percent interest if you put it with him at twenty days call, or three and a half if you want it on demand. He lives at the Crown and Thistle in Cheapside; his name is written on this piece of paper. But don't trust anyone else—above all don't trust a maid if you take one into service, and don't trust any strangers no matter how much you may like them. Now—" He turned and picked up his cloak. "I've got to go."

He spoke swiftly, giving her no chance to interrupt, and obviously was in a hurry to get out before she started to cry. But he had not taken three steps when she ran to throw herself before him.

"Bruce! Aren't you even going to kiss me?"

He hesitated for only an instant and then his arms went about her with a rough eagerness which suggested some reluctance within himself to leave her. Amber clung to him, her fingers clutching his arms as though she could hold him there by sheer force of superior strength, her mouth avidly against his, and already her face was wet with tears.

"Oh, Bruce! *Don't* go! Please don't go—please don't leave me—! Please—*please* don't leave me—"

But at last his fingers took hold of her wrists and slowly he forced her away. "Amber, darling—" His voice had a sound of pleading urgency. "I'll come back one day—I'll see you again—"

She gave a sudden cry, like a lonely desperate animal, and then she began to struggle with him, reaching out to grab hold of his arms, terrified. All at once he seized both her wrists, his mouth caught at hers again for an instant, and before she could quite realize what had happened he was gone through the room and out the door and it slammed behind him.

Stunned, she stood for a moment staring at the closed door. And then she ran to it, her hand going out to grab the knob.

"Bruce!"

But she did not quite reach it. Instead she stopped, brought up short by some hopelessness inside herself, and though for a moment her eyes continued to watch the door, at last she slumped slowly to her knees and her head dropped into her hands.

Chapter Six

THE DUKE OF YORK leaned gloomily against the fireplace. His hands were in the pockets of his breeches, his good-looking face was sulky, and he stared down at the floor. Across the room Charles was bent over a table, peering intently into a pewter pan set on an oil-lamp, in which boiled and bubbled a hundred different herbs. Now, carefully, he took up a spoon and measured in three heaping spoonfuls of dried ground angelica, stirring as he did so.

The brothers were in his Majesty's laboratory, surrounded on all sides by crucibles and alembics, retorts and matrasses. There were glass and earthenware jars full of powders, pastes, many-coloured liquids, oil of prima materia. Egg-shaped vessels of every size and substance lined the shelves. Piles of books bound in old leather, stamped with gold, stood on the floor or on the tables. Chemistry—which had not yet secured its divorce from the medieval witch-women, alchemy—was one of the King's chief interests. Even when he had had to beg a meal he had not been able to resist paying money out of his meagre store for almost every new nostrum recommended him by a passing quack.

"How the devil," said Charles now, stirring the mixture but not looking around, "did you let her get you into such a mess?"

York gave a heavy sigh. "I wish I knew. She isn't even pretty. She's as ugly as an old bawd. Eyes that pop and a shape like this—". His hands described an ungainly female form.

Charles smiled. "Perhaps that's what fooled you. It's my observation a pretty woman seldom thinks it's necessary to be clever. Anne Hyde is clever—don't you agree?" He seemed amused.

James shifted his weight, scowling. "I don't know what fooled me. I must have been out of my mind. Signing that damned marriage-contract!"

"And in your own blood. A picturesque touch, James, that one. Well—you've signed it and you've had her and she's pregnant. Now what?"

"Now nothing. I hope I never see her again."

"A contract of marriage is as binding as a ceremony, James, you know that. Whether you like it or not, you're married to her. And that child she carries is yours and will bear your name."

James heaved himself away from the fireplace, walked across the room and glanced at the concoction his brother had stirred up. "Ugh!" said the Duke. "How it stinks!"

"It does, I agree," admitted Charles. "But the fellow who sold me the recipe says it's the most sovereign thing for an ague ever discovered—and London and the ague, you know, are synonymous. This winter I don't doubt you'll be glad enough to borrow a dose of it from me."

Restless, discontented, angry, James turned and walked away. After a moment he once more took up the subject of his marriage. "I'm not so sure," he said slowly, "you're right about that, sir. The brat may not be mine after all."

"Now what've you been hearing?"

Suddenly James came back to him; his face was serious and growing excited. "Berkeley came to me two days ago and told me that Anne has lain with him. Killigrew and Jermyn have sworn the same thing since."

For a long moment Charles looked at his brother, searching his face. "And you believed them?"

"Of course I believed them!" declared James hotly. "They're my nearest friends! Why wouldn't I believe them?"

"Berkeley and Jermyn and Harry Killigrew. The three greatest liars in England. And why do you suppose they told you that? Because they knew it was what you wanted to hear. It is, isn't it?" Charles's dark eyes narrowed slightly, his face shrewd. He understood his brother perfectly, much better in fact than James understood himself.

James did not answer him for a long moment but at last he said softly, half-ashamed, "Yes. I suppose it is. But why the devil should I think Anne Hyde is more virtuous than another woman? They all have a price—"

"And hers was marriage." The King set the pan off the flame

and turned down the lamp. Then he took his doublet from where it had hung over a chair-back and slipped into it. "Look here, James—I'm no better pleased than you are with this business— The daughter of a commoner, even if he is my Chancellor, is no suitable wife for the heir to the English throne. But it would raise a damned peculiar smell all over Europe if you got her with child and refused to marry her. If she'd been anyone but the Chancellor's daughter we might have found a way around it. As it is I think there's only one course for you: Marry her immediately and with as good a grace as you can."

"That isn't what the Chancellor wants. He's locked her in her rooms and says he'd rather have her thrown into the Tower and beheaded than disgrace the Stuarts by marrying one of them."

"Edward Hyde was a good servant to my father and he's been a good servant to me. I don't doubt he's angry with her, but one thing you may be sure of—it's not only the Stuarts he's worried about. He knows well enough that if his daughter marries you he'll have a thousand new enemies. Jealousy doesn't breed love."

"If you say it's best, Sire, I'll marry her—but what about Mam?" He gave Charles a sudden desperate look that was almost comical.

Charles laughed, but put an arm about his brother's shoulders. "Mam will most likely have a fit of the mother that will go near to killing her." "A fit of the mother" was the common term for hysteria. "She's always hated Hyde—and her family pride is almost as great a passion with her as her religion. But I'll protect you, Jamie—" He grinned. "I'll threaten to hold off her pension."

They walked out together, James still thoughtful and morose, Charles good-humoured as usual. He snapped his fingers at a pair of little spaniels asleep in a square of sunshine and they scrambled to their feet and tore yapping out of the room, scuttling between his legs, turning to prance on their hind legs to look up at him.

James's marriage to Anne Hyde created a considerable excitement. The Chancellor was furious; Anne wept incessantly; and the Duke still thought he might find a way out. With the help of Sir Charles Berkeley he stole the blood-signed contract and burned it, and Berkeley offered to marry her himself and give the child his name. The courtiers were in a quandary, not knowing whether they should pay their respects to the new Duchess or avoid her altogether, and only Charles seemed perfectly at ease.

And then the Duke of Gloucester, who had fallen ill of small-pox but had been thought to be out of danger, died suddenly. Charles had loved him well, as he did all his family, and he had seemed a young man of great promise, eager and charming and intelligent. It was unbelievable that now he lay dead, still and solemn and never to move again. There had been nine children in the family. Two had died on the day of birth, two others had lived only a short while, and now there remained only Charles and James, Mary who was Princess of Orange, and Henrietta Anne, the youngest, still with her mother in France.

But even the death of Henry could not halt the festivities for long. And though the Court managed to show a decent face of sorrow in the presence of Charles or James, the balls and the suppers, the flirtations and the gambling went on as before, wildly, madly, as though it would never be possible to get enough of pleasure and excitement.

The great houses along the Strand, from Fleet Street to Charing Cross, were opened all day and far into the night. Their walls resounded with noisy laughter and the tinkle of glasses, music and chatter, the swish of silken skirts and the tap of high-heeled shoes. Great gilt coaches rattled down the streets, stood lined up outside theatres and taverns, went rambling through the woods of St. James's Park and along Pall Mall. Duels were fought in Marrowbone Fields and at Knightsbridge over a lady's dropped fan or a careless word spoken in jest. Across the card-tables thousands of pounds changed hands nightly, and lords and ladies sat on the floor, watching with breathless apprehension a pair of rolling dice.

The execution of the regicides, held at Charing Cross, were attended by thousands and all the quality went to watch. Those men who had been chiefly responsible for the death of Charles I now themselves died, jerking at the end of a rope until they were half-dead, and then they were cut down, disembowelled and beheaded and their dripping heads and hearts held up for the cheering crowds to see. After that their remains were flung into a cart and taken off to Newgate to be pickled and cured before being set up on pikes over the City gates.

A new way of life had come in full-blown on the crimson wings of the Restoration.

It was only a week after her brother's death that Princess Mary arrived in London. She was twenty-eight, a widow and mother—though she had left her son in Holland—a pretty, graceful gay young woman with chestnut curls and sparkling hazel eyes. She had always hated Holland, that sombre strait-laced land, and now she intended to live in England with her favourite brother and have all the lovely gowns and extravagant jewels for which she longed.

She embraced Charles enthusiastically, but she was cooler with James and only waited until the three of them were alone to speak her mind to him:

"How could you do it, James? Marry that creature! Heavens, where's your pride? Marrying your own sister's Maid of

Honour!" Anne and Mary had been close friends at one time, but that was over now.

James scowled. "I'm sick of hearing about it, Mary. God knows I didn't marry her because I wanted to."

"Didn't marry her because you wanted to! Why, pray, *did* you marry her then?"

Charles interrupted, putting an arm about his sister's waist. "I advised him to it, Mary. Under the circumstances it seemed the only honourable course to take."

Mary cocked a skeptical eyebrow. "Mam won't find it so honourable, I warrant you. Just wait until *she* gets here!"

"That," said Charles, "is what we're all waiting for."

It was not long until the Queen Mother Henrietta Maria arrived—not more than a week, in fact, after Anne Hyde's son was born. Most of the Court went to Dover to meet her and they stayed a day or two at the great old castle which for cenuries had guarded the cliffs of England.

Henrietta Maria was forty-nine but she looked nearer seventy, a tiny hollow-cheeked haunted-eyed woman with no vestige of beauty left. What little she had possessed had gone early, lost in the bearing of her many children, in the hardships of the Civil Wars, in her grief for her husband whom she had loved devotedly.

In repose her face was ugly, but when surrounded by people she was vivacious and gay, with all the superficial charm of her youth and the delightful manners in which she had so carefully schooled her children. She was dressed in the mourning-clothes which she had worn faithfully since her husband's death and never intended to leave off until her own. The gown was plain black with full sleeves and high neck, broad white linen collar and cuffs, and over her head was hung a heavy black veil. She still wore her dark hair in old-fashioned corkscrew curls; it was her one concession to the love of personal ornament and pretty things which had been so strong in her.

By nature she was domineering and since all her children were stubborn and self-willed there had been continual conflict in the family. Several years before she had quarrelled with Gloucester over his refusal to enter the Catholic Church and had warned him never to see her more; when he died they were still unreconciled. But in spite of her deep hurt over that situation she now accosted James, determined to rule him or to break off their relationship. The Duke and his mother had always been most friendly when apart and he had been dreading this encounter with her, for her tongue could be acid and spiteful when she was angry.

"Well, James," she said at last, when they were alone in her bedchamber to which she had summoned him. Her voice was quiet, and she had her hands clasped lightly before her, but her black eyes sparkled with excitement. "There's talk about you in France—talk of which I was, needless to say, deeply ashamed."

He stood across the room near the door and stared down at his feet, unhappy and ill-at-ease. He said nothing and would not look at her. For a long moment they remained perfectly silent and then he ventured to steal a glance, but instantly dropped his eyes.

"James!" Her voice was sharp and maternal. "Have you nothing to reply?"

With a sudden impulsiveness he crossed the room and dropped to one knee at her feet. "Madame, I beg your pardon if I have offended you. I've played the fool, but thank God now I've come to my senses. Mrs. Hyde and I are not married and I intend to think of her no more—I've had proof enough of her unworthiness."

The Queen Mother bent and kissed him lightly on the forehead. She was relieved and very pleased at the unexpected good sense he was showing—for knowing James she had anticipated a stubborn and bitter struggle. And so a part, at least, of what she had come for was accomplished.

She had two other purposes.

One was to secure a pension which would enable her to live out the rest of her life in comfort and security. She had begged too often from the tight-fisted Cardinal Mazarin, had lived too long in privation and want—sometimes without so much as firewood to heat her rooms. It would mean a great deal to her to have money again. Her other purpose was to get a suitable dowry for Henrietta Anne, who had suffered perhaps more than any of them during the years of exile. For with her father dead, her brother hunted out of his country, she had grown up as the poor relation of the grand Bourbons, a mere neglected little waif lost in the glitter of the French Court.

Now, however, King Louis's brother wanted to marry her.

Henrietta Anne, whom Charles called Minette, was just sixteen. Her features were not perfect, her figure was too slender and one shoulder was slightly higher than the other—but almost everyone who met her was immediately struck by her beauty. For they attributed to facial prettiness what was really the glow of a warm and tender charm; it was impossible to resist her. And Charles had for her a deep and sincere devotion which he had never felt for any of his numerous mistresses.

His sister's marriage to Philippe, Duc d'Orléans, would give him a valuable ally in the French Court, because Minette had already shown that she possessed a diplomatic talent which won admiration and respect from the most cynical statesmen. And she loved her brother with a passionate loyalty which would always place his interests first, those of Louis XIV second. Nevertheless Charles hesitated.

"Are you sure," he asked her, "that you *want* to marry Philippe?"

They had left the Banqueting Hall to stroll in the Privy Gardens, along the gravel paths which separated the lawns and hedges into formal squares. Though mid-November it was very warm, and the rose-bushes were still covered with leaves; Minette had not even troubled to throw a cloak over her gold-spangled ball-gown.

"Oh, yes, Sire! I do!" She answered him with an eager smile.

He glanced down at her. "Do you love him?" Charles was so eager for his sister's happiness that it troubled him to think of her marrying, as other princesses must, without love.

"Love him?" Minette laughed. "Mon Dieu! Since when did love have anything to do with marriage? You marry whom you must and if you can tolerate each other—why, so much the better. If not—" She shrugged. But there was no air of precocious cynicism about what she said—merely good common Parisian sense, and a willingness to accept the world for what it was.

"Perhaps," he said. "But nevertheless you're my sister, and I want to know. Do you love him?"

"Why—to tell you the truth, I don't know whether I do or not. I've played with him since we were children, and he's my cousin. I think he's pretty—and I feel a little sorry for him. Yes, I suppose you might say I love him." She put up one hand as a quick little breeze ruffled her hair. "And of course he's mad in love with me. Oh, he swears he can't *live* till we're married!"

"Oh, Minette, Minette—how innocent you are. Philippe's not in love with you—he's not in love with anyone but himself. If he thinks he loves you now it's because he sees that others do and imagines that if he marries you he'll get some of that affection himself. When he doesn't he'll grow jealous and resentful. He's a mean petty man, that Philippe—he'll never make you happy."

"Oh, you judge him too severely!" she protested. "He's so harmless. Why, all his concern is to find a new way of dressing his hair or tying his ribbons. The most serious thought in his life is who takes precedence over whom in a parade or at the banqueting-table."

"Or finding a new young man."

"Oh, well, *that!*" said Minette, dismissing so minor a fault with a graceful little gesture of one hand. "That's common enough—and no doubt he'll change when we're married."

"And suppose he doesn't?"

She stopped directly before him, looking up into his face.

"But, my dear!" Her voice was teasingly reproachful. "You're so serious about it. What if he doesn't? That's no great matter, is it—so long as we have children?"

He scowled. "You don't know what you're talking about, Minette."

"Yes, I do, my dear. I assure you I do, and I think the world overestimates love-making. It's only a small part of life—there are so many other things to do." She spoke now with a great air of confidence and worldly wisdom.

"My little sister—how much you have to learn." He smiled at her but his face was tender and sad. "Tell me, has a man ever made love to you?"

"No. That is, not very much. Oh, I've been kissed a time or two—but nothing more," she added, blushing a little and dropping her eyes.

"That's what I thought—or you wouldn't talk like that." Charles's first son had been born when Charles was Minette's age. "Half the joys and half the sorrows of this world are discovered in bed. And I'm afraid you'd find nothing but sorrow there if you married Philippe."

Minette frowned a little and gave a brief sigh; they started to walk again. "That may be all very true for men, but I'm sure it isn't for women. Oh, *please* let me marry him! You know how much Mam wants me to. And I want to too. I want to live in France, Sire—that's the only place I could ever be at home. I know Philippe isn't perfect, but I don't care—If I have France, I'll be happy."

Christmas was England's most beloved holiday, and nowhere was it celebrated with more enthusiasm than at Whitehall.

Every room and every gallery was decorated with holly, cypress and laurel. There were enormous beaten-silver wassail-bowls garlanded with ivy. Branches of mistletoe hung from chandeliers and in doorways, and a berry was pulled off for each kiss. Gay music sounded throughout the Palace, the staircases were crowded with merry young men and women, and both day and night there was a festival of dancing and games and cards.

The immense kitchens were busy preparing mince-pies, pickled boar's heads to be served on immense golden platters, peacocks with their tails spread, and every other traditional Yule-tide delicacy. In the Banqueting Hall the King's Christmas presents were on display and this year every courtier with a farthing to his name had sent one—instead of retiring into the country to avoid the obligation, as had once been common practice.

And then suddenly the laughter was hushed, the music ceased to play, gentlemen and ladies walked softly, spoke in whispers: Princess Mary was sick of the small-pox. She died the day before Christmas.

The royal family passed Christmas day quietly and sadly, and Henrietta Maria began to make preparations for returning to France. She was afraid to leave Minette longer in England for fear she too would contract the disease. And there was no real reason to stay longer, for though she had Minette's dowry and a generous pension for herself, she knew at last that she had failed with James.

Berkeley had finally admitted that his story had been a lie, Killigrew and Jermyn had done the same, and James had recognized Anne as his wife. But he made no mention of his decision to his mother and she was furious when she heard of it, refused to speak to him either in public or in private and declared that if that woman entered Whitehall by one door she herself would go out by another.

And then all at once her attitude changed completely and she told James that since Anne was his choice in a wife she was ready to accept her, and she asked that he bring the Duchess to her. James was relieved, though he knew what had prompted her sudden softening of heart. Cardinal Mazarin had written to tell her frankly that if she left England while still on bad terms with her two sons she would find no welcome in France. He was afraid that Charles would revoke her pension and that he, Mazarin, would have to support her.

The day before she left London Henrietta Maria received her daughter-in-law in her bedchamber at Whitehall. This was still the custom among great persons for that room was the most opulently furnished of all and differed from a drawing-room only because it contained the immense four-poster tester-covered bed-of-state. The reception was a large one, for Henrietta Maria was popular at Court if nowhere else, and in spite of widespread sickness they had been drawn there by curiosity to see how Queen and Duchess would greet each other. All wore sombre black and most jewels had been reluctantly left at home. The room smelt of unwashed bodies and a nostril-searing stench of burnt brimstone and saltpetre which had been used to disinfect the air. In spite of that precaution Henrietta Maria had not been willing for Minette to run the risk, and she was not there.

The Queen Mother sat in a great black velvet chair, a little mantle of ermine about her shoulders, talking pleasantly with a group of gentlemen. The King stood just beside her, tall and handsome in his royal-purple velvet mourning. But everyone was growing impatient. The prologue had been too long—they were eager for the play to begin.

And then there was a sudden commotion in the doorway. The Duke and Duchess of York were announced.

A hushed expectant murmur ran through the room and many pairs of eyes glanced quickly to Henrietta Maria. She sat perfectly still, watching her son and his wife approach, a faint smile on her mouth; no one could have told what she was thinking. But Charles, glancing down at her, saw that she trembled ever so slightly and that one veined taut-skinned hand had a tight hold on the arm of her chair.

Poor Mam, he thought. How much that pension means to her!

Anne Hyde was twenty-three years old, dark and ugly with a large mouth and bulging eyes. But she walked into the room —stared at by dozens of pairs of curious jealous critical eyes and facing a mother-in-law she knew hated her—with her head held high and a kind of courageous grandeur that commanded admiration. With perfect respect but no slightest hint of servility she knelt at the Queen's feet, bowing her head, while James mumbled a speech of presentation.

Henrietta Maria smiled graciously and kissed Anne lightly on the forehead, apparently as well-pleased as though she had made the choice for James herself. Behind her the face of the King was impassive—but as Anne gave him a quick look of gratitude his black eyes sparkled at her with something that was very like a reassuring and congratulatory smile.

Chapter Seven

THE DAY AFTER Lord Carlton's departure Amber had moved almost a mile across town to the Rose and Crown in Fetter Lane. She could not stand the sight of the rooms where they had lived, the table where they had eaten, and the bed they had slept in. Mr. Gumble who gave her a bleak, sympathetic look, the chambermaid, even the black-and-white bitch with her litter of pups, filled her with lonely sickness. She wanted to get away from it and, just as much, she wanted to avoid the possibility of seeing Almsbury or any other of his Lordship's acquaintance. The Earl's promise of friendship should she need it meant nothing to her now but the dread of raking over her misery and shame. She wanted to be left alone.

For several days she shut herself up in the single room she had taken.

She was convinced that her life was over and the future that lay before her was arid and hopeless. She wished that she had never seen Bruce, and forgetting her own willful part in what had happened to her, blamed him for all her troubles. She forgot that she had eagerly wanted to have a child and hated him for leaving her pregnant, frightened and baffled by the knowledge that imprisoned within her body, growing with each day that passed, was proof of her guiltiness. One day she would no longer be able to conceal it—and what would happen to her then? She forgot that she had despised Marygreen and wanted to leave it, and blamed him for having brought her to this great city where she had no friends and every strange face looked like an enemy's. A hundred times she decided that she would go back home, but she did not dare. For though she might be able to explain to Sarah what had happened, her uncle, she knew, would very likely refuse her the house. And certainly would turn her out when he found her with child.

Amber mulled wretchedly over her problems, but there

seemed no solution to them and no end. She would never again be young and gay and free. And all because of *him!*

But in spite of herself Lord Carlton sometimes—and more often as the days passed—stepped out of his role as Devil. She was still wholly infatuated and she had a passionate painful longing for him that was something more than desire. It was awe, bedazzlement, admiration as well.

But gradually, as time passed, she began again to take an interest in merely being alive. Her meals tasted good to her. There were so many things to eat here in London that she had never had before: elaborate sweets called marchpanes, olives imported from the Continent, Parmesan cheese and Bayonne bacon. And she began to feel a kind of curious wonder at the strange and mysterious functioning of her own body in pregnancy. She even began to care something about her appearance again. And once when she had idly dusted some powder over her cheeks, she went on opening one jar after another, until she had painted all her face, and she could not help being pleased with the result.

She almost felt then that she was too pretty to mope away the rest of her life alone.

Her windows overlooked the street, which was in a somewhat fashionable neighbourhood, and she began to spend more and more time there, wondering who the handsomely gowned lady was, getting out of her coach attended by four gallants, where the good-looking young man who stared up at her was going and what he thought of her. London was just as exciting as it had ever been.

But *I'm* going to have a baby!

That was what made the difference. Even more than Lord Carlton's departure.

But she could not stay indoors forever, and so one day when Carlton had been gone for about a fortnight she made herself ready again with great care and went out. She had no plan or specific intention but wanted only to get away from her room, perhaps to ramble through the streets in her coach, to feel in some way that she was a part of the world.

The coachman whom Lord Carlton had hired had fallen sick of the small-pox not three days after his Lordship left and Amber had paid him his salary for the year and—scared of the disease—sent the footman away. The host at the Rose and Crown found two others to take their place. Now while she waited for her coach she stood in the doorway of the inn pulling on her gloves, and was unable to keep back a pleased smile as two flaxenhaired beribboned young fops went by and craned their necks to stare at her. She was sure that they thought her some person of quality. And then, to her surprise, she heard her own name spoken and gave a start. Turning quickly she saw that a strange woman had come up behind her.

"Good morning, Mrs. St. Clare. Oh, I'm sorry! I didn't mean

to affright you, madame. I wanted to ask how you were doing. My apartments are just next yours and the landlord told me you'd been abed with an ague. I have a decoction that does wonders for an ague—"

Her eyes and smile were friendly and she looked at Amber as though she admired her beauty and her clothes. Instantly grateful for the attention and glad to have someone to talk to, if only for a moment, Amber made her a little curtsy.

"God-a-mercy, madame. But I think the ague's near gone by now."

At that instant her coach drove up and stopped before them; the footman opened the door, turned down the folding iron steps and stood ready to hand her in. Amber hesitated for just a moment. The jolt her self-confidence had had and two weeks of complete seclusion had made her a little shy. But she was desperately lonely and this lady looked kind—and not too critical. She would have been afraid of one of the glossy tart-voiced young women her own age whom she had seen and admired and half-consciously begun to imitate. But she was not able to think of anything more to say and so made her a slight curtsy and started toward the coach.

"Why!" cried the stranger then. "Is that your family madame?" She referred to Bruce's crest, which Amber had not removed from the door.

"Aye," said Amber without hesitation. But she was hoping that the woman could not tell one from another. To her, at least, they all looked alike with their absurd clawing dog-faced lions, their checkerboards and stripes.

"Why, then I know your father well! My own country-seat is near Pickering in Yorkshire!"

"I come from Essex, madame. Near Heathstone." She was beginning to wish that she had not lied about it, for it seemed likely she might be caught.

"Why, of course, Mrs. St. Clare! How furiously stupid of me! But your crest is so similar to that of a near neighbour of mine—though now I look closer I see well enough what the difference is. May I present myself, madame? I'm Mrs. Goodman."

"I'm glad of your acquaintance, madame." She bowed, thinking how much like a fine lady she was behaving, for she had learned those little niceties from her French master and by watching Lord Carlton and his friends. "Can't I carry you somewhere?"

"Why, faith, my dear, I wouldn't care to put you to the trouble. I was only going to pick up a trifle or so in the 'Change."

The 'Change, Amber knew, was a fashionable lounge and meeting-place for the gallants and ladies, and that now seemed to her as good a place as any for her excursion. "I am going there myself, madame. Pray ride along with me."

Mrs. Goodman did not hesitate and they both got in, spreading their full skirts about them, ruffling their fans, commenting on the September heat. The coach started off across town, jogging about on the cobble-stones, and from time to time they were held up in a dispute with a hackney over the right of way or had to wait while a procession of colliers carts filed slowly by. Amber and Sally Goodman sat inside talking animatedly, and Amber had almost forgotten that she was a jilted woman carrying in her body a bastard child.

Sally Goodman was plump with pink over-fleshed arms and a bosom that bulged out of her low-necked gowns. Her skin was badly pock-marked, though she did what she could to remedy this defect by the application of a thick layer of some pink-white cosmetic, and her hair was two or three shades of light yellow so that it was plain she aided nature in this respect also. She admitted to twenty-eight of her thirty-nine years and, for that matter, she did contrive to look younger than she was. Her clothes had a sort of specious elegance, though a practiced eye might have known immediately that they were made of second-rate materials by a second-rate sempstress, and there was precisely the same quality in her manner and personality. But she had a hearty good-natured joviality that Amber found both warming and comforting.

Mrs. Goodman, it seemed, was a person of quality and means, making a short stay in London while her husband was abroad on business. Evidently judging Amber by her accent, clothes and coach, she assumed her to be a country heiress visiting in the city and Amber—pleased with this identity—agreed that she was.

"But, Lord, sweetheart!" said Mrs. Goodman. "Are you all alone? A pretty young creature like you? Why, there's dozens of wicked men in London looking for just such an opportunity!"

Amber almost surprised herself with the readiness of her reply. "Oh, I'm visiting my aunt—that is, I—I'm going to visit her as soon as she gets back. She's still in France— She was with his Majesty's court—"

"Oh, of course," agreed Mrs. Goodman. "My husband was there too, for a time, but the King thought he could do more good back here, organizing plots. Where does your aunt live, my dear?"

"She lives in the Strand—oh, it's a mighty fine house!" Almsbury had once driven her by his home which was located there, though not yet returned to his possession.

"I hope she comes back soon. I'm afraid your parents would be uneasy to have you here alone for very long, my dear. You're not married, I suppose?"

Amber felt a sudden hot blush at that question and her eyes retreated to her closed fan. But she found another nimble lie conveniently at her tongue's end.

"No—I'm not— But I will be soon. My aunt has a gentleman for me—an earl, I think she said. He's on his travels now but he'll likely come home when she does." Then she remembered what Almsbury had told her about Bruce's parents and added: "My father and mother are both dead. My father was killed at Marston Moor and my mother died in Paris ten years ago."

"Oh, you poor dear child. And have you no guardian, no one to care for you?"

"My aunt is my guardian when she's here. I've been living with another aunt since she went abroad."

Mrs. Goodman shook her head and sympathetically pressed Amber's hand. Amber was passionately grateful for her kindly interest and understanding, for the mere fact that here was another human being she could talk to, share small experiences with—she had always felt miserable and lost when alone.

The Royal Exchange stood at the junction of Corn Hill and Threadneedle Street, not far from the Royal Saracen Inn. The building formed an immense quadrangle completely surrounding a courtyard and the galleries were divided into tiny shops attended by pretty young women who kept up a continual cry: "What d'ye lack, gentlemen? What d'ye lack, ladies? Ribbons, gloves, essences—" The gallants loitered there, flirting with the 'Change women, lounging against a pillar to watch the ladies walk by and calling out boldly to them. The courtyard itself was crowded with merchants, soberly dressed, intent on business, talking of stocks and mortgages and their ventures at sea.

As they went inside and began to mount the stairs Amber reluctantly followed Sally Goodman's example and put on her vizard. What's the good of a pretty face, she thought, if no one's to see it? and she let her cloak fall back, showing her figure. But in spite of the mask there was no doubt she attracted attention. For as they walked along, pausing now and then to examine a pair of gloves, some embroidered ribbons, a length of lace, enthusiastic comments followed them.

"She's handsome—*very* handsome! By God, but she is!"

"Those killing eyes!"

"As pretty a girl, for a fortnight's use or so, as a man could wish."

Amber began to feel pleased and excited and she cast furtive sidelong glances to see how many men were watching her and what they looked like. Mrs. Goodman, however, took another view of the compliments. She clucked her tongue and shook her head.

"Lord, how bawdy the young men talk nowadays!"

Somewhat abashed at this Amber guarded her eyes and frowned a little, to show that she was displeased too. But the frown did not last long—for she was half-intoxicated by the sights and sounds all about her.

She wanted to buy almost everything she saw. She had little

sense of discrimination, her acquisitive instincts were strong, and she felt so boundlessly rich that there seemed no reason why she might not have whatever she desired. Finally she stopped before a stall where a plump black-eyed young woman stood surrounded by dozens of bird-cages, painted gold or silver or bright colours; in each one was a brilliant bird, canaries, parrots, cockatoos brought back by the East India Company or some merchant fleet.

While she was making her selection, unable to decide between a small turquoise-coloured parakeet and a large green squawking bird, she heard a man's voice in back of her remark: "By God, she's tearing fine. Who d'ye think she is?"

Amber glanced around to see if he was speaking of her, just as the other replied, "I've never seen her at Court. Like as not she's some country heiress. By God, I'll make her acquaintance though I perish for it!" And with that he stepped forward, swept off his hat and bowed to her. "Madame, if you'll permit me, I should like to make you a present of that bird—which is, if I may be permitted the observation—no more gorgeous than yourself."

Delighted, Amber smiled at him and had just begun to make a curtsy when Mrs. Goodman's voice cut in sharply: "How dare you use a young woman of quality at this rate, sir? Begone, now, before I call a constable and have you clapped up for your impertinence!"

The fop raised his eyebrows in surprise and hesitated a moment as if undecided whether to challenge the issue, but Mrs. Goodman faced him so stoutly that at last he bowed very ceremoniously to the disappointed Amber and turned to go off with his friend. As they walked away she heard his scornful remark:

"Just as I thought. A bawd out with her protégée. But apparently she intends to save her for some gouty old duke."

At that Amber realized she had seemed too eager to make the acquaintance of strangers, and she began to fan herself swiftly. "Heaven! I swear I thought he was a young fellow I'd seen sometime at my aunt's!" She drew her cloak about her and went back to the business of selecting her bird, but now she kept her eyes decorously within the shop.

She paid for the gilt cage and little turquoise parakeet with a random coin which she fished out of her muff. And once again Mrs. Goodman's quickness came to her rescue, for as she was scooping the change back into her hand, Sally caught hold of her wrist.

"Hold on, sweetheart. I believe you're lacking a shilling there."

The girl behind the counter quickly produced one, giggling, saying that she had miscounted. Mrs. Goodman gave her a severe frown and she and Amber left, going downstairs then to get into the coach.

On the ride back Mrs. Goodman undertook to warn Amber

of the dangers a young and pretty woman unaccustomed to town life, must encounter in the city. The times were wicked, she said; a woman of virtue had much ado to preserve not only her honesty but even the appearance of it.

"For in the way of the world, sweetheart," she warned, "a woman loses as much by the appearance of evil as she does by the misdeed itself."

Amber nodded solemnly, her own guilty conscience writhing inside her, and she wondered miserably if her behaviour had given the strait-laced Mrs. Goodman some clue to her predicament. And then, as the coach stopped, she looked out the opened window and gave a sharp horrified cry at what she saw: Trudging slowly along was a woman, naked to the waist and with her long hair falling over her breasts, moaning and wincing each time a man who walked behind her slashed his whip across her shoulders. Following in her wake and trailing beside her was a considerable crowd—laughing jeering little boys, grown men and women, who mocked and taunted.

"Oh! Look at that woman! They're beating her!"

Sally Goodman glanced at her and then away, her face complacently untroubled. "Don't waste your sympathy, my dear. Wretched creature—she must be the mother of a bastard child. It's the common punishment, and no more than the wicked creatures deserve."

Amber continued to watch with reluctant fascination, turning her head to look as the procession passed. There were streaks of blood laced across the woman's naked shoulders. And then suddenly she turned back again and shut her eyes hard. For a moment she felt so sick that she was sure she would faint, but fear of Mrs. Goodman made her take hold of herself again. But all her gaiety was gone and she was aware as never before that she had committed a terrible crime—a punishable crime.

Oh, Gemini! she thought in frantic despair. That might be me! That *will* be me!

The next morning Amber was up, wearing her dressing-gown and eating a dishful of gooseberry jelly, which was supposed to cure her nausea, when there was a rap at the door and Mrs. Goodman's cheerful voice called her name. Quickly she shoved the dish under the bed and ran to let her in.

"I was just putting up my hair."

Mrs. Goodman followed her back to the dressing-table. "Let me help sweetheart. Has your maid gone abroad?"

Amber felt her fingers working competently, making a thick braid, twisting it into a chignon high on her head, then sticking in gold-headed bodkins to hold the heavy scroll in place. "Why—I had to turn my maid off. She—she got herself with child." It was the only excuse she could think of.

Mrs. Goodman shook her head, but her mouth was too full

of bodkins to cluck her tongue. "It's a wicked age, I vow and swear. But Lord, sweetheart, how'll you shift, without a maid?"

Amber frowned. "I don't know. But my aunt'll have dozens, when she comes."

Mrs. Goodman had finished now and Amber began combing out the long thick tresses at the sides of her face, rolling the ends into fat curls that lay on her shoulders.

"Of course, sweetheart. But until then—Heaven, a lady can't do without a serving-woman."

"No," agreed Amber. "I know it. But I don't know where to get one—I've never been in London before. And a woman alone must be mighty careful of strangers," she added virtuously.

"She must, my dear, and that's the truth on it. You're a wise young creature to know it. But perhaps I can help you. A dear friend of mine has just removed to her country-estate and left some of her serving-maids here. There's one of 'em I have in mind in particular—a neat modest accomplished young creature she is, and if she's not already found a new place I can get her for you."

Amber agreed and the girl arrived in less than an hour, a plain-faced plump little thing in neat dark-blue skirt, tucked-up fresh white apron and long-sleeved white blouse with a linen cap that covered her hair and tied in a knot beneath her round chin. She curtsied to Amber, her eyes lowered modestly, and she spoke in a soft voice that suggested she would never try to bully whoever took her into service. Her name was Honour Mills and Amber hired her promptly at two pounds a year, with her room and board and clothing.

It made her feel very fashionable and elegant, having a maid to brush her hair and lay out her clothes, run small errands and walk behind her when she went out of doors. And she was grateful, too, for the girl's company. Honour was quiet and well-behaved, always neat in her appearance, always good-tempered, and a most satisfactory audience for her mistress whom she seemed to admire greatly.

But nevertheless Amber remembered Lord Carlton's advice, kept her money well-hidden and did not confide her private affairs to her. She had not, however, taken the five hundred pounds to Shadrac Newbold, as he had suggested, for she had never heard of a goldsmith before and was distrustful of putting her money into the hands of a complete stranger. She thought herself quite competent to manage it. Nor did she intend to go to either of the two women he had suggested until she was forced by her own appearance to do so.

Amber and Mrs. Goodman became constant companions. They ate dinner together, usually in one of their own apartments; they went riding in Hyde Park or the Mall, but did not get out; they shopped in the Royal Exchange or at the East India House. Once Amber suggested that they go to a play, but Mrs. Goodman had some severe things to say about the debauchery of the theatres, and after that she did not dare make any more suggestions.

Mrs. Goodman's husband was detained longer on the Continent, for his business matters were badly tangled. And Amber said that she had received a letter from her aunt, telling her that it would be two weeks or more before she could leave France. If necessary she did not doubt that she could think of another excuse at the end of that time. She was already convinced that people had a better opinion of you if you pretended to be something more than you were than if you used them honestly.

They had been acquainted for perhaps a fortnight when Sally Goodman told Amber about her nephew. Just returned from church, for it was Sunday, they were in Amber's room, eating a dishful of hot buttered shrimps with their fingers and washing them down with Rhenish. Honour was busily using a pair of bellows to make the fire go, for the day had suddenly turned chill and heavy fog hung over the city.

"Faith," said Mrs. Goodman, not looking up, for she ate with an almost impartial attention to her plate, "but I'll vow it was worth a Jew's eye to hear my silly nephew going on about you last night. He swears you're the most glorious creature he's ever seen."

Amber, popping a crisp plump shrimp into her mouth, glanced over at her swiftly. "When did he see me?"

She had not made the acquaintance of a single young man, though she had had opportunities aplenty; she was convinced that she would never fall in love again but nevertheless she longed for masculine company. Being with a woman she thought was flat and unexciting as a glass of water. But she had almost never met the man who did not seem to have at least one redeeming quality.

"Yesterday, when you alighted from your coach out in the yard. I thought the young simpleton would fall out the window and break his noddle. But I told 'im you're intended for an earl."

Amber's smile disappeared. "Oh. You shouldn't 've done that!"

"Why not?" Mrs. Goodman now turned to a French cake, split and covered with melted butter and rose-water, sprinkled with almonds. "You are, aren't you?"

"Well—yes. But then, he's your nephew. Heavens, you've been mighty kind to me, Mrs. Goodman, and if your nephew wants to make my acquaintance—why, what harm is there in that?"

Luke Channell was to call on his aunt that evening and Mrs. Goodman said that she would bring him to meet her. He was, she said, just returning from his travels and on his way to his country-seat in Devonshire. Amber, very much excited and hoping that he would be handsome, changed her gown and had

Honour dress her hair again. She did not expect a man like Lord Carlton, for she had seen none other in London like him, but the prospect of talking to a young man again, perhaps flirting a little, seeing his eyes light with admiration, was an exhilarating tonic.

Luke Channel, however, was a serious disappointment.

Not very much taller than she, he was stockily built with a broad flat snub-nosed face, and his two front teeth had been broken off diagonally; there was a kind of slippery green moss growing along the edges of his gums. But at least he was quite well-dressed, with a profusion of ribbon-loops at his elbows, hips, and knees, his manner was self-assured, and he seemed tremendously smitten by her. He grinned incessantly, his eyes scarcely left her face, and at times he even seemed so nonplussed as to lose his trend of thought in the middle of a sentence.

Like most young men who went abroad he had brought back his quota of French oaths, and every other word was "Morblew" or "Mor-dee." He told her that the Louvre was much larger that Whitehall, that in Venice the prostitutes walked the streets with their naked breasts on display, and that the Germans drank even more than the English. When he left he invited Amber and his aunt to be his guests at the Mulberry Gardens the next evening and she accepted the invitation with a smiling curtsy.

They had scarcely closed the door when Honour asked her: "Well, mem, what d'ye think of him? A mighty spruce young fellow, I'd say."

But Amber felt suddenly tired and discouraged; the tendency to gloom and moroseness which had come with her pregnancy began to settle. Listlessly she shrugged her shoulders. "He's no great matters to brag of."

And all at once it washed down over her—the disappointment and loneliness, the aching longing she had for Bruce, the hopelessness of her situation, and she flung herself onto the bed and began to cry. She could feel her pregnancy closing in on her, seeming to shut her into a room from which there was no escape, and she was as terrified as though menaced by some looming monster.

Oh, what'll I do. What'll I *do!* she thought wildly. It's growing and growing and *growing* inside me! I can't stop it! It's going to get bigger and bigger till I swell up like a stuffed toad and everyone will know— Oh! I wish I was dead!

Chapter Eight

AMBER AND LUKE CHANNELL were married in mid-October, three weeks after they had met, in the old church of the parish where the Rose and Crown was located. As was customary,

Amber bought the wedding-ring and she got a very handsome one with several little diamonds, for which she told the jeweller to send a bill. She had discovered that it was possible to do business that way and now made a practice of it, for her ignorance of money-values was otherwise a serious handicap.

Amber had not been at all eager to marry Luke. She considered him to be one of the least attractive men she had ever known and nothing but the eternal nagging awareness of pregnancy could have persuaded her to consider him for a husband. He seemed to have just one redeeming quality, and that was a violent infatuation for her.

But by the next morning she knew that she had been cheated in that too.

His obsequious adoring manner had vanished altogether and now instead he was insolent, crude, and overbearing. His vulgarity shocked and disgusted her and he would allow her neither privacy nor peace but set upon her at any hour of the day or night. From the first day he was gone most of the time, drank incessantly, harangued her to send for the rest of her money, and displayed almost without provocation a violent and destructive bad-temper.

Mr. Goodman's financial affairs continued unsolved and he began to seem almost as nebulous a figure as Amber's aunt, though both women made new excuses to each other whenever the time limit of the old one had run out. As soon as Amber and Luke were married the two apartments were flung together and presently Sally was borrowing Amber's fans and gloves and jewels and even tried without success to squeeze into her gowns. Amber began to feel that somehow she was caught between these two, aunt and nephew, who seemed to have gained an advantage over her—though she was at a loss to know just when or how it had happened.

Honour remained as quiet and self-effacing as ever, though she became slovenly and Amber had to tell her over and over again to wear her shoes in the house and not to go out in a soiled apron. When Luke was at home she stared at him with a sheepish longing that turned Amber sick; when he was drunk she held his head, cleaned up his vomit, undressed him and put him to bed. Such tasks were routine for a servant, but Honour performed them with a kind of fawning wife-like devotion. Luke, however, showed her no gratitude, nagged at her persistently, gave her a cuff or a kick whenever he was annoyed—which was often—and handled her familiarly even before Amber.

When they had been married scarcely two weeks Amber came into the room one day and surprised Honour and Luke on the bed together. Stunned and disgusted Amber stood there for a moment, mouth and eyes wide open, before she slammed the door. Luke gave a startled jump and Honour, with a terrified shriek, scrambled up and ran into Sally's room, whimpering as she went.

Luke glared at her. "What in hell blew you in here?"

She was on the verge of crying, not because she cared if he seduced the maid, but because she was nervous and distraught. "How was I to know what you'd be about!"

He did not answer but got into his doublet, buckled on his sword and smacking his hat onto his head slammed out of the room. Amber stood for a moment, glaring after him, and then she went to find Honour. The girl was in Sally's room, huddled in a far corner behind the bed, rocking and sobbing with her hands held protectively over her head. A master or mistress had the right to beat unruly servants and that was obviously what she expected.

"Stop that!" cried Amber. "I'm not going to hurt you!" She tossed a coin into her lap. "Here. And I'll give you another for every piece-of-mutton he gets from you. Maybe he won't worry me so much then," she added in a mutter, and swirling her skirts about walked away.

But her own loathing of Luke and his unpleasant personal habits was by no means the only source of Amber's trouble with her husband. Both he and his aunt were spending a great deal of money—almost every day new packages arrived for one or both of them—but they paid for nothing. She brought the subject up one day when she was setting out on a shopping tour with Mrs. Goodman.

"When's Luke going to get some money from home? If he so much as takes his dinner at a tavern or goes to the play he asks me for some."

Sally laughed and fanned herself industriously, looking out into the crowded street. "See that yellow satin gown just across the way, sweetheart? I've a mind to have one like it. Now what's that you were saying? Oh, yes—Luke's money. Well, to tell you truly, sweetheart, we wanted to keep this from you, but since you ask you may as well know: Luke's father is furious he married without his leave. Poor Luke—married for love and now it seems he may be cut off without so much as a shilling. But then, my dear, with all *your* money no doubt the two of you could shift well enough?" She gave Amber an ingratiating grin, but her eyes were hard and searching.

Amber stared at her, shocked. Luke cut off and the two of them to live on her five hundred pounds! She had begun to learn already that five hundred was less than the illimitable fortune she had at first imagined it to be, particularly when spent at the reckless rate they three were going.

"Well, now, why the devil *should* he be cut out of his father's will?" The question was a sharp challenge, for she and Sally were by no means as polite as they had once been and several times had come close to quarreling. "I suppose I'm not a good enough match for 'im?"

"Oh, Lord, sweetheart, I protest! I didn't say that, did I? But his father had another girl in mind— Wait till he sees you. He'll come around then fast enough, I warrant. And by the way, my dear, that thousand pound you sent for to your aunt's lawyer—isn't it mighty long in coming?" Sally's voice was once more silky, soothing, as when she asked Luke to curb his temper, not to tear up the cards when he lost a hand, and to treat Honour more gently.

But Amber stuck out her lower lip, refused to look at her, and answered sullenly. "Maybe the lawyer won't send it at all—now I'm married!"

Little by little her money was dribbling away. It went to Luke for pocket money, to Mrs. Goodman, who always promised to repay the instant her husband returned from France, or to a tradesman who came to the door dunning her for a bill two or three months in arrears.

What'll I do when it's gone? she would think desperately. And, overwhelmed with fear and foreboding she would begin to cry again. She had cried more often in the weeks since Lord Carlton had left than in all the rest of her life. If Luke flew into a temper, if the laundress did not return her smocks in time—the slightest upset, the smallest inconvenience was now enough to start the tears. Sometimes she wept dismally, mournfully, but other times the tears came in a torrent, noisy and splashing as a summer storm. Life was no longer a gay and buoyant challenge but had become empty and hopeless.

There was nothing left to look forward to. This baby would be born and others would follow in a succession down the years. Without money, with children to care for, a brutal husband, hard work, her prettiness would soon be gone. And she would grow old.

Sometimes she woke at night feeling as if she were struggling in some growing living net. She would sit up suddenly, so scared that she could not breathe. And then she would remember Luke beside her, sprawled over three-fourths of the bed, and hatred made her long to reach down and strangle him with her own hands. She would sit there staring at him, thinking with pleasure of what it would be like to stab him to death, to have him pinned there to the bed flopping helplessly. She wondered if she could poison him—but she knew nothing of the process and was afraid of being caught. A woman guilty of husband-murder was burnt alive.

So far apparently none of them had guessed at her pregnancy, though it had now passed the end of the fifth month. Her numerous starched petticoats and full-gathered skirts helped to disguise her in the daytime and ever since her stomach had begun to swell she had contrived to dress when no one was around or to keep her back turned. The lights were always out at night because Honour slept in the same room they did, on a little trundle-bed which was pushed under the large one in the daytime. But nevertheless they were sure to find out soon, and she knew she could never make them believe the child was Luke's. She had no idea what she would do then.

From time to time Amber had changed the hiding-place of her money, leaving out only a few coins at one time, and she congratulated herself that the system was a very clever one. One day she went to her cache; the wallet was gone.

She had hung the strings of the leather bag over a nail hammered into the back of a very heavy carved oak chest which stood against one wall and was never moved. Now, with a little gasp, she got down onto her hands and knees to look underneath it, reaching back to feel about in the thick rolls of dust, suddenly scared and sick. She turned and shouted over her shoulder at Honour, who was in the next room, and the girl came on the run, stopping suddenly when she saw Amber glowering there beside the chest. Then she made a demure little curtsy and opened her eyes wide.

"Yes, mem?"

"Did you move this chest?"

"Oh, no, mem!" Her hands were holding to the sides of her skirts, as though for moral support.

Amber decided that she was lying, but thought it most likely that whatever her part in the theft had been she had been prompted by Luke. She got up wearily, discouraged, but still less surprised than she would have expected to be, and went to the door where a tailor stood waiting with his bill in his hand. He was most courteous, however, when she told him that she had no money in the house, and said that he would call again. Mr. Channell had been an excellent customer and he had no wish to antagonize him.

Luke came home late, too drunk to talk, so that Amber had no alternative but to wait. When she woke the next morning, however, the room was empty and the door into Sally's apartment closed, but she could hear low voices coming from it. Quickly she slipped out of bed and ran to get into her clothes, intending to dress and then go in to talk to him before he left.

She had just pulled the sheer linen smock over her head and settled it about her when Luke opened the door. Quickly she reached for a petticoat. But he crossed the room swiftly, grabbed her by one elbow and swung her about, jerking the petticoat out of her hand and flinging it aside.

"Not so quick there. I hope a husband may be permitted to look at his wife sometimes?" He eyed her swollen belly. "You're mighty modest—" he said slowly, his face unpleasant, "for a bitch who was three months gone with child when she got married."

Amber stared at him, unmoving, her eyes cold and hard. Suddenly all her worry and indecision were gone. She felt only a bitter contemptuous hatred so strong it blotted out every other sense and emotion.

"Is that what you married me for, you lousy trull? To furnish a name for your bastard—"

All at once Amber struck him a hard, furious blow, with all the strength of her body, across the side of his face and left ear. Before she could even move he grabbed her by the hair, giving her head a vicious cracking jerk as his free hand smashed across her jaw. Suddenly terrified, seeing murder in his face, Amber screamed and Sally Goodman rushed into the room, shouting at him.

"Luke! Luke! Oh, you fool! You'll spoil everything! Stop it!"

She began to struggle with him as Amber cowered, not daring to fight back for fear some blow or kick would kill the baby, trying to protect herself with her hands and arms. But he struck at her again and again, his hands and fists hitting her wherever he could, swearing between his teeth, his face livid and writhing with rage. And then at last Sally succeeded in dragging him off and Amber crumpled to the floor, retching violently, moaning and gasping and almost hysterical.

"Oh, damn you, Luke!" she heard Sally cry. "Your temper will ruin us all!"

He ignored her, shouting at Amber: "Next time, you damned slut, I won't let you off so easy! I'll break your neck, d'ye hear me?" He made a short vicious kick at her and Amber screamed, arms covering her belly, eyes shut. He left the room, slamming the door with a crash.

The two women rushed immediately to Amber and helped her into the bed. She lay there for several minutes, still sobbing, trembling violently but more with rage and hatred and humiliation than from any pain she suffered. Sally sat on the bed chafing her hands, talking to her in a low soothing tone, while Honour hung over her with a sort of wide-eyed sympathetic stupefaction.

But as Amber began to recover her senses she became conscious of sharp little thrusting movements within her, and putting her hands to her stomach she could feel the baby stir. "Oh!" she cried furiously. "If I lose this baby I swear I'll see that son of a whore set up on a gibbet on Tyburn Hill!" Though a great many times she had half-hoped that some accident would bring on a miscarriage, now she realized that more than anything else she wanted to bear this child—for he was all that was left to her of Lord Carlton.

"Lord, sweetheart! How you talk!" cried Sally.

Nevertheless she sent Honour to an apothecary to get something which would prevent abortion and when the girl returned she brewed the packet of herbs into a tea. Amber drank the stinking decoction, holding her nose and making a face. The day wore on and as no symptoms of a miscarriage appeared Amber began to feel easier, for though she was sore and bruised she had not been otherwise seriously hurt. But she could think of nothing but Luke Channell and how she hated him, and she was determined that as soon as she got her money back she would leave him—go away from London to some other town and hide. She lay on the bed for several hours with her eyes shut, absorbed in making her plans.

Sally was most solicitous and even when Amber pretended to be asleep she continued to question her, to bring her something to eat, to suggest that she would feel better if she sat up for a little while and played some game to amuse herself. Finally, with a bored sigh, Amber agreed and they started a game of ombre, playing on a board which rested across their laps.

"Poor Luke," Sally said after a few minutes. "I fear the dear boy inherited his father's fits. Sometimes, I swear, I've seen Sir Walter Channell lie foaming at the mouth and stark rigid for minutes at a time. But when it passes, he's the pleasantest man alive—just like Luke."

Amber, giving Sally a skeptical glance, put down her queen and took the trick. "Just like Luke?" she repeated. "Then I'm mighty sorry for Lady Channell."

Sally pursed her lips primly. "Well, my dear—sure, now, you wouldn't expect any man to be pleased to find his wife with child by another man's offices? And d'ye know—" She played a card, took the trick, and as she was placing it slantwise along the board looked across at Amber. "It would almost seem you must 've known what your condition was when you married 'im."

Amber smiled maliciously. "Oh, would it?" Suddenly her eyes flashed and she snapped out, "Why else would I marry that daggle-touthed lout?"

Sally looked at her, took a deep breath, and then began counting the tricks. She shuffled the cards, dealt, and they played for a while in silence.

All at once Amber said: "I'm missing a wallet that had a deal of money in it. It was on a nail behind that chest and someone stole it."

"Stole it! Thieves in these rooms! Oh, heaven!"

"I think the thief was Luke!"

"Luke? A thief? Lord, child, how you talk! Why, there's never an honester man in London than my nephew! And anyway, my dear, how could he *steal* money from you? A wife's money belongs to her husband the moment they leave the altar. I must say, sweetheart, I'm surprised you'd hide a few paltry pounds from 'im."

"A few paltry pounds! That wasn't a few paltry pounds! It was everything I had in the world!"

Sally looked at her quickly. "Everything you had? Then what about your inheritance? What about your five thousand pound?" She was staring at her, her blue eyes narrowed and hard, all the placid good-humour gone from her face.

"What about *his* inheritance?"

Sally refused to let go of her patience. "I explained that to you, my dear. And now am I to understand that you've swindled my nephew—made him think you were a person of some fortune when five hundred was all you had?"

Suddenly Amber slammed her handful of cards across the room and swept the board onto the floor. "Understand what you damn please! That wretch stole my money and I'll have 'im before a constable for it!"

Sally got up, bowed to her with an air of injured dignity, and went into her own room where she closed the door and remained throughout the rest of the day. Honour stayed with her mistress. Quietly she went about her usual duties. She served Amber her supper on a tray, brushed her hair, and when Amber got up to wash her face and clean her teeth she smoothed out the sheets with a bed-staff. She listened with sympathy but made no comment upon Amber's grumbling about her husband and his aunt and seemed not very much surprised by Amber's statement that she intended to leave him as soon as she could force him to give her money back.

Though she did not intend to, Amber fell asleep before Luke came home. Some time in the middle of the night she wakened to hear voices in the next room—his and Sally's—and though she waited for some time in cold angry apprehension the door between their rooms remained closed. And at last the sound of their voices ceased. She fell asleep again.

When she awoke the next morning there was a bright fire going and the room had an almost surprising air of contented domesticity. Sally, humming a tune beneath her breath, was arranging a bowlful of green leaves. Honour was dusting the furniture with more enthusiasm than she usually showed for such tasks. And Luke stood knotting his cravat before a mirror, regarding himself with smug approval.

The moment she pulled back the bed-hangings Sally saw her.

"Why!" she cried pleasantly. "Good morning to you, sweetheart!" Briskly she crossed the room and kissed her on the cheek, ignoring the face Amber made. "I hope you've slept well! Luke slept on the trundle in my room so as not to disturb you." She had never been more pleasant and now she turned a beaming smile upon her nephew, like a mother prompting her child in the presence of guests. "Didn't you, Luke?"

Luke gave her a broad grin, the same one he had used during their courtship. Amber lay propped on one elbow and regarded him sourly. She was determined somehow to get her money back, but the mere sight of him infuriated her so that she lost hold of all her schemes and plans. He started toward her, still grinning, though Amber watched him with sullen distrust.

"What d'ye suppose I've got here for you?" He had picked something off the mantel and kept one hand behind his back.

"I don't know, and I don't care! Get away from me!" she

cried warningly, as he stooped to kiss her, and she flung the covers up over her head.

An ugly look came swiftly to his face but Sally reminded him with a nudge and jerk of her head. He sat down on the bed and reached out a tentative hand to touch her. "Look here, duckling—look what a fine present I've brought you. Heavens, sweetheart, you a'nt going to stay mad at poor Luke, now are you?"

She could hear him open a box and jingle something which sounded like jewellery and at last out of curiosity she peeked over the top of the blankets. He was holding toward her, temptingly, a bracelet with several diamonds and a ruby or two winking on it. His voice continued to wheedle, though she was looking not at him but at the bracelet.

"Believe me, sweetheart, I'm sorry for what I did yesterday. But truly at times it seems I'm not master of myself. My poor old father had those fits. Here—let me fasten it on your wrist—"

The bracelet was a handsome one, and finally Amber permitted him to clasp it. She knew that she must make him think she liked him, or she would never get her money back. So she let him kiss her and even pretended to giggle with pleasure. She had such contempt for him it was easy to make herself believe that she could outwit him. Finally she got up and dressed and they drank the morning draught of ale, together with a few anchovies. Luke suggested that Amber ride out to Pancras with him and have dinner at a charming little inn he knew, and thinking that most likely he really was sorry for his behaviour and once more infatuated with her, she agreed. She put on her cloak—though at his suggestion she left the bracelet there because of the danger from highwaymen—and they set out.

Pancras, a tiny village to the northwest, was about two miles from the Rose and Crown, or some three-quarters of an hour by coach. But they had scarcely reached High Holborn when it began to rain—though the winter had been a dry and warm and dusty one—and within fifteen minutes the roads were splashing with mud and there was a strong smell of rotten garbage in the air, made more poignant by the wet. Two or three times the wheels stuck and the coachman and footman had to pry them out, using an iron bar, which all coaches carried for that purpose.

To Amber, lurching and jogging inside the springless carriage, the ride seemed interminable and she wished miserably that she had stayed at home. But Luke was cheerful and talkative as he had not been for weeks, and she tried to pretend that she was enjoying the outing and his company. His hands roamed over her persistently, and he urged her to reciprocate his attentions. Amber laughed and tried to push him off, pretending she was afraid that the coach might overturn and spill them out for everyone to see; the touch of his fingers made her flesh crawl and turn cold with loathing.

The inn she found to be a little greasy place and the room to which the host showed them was cold and unaired. He lighted a fire and then Luke went below with him to order the dinner while Amber stood at the window, looking out at the pouring rain and watching the bedraggled red rooster moving majestically across the courtyard, carefully picking up his claws as he went. She kept her cloak on, shivering a little, unhappy and listless, a sense of depression dragging at her.

The dinner was a bad one, a stringy slightly warmed chunk of boiled beef, boiled parsnips, and boiled bacon. Amber was disgusted with such fare and could scarcely force herself to take a bite but Luke, who was never discriminating, ate with gusto, a trickle of greasy juice running over his chin. He smacked his lips noisily, picked at his teeth with his fingernails, and spat on the floor until Amber, queasy with her pregnancy, thought that she would be sick.

He had scarcely done eating when he set upon her again, mauling her and pulling at her clothes. A moment later there was a knock and the landlord called his name; without a word he left her and went out the door.

For a moment Amber lay, surprised and relieved, half wondering what had happened. Suddenly she burst into tears of anger and loneliness and revulsion. I won't do it again! she thought. I won't if he kills me! She rolled over onto her side, crying drearily, and waited for him to come back.

She waited a long time. At last she got up, rinsed her face in cold water and combed her hair. She wondered where he had gone and what kept him, but she did not care very much. For when he did return they would only drive back and she would spend the rest of the afternoon talking to Sally or, if Luke stayed home, playing ombre or gleek and she would be sure to lose because they cheated and she did not know how.

Finally she began to grow uneasy and the suspicion sneaked into her mind that he had taken the coach and gone off leaving her to get back however she might. It would be like him to take some such means of repaying her for having slapped him. And she had not so much as a farthing with her. She snatched up her fan and muff and mask, flung on her black velvet cloak, and went out of the room and downstairs. The host was leaning over the counter, talking to some booted muddy stranger, and both men were smoking pipes and drinking ale.

"Where's my husband?" she demanded, halfway down the stairs.

They looked up at her. "Your husband?" repeated the host.

"Of course! The man I came here with!" she cried impatiently, crossing the floor toward him now. "Where is he?"

"Why, he's gone, mem. He said you was a lady wanted to elope with 'im and told me to call 'im at half-after-one. He went off in the coach soon's he came down—said you'd pay the reckoning," he added significantly.

Amber stared at him in astonishment and then she ran to the door to look out. It was true. Her coach was gone. She turned and faced him, angry and worried. "I've got to get back to London! How can I do it? Is there a stage-coach that stops here?"

"No, mem. Few enough of any kind stops here. The dinner was ten shillin's and the room ten shillin's. One pound in all, mem." He held out his hand.

"One pound! Well, I haven't got it! I haven't got a farthing! Oh, damn him!" It seemed to her that no one had ever had such scurvy luck, no one had ever suffered such trials as had beset her constantly since she had come to London. "How 'm I to get home?" she demanded again, desperate now. Certainly she could not walk in that pouring rain and the mud.

For a moment the host was silent, measuring her, deciding at last in her favour because of her fine clothes, "Well, mem, you look an honest lady. I've got a horse I can let you take and my son can show you the way—if you'll pay him the reckoning when you get there."

Amber agreed and she and the innkeeper's fourteen-year-old boy set out on a pair of swaybacked nags that could not be kicked or coaxed out of a plodding trot. Though not yet two-thirty it was dark and the rain came down steadily, soaking both of them through before they had gone a quarter-mile.

They rode silently, Amber clenching her teeth, wretchedly uncomfortable with the heavy jogging of her belly and the feel of wet clothes and hair clinging tight to her skin. She was wholly obsessed with Luke Channell and how she despised him. And the farther they rode, the more her stomach stabbed and ached, the more chilled she became—the more savagely she hated him. She promised herself that she would murder him for this, though she burnt alive for it.

When they got back into the City the streets were almost deserted. Men with their cloaks wrapped up about their mouths and their hats pulled low leant against the wind. Wet skinny dogs and miserable cats crouched in the doorways, and the kennels down the middle of the streets were rushing torrents of water and refuse.

The boy helped her to dismount and followed her as she ran inside, her skirts sticking to her legs, her soaked hair hanging down her shoulders in long twining tendrils. She looked like some weird water-witch. She ran through the parlour without glancing at anyone—though every eye there turned to follow her in amazement—rushed up the steps two at a time, then down the hallway to burst into her room with a hysterical scream.

"Luke!"

No one answered. For the room was empty, her bed still

unmade, and everywhere were signs of hurried departure. Drawers were open and empty; the wardrobe where her clothes had been stood ajar, but nothing was in it; the top of her dressing-table had been wiped clean. The mirrors she had bought were gone from the walls. A pair of silver candlesticks had been taken from the mantel. In his pretty gilt cage the little parakeet cocked an eye at her, and she saw the earrings Bruce had bought at the May Fair lying on the floor, as though flung away in contempt.

She stood there, staring, stunned and helpless. But even while she stared there began to come over her a feeling of relief and she was glad to be rid of them—all three, Luke and Sally Goodman and simple little Honour Mills. Slowly she reached up one hand and took out the bodkins that held up her back hair—they had gold knobs on the ends with a pattern of tiny pearls. She held them toward him.

"My money's all gone," she said wearily. "Here. Take these."

He looked at her doubtfully for a moment, but finally accepted them. Slowly Amber pushed the door shut. She leaned back against it. She wanted nothing but to lie down on the bed and forget—forget that she was even alive.

PART II

Chapter Nine

THE FLOOR OF the room was covered with rushes which smelt sour and old, and rats came out boldly to dart about searching for morsels of food, their eyes bright and black as beads. The walls were stone, moist and dripping and green with a mossy slime; sunk into them were great ring-bolts from which hung heavy chains. Boarded beds ranged the walls as in a barracks. Though only mid-morning it was dark and would have been darker but for a tallow-candle which burnt with a low sullen flame, as though oppressed by the stinking air. It was the Condemned Hold at Newgate where prisoners were kept until they had paid the price of better quarters.

There were four women in the room, all of them seated, all of them shackled with heavy chains on wrists and ankles, all of them perfectly quiet.

One was a young Quaker girl in sober prim black, a starched white collar about her throat and a linen cap covering her hair; she sat motionless, concentrating on her feet. Across from her was a middle-aged woman who looked like any of the dozens of housewives seen every day in the streets going to market with a basket over one arm. Not far from her sprawled a morose slattern who stared dully at the others, one side of her mouth screwed up in a faint cynical smile. There were large open sores on her face and breasts and now and again she coughed with a hollow, racking sound as if she would bring up her very guts. The fourth woman was Amber, and she sat wrapped in her cloak, one hand tightly clasping the bird-cage set on her lap, the other inside her muff.

She looked strangely out of place there in that mouldering sty, for though all her garments were somewhat the worse for the soaking they had had two weeks before, the materials were good and the style fashionable. The gown, which had been made by Madame Darnier, was black velvet, caught up in back over a stiff petticoat of dark red-and-white-striped satin. Pleated frills of sheer white linen showed about the low neckline and at the elbows of the puffed sleeves. Her silk stockings were scarlet and her square-toed shoes black velvet with large sparkling buckles. She wore her black-velvet cloak, carried her fox muff, her gloves and fan and mask.

She had been there for perhaps an hour—though it seemed

a great deal longer—and so far no one had spoken a word. Her eyes roamed about restlessly, searching in the darkness, and she was beginning to fidget nervously. From everywhere about them, overhead, beneath their feet, from either side, came the muffled sounds of shouts and groans, screams and curses and laughter.

She looked at the housewife, then at the Quakeress, finally at the dirty slut across the room, and the last she found watching her with grum insolent amusement. "Is this the prison?" asked Amber at last, speaking to her because neither of the others seemed conscious of her or their own whereabouts.

For a moment she continued to squint near-sightedly at Amber and then she laughed and suddenly began to cough, leaning over with her hand against her chest until she spat out a great clot of bloody phlegm. "Is this the prison?" she repeated at last, mimicking. "What the hell d'ye think it is? It ain't Whitehall, me fine lady!" Her accent was strong and harsh and her voice had the dreary whine of a woman who has been tired for years.

"I mean is this *all* the prison?"

"Jesus, no." She gave a weary sweep of one arm. "Hear that? It's over us and under us and all around us. What're *you* here for?" she asked abruptly. "We ain't used to havin' the quality for company." She sounded sarcastic, but too tired to be dangerously malicious.

"For debt," said Amber.

The morning after Luke and his aunt and the maid had left her Amber had wakened with a bad cold, her throat so sore she could scarcely speak. But she was half relieved to be sick, for at least she could do nothing until she got well and it was impossible for her even to imagine what she would do then. She had no clothes but the ones she had been wearing, not a penny in cash, and her only negotiable assets were her wedding-ring, the string of pearls she had worn around her neck, a pair of pearl ear-drops, and the earrings Bruce had bought for her at the Fair. Luke had stolen everything of value, including the reconciliation bracelet and the silver-handled toothbrush Bruce had given her.

As Amber lay in bed, coughing and blowing her nose, her very bones seeming to ache and her head feeling as though it was stuffed with cotton, she began to worry. She knew that she had been a fool, that they had played a trick on her that must be old as time and worn threadbare by usage. With her country-girl gullibility she had walked into their trap, as innocent as a woodcock. And she had nothing for consolation but the sureness that they had been almost as much mistaken in her. For now she was convinced that Luke had thought he was marrying a real heiress and that they had left only when the mistake was discovered.

By the third day the hall outside her room was aswarm with

creditors all of them demanding payment. And when Amber went to the door wrapped in a blanket and told them that her husband had run away and she had no money they threatened to bring action against her. At last she refused to answer any more and shouted at them to go away and leave her alone. Then this morning the constable had come, told her to get dressed and taken her off to Newgate. She would not be tried, he said, until the quarter-session and then—if found guilty of her large debt—she would be sentenced to remain in Newgate until it was paid.

"For debt," repeated the housewife. "That's why I'm here, too. My husband died owin' one pound six."

"One pound six!" cried Amber. *"I owe three hundred and ninety-seven pound!"* She felt almost triumphant at being in jail for such a stupendous sum, but that feeling was soon squelched.

"Then," said the slattern, "you ain't goin' out of here till they carry you out in a wooden box."

"What d'you mean? I had the money! I had *more* than that—but my husband rubbed off with it! When they catch him I'll get it back again!" She tried to sound confident but the woman's words had scared her, for it was not the first rumour she had heard of the kind of justice they dealt here in London.

Smiling, the other woman heaved herself away from the wall and came forward, bringing with her a stench that made Amber's nostrils flare in revulsion. She stood for a moment looking down at her with an expression that suggested both weary jealously of her youth and beauty and an almost friendly contempt for her *naïveté* and confident optimism. Then she sat down beside her.

"I'm Moll Turner. Where'd you come from, sweetheart? You ain't been long in London, have you?"

"I've been here seven months and a half!" retorted Amber defiantly, for it always hurt her pride when she was recognized for an outlander. "I came from Essex," she added, more meekly.

"Well, now, you needn't take such hogan-mogan airs with me, Mrs. Minx. I'd say anyone's had such a flam put upon 'em as you have stands in need of a little friendly counsel. And you'll need more before you been long in this place."

"I'm sorry. But to tell you truly, Mrs. Turner, I'm in such a mouse-hole I think I'll run mad. What can I *do?* I've got to get out of here! I'm going to have a baby!"

"Are you indeed?" She did not seem very much impressed or concerned. "Well, it won't be the first born in Newgate, believe me for that. Look here, sweetheart, most likely you ain't never goin' out of here. So listen to what I say and you'll save yourself a deal of trouble."

"Never!" cried Amber frantically. "Oh, but I am! I've got to! I won't stay—they can't keep me in here!"

Mrs. Turner seemed bored and impatient, and ignoring Amber's protests went on with what she had begun to say. "You'll have to pay garnish to the jailor's wife to get better quarters, garnish for lighter chains, garnish if you so much as puke in this place. And you can begin to get the feel of it by giving me them ear-drops—"

Amber gasped in horror and moved back a little. "I won't do it! They're mine! Why should I give 'em to *you*, pray!"

"Because, sweetheart, if I don't get 'em the jailor's wife will. Oh, I'll use you honestly. Give me the ear-drops—they don't look worth more'n a pound at the top—" she added, narrowing her eyes and peering at them closely, "—and I'll tell you how to live in this place. I've been here before, I'll warrant you. Come, now, before we're disturbed."

Amber stared at her for a long moment, frank skeptical distrust on her face, but finally she decided that it would be worth the earrings to have a friend who understood this strange place. She slid the pearls from her ears and dropped them into Mrs. Turner's outstretched palm. Moll tucked them into the bodice of her gown, somewhere between her stringy breasts, and turned to Amber.

"Now, my dear, how much money have you got?"

"Not a farthing."

"Not a farthing? My God, how d'you intend to live? Newgate ain't run for charity, you may be sure. You pay for everything you get here, and you pay dear."

"Well, *I* won't. Because I haven't got any money."

Amber's matter-of-fact tone sent Moll into another fit of violent coughing, but at last she straightened, running her forearm across her wet mouth. "Don't seem like you're old enough to be out of the house alone, sweetheart. Where's your family—in Essex? My advice to you is to send to 'em for help."

Amber stiffened at that suggestion, defensively lowering her black lashes. "I can't. I mean I won't. They didn't want me to get married and I—"

"Never mind, my dear. I think I know your plight well enough. You found yourself with child and so left home. Now your keeper's left you. Well, in London we don't give a damn—we've got troubles enough of our own without worryin' ourselves with our neighbours—"

"But I *am* married!" protested Amber, determined to have the credit of a respectable woman since she had gone to such length to be one. "I'm Mrs. Channell—Mrs. Luke Channell. And here's my ring to prove it!" She stripped the glove from her left hand and thrust it beneath Moll's nose.

"Yes, yes. Lord, my dear, I don't care if you're married or whore to forty men. I was myself, in better days. Now I'm so peppered a man wouldn't have me upon a pinch." She smiled faintly and shrugged, then stared off into space, forgetting her promise as she began to recall the disappointments of her own life. "That's the way I began. He was a captain in the King's army—a mighty handsome fellow in his uniform. But my dad didn't like to see his daughter bringin' a nameless brat into the family. So I came to London. You can hide anything in London. My boy died—more's the mercy—and I never saw my captain again. But I saw other men aplenty, I'll warrant you. And I had money for a while, too. Once a gentleman gave me a hundred pound for one night. Now—" She turned suddenly and looked at Amber, who had been staring at her with fascinated horror, finding it almost impossible to believe that this ugly emaciated sick creature had once been young and in love with a handsome man, just as she was. "How old d'ye think I am? Fifty? No, I'm thirty-two. Just thirty-two. Well, I've had my day, there's no denyin' that. I suppose I wouldn't trade it for something different—"

Amber was beginning to feel sick, seeing herself several years hence in Moll Turner. Oh, God! Oh, God! she thought frantically. It's just like Aunt Sarah said. Look what happens to a bad woman!

And then all of them started at the sound of a key in the lock; the great iron door began to swing open. Moll, putting her hand to her mouth, muttered quickly: "Sell that ring for whatever she'll give you."

A woman, perhaps fifty years old, came into the room. Her hair, almost white, was lifeless as straw and screwed into a hard knot high on the crown of her head. She wore a soiled blouse, a dark-blue woollen skirt with a long red apron tied over it, and slung about her hips was a leather thong to which were attached several very large keys, a pair of scissors, a wallet and a bull's pizzle—a short heavy wooden cudgel for maintaining discipline. She carried a candle stuck into a bottle, and before turning around to look at them she set it on a shelf.

A huge grey-striped cat followed her in, pushing against her legs, arching its back, giving out a low satisfied rumble. And then all at once it caught sight of Amber's parakeet and moved swiftly forward. But Amber, with a little scream, jumped to her feet and, holding the cage at shoulder-level, kicked out at the cat with one foot while her parakeet fluttered and clung terrified to the bars of its cage.

"Good morning, ladies," said the woman now, and her shrewd pitiless eyes went over them quickly, resting longest on Amber. "I'm Mrs. Cleggat—my husband is the Jailor. It's my understanding that you are all ladies of refinement who naturally would not care to take up your abode in a vault set aside for thieves, parricides, and murderers. I'm happy to say that from here you may be removed to a chamber the equal of that in any private house and there you'll be furnished with the best of conversation and entertainment—for a consideration."

"There's the rub," commented Moll, sprawled out with her arms crossed, her legs stretched before her.

"How much?" asked Amber, keeping an eye on the cat which now sat patiently at her feet, wide-eyed and flicking just the tip of his tail. If she could sell her wedding-ring she would have money enough to buy very good quarters—and she was still convinced that she would be out within a day or two.

"Two shillings six to get out of here. Six shillings for easement. Two shillings six a week for a bed. Two shillings a week for sheets. Six shillings six to the turnkey. Ten shillings six to the steward of the ward for coal and candles. That's all for now. I'll have one pound ten from each of you ladies." As they all looked at her and no one either moved or spoke she said briskly, "Come, now. I'm a woman of affairs. There's others here too, y'know."

Moll now lifted her skirt and from a pocket in her petticoat produced the required sum. "'Sblood, it seems I only steal enough to support myself in prison."

Amber looked around, waiting for one of the others to speak, but they did not and so she pulled the wedding-ring from her finger and extended it toward Mrs. Cleggat. "I haven't got any money. How much will you give me for this?"

Mrs. Cleggat took it, held it to the candle and said, "Three pound."

"Three pound! But I paid twelve for it!"

"Values are different here." She unbuttoned the wallet, counted out several shillings, handed them to Amber and dropped the wedding-ring into the leather pouch. "Is that all?"

"Yes," said Amber. She did not intend to part with the string of pearls Bruce had given her not long before he sailed.

Mrs. Cleggat looked at her sharply. "You'd better give me whatever else you've got right now. If you don't I promise you it'll be stolen before you've been here two hours."

Amber hesitated a moment longer and then, with a heavy sigh, she unfastened the clasp and drew the strand out of her cloak. Mrs. Cleggat gave her six pounds for them and promptly turned her attention to the other women. The Quakeress stood up and faced her squarely, but as she spoke her voice was soft and meek.

"I have no money, friend. Do with me as thou wilt."

"You'd better send out for some, Mrs. Or you go into the Common side which, though I say it myself, isn't fit for a baboon."

"No matter. I can get used to it."

Mrs. Cleggat shrugged and her voice was contemptuously indifferent. "You fanatics." (A fanatic, in the common understanding, was anyone who belonged to neither the Catholic nor the Anglican Church.) "Well enough then, Mrs. Give me your cloak for the entrance fee and your shoes for easement."

Out of doors it was almost warm for the winter had been a strange one, but in there it was chill and damp. Nevertheless the girl untied her cloak and took it off. Amber, looking from her to Mrs. Cleggat with growing indignation, now suddenly made up her mind.

"Here! Keep it on! I'll pay for you! You'll fall sick without it!"

Moll glanced at her scornfully. "Don't be a fool! You've little enough for yourself!"

But the Quakeress gave her a gentle smile. "Thank thee, friend. Thou art kind—but I want nothing. If I fall sick, it is the will of God."

Amber regarded her dubiously, then extended the coins toward Mrs. Cleggat. "Take it for her anyway."

"The girl will be a damned nuisance to me if she's made comfortable. Keep the money for yourself. It'll go quick enough." She turned to the housewife, who admitted that she had not so much as a farthing. Amber looked at Moll to see if she would not offer to share the woman's expenses with her, but Moll was glancing idly about the room and whistling beneath her breath. "Well, then—I'll pay for her."

This time the offer was accepted and the woman thanked her profusely, promising to repay her as soon as she was able—which would apparently be never if she was to be kept in prison until her debt was cleared. And then a man came in to put on the lighter shackles. They consisted of bracelets which fitted loosely about the wrists and ankles with long chains stretching between, and though they were awkward and clanked dismally they did not seem to be otherwise uncomfortable.

"Take the fanatic to the Common Felon's side," said Mrs. Cleggat to the man when he had done. "Come with me, ladies." They trooped out of the room after her, first Moll, then Amber holding the bird-cage on her shoulder, and then the housewife.

Mounting a dark narrow stairway they reached a big room where the door stood open; above it was nailed a skull-and-crossbones. Mrs. Cleggat went in first with her candle and as they followed they could see two large flat beds, covered with flock mattresses and some grey rumpled bedding, a table, scarred stools and chairs, and a cold fireplace above and beside which hung some blackened kettles and pans and a few pewter mugs and dishes. Certainly there was nothing in this barren dirty room to suggest the luxurious quarters Mrs. Cleggat had painted.

"This," she said, "is the Lady Debtors' Ward."

Amber looked at her in angry astonishment, while Moll smiled. "This!" she cried, forgetting her manacles and giving a sweep of one arm. "But you told us—"

"Never mind what I told you. If you don't like it I can take you to the Common Side."

Amber turned away, disgusted, and Mrs. Cleggat prepared to leave with Moll, who would go to the Lady Felon's Quarters. Oh, she thought furiously. This nasty place! I won't stay here a day! Then she swung around.

"I want to send a letter!"

"That'll cost you three shillings."

Amber paid it. "Are we the only prisoners?" She could still hear the voices, the incessant sounds that seemed to come from the very walls, but they had seen no one else.

"Most of the others are down in the Tap-Room. It's Christmas Eve."

The letter, written by an amanuensis, was sent to Almsbury, and she was very confident that he would have her out of there within twenty-four hours. When she got no immediate reply she told herself that since it was Christmas Day he had very likely been away from his lodgings. Tomorrow, she promised herself, he'll come. But he did not, and the days passed and at last she was forced to realize that either he had not received the letter or was no longer interested in her.

The Lady Debtors' Ward was the least crowded one in Newgate, but even so she and the housewife, Mrs. Buxted had to share those scant accommodations with a dozen other women. In many wards, however, thirty or forty were crowded into the same space and there were more than three hundred prisoners in a building intended for half that number. It was impossible for everyone to lie on the beds at once and they had to use cooking utensils and dishes in turn. Usually these were merely scraped off between meals, for water cost money and was always stale and stinking and afloat with vegetation and specks of sewage. This encouraged them to spend what they could on ale or wine.

The entire prison lay in an eternal half-gloom, for the windows, deep-set and narrow, opened only upon dark passages. Links and tallow-candles were bought by the prisoners and they burnt all day long. Large ugly cats and numerous dogs, half-naked with mange, roamed the hallways and contested with the rats for every shred of refuse; Amber had to keep a constant eye on her parakeet. The smells were thick and almost palpable, product of the accumulated rot of centuries, and sometimes there was another strange and sickening odour which she learned came from the heads being boiled by the hangman in his kitchen below their ward. She had not been there an hour when she started scratching furiously. She caught the plump lice between her fingers, squashing them like boiled peas.

Newcomers were automatically assigned the duties of chamber-maid. The first morning Amber and Mrs. Buxted carried the slop-jars down the hall and emptied them into the cesspool below. The stench of the heavy fumes made Amber almost faint. After that she paid another woman two pence a week to do the job for her.

The prison was considered to be a place of detention, not of correction, and from eight o'clock in the morning until nine at night all inside doors were opened and each was free to follow his inclination.

Those who had been arrested because of their religious beliefs were now permitted to hold services, make what converts they could, or preach sedition. Whoever had money usually spent it in the Tap-Room, drinking and gambling. Well-to-do inmates sometimes gave large entertainments attended by people of the first quality, for some criminals enjoyed considerable popularity. Visitors were admitted to the Hall and swarmed there by the hundreds. A man might have his wife and children to keep him company—sometimes for years—or, if he preferred and had the price, he could take his choice of the prostitutes who daily came from outside.

Thievery was common and fights went on continually, for discipline was maintained by the prisoners themselves. Some went mad and were heavily chained, but usually not segregated. Babies were born but seldom lived long, and the death-rate among all prisoners was high.

Amber remained as aloof from the life of the jail as she could; this was one place where she desired no popularity. She did not go to the Tap-Room and of course she had no visitors, so that the only time she left her own ward was on Sunday when everyone was herded up to the third-floor Chapel.

Most of the women in the Lady Debtors' Ward were the victims of misfortune and all of them expected soon to be released. They sat by the hour talking of the day when their debt would be paid—by a father or brother or friend—and they would go free. Amber listened to them, wistfully, for she had no one to pay her debt and no reason to hope for freedom, though she continued stubbornly to do so.

With aching homesickness her memories went back to the Goodegroome cottage. She took pleasure in remembering many things she had not known she cared for. She remembered how the dormer windows of her bedroom were wreathed in roses, and the delicious summer scent they had had. She remembered how the overhanging eaves were full of sparrows so that every morning she woke to the sound of their twirring and twittering. She remembered Sarah's wonderful rich food, the clean-scrubbed flagstones of the kitchen floor and the rows of glossy pewter lining the shelves. She longed passionately for a sight of the sky, a breath of fresh air, the smell of flowers and hay new-mown, the sound of a bird's song.

The holidays were dreary as she had never known they could be.

She remembered what Christmas had been the year before when she had helped Sarah to make mince-pies and plum-pottages; she and all her cousins had dressed up to go mumming; and everyone on the farm had toasted the fruit trees in apple-cider, according to the old old custom. On New Year's Eve she spent several shillings of her fast-dwindling supply for

Rhenish wine and the Lady Debtors drank it, proposing a toast to the new year. Just before midnight the bells began to ring from every steeple in London and Amber burst into lonely frightened tears, for she was sure that she would never live to hear them ring in another year.

A week later Newgate was swept with frenzied excitement: A rebellion had broken out in the city, led by a band of religious zealots, and for three days and nights they ran riot through the streets. Bellowing for King Jesus, they shot down whoever opposed them. Inside the prison they heard the bells banging out an ominous warning, confused shouts and cries and the sound of flying hoofs. The prisoners gathered anxiously in groups, talking of massacre and fire, discussing means of escape; the women became hysterical, screamed at the gates and begged to be set free.

But the Fifth Monarchists were hunted out, killed or captured, and within a few days twenty of them had been hanged, drawn and quartered. Their remains were brought to Newgate and dismembered legs and arms and torsos lay in the courtyard while Esquire Dun was at work in his kitchen pickling the heads in bay-salt and cumin seed. Prison life settled back into the normal rut of drunkenness and gambling, quarrels and venery and theft.

When the quarter-sessions were held Amber was brought to trial along with Mrs. Buxted and Moll Turner and a great many others and—like most of them—found guilty. She was sentenced to remain in Newgate until her debt had been paid in full. She had been so hopeful she would be released after the trial that it was a severe shock and for several days she was sunk in despondency; she would have been almost glad to die. But gradually she began trying to persuade herself that her position was not so desperate as it seemed. Why—any day Almsbury might arrive and rescue her. It always happens, she assured herself, when you least expect it; and she tried very hard to stop expecting Almsbury.

She often saw Moll Turner, who wandered in to talk to her and to urge her to come out and mingle with the others. "Christ, sweetheart, what can you lose? D'ye want to rot in here?"

"Of course not!" said Amber crossly. "I want to get out of this damned place!"

Moll laughed and went to the fireplace to light a pipeful of tobacco. Many of the prisoners, both men and women, smoked incessantly for the tobacco was supposed to protect them against disease. She came back puffing and sat down opposite Amber, ostentatiously drumming one hand on the table-top.

"See that?" On her middle finger she wore a large diamond. "Got that off a lady was here visitin' day before yesterday. We gave her the budge, and when she caught her balance I had the fambles cheat and somebody else had the scout." Moll often talked in an underworld cant, of which Amber had begun to pick up a few words. A "fambles cheat" was a ring and a "scout" was a watch. "Oh, I tell you, my dear, the Hall's a mighty profitable place. At this rate I can buy my way out of here in another month. "Well—" She heaved herself up. "Stay in here if you like—"

Amber, half-convinced by Moll's tales of facile theft, ventured out into the hallway a time or two, but she was always accosted so swiftly and roughly that she would pick up her skirts and run as hard as she could go for the comparative privacy of the Lady Debtors' Ward. Moll laughed at this too and told her that she was a fool not to take advantage of what she could get.

"Some of those gentlemen are mighty rich. In time I don't doubt you could earn your way out. Of course," she would admit, with her lop-sided smile, "four hundred pound ain't come by very quick, and there's a dozen half-crown sluts they have the pick of any day in the week."

Several times she brought Amber offers of specific sums from one or another of the men, but it was never enough that Amber cared to make the venture. Moll's condition was sufficient warning and she was in mortal fear of being peppered herself. Nevertheless she would have done anything to get out of Newgate—taken any wild chance that might keep her baby from being born there.

By the end of a month her money had dwindled to less than two pounds, for everything had a price and it was invariably a high one. She had been paying to have her food sent in—the alternative was to eat the prison-fare, mouldy bread and stale water, with charity-meat once a week—and she had also paid for Mrs. Buxted's meals because otherwise the woman would have had none. When a midwife who shared the ward told her that she was too thin for a pregnant woman and that the baby was getting all she ate, she decided that she must sell the gold ear-rings.

Mrs. Cleggat gave them one scornful glance. "Those things? Brass and Bristol-stone! They're not worth three farthings! Where'd ye get 'em—St. Martin's?" A great deal of cheap imitation jewellery was sold in the parish of St. Martin-le-Grand.

Hurt, Amber did not answer her. But she had begun to notice herself that the thin gilt was wearing and showed a grey metal beneath. She was almost glad that they were too worthless to sell.

At the end of her fifth week in Newgate Amber sat in one of the boxes of the chapel, stared at her dirty fingernails, and worried about how she would eat a month from then. For days she had been trying to find courage to tell Mrs. Buxted that she could not feed her any longer. But she had not been able to do it, for every day Mrs. Buxted's daughter came and brought her the youngest child to nurse. As usual, Amber had not heard a word of the sermon, though it had been going on for a long while.

Now Moll Turner gave her a sharp nudge. "There's Black Jack Mallard!" she whispered. "And he's got his eye on you!"

Amber glanced sulkily across the room where she saw a gigantic black-haired man sitting staring at her, and as she did so he smiled. Cross at being interrupted in her worries, she scowled at him and looked away. Moll, thoroughly disgusted, nudged her several times but Amber refused to pay her any attention.

"Oh, you and your hogan-mogan airs!" muttered Moll as they left the chapel. "Who d'ye expect to find here in Newgate, pray? His Majesty?"

"What's so fine about him, I'd like to know?" She had thought him too dark and ugly.

"Well, Mrs., whatever you may think, Black Jack Mallard *is* somebody! He's a rum-pad, let me tell you."

"A highwayman?"

Highwaymen, she had discovered, were the élite of the criminal world, though this man was the first she had seen. She did remember, though, one of that brotherhood who had hung, a mere clean-picked skeleton, in a set of gibbet-irons at the Marygreen crossroads, mute warning to others of his kind. And in a slight breeze the bones and irons had had an eerie clank that sent the villagers home before sundown to avoid him in the dark.

"A highwayman. And one of the best, too. He's already broke out of here three times."

Amber's eyes opened with a snap. "Broke out of here! How!"

"Ask 'im yourself," said Moll, and went off, leaving Amber at the door of her own ward.

Staring dazedly, Amber walked inside. Here was the chance she had been waiting for! If he'd got out before, he'd get out again—perhaps soon. And when he did— She was suddenly excited and full of optimism— But all at once her hopes collapsed.

Look at me! I'm fat as a barn-yard fowl and stinking dirty. The Devil himself wouldn't have a use for me now.

There was no doubt her appearance had suffered sad changes during the past five weeks. Now, at the end of her seventh month of pregnancy, she could no longer button her bodice, the once pert frills had wilted, and her smock was a dirty grey. Her gown was stained in the armpits, spotted with food, and her skirt hung inches shorter in front. She had long ago thrown away her silk stockings, for they had been streaked with runs, and her shoes were scuffed out at the toes. She had not seen a mirror since she had been there, nor taken off her clothes, and though she had scrubbed her teeth on her smock she could feel a slick film as she ran her tongue over them. Her face was grimy and her hair, which she had to comb with her long finger-nails, snarled and greasy.

Despair on her face, Amber's hands ran down over her body. But she was sharply aware that this might be her one chance, and that made her determination begin to rise. It's dark in here, she told herself. He can't see me very well—and maybe I can do something, maybe I can make myself look a little better someway. She decided that she would do what she could to improve her appearance and then go down to the Tap-Room, on the chance of seeing him, though admission there would cost her a precious shilling and a half.

She was scrubbing her teeth with some salt and a piece torn off her smock—rinsing her mouth out with ale and spitting into the fireplace—when a man appeared at the door, and told her that Black Jack wanted to see her in the Tap-Room. She gave a start and turned quickly.

"Me?"

"Yes, you."

"Oh, Lord! And I'm all unready! Wait a moment!"

Not knowing what to do, she began smoothing her dress and rubbing her hands over her face in the hope of taking off some of the dirt.

"I'm paid to light you down, Mrs., but not to wait here. Come along." He gave a wave of the link and started off.

Amber paused just long enough to open her smock low over her breasts, muttered swiftly to Mrs. Buxted, "Watch my bird," and then picking up her skirts she hurried after him. Her heart was pounding as though she had been going to be presented at Court.

Chapter Ten

BARBARA PALMER was a woman of no uncertain desires or ambitions. Almost from the moment she had been born she had known what she wanted and had usually contrived to get it, whatever the cost to herself or others. She had no morals, knew no qualms, did not trouble herself with a conscience. Her character and personality were as glittering, as elemental, as barbaric as was her beauty. And now, just twenty-one years old, she had found what she wanted more than anything else on earth.

She wanted to be the wife of Charles Stuart; she wanted to be Queen of England. She refused to believe that such an idea was absurd.

Barbara and Charles had met at the Hague a few weeks before the Restoration, when her husband was sent there to take a gift of money to the King. Charles, who was invariably attracted to beautiful women, was instantly and strongly attracted to her. And Barbara, both flattered to be sought by a king and glad of an opportunity to revenge herself on a jilting lover—the Earl of Chesterfield—quickly became his mistress. Everyone agreed that Charles, not surprisingly, was more deeply infatuated than he had ever been during the many years of his gallantry, and Barbara began to be a woman of considerable importance.

The Roger Palmers, who had been married less than two years, lived in one of the great houses on King Street, a narrow muddy but highly fashionable thoroughfare which ran through the Palace grounds and served to connect the villages of Charing and Westminster. Inns massed the west side of the street, but on the east were great mansions, whose gardens led down to the unembanked Thames. It was in her husband's home, at the end of the year, that Barbara began to give suppers which were attended by the King and most of the gay young men and pretty women of the Court, his Majesty's closest companions.

For a while Roger obediently appeared and pretended to be host. But at last he balked at the ridiculous role he was expected to play.

He came one January evening and knocked, as he had been told to do, at the door of his wife's bedroom. He was a medium-sized man of no pretentious appearance or manner but there was a look of good-breeding on his face and intelligence in his eyes. Barbara called out to him to enter and then, as he did so, merely glanced around carelessly over her shoulder.

"Oh. Good-evening, sir."

She was sitting before a table above which hung a mirror with candles affixed, and a maid was brushing her long mahogany-coloured hair while she tried several different pairs of dangling ear-rings to see which effect she liked best. Her elaborate gown was made of stiff black satin so that by contrast the skin of her arms and shoulders and breasts looked chalk-white, and there were diamonds at her throat and about her wrists. She was in the eighth month of her first pregnancy but seemed scarcely conscious of her unusual bulk, and she looked robustly healthy.

Now, as he entered and crossed the room the maid curtsied and went on with her brushing while Barbara turned her head from one side to the other, making the diamond pendants dance and catch the candle-light. At his appearance a subtle boredom, a kind of polite contempt, had come upon her face. And as he stood looking down at her in obvious perplexity she paid him no further attention, though she knew that he was trying to speak and wanted her help.

"Madame," he began at last, after taking a deep swallow into his dry throat. "I find that it will be impossible for me to have supper with you this evening."

"Ridiculous, Roger! His Majesty will be here. He'll expect you."

She had finally satisfied herself as to the ear-rings and now began to stick on several small black patches, hearts and diamonds and half-moons; one went beside her right eye, another on the left side of her mouth, a third high on her left temple. She had not glanced at him again after the first careless greeting.

"I think his Majesty will understand well enough, if I'm not present."

Barbara rolled her eyes, heaving a pained but patient sigh. "Heigh ho! Are we to go through this again?"

He bowed. "We are not, madame. Good-night."

As he turned and went to the door Barbara sat drumming her nails on the edge of the table, her eyes taking on a dangerous sparkle, and then all at once she pulled away from the maid and got to her feet, raising her arm to secure the last bodkin herself.

"Roger! I want to speak to you!"

His hand on the knob, he turned and faced her. "Madame?"

"Get out of here, Wharton." She gave a wave of her hand at the maid but started to talk before the girl had had time to leave. "I think you'd better come tonight, Roger. If you don't his Majesty will think it damned peculiar."

"I don't agree, madame. I think his Majesty must find it more peculiar that a man should be content to go tamely and parade his wife's whoredom before half the Court."

Barbara gave an unpleasant laugh. "The mistress of a King is not a whore, Roger!" Her eyes suddenly narrowed and hardened and her voice rose. "How often must I tell you that!" Then it fell again to become soft, purring, sarcastic. "Or can it be you haven't noticed I'm treated with twice as much respect now as I got when I was only the wife of an honourable gentleman?" The inflection she gave the last two words showed her contempt of him and of her own insignificant station as his wife.

He looked at her coldly. "I think there's a better word for it than respect."

"Oh? And what's that pray?"

"Self-interest."

"Oh, a pox on you and your damned jealousy! I'm sick of your bellow-weathering! But you'll come to the supper tonight and act as host or by Jesus you'll smoke for it!"

Suddenly he crossed to her, his pose of indifference gone, his face flushed and contorted with anger. He caught hold of her fore-arm. "Be quiet, madame! You sound like a fish-wife! I was a fool not to have taken you to the country when I first married you—my father warned me you'd disgrace us all! But I've learned since then, and I've discovered that to some women freedom means license. It seems that you're one of those women."

Her eyes, almost on a level with his, stared at him tauntingly. "And if I am," she said slowly, "what of it?"

All the uncertainty he had shown before her at first had now vanished completely, leaving him poised and determined. "Tomorrow we shall leave for Cornwall. I don't doubt that two or three years of country quiet will do much to restore your perspective."

With a sudden swift wrench she jerked away from him. "You damned noddy! Just you try spiriting me away to the country and we'll make a trial of what good it does me to have the King's favour!" They were standing silently, both breathing hard, staring fiercely into each other's eyes, when there was a knock on the door and a voice called:

"His Majesty, King Charles II!"

Barbara looked around. "He's here!" Automatically her hands went to her head to make sure that every hair was in place, her eyes moving swiftly and excitedly, and though her face still showed traces of anger it had cleared considerably. She went to pick up her black-spangled fan and then returned. "Now! Are you coming down to act as host, or no!"

"I am not."

"Oh, you fool!"

Her hand lashed out and slapped him stingingly across the face and then she picked up her skirts and hurried across the room, pausing a moment to compose her features before she opened the door. Then she went out and down the broad portrait-lined hallway to the staircase.

Below her stood the King in conversation with her cousin, Buckingham, but as she appeared both men stopped talking and turned to give her their attention. She came down slowly, partly because the precarious unbalance of pregnancy made her cautious, partly to let them admire her. And then as she reached the bottom she curtsied while both men bowed and the King, who alone might remain covered in his own presence, swept off his hat.

Barbara and Charles exchanged lingering smiles, deep intimate looks charged with memories and anticipation. And then she turned to the Duke who had been watching them with cynical amusement on his face.

"Well, George. I didn't expect you back so soon from France."

"I didn't expect to be back so soon. But—" He gave a shrug of his heavy shoulders, glancing at the King.

Charles laughed. "But Philippe flew into a jealous rage. I think he was afraid his Grace intended to follow in his father's footsteps."

It was notorious gossip in both kingdoms that the first Buckingham had been the lover of beautiful Anne of Austria, who was now Louis XIV's fat and old and ill-tempered mother.

And his son had made no secret of his violent admiration for Minette.

"It would have been a pleasure," said Buckingham, and made the King a half-mocking bow.

"Shall we go into the drawing-room?" asked Barbara then, and as they walked toward it she looked up at Charles, her face appealing, soft and almost childish. "Your Majesty, I'm in a most embarrassing position. There's no host for the supper tonight."

"No host? Where's— You mean he didn't care to come?"

Barbara nodded and dropped her black lashes, as though deeply ashamed of her husband's bad manners. But Charles had another view of the matter.

"Well, I can't say that I blame him, poor devil. Ods-fish, it seems a man with a beautiful wife is more to be pitied than envied."

"If he lives in England, he is," said the Duke.

Charles laughed good-humouredly. He could not be offended on the subject of his own habits for he did not try to fool himself about them.

"Still, every party needs a host. If you'll permit me, madame—"

Barbara's purple eyes gleamed with triumph. "Oh, your Majesty! If you would!"

Now, as they entered the doorway and paused for a moment, the roomful of people swung to face them as though magnetized. The hat of every man came off in a sweeping bow and the ladies bent gracefully to the ground, like full-blown flowers grown too heavy for their stems. Barbara had already become so successful and important a hostess that she did not find it necessary to welcome her guests as they arrived. Everyone of any ambition, whether social or political, was delighted to receive an invitation from Mrs. Palmer and would not have complained whatever her manners might be. For many were convinced she would one day, perhaps soon, be Queen of England.

A year ago Barbara would have thought it incredible that she would ever have in her home all at one time these men and women she now used so carelessly.

There was Anthony Ashley Cooper, small, emaciated and sick, related to many of the most powerful families in the nation. By some sleight-of-hand performance he had contrived to transmute himself into a loyal Cavalier at just about the time of the Restoration. The feat however, was no very unusual one. Sympathizers with or active workers in the old régime had by no means all been hanged and quartered or harried into exile—many of them now supported the Monarchy and, in fact, formed the basis of the new Government. Charles was too practical and too well-versed in politics to have imagined that his Restoration could mean a complete overthrow of everything that had been done these past twenty years; the recent change had been mostly superficial. Cooper, like many another, had adopted a new set of manners which matched better with Charles's Court, but he had relinquished neither principles nor fundamental intentions.

There was Cooper's good friend, the Earl of Lauderdale, a huge red-faced red-haired Scotsman whose brogue was thick even though most of his forty-five years had been spent in England. He was ugly and coarse and boisterous, but he had an amazing education in Latin, Hebrew, French, and Italian which he had laboriously acquired during his years of imprisonment under the Commonwealth. Charles found him amusing and the Earl had a deep affection for his King.

George Digby, Earl of Bristol, was a good-looking man of almost fifty, vain and unreliable, but he had in common with Cooper and Lauderdale a violent hatred of the Chancellor. That hatred, founded on envy and jealousy, served to unite most of the ambitious men at Court. To put Chancellor Hyde out of the way was their highest aim, their greatest hope. Barbara's house gave them a rallying-ground, for here they might meet the King when he was at his leisure and most accessible.

But many of them were merely gay young people interested in nothing more serious than their love-affairs and gambling, in learning the latest dance or keeping apace with the French fashions.

Lord Buckhurst, only twenty-three, lived at Court but had no use for it, and refused to exert himself to become a man of power. Henry Jermyn was a big-headed spindle-shanked fop who was enjoying a considerable amatory success because many persons believed he had been married to the dead Princess Mary. Among the ladies was the voluptuous cat-like Countess of Shrewsbury; Anne, Lady Carnegie, flagrantly over-painted, now famous because she had shared Barbara's first lover with her; Elizabeth Hamilton, a tall gracious cool young woman, newly arrived at Court, whom it was the fashion to admire. They were all about Barbara's age, twenty or younger, for the men were outspoken in their opinion that a woman had begun to decay at twenty-two.

The immense drawing-room was furnished well, hung with heavy draperies of gold-green, lighted by dozens of candles burning in wall-sconces and in brass chandeliers overhead. The floor was uncovered and the high heels made a melodious tapping upon it. Laughter seemed to fill the air to the very ceiling; a band of musicians played in one corner; silverware and dishes rattled together.

An adjoining room was set with a buffet-table, in the French style which Charles preferred, and footmen swarmed everywhere. The dishes piled upon it might have done justice to a cathedral builder: pompous confections decorated with candied roses and violets; little dolls in full Court dress spinning about on cake tops; great silver porringers containing steaming ragouts of mushrooms, sweetbreads, and oysters. Bottles of the new drink, champagne, crowded the tables. No more was an Englishman to be satisfied with boiled-mutton and pease and ale. He had learnt better in France and would never be reconciled to the old fare again.

The King's role as host created a sensation, for many of them were sure that it was a subtle way of showing his future intentions. Barbara was sure too and she moved about the room like a flame, charming, amazingly beautiful, full of the confidence of her power. Their eyes followed her and their whispers discussed her. But Barbara was not fooled, for she knew well enough that obsequious though they all were now it would take no more than a hint that the King was losing interest and out would come the sheathed claws, every honeyed word would turn to acid, and she would find herself more alone than she had ever been in the days before her dangerous glory.

It had happened before. But it won't happen to me, she told herself. To all the others, perhaps, but not to me.

Gambling-tables were set up in a third room and there they were soon congregated. Charles sat down to play for a short time, but in less than half an hour he had lost a couple of hundred pounds. He glanced up at Lauderdale who hung over his shoulder.

"Take my place, will you, John. I always lose and I'm a bad loser— What's worse, I can't afford it."

Lauderdale guffawed appreciatively, splattering the King as he did so for his tongue was too big for his mouth, but he took his seat and Charles strolled into the next room to listen to the music. Barbara promptly left her own table and met him just as he was going out the door. Her arm linked with his and he bent to kiss her lightly on the temple, while behind them significant glances were exchanged and some wagers laid.

"It's my opinion Mrs. Palmer is mad enough to think she might be Queen," said Dr. Fraser. He was a personal favourite of the King and, since he could with equal dexterity perform an abortion, cure a clap, or administer a physic, his services were much in demand at Whitehall.

"The lady has a husband, you know," murmured Elizabeth Hamilton, not glancing away from her cards.

"A husband is no obstacle where a king has set his heart."

"He'll never marry her," said Cooper positively. "His Majesty is no such fool as that." Cooper had acquired a considerable reputation for sagacity by guessing far ahead of anyone else that York was married to Anne Hyde.

Barbara's old chum, Anne, gave him a malicious smile. "Why, whatever do you mean by that, sir? Sure, now, you don't think she'd be an unlucky choice?"

"I do not, madame," he assured her coldly. "But I think that the King will marry where political expediency dictates—as kings have always done."

By the time they had left, Barbara was thoroughly relieved. She was tired. The muscles in her legs ached and trembled. But she was happier than she had ever been and perfectly convinced that her hopes and expectation—wild as they might have seemed—would soon be fulfilled.

As she and Charles entered the bedroom together Wharton, asleep in a chair by the fire, jumped to her feet and curtsied, looking at her mistress with frightened apprehension. But Barbara smiled and spoke to her kindly.

"You may go, Wharton. I won't need you again tonight." Then, just as the girl was leaving, she called after her, "Wake me by half-after-eight. There's a 'Change woman coming to show me some lace and if I don't get it first, Carnegie will." Barbara smiled at Charles as though she were a naughty little girl. "Isn't that selfish of me?"

He answered the smile but not the question, and took a chair. "That was good food, Barbara. Haven't you a new head-cook?"

She had gone to the dressing-table and was beginning to unfasten her hair. "Isn't he a marvel? Guess were I got him. I took him away from Mrs. Hyde—she brought him from France with her. D'you know, Charles, that woman hasn't *once* paid me a call?" She shook out her hair and it tumbled in long ripples like dark-fire running down her back; over her shoulder she threw him a quick, petulant glance. "I don't think the Chancellor likes me—or his wife would have called long since."

"Well," said Charles easily, "suppose he doesn't."

"Well! Why shouldn't he! What harm have I done him, pray?" Barbara thought that her new position should command not only the deference but the liking of every man and woman at Court, and she intended to get it, one way or another.

"The Chancellor belongs to the old school of statesmen, my dear. He'll neither pimp nor bribe, but thinks it's possible to get along in this world by honest hard work. I'm afraid there's a new model politician likely to prove too hard for him."

"I don't care what his morals are! He was good friends with my father and I think it's damned bad manners his wife doesn't make me a call! Why, I've heard he even tells you you shouldn't waste your time on a jade like me!"

Charles smiled, one arm over the back of the chair and his legs crossed, his eyes lazily admiring as he sat watching her undress. "The Chancellor has been telling me what I may and may not do for so many years I believe he half thinks I pay him some attention. But he's a very good old man and very loyal, and his intentions are the best even if his understanding is sometimes faulty. However, I wouldn't trouble myself with whether or not his wife calls, if I were you. I assure you she's a dull old lady and no very entertaining company."

"I don't care whether she's dull or not! Don't you understand? It's just that she *should* call on me!"

He laughed. "I understand. Let's forget it—"

He got up and went toward her and Barbara turned, just slipping her smock down over her breasts, to look at him. Her eyes lighted with a bright passion that was perfectly genuine, and as his hands reached out a shudder of expectation shook her, driving everything else from her mind. But not for long.

As they lay in the bed, her head resting on his shoulder so that she could feel beneath her cheek the pulsing of his blood, Barbara said softly, "I heard the most ridiculous rumour today."

Charles was uninterested and merely murmured, "Did you?"

"Yes—someone told me that you're already married to a niece of the Prince de Ligne—and have two sons by her."

"The Prince doesn't even have a niece, so far as I know. None I've married, anyway." His eyes were closed and he lay flat on his back, a faint smile on his mouth. But he was not thinking of what they were saying.

"Someone else told me that you're contracted to the Duke of Parma's daughter."

He did not answer and now, raising herself on one elbow, she said anxiously: "You're not, are you?"

"Not what? Oh, no. No, I'm not married."

"But they want you to marry, don't they? The people, I mean."

"Yes, I suppose they do. Some fat squint-eyed straight-haired antidote, no doubt," he said lazily. "Odsfish, I don't know how I'll ever get an ugly woman with child."

"But why should you marry an ugly woman?" With one pointed forefinger she was tracing a pattern in the matted black hair on his chest.

He opened his eyes and looked up at her, and then his face broke into a grin and he reached out his hand to stroke her head. "Princesses are always ugly. It's a tradition they have."

Barbara felt the excitement begin to mount within her, and her heart was pounding at a furious rate. Unable to look him full in the face, she dropped her eyes before she spoke. "But—Well, why marry a princess if there's none you like? Why not—" She took a deep quick breath and her throat felt dry; a sharp pain stabbed at the base of her skull. "Why not marry me?" Then she raised her eyes quickly and looked at him, searching.

Instantly Charles's face grew wary, the smile faded, and it settled once more into the old lines of moody cynicism. She could feel him draw away from her, though actually he had not moved at all. Barbara was shocked and she looked at him with horrified disbelief on her face. She had been so sure, so perfectly confident that he loved her madly, even enough to make her his wife.

"Sire," she said softly, "hasn't that ever occurred to you?"

He sat up and then left the bed to begin dressing. "Now come, Barbara. You know as well as I do that it's impossible."

"Why?" she cried, growing desperate. "Why is it impossible? I've heard it was you who made the Duke marry Anne Hyde! Then why *can't* you marry me—if you want to. If you love me." She felt her temper getting away from her and caught at it frantically, telling herself that this was too important to throw away because she couldn't hold her tongue. She still thought that she could wheedle him into anything.

Someway I'll make him marry me. I know I will. He's got to. He's got to!

With his breeches on he pulled the thin white linen shirt over his head and fastened the full sleeves at the wrist. He was eager to get away from her, bored and impatient at the prospect of a useless quarrel. He was, and he knew it, thoroughly infatuated with her, for he had never found a woman more exciting to lie with. But if she had been Queen of Naples he would not have cared to marry her—he knew her too well for that, already.

"The two cases aren't exactly comparable, my dear," he said now, his warm voice low and soothing, hoping to lull her into quiet and then get away. "My children will succeed to the throne. James's, most likely, never will."

Certainly that seemed perfectly reasonable for Charles had already recognized at least five illegitimate children, while Barbara herself was convinced that the child she carried was his and not her husband's—or Chesterfield's.

"Oh, but what's to become of *me* if you marry another woman? What will *I* do?" She was close to tears.

"I think you'll do very well, Barbara. I see no reason why you shouldn't. You're not exactly a helpless person, you know."

"But that isn't what I mean! Oh, you see how they all run after me now—Buckingham and Cooper and the rest of that crew— But if you marry someone else and fob me off— Oh, I'd die! You can't think how they'd use me! And the women would be even worse than the men! Oh, Charles, you can't, you *can't* do that to me!"

He paused now and looked at her sharply; then all at once his face softened and he sat down beside her again, taking her hands into his. Her face was wet with tears that welled out of her eyes and slid over her cheeks in great drops, splashing off onto the satin-covered blankets beneath her.

"Don't cry, darling. What the devil do you take me for—an ogre? I won't desert you, Barbara, you can be sure of that. You've given me a great deal of happiness, and I'm grateful. I can't marry you, but I'll see that you're taken care of—very well."

She was sniffling and her chin quivered but she was again conscious of her appearance and trying to weep attractively. "How? With money? Money won't help—not in the case I'll be in."

"What would help?"

"Oh, Sire, I don't know! I don't see how I can—"

He interrupted her quickly, to stem another flood. "If I make you a Lady of my wife's Bedchamber—would that help?"

He spoke to her like an indulgent uncle holding out a sweetmeat to a small girl who had fallen and skinned her knee.

"I suppose it would. If you really do it. You won't change your mind and just—just— Oh—"

Now, suddenly overwhelmed with the knowledge of her defeat, she burst into shaking sobs and flung herself toward him. He held her against his chest for a moment, patting her shoulder while she cried, and then very gently he disengaged himself and got up.

While she lay on the bed and sobbed he swiftly slid into his doublet, knotted his cravat, buckled on his sword, and taking up his hat came to stand above her. Charles, who could not do without women though he could very easily do without any one woman, was often inclined to wish that it was never necessary to see any of them out of bed.

"Barbara—I swear I've got to go now. Please don't cry any more, darling. Believe me, I'll keep my promise—"

He bent and kissed the top of her head and then turned and went to the door. He glanced back just in time to see her look around at him, red-faced and swollen-eyed; he gave her a hasty wave and went out.

She sat up slowly, her face wrenched into a scowl, one hand to her aching head. And then all at once she opened her mouth and gave a high uncanny scream that made the veins in her neck stand out like purple cords, and picking up a vase from the bedside table she hurled it with all her strength at the mirror across the room.

Chapter Eleven

To GET TO the Tap-Room, which was a floor and a half below the Lady Debtors' Ward, Amber had to follow the candleman down a black narrow flight of stairs. But when they had gone only part way he turned suddenly and blocked the passage and she stopped three steps above him, angry and frightened at the look she saw on his face, for her advanced pregnancy gave her a sense of clumsy helplessness.

"Go on!" she cried. "What are you stopping for?"

He made no answer but lunged swiftly forward; one hand caught hold of her skirts and dragged her toward him. With a scream Amber knocked the candle out of his hand. Suddenly she found that he had given way and she was going swiftly down the steps, her hands reaching out blindly toward the walls, but the short chains on her wrists and ankles caught with a jerk. She lost her footing and toppled headlong, twisting desperately to protect her belly and yelling with terror as she plunged toward the bottom of the stair-well.

But even as she stumbled Black Jack Mallard started up, and he caught her before she had hurt herself. She could not see him but she felt with passionate relief a man's powerful hands and arms, his great protecting body, and she heard the violent angry thunder of his voice bellowing curses at the candleman whose footsteps went pounding on up to the second story.

"What did he do to you? Are you hurt?" he demanded anxiously.

Spent with fear, Amber relaxed against him. "No—" she panted. "I think I'm—"

From above, the candleman shouted something unintelligible and with a snarl of rage Black Jack let her go and started after him. "You stinking son-of-a-whore, I'll "

Suddenly his warmth and protectiveness were gone. Amber's eyes opened and she reached out frantically. "Don't leave me! Please—don't leave me!" She was afraid of other unseen dangers hiding there in the dark.

Instantly he was back again. "I'm here, sweetheart. Don't be scared. I swear I'll slit his gullet next time I see him, the turd-coloured dog!"

"I wish you would," she muttered, pressing her hands to her swollen stomach.

Fright had left her crumpled and weak and she let him half carry her to the bottom of the staircase where he gently set her on her feet again. The Tap-Room was nearby and they stood in a kind of smoky twilight; she could feel him watching her. And finally, forcing herself to look up, she saw his eyes going over her face and shoulders and breasts with an expression of pleased contemplation. All at once she felt pretty again; she could almost forget her stringy hair and the lice crawling on her skin and the dirt packed beneath her finger nails. The corners of her mouth went up in a faint smile and her eyes slanted flirtatiously.

Black Jack Mallard was the biggest man Amber had ever seen. He was at least six feet five, his shoulders were massive and the muscles in his calves thick and powerful. His coarse black hair, shiny with oil, hung to his shoulders and there was a slight wave in it. She could see the glint of gold as a vagrant light touched the rings he wore in either ear—it was a fashion much affected by the fops, but on this giant the jewels seemed only to accentuate his almost threatening masculinity. His forehead was low and broad, his nose wide at the nostrils, and while his upper lip was narrow and tightly drawn the lower rolled out in a heavy curve.

His clothes were in the latest mode: A blue velvet suit consisting of short doublet and wide-legged knee-length breeches, white shirt, white linen-and-lace cravat. Garnet-coloured satin ribbons hung in loops at his waist and sleeves and shoulders, there was a feather-loaded Cavalier's hat on his head and he wore calf-high riding boots. Only the boots would not have been acceptable in the King's own Drawing-Room. The clothes were obviously expensive and certainly no cast-off garments but they were soiled, somewhat wrinkled, and he wore them with an air which suggested contempt of such finery.

Now he grinned at her, showing even, square teeth so white they glistened, and made a bow. For all his great bulk he was controlled and graceful as a cat. "I'm Black Jack Mallard, madame, of the Press Yard." The Press Yard was the élite quarter of the jail, reserved for the rich.

She curtsied, delighted to be once more in the presence of a man who was not only susceptible to her charms but worthy of them. "And I, sir, am Mrs. Channell of the Lady Debtors' Ward, Master side."

Both of them laughed and bending over he gave her a casual kiss, the customary salute upon formal introduction. "Come in here," he said, "and we'll have a bouse on that."

"A what?"

"A bouse, sweetheart—a drink. I don't suppose you know our Alsatian cant." He took her arm and she noticed that he wore no fetters and even had a sword slung at his hip.

The Tap-Room was dimly lighted with several tallow candles, but the smoke that hung over it was thick as a morning fog on the Thames. At one end was a bar. Stools and tables and chairs were packed in closely, leaving little room to pass between them, and the ceiling was so low that Black Jack had to hunch his shoulders as he walked along, going toward a table in one far corner. He exchanged several greetings as he went and Amber was aware that every eye there turned to survey her, searching curiously over Black Jack's new wench; she caught some whistles from the men and low-murmured spiteful comments from the women.

But he evidently had a position of some authority, for they moved respectfully aside to let him pass, several of the women gave him inviting smiles, and one or two men complimented his choice. His own attitude toward them was that of good-natured camaraderie—he slapped the men on the back, stroked one woman's hand and another's cheek as he passed—and seemed as much at his ease as though they had been in the tap-room of the Dog and Partridge.

Amber sat down with her back to the wall, and Black Jack, after asking her what she wanted, ordered Rhenish for her and brandy for himself. When they had examined her thoroughly the others went back to what they had been doing. Bottles were raised, cards shuffled and dice rolled, prostitutes wandered from table to table soliciting business; the room swelled with voices—laughter, songs and shouts, the occasional cry of a child. Amber exchanged a smile with Moll Turner but averted her eyes swiftly from the sight of a blowzy fat woman sprawled at a table, holding a fan of cards in her hand while a sleeping baby had its mouth fastened to one brown teat.

"Oh, my God! she thought with horror. Two more months and I'll— She looked quickly at Black Jack, and found him smiling down at her.

"You're a mighty dimber wench," he said softly. "How long 've you been here?"

"Five weeks. I'm here for debt—four hundred pound."

He was less impressed than the Lady Debtors had been. "Four hundred. God's blood, I can take that much in an easy night's work. What happened?"

"My husband stole every penny I had and ran off and left me with the debts—"

"And the lullabye-cheat." He glanced significantly at her belly. "Well—" He poured a glass of white wine for her and a smaller one of brandy for himself and flipped a coin to the waiter, giving a casual salute to the brim of his hat. "Here's to you! May he come back soon and get you out of crampings." He tossed it down at a gulp, as a gentleman should, poured another glass and turned to look at her shrewdly.

Amber drank hers down too, for she was thirsty, but a scowl puckered her eyebrows. "He'll never come back. And I hope he never does—the ungrateful pimp!"

Black Jack laughed and gave a low whistle. "You say that with such spleen I'd go near to believe you really are married."

She stared at him, her eyes sparkling. "Well! And why shouldn't you believe it, pray! Why the devil does everyone think that's just some tale I tell!"

He poured another glass for each of them. "Because sweetheart, a girl like you who says her husband left her, probably never had one at all."

She smiled then and her voice purred. "The way I look now I think I'd fright away a better man than a husband."

"My eyes are good, sweetheart. They see under six layers of dirt—and they see a tearing beauty." For a moment they sat looking at each other and then at last he said, "I've got a room with a window on the third floor. Would you like to smell some fresh air and look at the sky?" He half-smiled at the invitation but got to his feet and reached down his hand to help her.

As they walked out the entire room set up a bellowing and laughing, shouting obscenities and advice to Black Jack, who waved his hand at them but did not glance around.

The rooms were furnished like those in a low-class tavern catering to gay parties, the furniture scarred and much initialled, but certainly luxurious compared to the rest of the jail. The walls were covered with ribald words and sentences, crude drawings, names, and dates. Black Jack told her that the quarters had cost him three hundred pounds. Every man who bought the office of Jailor at Newgate went out of it rich, if not beloved.

Black Jack was often gone, for he had a great many visitors and social obligations to fulfill. But each time he came back they would laugh together over the fine lady—masked of course—who had hinted that she was at the very least a countess and had offered to solace his lonely hours. Once he stole a gold bracelet from some admirer and gave it to her. The highwaymen were the aristocrats of the underworld and they enjoyed a general popularity. Their names were well-known, their exploits discussed in taverns and on street-corners, they were much visited when in jail and when they took their last ride in a cart up Tyburn Hill they were attended by great and sympathetic crowds.

Amber spent most of her time at the window, swallowing in the fresh air as though she could never get enough, standing with her arms braced on the window-sill and looking out over the city. She could see the favoured prisoners down below in the courtyard, walking or standing in groups, some of them playing hand-ball or pitch-and-toss for though it was now the end of January the weather continued mild and the streets were dusty. The tar-smeared quarters of the men hanged after the fanatic uprising earlier that month still lay exposed there and flies and wasps buzzed over the heap in angry masses.

Four days after Amber had met him Black Jack made another of his miraculous escapes, and she went with him. Every bolt, every door, every gate had been liberally greased with the King's coin and each swung open at a touch. In the street a hackney waited, the door ajar; they got in swiftly and rattled off down Old Bailey Street. Black Jack, settling into the seat beside her, slapped his thigh and gave one of his thunderous laughs.

Suddenly a woman's voice spoke, tart and peevish. " 'Sdeath, Jack! That's a fine stink you've got! You bring it out every time you go into that damned jail!"

That, Amber knew, must be Bess Columbine, whom he called his "buttock." Now he introduced them, saying, "Bess, this is Mrs. Channell."

The two women exchanged cool murmurous greetings and all three of them lapsed into silence. It was only a few minutes, however, until the coach stopped, and as she got out Amber saw that they were at the edge of the river. They climbed swiftly into the barge that waited there and the waterman started upstream; it was perfectly black and moonless and though none of them could see the others Amber felt Bess staring insistently at her and could sense her jealous hostility.

Much I care, she thought, if she likes my company or not!

But she did not expect to stay long with Black Jack. For somehow, she was sure, she could get him to give her four hundred pounds. He seemed to have so much money, and so little use for it, she was convinced she would have it from him in less than a fortnight. And then she would leave him—though what she would do or where she would go she had no idea. She had even lost the names of the women Lord Carlton had said would take care of her during her lying-in.

At the foot of Water Lane they disemberked and Bess started out ahead up the steep stone steps to the street level. Amber, holding the bird-cage in one hand and her skirts in the other, cautiously felt her way along until all at once Black Jack—who had been delayed while he paid the bargeman—come up behind her, swung her into his arms and went up as swiftly as though it had been broad daylight. They passed through the gardens which had belonged to the old Carmelite monastery that had once stood there, and finally came into a narrow street.

Here, there was light and noise, and great street signs indicated that almost every other building was a tavern. Through the square-paned windows they could see men playing cards, a naked woman dancing, two other women stripped to the waist and fighting before a crowd of onlookers that cheered and threw coins. The sound of fiddles blended with screams and laughter and the wailing of babies. They were in Ram Alley, Whitefriars, a part of the district which gave the privilege of sanctuary to criminals and debtors. Those who lived there preferred to call it, ironically, Alsatia.

They stopped before one of the houses, Bess opened the door with a key and Black Jack set Amber down. She stepped inside and instantly the two women turned to look at each other.

Bess, Amber saw, was no more than her own age, and of about the same height. Her hair, which was abundant, was dark brown and curly and fell below her shoulders; her eyes were blue and she had a small piquant face, somewhat too broad at the cheekbones, with a nose that turned up saucily. Her figure was round almost to plumpness and her breasts were full-blown. Amber thought that she looked vulgar—an ill-bred slut.

But she was uneasy and angry herself to be put under the girl's scrutiny. For though she had used Black Jack's comb and scrubbed her face she was still miserably dirty, and now she could feel a louse begin to bite. But she would have died rather than reach down to scratch. As it was, Bess lifted her brows and smiled faintly to indicate that she considered her no very formidable rival.

below her knees. Then, giving her a wink, Jack went to a chest and lifted out a large box which he put into her hands. She took it and glanced at him questioningly. He was standing there with his hands thrust into his pockets, rocking back on his heels and grinning broadly, waiting for her to open it.

Excited at the prospect of a present, Amber laid the box on a chest, untied the strings and tossed the crackling papers aside. With a cry of delight she took out a green taffeta gown sewn with appliquéd scrolls of black velvet. Underneath lay a black velvet cloak, a smock and two petticoats, green silk stockings and green shoes.

"Oh, Black Jack! It's beautiful!" She reached up to kiss him and he bent rather awkwardly, like a bashful boy, for he was always afraid of hurting her. "But how'd you ever get it so quick?" Madame Darnier had never completed a gown in less than a week.

"I was abroad early this morning. There's a second-hand dealer in Houndstitch where the quality sell their clothes."

"Oh, Black Jack—and just the colour I love!" She slipped off the robe and began to dress hastily, chattering all the while. "It looks like the leaves on the apple-tree that used to grow outside my bedroom window. How'd you know green's my favourite colour?"

But a moment later her face fell in disappointment. The gown would not fasten over her stomach and the sight of herself in a mirror—something she had not seen for over a month—made her want to cry. It seemed to her that she had been pregnant forever.

"Oh!" she cried in exasperation, and stamped her foot. "How ugly I look! I *hate* having a baby!"

But Black Jack assured her soothingly that she was the prettiest thing he had ever seen, and they went downstairs to meet Mother Red-Cap. They found her seated at one of the tables with her back to them and a candle at her elbow, writing in an enormous ledger which lay spread open before her. As Black Jack spoke to her she turned and then immediately got to her feet and came forward. She gave Amber a friendly kiss on the cheek and smiled her approval at Black Jack, who stood there proudly beaming over both of them.

"A gentry-more she is, Jack." She glanced over her figure. "When do you reckon?"

"About two months, I think."

Amber was looking at her wide-eyed, amazed to find that she bore no resemblance at all to the dissolute old harridan she had been expecting. She did not, in fact, look any more vicious than Aunt Sarah. Mother Red-Cap was fifty-five years old but her skin was clear and smooth and her eyes snapped brightly. Smaller than Amber, her body was trim and compact, and all her movements suggested a fund of unexpressed energy. The clothes he wore were plain neat ones made of cotton and wool with starched collar and cuffs and apron, and there was not a jewel in sight. A bright red cap covered every wisp of hair and Black Jack had told Amber that in almost ten years he had never seen her without it.

"I'll have a midwife for you in good time, then," she said, "and we'll find a woman to take the baby."

"Take the baby where!" cried Amber, suddenly on the defensive.

"Don't be alarmed, my dear," said Mother Red-Cap reasonably, and the accent with which she spoke reminded Amber of Lord Carlton and his friends. "Who'd want a baby to live in the friars? Most of those who do die before their first year is out. We can get a cleanly responsible cottager's wife who will care for the child and let you visit him whenever you like. Oh, it's a very satisfactory arrangement—many women do it," she assured her, as Amber still did not look convinced. "Now," she turned briskly and went back to her ledger. "Tell me your full name."

Black Jack spoke up quickly. "Mrs. Channell is all she wants to give. I'll pay the garnish-fee for her."

Amber had not told even Black Jack her real name and he did not seem to care for he said that his own was assumed and that any person of sense kept his name secret in Alsatia.

"Very well. No one here is interested in prying into the past. Black Jack tells me you're in debt for four hundred pound and want to pay it so that you can leave the Friars. I don't blame you—I think you're too pretty to stay here long, and I assure you I'll put the means of earning that sum in your way, just as soon as you're able to go abroad." Amber started to ask her how, but Mother Red-Cap went crisply on. "Meanwhile, we'll have to do something to get rid of that accent. A girl from the country is generally assumed to be a fool here in London, and that's a handicap to the best laid plans. I think that Michael Godfrey might make a good tutor for her, don't you, Black Jack? And now, my dear, make yourself comfortable with us and ask for whatever you want or need. I'll leave you now; this is the first of the month and I must call upon my tenants."

She closed the ledger, put it into a drawer of the table, and locked it with a key taken from her apron-pocket. Then tossing a cloak over her arm, she smiled at them both and went to the door. Once again she turned to give Amber a sweeping glance, shook her head slightly, and remarked, "A pity you're so far gone with child. Three months ago you'd have brought a hundred pound as a maidenhead."

She went out and though Black Jack burst into hearty laughter Amber turned to him with an angry light in her eyes. "What the devil does that old woman intend? If she thinks I'm going to earn my way out of here by—"

"Don't get excited. She doesn't—I'll see to that. But once a bawd, always a bawd. And Mother Red-Cap's such a matchmaker I'll swear she could have married the Pope to Queen Elizabeth."

What Mother Red-Cap's real name was, Amber never learned, but very obviously Black Jack not only liked her but had a strong masculine admiration for her success, her uncompromising determination, her ability to survive and prosper no matter what happened to others. But Amber could not understand why the woman lived so frugally when she did not need to, or why she had chosen a life of chastity after what must have been an exciting youth. For those reasons she felt a frank but unexpressed contempt for her and decided that she could not be so very clever after all.

But nevertheless she exerted herself to make Mother Red-Cap like her and believed that she was succeeding very well. For Black Jack had flatly refused, the first time she broached the subject, to give her money enough to pay her debt—and it had led to a quarrel between them.

"I think you *want* me to stay in this damned place!"

"I certainly do. What d'ye think I got you out of jail for? You're an ungrateful little bitch!"

"What if I am! Who wants to stay in this filthy hole all their life! I hate it! And I *will* get out! Just you wait and see! If you won't give it to me I'll ask Mother Red-Cap for the money! She doesn't use it and she'll lend me four hundred pound, I warrant you!"

He was a formidable giant who might have snapped her bones like toothpicks, but he threw back his head and laughed. "Go ahead and ask her if you like! But believe me, she'd as soon lend you four hundred of her teeth."

Chapter Twelve

ONE AFTERNOON while Black Jack was away Amber sought out Mother Red-Cap. When she was home, which was not often, she was almost always employed in working on her ledger, entering long columns, filling out bills and receipts by the dozen, and she did not like to be interrupted. Now, as Amber approached, she made her a signal to be silent and continued running her pen up a line of neatly written figures, her lips moving as she did so, and then finally she set down the total and turned to Amber.

"What is it, my dear? Can I do something for you?"

Amber had prepared and rehearsed her speech, but now she cried impulsively: "Yes! Lend me four hundred pound so I can get away from here! Oh, please Mother Red-Cap! I'll pay it back, I promise you!"

Mother Red-Cap observed her coolly for a moment, and then she smiled. "Four hundred pound, Mrs. Channell, is a large sum of money. What do you offer for security?"

"Why—I'll give you a promise, on paper, or anything you like. And I'll pay it back with interest," she added, for she had learned by now that Interest was both God and Sovereign to Mother Red-Cap. "I'll do anything. But I've *got* to have it!"

"I don't believe you understand the business of pawn-brokerage my dear. It may seem to you that four hundred pound is an insignificant sum to borrow. It is however, a very large sum to lend upon no better security than the promise of a young girl to repay. I don't doubt your intentions, but I think you would find it more difficult to come by four hundred pound than you imagine now."

Surprised, disappointed, Amber was angry. "Why!" she cried. "You said yourself you could have got a hundred pound for me!"

"And so I probably could. More than half that hundred however, would have been mine for arranging the match, not yours. But to be frank with you, it was merely an idle thought. Black Jack's told me very flatly he intends keeping you for himself and I believe, my dear, you should feel some gratitude toward him. It cost him three hundred pound to get you out of Newgate."

"Three hundred — Way, he never told me that!"

"And so I think that while Black Jack's here we won't be using you that way."

"While he's here? Is he going somewhere?"

"Not very soon, I hope. But someday he'll ride up Tyburn Hill in a cart—and he won't come down again."

Amber stared at her horror-struck. She knew that he had been burnt on the left thumb, which meant he was to hang for the next offense. But he had escaped again in spite of that and he had a reckless audacity which made her think of him as almost indestructible. Now, however, she was thinking not of him but of herself.

"That's what's going to happen to all of us! I know it is! We're *all* going to hang!"

Mother Red-Cap lifted her brows. "We might, I suppose. But we're far more likely to die of consumption here in Alsatia." She turned away and picked up her pen and though Amber lingered a few moments she knew that she had been dismissed, and went to climb the stairs back up to her bedroom.

She was discouraged but not beaten. She still intended to escape somehow, and comforted herself with the reminder that she had made the far more difficult escape from Newgate.

Alsatia lay just east of the Temple Gardens and could be reached from them by going down a narrow broken flight of steps. Low as it was and close to the river it was perpetually invaded by a thick dingy-yellow fog that hung to the very pavements, seeped into the bones, stuck in the nostrils and made it difficult even to breathe. Ram Alley, where Mother Red-Cap's house was, smelt of stinking cook-shops and the lye-soap used by the laundresses who made that street a headquarters.

Its courts and alleys were crowded with beggars and thieves, murderers and whores and debtors, a wild desperate rabble who lived in a constant internecine warfare but who invariably banded together to beat off any attempted intrusion by constable or bailiff. Children swarmed everywhere—almost as numerous as the dogs and pigs—starving little dwarfs with sunken eyes and husky high-pitched voices. Amber shuddered at the sight of them and looked swiftly away for fear her own baby would be marked before birth because she had seen them. She felt that living here she had left the world—the only world that mattered to her, the world where she might see Lord Carlton again.

It was Michael Godfrey, hired by Mother Red-Cap to teach her to speak as a London Lady of quality should, who gave her glimpses back into that life toward which her heart yearned.

He was a student at the Middle Temple where sons of many of England's wealthy families were to be found, supposedly acquiring a liberal education and learning how to manage their estates and preside at the sessions when they came into their property. Most of them, however, spent more time in taverns than they did in the class-room and more money on women than on books. Like many of the others, Michael had sometimes ventured into the Friars, impelled by curiosity and a desire to see how the wicked lived and looked. And also like many others, when his mode of living had far outrun his allowance and he found himself embarrassed with debts, he had come to borrow and thus he had made the acquaintance of Mother Red-Cap, the fabled witch-woman of the Sanctuary. Within a fortnight after Amber's arrival he had been engaged as her tutor.

He was just twenty years old, of medium height and size, with light-brown curling hair and blue eyes. His father was a knight with property in Kent and money enough to give his son all the customary advantages of his class: Michael had gone to Westminster School to learn Latin and Greek. At sixteen, the usual age for entering college, he had been sent to Oxford to master Greek and Roman literature, history, philosophy, and mathematics. That was supposed to be accomplished in three years, for too much education was not considered good for a gentleman, and a year ago he had enrolled in the Middle Temple. Two years or so there and he would go on his tour abroad.

While the rain dripped unceasingly—for the mild winter had been followed by weeks of wet—he and Amber would sit beside the fireplace in the parlour drinking hot-spiced buttered ale and talking. She was an eager and enthusiastic listener, appreciative of his jests, fascinated by the things he did and saw and heard.

She would laugh delightedly to hear of how he and his friends, "somewhat disguised" as the gallants liked to say when they had been drunk, had knocked over a watchman's stand where the old man sat sleeping, serenaded a bawdy-house in Whetstone Park and broken all the windows, and finally stripped naked a woman they met returning home late with her husband. Bands of young aristocrats scoured about the town every night, boisterous and destructive, the terror of all quiet peaceable citizens, who would as soon have been set upon by cutthroats or thieves. But Michael recounted his exploits with a zestful freshness and relish which made them seem the most harmless innocent childish pranks.

He told her that for the past three or four months women had been appearing on the London stage and were now in every play, overpainted, daringly-dressed young sluts, some of them already taken by the nobles as mistresses. He told her of seeing the rotten bodies of Cromwell and Ireton and Bradshaw pulled out of their graves and hanged in chains at Tyburn, and of how their pickled heads were now stuck atop poles on Westminster Hall and chunks of their carcasses exposed on pikes over the seven City gates. And he told her about the plans for his Majesty's Coronation which was to take place in April and was to be the most magnificent in the history of the British throne; he promised to describe for her every robe, every jewel, every word spoken and gesture made, after he had seen it.

Meanwhile she was losing the remnants of her country accent. Her ear was alert and her memory retentive, mimicry was natural to her and she had a passionate eagerness to learn. She stopped pronouncing power as pawer and yeo as yeow. She gave up both Gemini and Uds Lud and learned some more fashionable oaths. He taught her all the correct ways of making and receiving introductions, a few French phrases and words, that it was the mode to pronounce certain as sartin and servant as sarvant. Vulgarity was high-fashion at Whitehall and pungent words of one syllable interlarded the conversation of most lords and ladies. Amber absorbed all of it, and with it the cant of Alsatia.

Michael Godfrey, who was already sure he loved her, wanted to know her real name, who she was, and where she came from. She refused to tell him the truth but she embroidered upon her story to Sally Goodman and he accepted her for what she said she was: a country heiress run away from home with a man her family disliked, and now deserted by him. He was very sympathetic, indignant that a woman of her gentle breeding should have to live in such surroundings, and offered to get in touch with her family. But Amber shied away from that and assured him that they would never come to her aid in such a place as Whitefriars.

"Then come with me," he said. "I'll take care of you."

"Thanks, Michael, I wish I could. But I can't—not till I've laid-in, anyway. Lord, wouldn't it be a pretty fetch if I fell into labor in your quarters! You'd be turned out in a trice!"

They both laughed. "They've threatened me a dozen times. Mend your ways, sirrah, or out you go!" He drew down his brows and bellowed dramatically. Then all at once he leaned forward and took her hand. "But please—afterward—will you go with me then?"

"There's nothing I'd like better. But what about the constables? If they caught me I'd have to go back to Newgate." Michael lived on an allowance which did not cover his own expenses; he could never pay her debt.

"They won't catch you. I'll see to that. I'll keep you safe—"

Amber woke early in the morning on the 5th of April, conscious of a dull prodding ache in her back. She turned over to make herself more comfortable and then suddenly she realized what it was. She gave Black Jack a poke.

"Black Jack! Wake up! Go tell Mother Red-Cap it's started! Send for the midwife!"

"What?"

He grumbled sleepily, not wishing to be disturbed. But when she shook him—frantic, for she had heard of babies being born and no preparation made for them—he woke up, stared at her for a surprised instant, and quickly began to get into his clothes.

Mother Red-Cap came to see her and then went out on her perpetual round of business, confident that nothing would happen for several hours. The midwife arrived with her two helpers, made an examination and sat down to wait. Bess Columbine looked in once but was sent away, for there was a strong superstition that the presence of one whom the labouring woman disliked would impede the progress of birth. But Black Jack, though he poured sweat and seemed to suffer at least as much as she did, remained with her constantly, drinking one glass of brandy after another.

At last, about four o'clock in the afternoon, the baby's head began to appear, like a red wrinkled apple, and a few minutes later a boy was born. Amber lay in exhausted collapse on the bed, unable to feel anything but relief.

She was disappointed in the baby for he was long and thin and red and gave scant promise that he would ever resemble his handsome father, though Mother Red-Cap assured her that he would be very pretty in a month or two. But now his tiny face was screwed up in a continuous squall, for he was hungry. Amber had assumed that she would nurse him herself—in the country, women did not expect to look like virgins once they were married—but Mother Red-Cap was horrified at such a thought and told her that no lady of fashion would think of spoiling her figure. A wet-nurse would be found instead. Amber's vanity needed no urging and she agreed readily, but while they interviewed applicants the baby starved.

It took four days to find the woman who answered to Mother Red-Cap's exacting demands, but after that he was quiet and content and slept most of the time, in his cradle beside Amber's bed. She felt a passionate tenderness for him, far greater than she had ever expected or believed possible. Even so, she hoped that she would never have another baby.

She recuperated rapidly and by the time the wet-nurse arrived she was sitting up in bed, propped against pillows and wearing one of Black Jack's shirts, for that was supposed to cause the milk in the breasts to dry quickly. Michael Godfrey came to visit her and brought the baby a lavishly embroidered white-satin gown for his christening, and she received several other presents as well. Apparently she had made more friends in the Friars than she had realized.

One of them was Penelope Hill, a prostitute who lived just across the street. She was a large-boned young woman whose claims to beauty were a head of hair that was like a heavy skein of pale yellow silk, and ample melon-shaped breasts. Rusty sweatstains showed in the armpits of her soiled blue-taffeta gown and all her body gave out a strangely inviting promise of lushness and fulfillment. She was languid and cynical and regarded all men with a kind of amused contempt; but she warned Amber that a woman had no chance of succeeding in a man's world unless she could turn their weaknesses to her own advantage.

Such philosophical advice, however, meant less to Amber than did her practical information on another subject. From Penelope she learned that there were a great many means of preventing perpetual child-bearing—or abortions—and she learned what they were. In possession of the knowledge, Amber wondered how she had ever been so stupid as not to have guessed at it long since; it seemed so perfectly obvious.

When the baby was two weeks old he was christened with the single name—Bruce. It was customary to give a bastard his mother's surname, but she could not use hers and would not use Luke Channell's. Afterwards she had a christening feast, which was attended by Mother Red-Cap and Black Jack, Bess Columbine and Michael and Penelope Hill, an Italian nobleman who had fled his country for reasons he did not disclose and who knew no word of English, the coiner and his wife from the third floor, two men who accompanied Black Jack on his expeditions out of town—Jimmy the Mouth and Blueskin—and an assortment of cutpurses, bilks, and debtors. While the men drank and played cards the women sat and discussed pregnancy and miscarriages and abortions with the same ravening interest they had in Marygreen.

A week after that the woman Mother Red-Cap had hired to take the baby came for him. She was Mrs. Chiverton, a cottager's wife from Kingsland, a tiny village lying out of London some two and a quarter miles, but almost four miles from

Whitefriars. Amber liked and trusted her immediately, for she had known many women of her kind. She agreed to pay her ten pounds a year to feed and care for the baby, and gave her another five so that she could have him brought to see her whenever she wanted.

She did not wish to part with him at all and would have kept him there with her in Whitefriars if it had not been for Mother Red-Cap's insistence that he would probably die in that unhealthy place. She loved him because he was her own—but perhaps even more because he was Bruce Carlton's. Bruce had been gone now for almost eight months, and in spite of the violent feeling she still had for him, he had grown unceasingly unreal to her. The baby, a moving breathing proof of his existence, was all that convinced her she had ever known him at all. He seemed to be a dream she had had, a wish that had almost, but not quite, come true.

"Let me know right away if he falls sick, won't you?" she said anxiously as she put him into Mrs. Chiverton's arms. "When will you bring him to see me?"

"Whenever ye say, mem."

"Next Saturday? If it's a good day?"

"Very well, mem."

"Oh, please do! And you'll keep him warm and never let him be hungry, won't you?"

"Yes, mem. I will, mem."

Black Jack went along to see her safely into a hackney, but when he came back Amber was sitting alone in a chair by the table, staring morosely into space. He sat beside her and took her hands into his; his voice was teasing but sympathetic. "Here, sweetheart. What's the good of all this moping and sighing? The little fellow's in good hands, isn't he? Lord, you wouldn't want 'im to stay here. Would you now?"

Amber looked at him. "No, of course not. Well—" She tried a little smile.

"Now, that's better! Look here—d'ye know what day this is?"

"No."

"It's the day before his Majesty's coronation. He rides through the City on his way to the Tower! How would you like to go see 'im?"

"Oh, Black Jack!" Her whole face lighted eagerly and then suddenly collapsed into a discontented frown. "But we can't—" She had come to feel that she was as much a prisoner in Whitefriars as she had been in Newgate.

"Of course we can. I go into the City every day of my life. Hurry along now, into your rigging and we'll be off. Bring your mask and wear your cloak," he called after her, as she whirled and started out on a run.

It was the first time Amber had left Alsatia since she had come there two months and a half before, and she was almost as excited as she had been the first day she had seen London.

After weeks of rain the sky was now blue and the air fresh and clean; there was a brisk breeze that carried the smell of the outlying fields into the city. The streets along which the King's procession would pass had been covered with gravel and railed off on either side and the City companies and trainbands formed lines to keep back the eager pushing crowds. Magnificent triumphal arches had been erected at the corners of the four main streets and—as the year before—banners and tapestries floated from every house and women massed at the windows and balconies threw flowers.

Black Jack shepherded Amber through the crowd before him, elbowing one man aside, shoving his hand into the face of another, until finally they came to the very front. She dropped her mask—which was kept in place by a button held between the teeth—and could not stop to pick it up. Black Jack did not notice and in her own excitement she soon forgot that it was gone.

When they got to where they could see, the great gilt coaches, filled with noblemen in their magnificent Parliament robes, were turning slowly by. Amber stared at them with her eyes wide open, impressed as a child, and unconsciously she searched over each face, but did not see him. Lord Carlton had ridden the year before with the loyal Cavaliers returning from over the seas. But when the King approached she forgot even Bruce.

His Majesty was on horseback and as he rode along, nodding his head and smiling, hands reached out trying to touch him or the trappings of his horse. From time to time his attention was caught by a pretty woman somewhere in the crowd. And so he glanced once, then again, at a girl whose tawny eyes stared up at him in passionate admiration and awe, her lips parted with a sudden catch of breath as his gaze met hers. And as he passed he smiled at her, the slow lazy smile that—for all its cynicism—was so strangely tender. Her head turned, following him, but he did not look back.

Oh! thought Amber, dizzy with exultation. He looked at me! And he smiled! The *King* smiled at me! In her excitement she did not even see the camel lumbering along bearing brocaded panniers from which a little East Indian boy flung pearls and spices into the crowd.

The King's swarthy face and the expression in his eyes stayed with her for hours as vivid as the moment she had seen him. And now she was more than ever dissatisfied with her life in the Sanctuary. The world of which she had half lost remembrance called to her again like an old and beloved melody and she yearned to follow it—but did not dare. Oh, if only somehow, *somehow* I could get out of this scurvy place!

That evening the four of them sat at the supper-table: Bess sullen and glowering because she had not been to the pageant; Amber eating in silent preoccupation; Black Jack laughing as he showed Mother Red-Cap the four watches he had stolen. Amber was conscious of the conversation but she paid no attention to what was being said until she heard Bess's angry protest.

"And what about me, pray? What am *I* to do?"

"You may stay here tonight," said Mother Red-Cap. "There'll be no need for you to go along."

Bess banged her knife onto the table. "There was a need for me once! But now Mrs. Fairtail's come I find I'm as unwelcome as a looking-glass after the small-pox!" She gave Amber a venomous glare.

Mother Red-Cap did not answer her, but turned to Amber. "Remember the things I've told you—and above all, don't be uneasy. Black Jack will be there when you need him. Keep your wits and there'll be no possibility of mistakes."

Amber's hands had turned cold and her heart was beginning to pound. During the discussions and rehearsals for these hold-ups she had always felt that she was merely pretending, that she would never really have to do any of those things. And now all of a sudden—when she had least expected it—the pretending was done. Mother Red-Cap *did* intend her to go. Amber could feel the noose about her neck already.

"Let Bess go if she wants to!" she cried. "I've got no great maw for the business! I dreamed about Newgate again last night!"

Mother Red-Cap smiled. Her temper was never ruffled, she never lost her cool, reasonable tone and manner. "My dear, surely you know that dreams are expounded by contraries. Come, now, I had expected great things of you—not only for your beauty but for your spirit, which I had thought would carry you undismayed through any adventure."

"Undismayed spirit, my arse!" snorted Bess.

Amber gave her a sharp hard stare across the table and then got to her feet. Without another word she left the room and went upstairs to get her cloak and mask, to powder her face and smooth a little rouge on her lips. A few minutes later she came down to find Bess and Black Jack quarreling. Bess was chattering furiously at him though he merely lounged in his chair with a wine-bottle in his hand, and ignored her. Seeing Amber at the door he smiled and got to his feet. Bess whirled around.

"*You!*" she cried. "You're the cause of all my troubles—you jilting whore!" And suddenly she grabbed a saltcellar from the table and hurled it to the floor. "There! And the devil go with you!" She turned and rushed out of the room, sobbing as she went.

"Oh!" cried Amber, staring at the spilt salt with scared and anxious eyes. "We're cursed! We *can't* go!"

Black Jack, who had gone after Bess, now gave her a cuff with his great hand that almost knocked her off her feet. "You damned meddling jade!" he roared at her. "If we run into illluck I'll cut your ears off!"

But Mother Red-Cap scoffed at Amber's superstitious fears and assured her that it could be no ill omen because it had been done purposefully. She gave them some last-minute admonitions, Black Jack swallowed a glass of brandy and—though Amber was still reluctant and worried—they set out. By the time they had climbed the stairs and entered the Temple gardens she was beginning to feel excited and eager for whatever adventure might lie ahead; Bess and the spilled salt were already far out of her mind.

Chapter Thirteen

IN THE CITY the bells were ringing, and blazing bonfires sent up a glow against the sky. Every house was brightly lighted and crowds of merrymakers filled the streets; coaches rattled by and there were sounds of laughter and singing and music. Taverns were packed and the inns were turning customers away. It was the night of the Restoration all over again.

The Dog and Partridge was a fashionable tavern located in Fleet Street, frequented for the most part by gallants and the well-dressed, overpainted harlots who tracked them to their habitat. On this night it was jammed full. Every table was crowded with men—those who brought women usually took them to a private room upstairs; waiters were going among them with trays of bottles and glasses and foaming mugs of ale; a tableful of young men were singing; over in one corner some fiddlers scratched away, unheard and ignored. And just as Amber entered the door four young men started out, drunk and excited, going to fight a duel over some petty disagreement or imagined slight. They jostled against her but went on, troubling neither to stop nor to apologize, though by their dress they were obviously gentlemen.

Amber, masked and with her hood up, drew her cloak disdainfully about her and stepped aside. When they had gone she stood in the doorway and looked over the smoke-filled room, as though to find someone, and presently the host approached her.

"Madame?"

She knew by his manner that he took her for what she was supposed to be: a lady—Covent Garden variety. And she felt like one herself. She had spent hours at her window, both at the Royal Saracen and the Rose and Crown, watching them get in and out of their coaches, stop to speak to an admirer, fling a beggar a shilling. She knew how they picked up their skirts, how they pulled on a glove, spoke to a footman, used their fans. They were confident, careless ladies, sure of the world and of their position in it, ever so slightly scornful of those who lived apart. But it was not by mere mimicry that she could so successfully pretend to be one; it was an attitude toward life that seemed natural to her.

"I'm looking for a gentleman," she said softly. "He was to meet me here." She scarcely glanced at the host; her eyes were going over the room.

"Perhaps I can help you to find him, madame. What was he wearing? What is his appearance?"

"He's very tall and his hair is black. I think he wears a black suit with a gold braid garniture."

The host turned, looked over the room. "Can it be that gentleman? The one at the far right-hand table?"

"No, no. Not that one. Hang it, the rascal must be late!" She fluttered her fan in annoyance.

"I'm sorry, madame. Perhaps you would prefer to wait in some more private place?"

"I'd prefer it, but if I do he might miss me. I can't tarry long—you understand." He was to understand that she was a married woman come to an assignation with her lover and in some apprehension of being seen by her husband or an acquaintance. "Place me in some discreet corner then. I'll wait on the wretch a few minutes or so."

The host led her across the room, weaving his way through the hot, noisy crowd, and Amber was aware that for all she was concealed from top to toe several of the gallants turned and looked at her. Her perfume was alluring and her cloak—which Black Jack had stolen from some lady of quality—suggested wealth. He seated her at a table in the farthest corner, and though she declined to order anything to drink she put a silver coin into his hand.

"Thank you, sir."

Sitting down Amber let her cloak fall open just enough to reveal something of her low neckline, flared her fan, gave a bored little sigh and then a quick casual glance around the room. She met several pairs of eyes, a few smiles and one broad grin, and instantly she dropped her lashes. They were not to take her for a prostitute.

She was glad now that she had come; a quick excitement flowed through her veins, and she only wished that this was real life, no mere part she was playing.

Within a quarter of an hour she had sorted them over and found at least one young man apparently well suited to her purposes. He sat at a table some seven or eight feet away playing cards with four companions, but his head turned persistently and his eyes looked back at her again and again. When most women went masked in public places a man had to learn to judge beauty by very little detail—the colour and sheen of a curl escaping from a hood, the sparkle of a pair of eyes seen between narrow slits, the curve of a pretty mouth.

Now, as she felt him looking at her again she glanced across and let the faintest smile touch her lips, a smile that scarcely existed at all, and then she looked away. Immediately he put down his cards, shoved back his chair and started toward her, walking unsteadily.

"Madame—" He paused politely to hiccough. "Madame, will you permit me the honour of buying you a glass of wine?"

Amber, who had been looking in another direction, now glanced at him in apparent surprise.

"Sir?"

The boy was flustered. "Oh, I'm sorry, your Ladyship. I meant no offense—hic—but I thought you might be lonely—"

"I'm waiting for someone, sir. I'm not lonely at all. And if you take me for a whore you're quite mistaken. I think you'll find your luck better with that lady over there."

With her fan, which she held clasped in one hand as it lay on the table, she indicated an unmasked woman who had just come in and who stood surveying the room, her cloak open to show a pair of almost naked breasts. As he looked Amber noticed that he wore four rings, had gold buttons on his coat with tiny diamonds in the centers, that his sword case was silver and that he wore a large mink muff attached to a broad twisted satin girdle.

He gave her a bow, very stiff and dignified. "I beg your pardon, madame. That is not my game, I assure you. Your servant, madame." He turned and would have gone off but she stopped him.

"Sir!" He looked around and she smiled up at him, her tawny eyes coaxing. "Forgive my rudeness. I fear the waiting has set me on edge. I'll accept your offer of wine, and thanks."

He smiled, forgiving her instantly, sat down and summoned the waiter to order champagne for her and brandy for himself. He told her that his name was Tom Butterfield and that he was a student at Lincoln's Inn, but when he tried to find out who she was she grew cool and aloof, intimating that she was too well known to dare give her name. And she knew by the way he stared at her that he was trying to place her, wondering if she was Lady This or Countess That, and thinking that he was having a considerable adventure.

They sipped their drinks, chatting idly, and when a little herring-peddler came to the table to ask if she might sing a song for the lady they both agreed. The child was perhaps ten or eleven years old, a slovenly little waif with dirty fingers, snarled blonde curls and shoes worn through at the toes. But her voice was surprisingly clear and mature and there was about her a buoyant happy quality, refreshing as the taste of oranges on a stale tongue.

When she had done, Tom Butterfield munificently gave her several shillings, no doubt to impress her Ladyship. "You've a pretty voice, child. What's your name, pray?"

"Nelly Gwynne, sir. And thank ye, sir." She gave them both

a grin, bobbed a curtsy, and was off through the crowd, stopping at another table across the room.

Amber now began to seem impatient. "What provoking creatures men are!" she exclaimed at last. "How the devil does he dare use me at this rate? I'll see that he smokes for it, I warrant you!"

"He's an ignorant blockhead that would keep your Ladyship awaiting," agreed Tom Butterfield soberly, though his eyes no longer focused well and he looked half-asleep.

"Well, he'll not do it again, you may be sure!" She began to gather up her belongings, muff, fan, and gloves. "Thank you for your drink, sir. I'll go along now."

She dropped one glove and bent slightly to pick it up. He stooped at the same time to get it for her and as he did so stared down into her bodice; he was weaving on his feet as he straightened, and gave his head a vigorous shake to clear it.

"Let me see you to your coach, madame."

They went out the door, Tom Butterfield walking solemnly at her heels and ignoring the jocular hoots of his friends. "Where is your coach waiting, madame?"

"Why, I came in a hackney, sir," she replied, implying that no lady going to an assignation would be so foolish to ride in her own coach which might be seen and reported. "I believe there's one for hire over there. Will you call it for me?"

"I protest, madame. So fine a person as yourself travelling about after nightfall in a hell-cart? Tush!" He waggled an admonitory finger at her. "I have my coach just around the corner. Pray, let me carry you to your home." He put his fingers to his mouth and whistled.

They climbed in and the coach started off, jogging along Fleet Street to the Strand, and now Tom Butterfield sat in his own corner, hiccoughing gently from time to time and hanging onto the strap beside the window for support. Amber, afraid that he would fall asleep, finally said to him: "You still don't know me, do you, Mr. Butterfield?"

"Why, no, madame. *Do* I know you?" She could feel him lean toward her as though trying to see through the darkness.

"Well—you've smiled and bowed to me often enough at the play."

"How now, have I then? Where were you sitting?"

"Where? In a box of course!" No lady of quality sat elsewhere and her tone was indignant, but still teasing.

"When were you there last?"

"Oh, perhaps yesterday. Perhaps the day before. Don't you recall a lady who smiled kindly on you? Lord, I never thought you'd forget me so quick—all those amorous tweers you cast."

"I haven't forgot. My mind's been running on you ever since. You were in the fore of the king's box three days ago, dressed in a pretty déshabillé with your hair in a tour and your eyes had the most languishing gaze in all the world. Oh, gad, madame, I haven't forgot—not I. I'm mightily smitten with you, I swear I am. I'm in love with you, madame!"

As his impetuosity mounted Amber grew more coy, moving as far away as she could get and giving a low giggle in the darkness so that he made a grab for her. They started to tussle, she yielding a little and then pushing him off as he tried to draw her against him, giving a cry of dismay as his hand went into her bodice and caught one breast. He was panting excitedly, blowing his sour breath in her face, and all at once she gave him a brisk slap.

"What the devil, sir! Is this the way you handle a person of quality?"

Suddenly abashed, sobered by the slap, he drew away. "Forgive me, madame. My ardour outran my breeding."

"Indeed it did! I'm not accustomed to that kind of courtship!"

"My humblest apologies, madame. But I've admired you for a great while."

"How do you know? Perhaps I'm not the lady you have in mind at all."

"You must be the lady I have in mind. In fact, madame, I find myself so hot for you—" He reached for her again and they had begun to struggle once more, when the coach stopped. "Hell and furies!" he muttered, and she began to push him off.

"Sit up, sir, for God's sake!" She was straightening her clothes, pulling up her bodice, smoothing her hair, and then the door opened and Tom Butterfield staggered out and offered his hand to help her down.

The house before which they were stopped was a new one in Bow Street just a block from Covent Garden Square. At the door he caught hold of her to kiss her again and as he did so she took the key from her muff and slipped into the lock.

"My husband's abroad tonight," she murmured. "Will you come in, Mr. Butterfield—and drink a glass of wine with me?"

She pushed open the door and went in with him following close behind her. But when he would have detained her in the passage she disengaged herself and went on up the black staircase to another door, which she also opened. She went in first and turned to find him smiling, his eyes full of expectancy as he looked at her; a candle was burning and it gave just enough light to see by. And then as Black Jack's heavy cudgel smashed down upon his skull the smile froze on his face, his eyes glazed over, and he dropped to the floor, folding up in sections like a carpenter's rule. Amber gave an involuntary little scream, one hand to her mouth, for the look of accusation she had seen in his eyes filled her with guilt.

But Black Jack had already stuck the cudgel back into his pocket and was kneeling beside him, cutting the string of cat's gut on which the buttons of his coats were strung. While she stood and stared he went efficiently about his work, rolling him over to get the buttons in back, pulling off the rings, unbuckling the sword and muff, searching through his pockets. And then, as a dark narrow streak of blood began to run out of his hair and over his temple, Amber moaned aloud.

"Oh! You've killed him "

"Hush! He's not hurt." He looked up, giving her a broad grin. "What the hell, sweetheart! Scared by a little blood? A broken head may teach him better sense next time—if we hadn't fibbed the young prigster somebody else would have. Look at this scout—" He held up a gold watch. "Fifteen pound if it's worth a sice. It takes fine bait to catch a big fish. Now come along—let's rub off." He had the boy's wrists and ankles tied and they started out. Amber paused to look back once more, but Black Jack hurried her down the backstairs and into a hackney that was waiting.

The night's easy success was reassuring to Amber, who now believed that she might soon get money enough to leave the Friars. And she had enjoyed the adventure, too—all but the clouting of Tom Butterfield, for whose welfare she still felt a certain guilty concern. When she had drunk her morning draught of ale, brought to her by the shuffling Pall, she slipped into her dressing-gown and went downstairs. Mother Red-Cap and Black Jack were in the parlour, talking, and both of them seemed in high spirits.

Amber came in with a breezy greeting and wave of her hand—full of a vast self-confidence and ready to be congratulated. Mother Red-Cap gave her a warm smile.

"Good-morning, my dear! Black Jack's been telling me how like a veteran you handled matters last night! He says it was worth a Jew's eye to see the way you led the young cully into his trap. And now you've seen for yourself how easy it is, and safe, haven't you?"

Amber, thinking that now they had a need of her, was inclined to be independent. She shrugged. "I suppose so. Well—" She held out her hand. "Tip me my earnest."

"Why, my dear, there's nothing for you this time. I've applied your share on your bill."

"On my bill!"

"Of course. Or did you think it costs nothing to eat and lodge and give birth to a baby?"

She unlocked the drawer where her ledger was kept, took out a neatly written sheet and handed it to Amber who stood for a moment staring at it, nonplussed. She did not know what it said, for she had never been taught to read or write, but she was horrified to think that none of the money she had helped to steal was hers. For those expenses Mother Red-Cap had mentioned were not ones she had ever expected to pay. She felt that she had been cheated, and it made her angry. After a moment she looked up, her mouth opened to speak, and saw

Mother Red-Cap just removing her cloak from the peg where it hung beside the door; she put it on and went out.

"Here!" Amber thrust the bill at Black Jack. "Read it to me!"

He took it and read the items slowly. At each one her scowl intensified. Now she was in a fine pickle! Instead of being less in debt she was deeper than ever. A violent despair filled her.

The bill was carefully itemized.

		£.	s.	d.
1.	For 3 months lodging and diet...........	30	0	0
2.	Suit of childbed linen....................	4	4	0
3.	For the minister to christen the child......	2	10	0
4.	For the midwife's fees..................	3	3	0
5.	For the christening supper...............	6	0	0
6.	For the wet nurse for 15 days............	1	0	0
7.	For Mrs. Chiverton......................	10	0	0
8.	For Mrs. Chiverton to bring the child upon request	5	0	0
9.	For the dressmaker for altering the green gown	0	6	2
		£62	3	2

"Lord!" cried Amber furiously. "I'm surprised she doesn't charge me for the use of her pot!"

Black Jack grinned. "Never mind. She will."

Amber was as angry with Black Jack as she was with Mother Red-Cap. For he could have paid her bill—and the debt too—at no hardship to himself. She was so resentful over his refusal that she had lost all sense of gratitude at being out of Newgate. She would have pawned some of the jewellery he had given her, but it was not enough to clear the full debt and if part of it disappeared she knew that she would get no more. It seemed to her that she would be in Whitefriars forever.

And so when Michael Godfrey came the next afternoon and asked her again to go away with him she agreed without hesitating an instant.

"Wait here and I'll be right down. I want to get my cloak and I have a new gown—" She was already out of the room.

Michael called after her: "Let it go! I'll get you another!"

But she pretended not to hear him and ran on, for there were several things she wanted to take with her—a lace fan, a pair of green silk stockings, the imitation gold ear-rings, and her parakeet. She rushed about the room—the house was empty and she wanted to get away before someone should return—flung everything into a sheet and hastily tied it. "Come on," she said to the parakeet. "We've had enough of this damned sanctuary." And with the cage in one hand, the tied-up sheet in the other, she hurried out and down the stairs. Halfway to the bottom she stopped with a gasp, for the door swung open and Black Jack Mallard stood there, his great frame blocking out the light.

She gave a gasp of dismay. "Jack!"

It was dark down there and she could not see the expression on his face, but his voice was deep and hoarse. "So you were going to scour!" Slowly he started up the stairs toward her, and she could only stand there helplessly, watching him and waiting. All at once she was afraid of him; she had seen him lose his temper with Bess and knew that he could be violent. "You ungrateful little bitch, I should break your head for this—"

Amber's courage came back with a rush. "Get out of my way!" she cried. "I'm leaving this filthy place! I'm not going to stay here and hang with the rest of you!"

He was just below her now and she could see his face, the thin upper lip drawn tight against his teeth, his eyes dark and glittering. "You'll stay here as long as I want you to stay. Go on upstairs now. Go on, I say!"

For a long moment they stood staring at each other. Then suddenly she kicked out at his shins and threw herself against his arm, trying to break through. *"Michael!"* she screamed.

Suddenly Black Jack laughed. He picked her up with one arm, threw her over his shoulder, and started back up the stairs. "Michael!" he repeated contemptuously. "What good d'ye think that jack-straw could be to you?" He laughed again, a thunderous roar that echoed up the narrow stairwell, and he seemed scarcely to notice that Amber was screaming furiously, kicking and beating at him with her fists.

When he reached the bedroom he sat her down, so forcibly that the jar went from her heels up into her head. She recovered quickly.

"God damn you, Black Jack Mallard!" she yelled at him. "You're trying to kill me, *that's* what you're doing! You'll make me stay here till we *all* get caught! But I won't do it, d'ye hear? I'll get out if I have to—" She started for the door again, so furious that she would have run out of Whitefriars and into the arms of the first constable who saw her.

He reached out a hand and caught her as she would have gone by, jerking her to him as easily as if she were one of the dolls bought at Bartholomew Fair. "Stop it, you little fool! You gabble like a magery prater! You're not going out of the Friars—not while I'm here. When I'm gone do what you damned please—but I didn't give three hundred pound to get you out of Newgate so some other man could have the use of you!"

She stared at him with angry amazement, for she had always believed that he was in love with her; and it had long been her opinion that it was very easy for a woman to take advantage of a man in love. Now she realized that the only distinction he made between her and Bess was that she was newer and more ornamental and evidently pleased him better in bed. It was a sharp and humiliating cut to her pride, and all of a sudden she despised him.

When she answered him her voice was low and tense, full of enraged scorn. "Oh, you gormandizing vermin, Jack Mallard, I despise you! I hope you *do* get caught! I hope they hang you and cut you up in pieces—I hope—Oh!" She whirled about and flung herself on the bed, bursting into sobs, and in a moment she heard the door slam behind him.

She stayed in her room the rest of the day, refused any supper, and was still sulking the next morning when someone knocked. Thinking that it was probably Black Jack, coming with a gift to beg her pardon and try to make up the quarrel, she called out for him to come in. She was at the dressing-table, cleaning her nails, and did not glance around until she saw Bess's face appear in the mirror. Then she turned swiftly.

"What are you doing here!"

Bess was unexpectedly sweet and agreeable. "I only came to wish you a good morning." Amber thought she had most likely come to gloat because Black Jack had spent the night with her, and she turned away. But now Bess leaned over, close to her shoulder.

"I heard you and Jack yesterday afternoon—"

"Did you now!"

"If you really want to leave the Friars—if you'll promise to go away and never come back—I can get that money for you."

Amber jumped to her feet, one hand reaching out to grab Bess's wrist. "If I'll promise to go! My God! I'll go so fast I'll—Where is it?"

"It's mine. I've saved it up to have if Black Jack should ever need it. Mother Red-Cap keeps it for me, but I can get it by tomorrow night. I'll put it in the food-hutch in the kitchen."

But the money was not there and when next Amber saw Bess she had a purple bruise across one eye, and the side of her face and her lower lip was swollen—obviously Black Jack had discovered their plot. After that Bess never troubled to conceal her hatred and jealousy and only a few days later Amber found the house-cat with turquoise feathers clinging to its jowls and paws. Bess insisted that she was completely innocent of any connection with the cat's crime, but Amber had always kept her parakeet's cage safely out of reach and knew the little bird could not have been caught without help from someone.

Chapter Fourteen

Though she at first intended to, Amber discovered it would not be possible to stay on bad terms with Black Jack forever. She depended on him for too much. And so—even if she continued to harbour her resentment against him—within four or five days after the quarrel they seemed as close as before.

She had declared to Mother Red-Cap and all of them that she would never venture her carcass again for so paltry a fee—twelve pounds was her share from the first night—but she soon did. For it was the only possible chance she had of ever getting out of the Friars. And in spite of the danger she enjoyed their escapades: playing at being a fine lady, venturing up into the City, even the excitement of running great risks.

For the most part their luck was as good as it had been the first night. It seemed that every young coxcomb in London was ready to believe a beautiful stranger had fallen in love with him at the play or in Hyde Park or the Mulberry Gardens, and was more than eager to help her cuckold her foolish old husband. Both Black Jack and Mother Red-Cap attributed much of their success to Amber's own skill at portraying a fashionable woman. Bess, they said, had too often spoiled the whole scheme by being taken for a whore in disguise—which made the gentlemen wary, for it was well known that those ladies were frequently in league with a gang of bullies.

One of their most consistently successful tricks was the "buttock and twang"—a simpler form of what they had done the first night. Amber would go masked into a tavern, find her victim and lure him outside into some dark alley. When she had picked his pocket a cough or sneeze summoned Black Jack who would come staggering along and pretending to be drunk, knock him over, and make off with whatever she had stolen. Concealed by the darkness she would also disappear, join Black Jack, and return to Alsatia. A time or two she went "upon the question lay." Dressed well, though discreetly, and carrying in her hand an empty bandbox she would go to some great house and pretend to be the 'Change-woman come with the ribbons my lady had bespoke the day before. While the maid was gone to see if the lady was awake she could put a few small valuable objects into her box and depart.

But Amber did not care for that kind of sport. She preferred to play the lady of quality herself and told them flatly this dodge was a trick better suited to Bess's talents than her own.

Once Amber went into a house in Great Queen Street where a masquerade was in progress, and after a while she and one of the young men sought a quiet room. But as they were walking down a dark hallway she felt stealthy fingers at the nape of her neck and moved swiftly. "You're a thief!" she whispered, afraid to cry out for fear a constable actually would come. He protested and was about to run off when he discovered that the buttons on his coat had been cut. They both laughed, he admitted he had been mistaken in her too, and so they parted, to cast for other fish.

She had only one serious scare and that occurred the night she went to an upstairs-room in a tavern with their victim and found that Black Jack had not yet arrived. For more than half an hour she was capricious and teasing, holding him off; but at last he grew impatient, began to suspect what she was about and when he tried to pull off her mask she grabbed up a pewter candlestick and struck him with it. Then, not stopping for his sword or watch or even to see whether or not he was dead, she rushed out of the room, down the hallway and the stairs and was halfway through the taproom when she heard a voice bellow: "Stop that woman! She's a thief!" He had recovered consciousness and come after her.

Amber felt an agonizing terror that seemed to freeze blood and muscle, but somehow in spite of herself she ran on at full speed through the roomful of dumfounded patrons. She had just reached the door to the street when a man sprang up from one of the tables and started after her, shouting that he would bring her back. It was Black Jack. They got safely to the Sanctuary where he told the story to everyone with shouts of laughter—but Amber refused to stir out of the Friars again for more than a fortnight. She had felt the gallows noose too plain that time.

But in spite of all these activities she was not able to save much money. She had to have numerous gowns and cloaks, so that she could not come to be recognized by what she wore, and though she bought them seconded-hand in Houndstitch or in Long Lane and soon sold them again, she spent a good deal. She also had to defer the cost of her lodging and food and other incidental expenses. And every time Mrs. Chiverton brought the baby in she had a dozen gifts for him. She had come to feel that there was a wall around Alsatia over which it would never be possible to climb—most who came there, she knew, stayed.

Black Jack was himself a good example.

Whatever his real name, he was the son of a country-squire and had come to London eleven years before to attend the Middle Temple. At that time the King had just been beheaded and the Puritans were rabidly punishing vice and praising virtue; but the young men nevertheless contrived to live very much the same carefree reckless lives they always had. A hypocritical cloak of modesty served its purpose for them. Thus he ran himself into debt, far beyond his father's ability to pay even had the old man wished to do so. It was never permissible for impecunious gentlemen to beg of their relatives and friends, and so when his creditors became too pressing he moved into Whitefriars to avoid arrest. And there he had found, as did many another bankrupt young man of good family, that the King's highway offered an easy and exciting livelihood.

"When it's so easy to steal money," he said, "a man's a fool to work for it." Amber was half inclined to agree with him—

or would have had she been able to keep all and not merely a small part of what she took.

Early in June Black Jack went back to the roads again. Winter was the gay social season in London and many of the nobility returned to their country homes to spend the summer months. Then the roads swarmed with highwaymen and numerous inn-keepers were in their pay; but in spite of the well-known dangers most persons rode without sufficient protection.

Amber's part was a simple and safe one. With Bess, who went along dressed as her serving-woman, she would ride out to the inn from which Mother Red-Cap had had information and there make the acquaintance of the traveller and his family. Pretending to be a lady of quality just going out of or coming into town, she would tell them that her coach had been overturned and wrecked; and when they offered to let her ride with them she could manage the time of departure to Black Jack's advantage. For though many inn-keepers were willing to give information, very few would allow a robbery on the premises—too many such incidents would put them out of business. Amber was well satisfied with this arrangement, but Bess was not—for she had been accustomed to acting the part of lady herself and was furiously resentful at having been demoted.

There was seldom any scuffle when the bandits appeared, for even if all members of a party were armed they usually preferred giving up the master's valuables to risking a wound. One man, however, told Black Jack that he would never have got the money if he had not taken him unawares, and Black Jack offered to shoot it out with him. Armed with pistols, they walked into the nearby field, counted off ten paces, and fired. The man dropped dead. Amber, who had been watching with anxiety and trying to think what she should do if Black Jack was killed, felt a passionate relief—but afterward she was more in awe of him than she had been.

But he was a good-natured thief and always left the coachman half-a-crown to drink his health. Once he robbed an old Parliamentarian just returning from a trip into the country with his whore, stripped them both naked and tied them to a tree, back to back; over their heads he put a sign informing all passers-by that here were two Adamites.

As the summer weeks passed Amber's savings began to mount; by mid-August she had accumulated two hundred and fifty pounds. They had had no new scares and she became brazenly confident and almost began to enjoy the life she was living. She still had an uneasy restlessness to leave Alsatia, a feeling that she was missing something of great importance going on out in the real world, but the days faded one into another and she was half content.

Then one day she got a crude and sickening shock.

Coming into the parlour she found Black Jack standing between Blueskin and Jimmy the Mouth—leaning with his great arms upon their shoulders—while they looked at something laid out on the table before them. Their backs were to her and she could not see what it was but they were talking together in low voices which now and then burst into a laugh.

Amber walked up and saw that it was a large sheet of paper with his Majesty's coat-of-arms and two long lines of printing upon it. She frowned, suddenly suspicious.

"What's that?"

They looked around, surprised to find her there.

"Black Jack's a famous man," said Blueskin. "He's been named first in a proclamation for taking twenty-two highwaymen." Black Jack grinned, pleased with the honour.

But Amber stared, open-mouthed and horrified. She wanted violently to live, and at a time like this, when she saw how close death stood beside her, she grew frantic with terror.

"What's the matter?" demanded Black Jack, a kind of sharpness in his voice.

"You know what's the matter! They're looking for you and they'll catch you! They'll catch all of us, and hang us! Oh, I wish I was still in Newgate! There at least I was safe!"

"And so do I wish you were still in Newgate! Of all the complaining jades I've ever known— What the hell did you expect when I brought you here? You'd better get it through your head the whole world doesn't function for your benefit! But you can stop worrying about your neck! A woman's always got one alibi—you can plead your belly. Why," he continued—and now his voice had turned sarcastic, his eyes went over her with mocking amusement—"I once knew a woman put off the hangman for ten years—no sooner was she delivered of one brat than they found her quick again."

Amber scowled and her mouth gave a sneer of repugnance. "Oh, did she, indeed? Well, that's all very well—but not for me!" She finished the sentence with a shout, leaning toward him, fists clenched and the cords in her throat straining. "I've got other things to do with *my* life, I'll have you know—!"

At that moment Bess came in the door, and saw that there was trouble between them. She grinned maliciously. "What's the quarrel here? Sure, now, Jack, you've not fallen out with our fine Mrs. Fairtail?"

Amber turned, her nostrils flaring with anger, and gave her a sweeping glance of lazy insolence. "Marry come up, Bess Columbine, but you're as jealous as a wife of her husband when she lies-in!"

"Jealous? *Me* jealous of *you!*" yelled Bess. "I'll be damned if I am, you scurvy wench!"

"Don't call *me* names!"

Suddenly Amber reached out, grabbed her by the hair, and gave a violent jerk. With a shriek of rage Bess seized a fistful of curls and the two women would have flown into deadly battle—but for the unexpected appearance of Mother Red-Cap.

The men merely stood looking on and smiling, but she rushed forward, took them by the shoulders and gave each a vigorous shake.

"Stop!" she cried. "I won't have any brawling under my roof! Just once more, Bess Columbine, and out you go!"

"Out *I* go!" protested Bess, while Amber, with a superior smile, reached up to pin back the long heavy curls that had come loose. "What about her! What about that—"

"Bess!"

For a long time Bess and Mother Red-Cap stood with locked stares, but Bess was finally forced to yield. Nevertheless, as she turned to leave the room she knocked into Amber, giving her a hard jar. Without an instant's hesitation Amber turned her head and spat onto her gown. Bess stopped abruptly, the two women once more face to face like a pair of bristling cats; but at another warning from Mother Red-Cap Bess whirled around and stalked out.

For several days after that Black Jack ignored Amber as though she did not exist, and Bess was insultingly triumphant; she flouted his preference whenever they met. But however little Amber cared for Black Jack or his company, she did not intend to let Bess get the better of her. She began a new flirtation with him which was presently successful——and after that Bess's hatred was so intense and so sullen that she half expected to get a knife stuck into her ribs. She believed, and with good reason, that it was only Bess's fear of Black Jack which secured her own life.

Early in September, Bess, convinced that she was pregnant, told Black Jack about it and asked him outright to marry her. He gave her an insulting snort.

"Marry you? You must take me for a dommerer. I suppose you think I don't know every man that's come into this house has had a lick at you!"

He was sitting at the dinner-table, as he always did, long after everyone else had left, gnawing at a chicken-leg he had in one hand and washing it down with swallows from a wine-bottle held in the other. He was slumped far down on his spine, perfectly easy and relaxed and unconcerned, not even troubling to glance up at her.

"That's a damned lie and you know it! I never so much as spoke to another man until you brought that slut in here! And anyway I haven't laid with anyone but Blueskin—and that only a few times! This brat is yours and you know it, Black Jack Mallard, and you'll own it or I'll—"

He tossed the bone aside and leaned forward to pick up a cluster of purple Lisbon grapes. "For God's sake, Bess, stubble it! You sound like a beggar's clack-dish! I don't care what you do. Lay with who you damned please, but don't bother me about it."

His back was half-turned and for a moment she stood staring at him, her eyes like glass, her whole body beginning to tremble with rage. And then with an animal-like cry she lunged for him, snatching up a knife off the table. A quick look of surprise crossed his face as he saw the swift descending flash of the blade and his arm went up to defend himself, thrashing out then and giving her a violent blow that sent her sprawling across the room.

She was crouched on the floor, staring ferociously up at him where he loomed above her, when Mother Red-Cap rushed in from her room down the hallway. "What is it? she cried. "Oh!" She put her hands on her hips. "Well. I've warned you before, Bess, and now you go. Get your belongings and leave this house!"

Bess glared up at her with sulky defiance, but got slowly to her feet. For a long moment she stood there without moving.

"Go on!" repeated Mother Red-Cap. "Get out of here!"

Bess started to protest and then she gave a sudden furious scream. "Don't say it again! I'm going! I'm going away from here and I'll never come back! I wouldn't come back if you got on your knees and begged me! I hate you! I hate every one of you and I hope you—" Suddenly she whirled about and ran from the room and they could hear her feet pounding up the stairs.

Black Jack gave a low whistle and glanced at the knife where it lay on the floor, knocked out of her hand when he had struck her. "Whew! The crafty little gypsy. She'd have slit my throat, I think." He gave a shrug and went back to take up the cluster of grapes, picking them off and tossing them one at a time into his mouth.

Mother Red-Cap went to the table, got out her ledger, and sat down to settle Bess's account. "I'll be glad to be done with her. She's never been much use to me, and ever since Mrs. Channell came she's been an infernal nuisance. Oh, well—you can't make a whistle of a pig's tail."

Presently Black Jack went into the kitchen to tease Pall, who adored him though she blushed and stammered and scratched nervously at her lice whenever he appeared. The house was quiet for several minutes and then Amber came in the front door. She was wearing a thin pale-green silk dress with her hair tumbling about her shoulders and tied with a ribbon, and she had two of Penelope Hill's choicest yellow roses stuck into the low-cut neckline.

"Ye gods! I swear this is the hottest day in an age!" She dropped into a chair, fanning herself with her lace-trimmed handkerchief, and Mother Red-Cap went on with her work. After a few moments Amber got up and started for the doorway that led into the hall where the stairs were.

"I don't think you'd better go up there, my dear," said Mother Red-Cap, dipping her pen into a pewter inkwell, but neither turning nor looking around. "I just sent Bess to pack her rigging and she's in a tearing rage."

Amber glanced back, smiling. "Bess is going?" She shrugged. "Well, much I care if she's in a rage or no. Let her just say something to me and I'll—"

"Never mind, my dear. I don't want another brawl in my house. Go into the kitchen with Black Jack and Pall until she's gone."

Amber hesitated for a moment but finally turned and went into the other room. After a few minutes they heard Bess's high-heeled shoes coming down the stairs, Mother Red-Cap's voice talking to her, though Bess did not answer, and then with a bang she was gone. Black Jack proposed a toast to the peaceful life, and he and Amber presently wandered back into the parlour and sat down to play a game of cards.

They had spent interminable hours at cards and dice, for they did not go out on business more than once or twice a week—sometimes even less—and the long days and nights had to be passed somehow. Black Jack had taught her every trick in a gambler's repertoire—palming, slurring, knapping, the brief—and in seven months she had attained to a very creditable proficiency. She felt that she could hold her own now at a table with any lord or lady in the kingdom.

After a while Blueskin came in and they started to play at putt, the favourite tavern game and one which had probably been the undoing of more country-squires' sons than any other. It was three or four hours before she went upstairs to her own room, and there she found Bess's final gesture to the rival she despised. Her smocks and gowns and petticoats littered the room, ripped and slashed to pieces. There were torn fans, gloves cut in two, cloaks backed by scissors, and she had dumped the contents of the chamber-pot onto the remnants of Amber's finest gown.

Black Jack promised to find Bess and give her the beating she deserved, but she had disappeared from Sanctuary and left not a trace, and they all knew it would never be possible to seek her out in the great sprawling city with its half-million inhabitants. She could lose herself in the warrens of Clerkenwell or St. Pancras, in the glutted seafaring center of Wapping, or in the alleys and courts of the Mint across the river in Southwark.

It was a bad shock to Amber; she decided that her life was cursed and that she would never get out of Whitefriars. She became gloomy and despondent, trailed listlessly about the house, and was sullenly bad-tempered with all of them. She hated Bess and Black Jack and Mother Red-Cap, Pall and Blueskin and the house-cat, even herself.

No matter what I do, she thought, no matter how hard I

work and how much I save, there's always *something* happens! I'll never get out! I'll die in this stinking hole!

Three days after Bess had gone Mother Red-Cap came into the bedroom and found Amber lying on her back, stretched out straight with her hands behind her head. She had been awake for at least two hours, mulling over her troubles, and the longer she thought about them the more insurmountable they became. She gave Mother Red-Cap a sulky glare, annoyed at being interrupted, but she did not speak.

"Well, my dear," said Mother Red-Cap, as cheerfully as though Amber had greeted her in good humour. "This is no ordinary day for us, you know."

Every morning she got up punctually at five, like an apprentice, put on her plain, neat dress, and began to go about her numberless tasks. From the moment she woke she was brisk and alert and ready for the day. The sight of such determined activity was irritating to Amber.

"It's an ordinary day for me," she said crossly.

"How now! Surely you've not forgot this is the day you're going to Knightsbridge."

"It's not the day *I'm* going to Knightsbridge!"

"But, my dear child, this is most important. There's a great deal of money involved."

"It isn't the first time there's been a great deal of money involved—but *I* never saw much of it!" The subject had been discussed between them before, always with considerable bitterness, for though Amber protested she was being cheated of her rightful share Mother Red-Cap insisted that she got exactly what her services warranted, and Black Jack agreed. "Anyway, it'd be like Bess Columbine to have the constables waiting on us. She knows all our plans."

"Nonsense, my dear. I think I know Bess better than you do, and I assure you she's no such desperate creature as that. She hates the sight of a constable worse than a fishmonger hates a hard frost. But as for the money—I came up here to tell you I'll double your earnest this time, to make up for the loss of your clothes." Considering the matter settled she started toward the door. "Black Jack is below with Jimmy and Blueskin. They intend setting out within the hour."

But as she went Amber flounced over on her side, scowled and called after her, "I'm *not* going!"

Mother Red-Cap did not reply, but within a few minutes Black Jack appeared and after half-an-hour's coaxing and wheedling and assuring her that they had changed their plans so that Bess could not catch them if she tried, she got up and began to dress. Even so she would not leave before she had gone to consult an astrologer who lived in Mitre Court. Upon his assurance that the day was a propitious one for her she borrowed a cloak from Mother Red-Cap and, still sulking, left the Sanctuary with Pall and the three men.

Knightsbridge was a quiet little village on the West Bourne just two miles and a half out of the city, and they reached it by taking a barge up the river to Tuthill Fields and then hiring a coach to the village. Because of its convenient situation Knightsbridge was much frequented by highwaymen who attacked travellers leaving or entering the city. Mother Red-Cap had had a message from the inn-keeper in her employ there that an old gentleman, Theophilus Bidulph, who came into London twice a year, was expected on the 8th of September.

Sometimes they had to wait two or three or more days for a victim to appear, but Amber heartily hoped that this time it would not be necessary. They went upstairs to the room assigned to them and Pall immediately took off her shoes, complaining—as she had ever since leaving home—that they hurt her feet. Having nothing else to do Amber sat down to arrange her hair all over again, a process which could easily take half-an-hour, and when that was done she plagued Pall until the miserable girl finally admitted that she was with child by Black Jack Mallard. By nightfall she was distractedly bored, pacing uneasily about the room, hanging out the window and tapping her fingers on the sill, wishing she was anyone but who she was and anywhere in the world but there.

But at last she heard the pounding of horses' hoofs, the clatter and bang of a coach; dogs began to bark and the ostlers ran out into the courtyard to greet the arriving guest. A few moments later there was a hasty tap at her door and the host told her Theophilus Bidulph had come and was ordering his supper downstairs. Amber waited about a quarter of an hour and then she went down herself.

Mr. Bidulph was standing beside the fireplace drinking a glass of ale and talking to the host and he did not see her until she spoke his name. Then he turned about in some surprise. He was a short merry-faced old gentleman with great bushy pointed eyebrows and the look of a good-natured imp.

"Why, Mr. Bidulph!" she cried, giving him a sparkling smile and holding out her hand.

He took it and made her a bow. "Your servant, madame." In spite of his courtesy he was franky puzzled, though he looked at her with interest.

"I vow I think you've forgotten me, sir."

"By the mass, madame, I fear I have."

"I'm Balthazar St. Michel's eldest daughter, Ann. Last time we met I was no more than so high." She bent a little, indicating with her flat palm a very tiny girl. "Surely you remember me now, sir? You used to dandle me on your knee." She continued to smile at him.

"Why—uh—of course, madame—my dear, I mean. And how is your father, pray? It's some years since we've met and —uh—"

Her face fell a little. "Oh, Mr. Bidulph, he's not well. The old gout again. Sometimes he's in bed for days." She gave him another quick smile. "But he speaks so often of you— He'll be so pleased I chanced to see you."

Mr. Bidulph drank down his ale. "You must give him my regards, child. But what are you doing all alone out here?"

"Oh, I'm not alone, sir. I'm traveling with my woman. I'm going into town to visit Aunt Sarah—but one of our horses lost a shoe and we stopped here for the night. They say the ways are thick with highwaymen nowadays."

"It's true the wretches are everywhere—much worse than when I was a young fellow, let me tell you. But then, of course, nothing is as it was. But won't you ride in with me in the morning? I'll see you get there safe and sound."

"Oh, thank you, sir! How kind that is! For the truth on it is, those cutthroats everywhere about have me uneasy as a witch."

While they talked Amber saw some of his footmen going through the room bearing trunks and boxes on their backs; evidently the old gentleman did not intend to trust his belongings to the surveillance of the stable-boys. But at least that would make it possible for Black Jack to take what he wanted, while she occupied Mr. Bidulph's attention. And, long before morning, all five of them would be in Whitefriars again. Amber was eager to have it over and done and to be back in safety once more—for Bess's jealousy hung above her like an ominous threat. She thought the girl was mad enough to do anything for her revenge.

At Mr. Bidulph's invitation Amber sat down to have supper with him, and they lingered thereafterward while she listened to his tales of the Civil Wars. She heard of numerous instances demonstrating his and everyone else's heroic valour, of the dead King's nobility and martyrdom, the magnificent leadership of Prince Rupert. Nothing, he assured her again and again, could have been more glorious than the way the Royalists had lost the war.

Amber kept an eye on the clock.

By ten she was beginning to grow nervous and had to force herself to sit still and smile and ask questions. They had been there at the table for more than three hours, and certainly Black Jack should have finished his work by now and made her a signal to join them. A feeling of panic was rising in her, and her stomach turned over and over, fluttering like a captive bird.

Oh! she thought wildly. Where is he! Why doesn't he come! *What* can have happened!

Then all at once she heard a noisy commotion from outside. The dogs began to bark again, horses' hoofs beat along the roadway, and there was a babble of voices—men shouting, a woman's scream. Pall opened their door at the head of the stairs to wave frantically at her. And Amber, suddenly terrified, thinking that Bess had arrived with a party of constables, leaped to her feet.

"Good Lord, madame! What's amiss?"

"It's thieves!" cried Amber wildly. "Quick! Put out the lights!"

She darted across to snuff out the candles burning in wall-sconces, and as she did so Pall burst from the room above and came running down, wailing with fear. "Shut up!" cried Amber frantically. At that moment she heard the unmistakable sound of Bess Columbine's voice and a bellow of rage from Black Jack.

The voices were nearer now and Amber—able to think of nothing but saving herself—started for the front door. She heard Pall bawling her name, and Mr. Bidulph, catching the contagion of excitement, went stumbling around in the dark, calling out, "Mrs. Ann! Mrs. Ann! Where are you!" By mistake he grabbed hold of Pall and she shrieked with terror.

Amber rushed on and then, just as she got outside, she heard footsteps coming that way and saw the flare from their torches. Bess's voice screamed: "She's in here! Let him go—*He's* not the one! The woman's inside!"

Amber whirled and ran back inside, heading for the kitchen. Mr. Bidulph was still floundering about and calling her name while Pall screamed but could not decide what to do; as Amber ran by he reached for her and caught hold of her skirt. She jerked it free, hearing it tear, and rushed on, reaching the narrow little hallway below the stairs just as a torch brightened the room. Pall gave a shriek of agony as she was seized and Mr. Budulph indignantly demanded to know what was going on.

Amber burst into the kitchen, panting so that she could scarcely breathe, and gave a scared start as she heard a voice.

"Mrs. Channell? It's the host."

She stopped still. "Oh, my God! Where can I go! Where can I hide? They'll be here next!" Her teeth were chattering and her very bones seemed to shake.

"Quick! Get into this food-hutch! Give me your hand!"

Amber reached out gropingly. He caught hold of her hand, threw up the top of a great oaken chest, and she climbed in. The lid had just shut down when Bess and the constables came through the hallway; the host turned and ran out of the room, slamming the door behind him.

"There she goes!" yelled Bess. And through the air-holes bored in the chest Amber saw a flare of light and heard the rush of their feet as they went by, Bess swearing when she knocked her ankle against a stool.

Amber waited only until the last one was gone and then she flung back the lid and got out, picked up her skirts, and ran after them. Still on the trail of the host they had rounded the corner into the courtyard, and since the kitchen formed a separate wing of the house it was dark when she got outside. The confusion was greater than ever and she knew they had captured all three men for she heard Bess yelling: "Let him go, you damned fools! He's the ostler here! Get that woman!"

Amber did not pause an instant but struck off in the other direction, toward the river, hoping only to get away where it was so dark she could not be seen. Reaching the bank she plunged down it. She was unable to see at all, for the moon had disappeared and the sky was black with storm-clouds, but she ran blindly ahead—like one in a dream who, no matter how hard the legs churn, cannot seem to make any progress. The sounds were growing fainter, but she dared not stop or look back.

Her shoes were soaked through in a moment and the rocks on the streambed bruised the soles of her feet. Her wet skirts flopped and clung to her ankles; brambles scratched her face and bare arms and caught in her hair. A hard pain seared her left side, her legs felt wooden and her lungs were beginning to burn. But she ran on and on.

It was quiet down there and after several minutes she could hear nothing at all from the inn, only the occasional plop of a frog into the water or the frightened scurrying of an animal. At last she could run no more and stopped, heaving, sagged helplessly against a tree.

But as she began to get her breath she also began to think and to wonder how she would get back. Following the Bourne, she knew, would lead her down to the Thames a great way from Whitefriars. She must go back to the road and hope to find a hackney—or walk; it was only about two miles and a quarter. She climbed the bank and started off across the fields, but did not return at once to the road, for fear they would come along searching for her. She alternately ran and walked, constantly looking back. Whenever a coach or a man on horseback approached, she flung herself flat and waited, but for the most part the night was quiet and she met no one.

Within a few minutes she had reached St. James's Park. She skirted the edge of it, and though here there were some late walkers, by keeping in the shadows and moving softly, she got through without molestation. Reaching the Strand she hurried along, holding onto her skirts to keep them from dragging in the street, clotted and littered as it was with animal dung and decaying vegetable refuse. She was afraid to be alone in the city, for she knew the menace of it and wished violently that a hackney would come along. And then all at once the banging clatter of a coach resounded through the night, lumbering heavily toward her as though in a great hurry to run her down and be on.

Seeing that it was a public vehicle she shouted. The driver hauled on the reins, came to a stop some yards beyond, and turned on his perch. "Want to hire a coach?"

Amber had already reached the door and pulled it open. "Temple Bar!" she cried. "And quick!" She jumped in and slammed it shut, so glad to be safe inside that she scarcely noticed how it smelt.

He drove so fast and so recklessly that she could only try to keep her seat as the coach careened along. The wooden seat on which she sat was covered with a thin hard pad and the jarring and vibrating of the springless compartment shook her to the heels. At Temple Bar he stopped. Almost before the wheels had quit turning she was down and off on a run toward the Temple, for she had not a farthing with her.

"Hey!" he yelled furiously. "Come back here, you cheating drab!"

And then as she ran on, disappearing into the darkness, he climbed down and started after her. But at the sight of a party of gay and drunken students, he apparently decided it was not worth the risk of losing his coach-and-horses for a one-shilling fare. He got back up on his perch and started off again.

Amber ran down Middle Temple Lane and cut into the Pump Court. Many lights were still burning, there were sounds of music and singing and laughter, and people were going and coming everywhere. Her head was down, because she was now too tired to hold it up, and she ran headlong into a group of some half-dozen students, one of whom caught her in his arms.

"Hey, there, sweetheart!" he cried gaily. "Where're you going in such haste!"

Amber did not answer him but began to struggle frantically, pounding at his chest with her fists, crying with exhaustion and terror. But the more she struggled the tighter he held her. And all the others had gathered around now, laughing and joking, thinking that perhaps they had caught a whore, since no respectable woman would be running about the streets at eleven o'clock in only a thin silk dress, and that torn and wet.

He bent her head back to kiss her and Amber felt them crowding closer and closer until such a terror swept over her she was close to fainting. Every one of them looked like a constable. At that moment she heard a familiar voice.

"Hey, just a minute! What's going on here! I know this lady— Let her go, you varlets!" It was Michael Godfrey, whom Amber had not seen for more than four months.

Reluctantly the young man released her. Amber looked up at Michael with tears streaking down her scratched and dirt-stained face, but she did not speak to him. Giving a quick shove she broke free and started off, but he followed her. When he caught her they had reached a dark corner leading into Vine Court, away from the lights of the torches.

"Mrs. Channell! For God's sake, what's the matter? What's happened? It's Michael—don't you remember me?"

He grabbed hold of her arm and brought her to a stop but

she jerked at him furiously, sobbing. "Let me go! Oh, damn you! Let me go or I'll get caught!"

"Caught by who! What is it? Tell me!" He gave her a little shake for she was not looking at him but tugging to free herself, trying to pry his fingers loose from her wrist, wild and desperate.

"The constables, you fool! Let me go!"

He turned suddenly, dragging her after him, and entered a doorway, which he closed. Amber slumped against the wall.

"Where's Black Jack?" he demanded.

"They've caught him. We were at Knightsbridge and the constables came—I got away but they're coming after me—" She made a sudden lunge. "Let me go! I've got to get back!"

He grabbed her shoulders, thrusting her against the wall, and she felt his arms go about her. "You can't go back there. Mother Red-Cap'll send you out again, and someday you'll get caught for sure. Come with me—" His mouth sought hers, his arms held her close, and Amber relaxed gratefully, so tired she could struggle no longer. He picked her up and started through the dark hallway toward the stairs.

Chapter Fifteen

THE THREE MEN, Black Jack and Jimmy the Mouth and Blueskin, were all hanged from the same arm of the three-cornered gallows, just ten days from the night they were taken. When the process of justice worked at all it was with devastating swiftness; they left him no time to pay his way out. Bess was sent to Bridewell, the house-of-correction for female offenders, to improve her morals. Pall, who pleaded her belly, was sent to Newgate to await the birth of her child and probable transportation to Virginia.

At the time of the execution Amber was alone in Michael Godfrey's rooms in Vine Court. Michael had gone to watch and when he came back he told her that all three men had been cut down and taken to lie at a tavern—where they might be viewed by mourners or whoever had a curiosity to look at them. All the corpses had been treated with respect and not, as often happened, carried through the streets and tossed about until mangled beyond recognition. Black Jack, he said, was very nonchalant to the end, and the last words of his farewell speech were: "Gentlemen, there's nothing like a merry life—and a short one."

But even then she could not believe it.

How could Black Jack Mallard be dead when she remembered him so well, everything he had done and said over the months she had known him? How could he be dead when he was so big, so powerful, so obstinately indestructible? She remembered his six feet five inches of male strength, hard-muscled and hard-fleshed, covered with wiry black hair that matted on his chest. She remembered the thunderous rumble of his laugh; his enormous capacity for wine—he had said that his nickname originated one night when he won a wager by drinking a blackjack of Burgundy without once putting down the vessel. She remembered a thousand things more.

And now he was dead.

She remembered how some of the men had wept at Chapel the day before they were to be executed. And, though she thought she had forgotten, she could, all too well, recall the expressions on their faces. She wondered how Black Jack had looked—and how she would have looked herself had she been sitting there beside him. She suffered agonies thinking of it. Whatever she was doing—enjoying her dinner, brushing her hair, leaning on the windowsill and laughing at the pranks of the young men down in the courtyard—the thought would come like the sudden shocking impact of a physical blow: I might not be here! I might be *dead!*

At night she would wake up, crying with terror and clutching at Michael. She had seen two of her cousins die, but this was the first time that any personal realization of death had come to her. She became very pious and repeated all the prayers she knew a dozen times a day.

But for the grace of God I'd not be here right now but in Hell, she would think, for she knew she had not been good enough to get into Heaven. Even before she had left Marygreen Uncle Matt had not thought it likely that Heaven was her destination. She believed in the existence of those two places with superstitious intensity, just as she believed that a hare was a witch in disguise, but the prospect of eternal damnation could not deter her from anything she really wanted to do.

For almost a month she did not once leave Michael Godfrey's apartment of two rooms. He bought a second-hand suit of boy's clothes for her to wear and she strutted about, swaggering, clacking her heels on the floor in imitation of the young fops she had seen in the streets, while he roared with laughter and told her that she was as good an actor as Edward Kynaston himself. She was supposed to be Tom, his nephew from the country, but none of his friends who visited them were very much fooled, though they all made a great jest of it and obligingly called her by that name.

He told her, however, that it would probably not be a great deal longer before her presence there became known and that when it did they would be forced to leave. But that threat did not trouble him for he seldom studied as it was and had no more interest in learning law than did most of the other young men whose fathers sent them to the Inns of Court. Now, more than ever, life was too distracting for a young man to give much time to books and lectures.

She told him her own name and the story of her misfortunes, though she omitted altogether Lord Carlton's part in it and pretended that the baby had been gotten by her husband. Luke Channell's name, since she had used it in Whitefriars, was no longer of any value to her and she made Michael promise to keep secret the fact that she had ever been married; she considered that that mistake was over and done and absolutely refused to think of Luke as her husband.

About a fortnight after Black Jack's death Michael went down to Ram Alley to visit Mother Red-Cap and convince her that Mrs. Channell had gone from London and would never return. He went partly out of curiosity, to see what the old woman's reaction to the recent events had been, and also because Amber begged him to get the imitation gold ear-rings she had left behind, telling him that her aunt had given them to her just before she had gone away. He brought them back, and some news as well.

"She's satisfied you're gone. I told her I'd had a letter from you and that you were back with your family and would never so much as think of London again."

Amber laughed, taking a bite out of a big red apple. "Did she believe you?"

"She seemed to. She said that you should never have left the country in the first place—and that London was no place for a girl like you."

"I'll warrant she's running distracted to have lost me. I made her a mighty good profit, let me tell you."

"Sweetheart, Mother Red-Cap wouldn't run distracted if she lost her own head. She's got another girl she's training to take your place—a pretty little wench she found somewhere who's with child and unmarried and full of gratitude for the kind old lady who's promised to help her out of her difficulties."

Amber made a sound of disgust, throwing the apple-core across the room into the fireplace. "That old fleshbroker would pimp for the devil himself if there was a farthing to be got by it!"

Most of her time, when she was alone, she spent learning to read and to write and she undertook both with the same enthusiasm she had had for her dancing and singing and guitar lessons. Hundreds of times she wrote her name and Bruce's, drawing big hearts around them, but she always burnt the papers before Michael should see them—partly because she knew it would not be tactful to let the man who was keeping her find that she was in love with someone else, but also because she could not bear the thought of discussing Bruce with anyone. Her own signature was a long sprawl of which only the initial letters were made large and distinguishable, and when she showed Michael specimens of her handwriting he laughed and told her it was so illegible it might be mistaken for that of a countess.

One wet early October afternoon she lay stretched out flat on her stomach on the bed, mouthing over the text of one of the bawdy illustrated books which he had given her to practice on, an English edition of Aretino's sonnets. Hearing the key turn in the lock and the door of the other room open, she called over her shoulder: "Michael? Come in here! I can't make this out—"

His voice, solemn for once, answered her. "Come here, nephew."

Thinking that he was playing some joke she leapt off the bed and ran to the doorway, but stopped on the threshold with a gasp of astonishment and dismay. For with him was an old man, a sour prim thin-nosed old gentleman with a forbidding scowl and a look of having been preserved in vinegar. Amber took a startled step backward and one hand went to the throat of her deeply opened white shirt, but it was too late. He could never mistake her for a boy now.

"You said that you were entertaining your nephew, sirrah!" said the old man sternly, drawing down his tufted brows and frowning back at Michael. "Where is he?"

"That is he, Mr. Gripenstraw," said Michael, respectfully but nevertheless with an air of whimsical unconcern.

Mr. Gripenstraw looked at Amber again, over the tops of his square-cut green spectacles, and he screwed his mouth from side to side. Amber's hand dropped and she spoke to Michael, pleading.

"I'm sorry, Michael. I thought you were alone."

He made a gesture, motioning her into the bedroom, and she went, closing the door but standing next to it so that she could hear what was said between them. Oh, God in Heaven! she thought despairingly, rubbing the palms of her hands together. *Now* what will happen to me? What if he finds out who I— Then she heard Mr. Gripenstraw's voice again.

"Well, Mr. Godfrey—and what excuse have you to make this time?"

"None, sir."

"How long has this baggage been on your premises?"

"One month, sir."

"One month! Great God! Have you no respect for the ancient and honourable institution of English law? Because of my regard for your father I have overlooked many of your past misdemeanours, but this is beyond anything! If it were not for the honour and esteem in which I hold Sir Michael I would have you sent to the Fleet, to learn a better view of the conduct befitting a young man. As it is, sirrah, you are expelled. Never show me your face again. And get that creature out of here—within the hour!"

"Yes, sir. Thank you, sir."

The door opened. "Let me tell you this, sirrah—there is

nothing a young man may get by wenching but duels, claps, and bastards. Good-day!" The door closed noisily.

Amber waited a moment and then flung open her own door. "Oh, Michael! You're expelled! And it's all my fault!"

She began to cry but he came swiftly across to take her into his arms. "Here, here, sweetheart! What the devil! We're well rid of this scurvy place. Come now, put on your hat and doublet and we'll find us lodgings where a man may live as he likes."

He took two rooms in an inn called the Hoops and Grapes, situated in St. Clement's Lane, which wound up out of Fleet Street. It was outside the City gates in the newer and more fashionable west-end of the town. Drury Lane was nearby, and Covent Garden, and not five minutes walk away was Gibbons Tennis Court in Vere Street, which had become the Theatre Royal.

He bought her some clothes, second-hand at first because she needed them immediately—though later she had some made—and she found herself precipitated into a whirl of gaiety and pleasure. She had met several of his friends while they were still at the Temple, but now she met many more. They were young men of good family, future barons and lords; officers in the King's or the Duke's guards; actors from one of the four public theatres. And she met, too, the women they kept, pretty girls who sold ribbons or gloves at the Royal Exchange, professed harlots, actresses, all of them wise and gay and no more than Amber's age—flowers that had bloomed since the Restoration.

They went to the theatres and sat in the pit where the women wore their masks and sucked on China oranges, bandying pleasantries with everyone in earshot. They went to the gambling-houses in the Haymarket and once Amber was thrown into a frenzy of excitement when a rumour swept through that the King was coming. But he did not and she was bitterly disappointed, for she had never forgotten his expression that day he had looked at her. They went to the New Spring Gardens at Lambeth and to the Mulberry Gardens, which was temporarily the height of fashion. They went to dinner at all the popular taverns, Lockets near Charing Cross which was always filled with young officers in their handsome uniforms, the Bear at the Bridgefoot, the notorious Dagger Tavern in High Holborn, a rough-and-tumble place that abounded in riots and noise but was famous for its fine pies. They went to see the puppet-play in Covent Garden, currently the resort of all the fashionable world. At night they often drove about town in a hackney, contesting as to who could break the most windows by throwing copper pennies through them.

And when they were not out their rooms were full of young people who came in at all hours of the day and night, ordered food and drink sent up, played cards and got drunk and borrowed their bed for love-making. None of them had a serious thought or occupation, beyond avoiding their creditors. Pleasure was their creed. The old views of morality had gone as much out of fashion as high-crowned hats and, like them, were now disdained and ridiculed. Indifference, cynicism, selfishness and egoistic opportunism were the marks of quality. Gentleness, honesty, devotion—these were held in contempt.

The gentlemen of the old school, of the decorus Court of Charles I, were blaming the present King for the manners and behaviour of the new generation. And while it was true that Charles neither wished nor tried to set up strict standards, the same conditions had existed during the late years of the Protectorate, though then more than half concealed under a mantle of hypocrisy. The Civil Wars, not his Majesty, had sowed the seeds for plants suddenly shot to full growth since his return.

But Amber was not even remotely aware of the force of trends and currents.

She was in love with this life. She liked the noise and confusion, the continued bustle and disorder, the reckless devil-may-care gaiety. She knew that it was wholly different from the country and was glad that it was, for here she might do as she liked and no one was shocked or admonitory. It never occurred to her that this was perhaps not the usual life of all gentlemen of all times.

None of the young men was interested in matrimony, which had fallen into such disrepute that it was considered only as the lest resort of a man so far encumbered by debt he could see no other way out. Good manners forbade a man and wife to love—scarcely permitted them to like—each other, and a happy marriage was regarded with scorn, not envy. This was Amber's view, for Luke Channell had convinced her that marriage was the most miserable state a woman could endure, and she talked as glibly as any rake about the absurdity of being a wife or husband. In her heart she held a secret reservation, for Bruce Carlton—but she was almost willing to believe now that she would never see him again.

Only once did her confident audacity receive a jar and that was when, about mid-October, she discovered that she was pregnant again. Penelope Hill had warned her that the most careful precautions sometimes failed, but she had never expected that they might fail her. For a time she was wildly distracted. All her pleasures would be ruined if she had to go again through the tedious uncomfortable ugly business of having a baby, and she determined that she would not do it. Even in Marygreen she had known women who had induced abortions when pregnancy recurred too often. She had wanted Bruce Carlton's child, but she did not want another man's now, or ever.

She talked to one of the girls she had met, a 'Change woman

named Mally, who was rumoured to have been given a great sum of money by no one less than the Duke of Buckingham: the girl directed her to a midwife in Hanging Sword Alley who she said had a numerous clientèle among young women of their class and way of life. Without telling Michael anything about it she went to the midwife, who set her for an hour or more over a pot of steaming herbs, gave her a strong dose of physic, and told her to ride out to Paddington and back in a hackney. To Amber's immense relief some one, or all, of the remedies had been successful. Mally told her that every twenty-eight days she followed the practice herself of taking an apothecary's prescription, a long soaking in a hot tub, and a ride in a hell-cart.

"Gentlemen nowadays," said Mally, "you'll find, have no patience with a woman who troubles 'em in that way. And, Lord knows, with matters as they stand a woman needs what good looks she can be mistress of." She lifted up her plump breasts and crossed her silken ankles, giving a smug little smile.

At first Amber was in considerable apprehension whenever she left the house—even though she habitually went cloaked and hooded and masked—for fear a constable would stop her. The memory of Newgate weighed on her like an incubus. But even more terrifying was the knowledge that if caught again she would very likely be either hanged or transported, and she was already so rabid a Londoner that one punishment seemed almost as bad as the other.

And then one day she learned something which seemed to offer her a solution, and an exciting new adventure as well. She had been surprised at the elegant clothes worn off-stage by all the actors she had seen, and one night she commented idly about it to Michael.

"Ye gods, they all look like lords. How much money do they get?"

"Fifty or sixty pound a year."

"Why, Charles Hart had on a sword tonight must have cost him that much!"

"Probably did. They're all head over ears in debt."

Amber, who was getting ready for bed, now backed up to have him unlace the tight little boned busk she wore. "Then I don't envy 'em," she said, jingling the bracelet on her right wrist. "Poor devils. They won't look so spruce in Newgate."

Michael was concentrating on the busk, but at last he had it unlaced and gave her a light slap on the rump. "They won't go to Newgate. An actor can't be arrested, except on a special warrant which must be procured from the King."

She swirled around, sudden eager interest on her face. "They can't be arrested! Why?"

"Why—because they're his Majesty's servants, and enjoy protection of the Crown."

Well—

That *was* something to think about.

This was not the first time, however, that she had cast covetous eyes toward the stage. Sitting with Michael in the pit, she had seen how the gallants all stared at the actresses and flocked back to the tiring-room after the play to paw over them and take them out to supper. She knew that they were kept by some of the greatest nobles at Court, that they dressed magnificently, occupied handsome lodgings and often had their own coaches to ride in. They seemed—for all that they were treated with a certain careless contempt by the very men who courted them —to be the most fortunate creatures on earth. Amber was filled with envy to see all this attention and applause going to others, when she felt that she deserved it at least as much as they.

She had looked them over narrowly and was convinced that she was better looking than any of them. Her voice was good, she had lost her country drawl, and her figure was lovely. Everyone was agreed to that. What other qualifications did an actress need? Few of them had so many.

Not many days later she got her opportunity.

With Michael and four other couples she was at supper in a private room on the "Folly," a floating house of entertainment moored just above the ruined old Savoy Palace. They sat over their cheesecake and wine, cracking open raw oysters and watching the performance of a naked dancing-woman.

Amber sat on Michael's lap; he had one arm hung over her shoulder with his hand slipped casually into the bodice of her gown. But all his attention was on the dancing-girl, and Amber, offended by his interest in the performance, got up and left him to sit down beside one man who had his back turned while he continued to eat his supper. He was Edward Kynaston, the fabulously handsome young actor from the King's Theatre, who had taken women's parts before the hiring of actresses had begun.

He was very young, no more than nineteen, with skin like a girl's, loosely waving blond hair and blue eyes, a slender but well-proportioned body. There was nothing to mar his perfection but the sound of his voice which, from long practice of keeping it high-pitched, carried a kind of unpleasant whine. He smiled at her as she took a chair next to his.

"Edward, how d'you go about getting on the stage?"

"Why? Have you a mind to acting?"

"Don't you think I could? I hope I'm pretty enough." She smiled, slanting her eyes.

He looked her over thoughtfully. "You certainly are. You're prettier than anyone we have—or anyone Davenant has, either, for the matter of that." Davenant managed the Duke of York's Theatre, for there were only two licensed companies (though some others continued performing), and rivalry was sharp between His Majesty's and His Highness's Comedians. "I suppose you think to show yourself on the boards and get some great man for a keeper."

"Maybe I do," she admitted. "They say there's a mighty fine profit to be got that way."

Her voice had a soft tone of insinuation, for Kynaston, everyone knew, had numerous admirers among the gentlemen and had received many valuable gifts from them, most of which he shrewdly turned into money and banked with a goldsmith. Among his lovers he was said to number the immensely rich Buckingham, who had already begun the ruin of the greatest fortune in England, squandering what he had as recklessly as if it came out of a bottomless well.

Kynaston did not take offense at her suggestion, but he had a kind of feminine modesty which, for all that he sold himself in the open market, lent him the appearance of dignity and virtue.

"Perhaps there is, madame. Would you like me to present you to Tom Killigrew?" Thomas Killigrew was a favourite courier and manager of the King's Theatre.

"Oh, would you! When?" She was excited, and a little fearful.

"Rehearsal will be over about eleven tomorrow. Come then if you like."

Amber dressed with great care for her interview and, though it was a cold dark early-November morning with no shred of sun filtering through the heavy smoke and fog, she put on her finest gown and cloak. All morning long her stomach had been churning and the palms of her hands felt wet. In spite of her eagerness she was miserably nervous, and at the last moment such a panic of doubt swept through her that she had to bully herself into going out the door.

When she reached the theatre, however, and took off her mask the attendant gave a low whistle; she laughed and made him an impudent face, suddenly relieved.

"I've come to see Edward Kynaston. He's expecting me. Can I go in?"

"You're wasting your time, sweetheart," he told her. "Kynaston doesn't give a hang for the finest woman that wears a head. But go along if you will."

The stage was just clearing and Killigrew was down in the pit talking to Kynaston and Charles Hart and one of the actresses who stood on the apron-shaped stage above them. It was dark inside, for only the candles in the chandelier that hung above the stage were lighted, and the cold seemed to bring out a strong sour smell. Orange-peelings littered the aisle and the green-cloth-covered benches were dirty with the footmarks of the men who had stood upon them. Empty now of people and of noise there was something strangely dismal and shabby, almost sad, about it. But Amber did not notice.

For a moment she hesitated, then she started down the aisle toward them. At the sound of her heels they looked around, Kynaston lifting his hand to wave. They watched her come, Kynaston, Charles Hart, Killigrew, and the woman on the stage, Beck Marshall. She had met Charles Hart, a handsome man who had been on the stage for many years, often risking imprisonment to act during the dour years of the Commonwealth. And once she had been casually introduced to Beck Marshall who stood now, hands on her hips, looking her over, not missing anything about her gown or hair or face, and then with a switch of her skirt walked off. The three men remained.

Kynaston presented her to Killigrew—an aristocratic, middle-aged man with bright-blue eyes and white hair and an old-fashioned, pointed chin-beard. He did not look as though he would be the father of the notorious Harry Killigrew, a bold rash drunken young rake whose exploits caused some surprise even at Court. Amber had seen Harry once, molesting the women in St. James's Park, but she had been masked and well muffled and he had not seen her.

She made her curtsy to Killigrew, who said: "Kynaston tells me that you want to go on the stage."

Amber gave him her most alluring smile, which she had practiced several times in the mirror just before leaving home. But the corners of her mouth quivered and her chest felt tight. "Yes," she said softly. "I do. Will you give me a part?"

Killigrew laughed. "Take off your cloak and walk up onto the stage, so I can have a look at you."

Amber pulled loose the cord which tied in a bow at her throat, flung back the cloak, and Charles Hart offered his hand to lift her onto the platform. Ribs held high to show off her pert breasts and little waist, she walked the length of the stage, turning, raising her skirts above her knees to let him see her legs. Hart and Killigrew exchanged significant glances.

At last, having appraised her as carefully as any man buying a horse, he asked: "What else can you do, Mrs. St. Clare, besides look beautiful?"

Charles Hart, stuffing his pipe with tobacco, gave a cynical snort. "What else *should* she do? What else can any of 'em do?"

"What the devil, Hart! Will you convince her she needn't even *try* to learn to act? Come, my dear, what else do you know?"

"I can sing, and I can dance."

"Good! That's half an actress's business."

"God knows," muttered Charles Hart. He could act himself and thought the theatre was running amuck these days with its emphasis on nothing but female legs and breasts. "I don't doubt to see 'Hamlet' put on one day with a Gravediggers' dance."

Killigrew gave her a signal and Amber began to dance. It was a Spanish saraband which she had learned more than a year before and had since performed many times, for Black

Jack and his friends in Whitefriars, more recently for Michael and all their acquaintance. Twirling, swaying, dipping, she moved swiftly about the stage, all her self-consciousness gone now in her passionate determination to please. After that she sang a bawdy street-ballad which burlesqued the old Greek fable of Ariadne and Theseus, and her voice had a full voluptuous quality which would have made a far more innocent song seem sensual and exciting. When at last she sank to a curtsy and then lifted her head to smile at him with eager questioning, he clapped his hands.

"You're as spectacular as a show of fireworks on the Thames. Can you read a part?"

"Yes," said Amber, though she had never tried.

"Well, never mind about that now. Next Wednesday we're going to give a performance of 'The Maid's Tragedy.' Come to rehearsal tomorrow morning at seven and I'll have a part in it for you."

Half delirious with joy, Amber ran home to tell Michael the great news. But though she did not expect to play the heroine, she was nevertheless seriously disappointed the next morning to learn that she was to be merely one of a crowd of Court ladies-in-waiting, and that she had not so much as a single word to speak. She was disappointed, too, at her salary, which was only forty-five pounds a year. She realized by now that the five hundred pounds given her by Bruce Carlton had been a considerable sum of money, if only she had had the wit to keep it.

But both Kynaston and Charles Hart encouraged her, saying that if she attracted the attention of the audience as they knew she would, he would put her in more important parts. An actress had no such period of long training and apprenticeship as did an actor. Pretty young women were very much in demand for the stage, and if the men in the audience liked them they could sound like screech owls and act no better than puppets.

She quickly established a gay friendliness with the actors and was prepared to do likewise with the women, but they would have none of it. Despite the fact that women had been on the stage for no more than a year they had already formed a tight clique, and were jealous and distrustful of any outsider trying to break into their closed ranks. They ignored her when she spoke to them, tittered and whispered behind her back, hid her costume on the day of the dress rehearsal, all in the obvious hope of making her so miserable that she would quit. But Amber had never believed that other women were important to her success and happiness, and she did not intend to let them trouble her now.

The stage fascinated her. She loved everything about the theatre: The hours of rehearsal, when she listened and watched intensely, memorizing the lines of half the other characters. The thrilling day when she was sworn in at the Lord Chamberlain's Office as his Majesty's servant. The occult mysteries of stage make-up, into which she was now initiated, black and white and red paint, false-noses, false-beards, false-hair. The marvellous collection of scenery and other apparatus which made it possible to show the moon coming up at night, to reveal the sun breaking through a mist, to simulate a bird's song or the rattle of hail. The costumes, some of which were gorgeous things given by the nobles, others mere cheap imitations made of shoddy and bombazine. She took it to her heart, made it a part of her, in the same way she had London.

At last the great day arrived and, after a restless turning night full of apprehension and doubts, she got up and dressed and set out very early for the theatre. On the way she saw one of the play-bills nailed up on a post and stopped to read it: "At the Theatre Royal this present Wednesday, being the Ninth day of December will be presented a play called: The Maid's Tragedy beginning exactly at three after Noon. By His Majesty's Servants. Vivat Rex." And when she reached the theatre a flag was already flying from the roof to announce that there would be a performance that day.

Oh, Lord! she thought. What ever made me think I wanted to go on the stage?

It was still so early that she found the entire theatre empty but for a couple of scene-shifters and the tiring-woman, Mrs. Scroggs, a dirty profane drunken old harridan whose daughter Killigrew hired at twenty shillings a week for the use of his actors. With her easy camaraderie and frequent gifts of money Amber had purchased her friendship at least, and Scroggs was as ardently partisan in her favour as the women were violently antagonistic. By the time the other actresses began to arrive she was painted and dressed and had gone out to watch the audience from behind the curtains.

The pit was already crowded, fops, prostitutes and orange-girls, all of them noisy and laughing, shouting to acquaintances all over the theatre. The galleries were spotted with men and women, and 'prentices were trying out their cat-calls. Finally the boxes began to fill with splendidly gowned and jewelled ladies, languid dreamy creatures who were bored with the play before it had even begun. The very boards and walls seemed now to have changed, enchanted by the glamour and richness of the audience.

Amber stood looking out, her throat dry and her heart beating with anticipation, when suddenly Charles Hart appeared behind her, slipped an arm about her waist and kissed her cheek. She gave a startled little jump.

"Oh!" She laughed nervously and swallowed.

"Now, now, sweetheart!" he said briskly. "Ready to lay the town by its ears?"

She gave him a pleading look. "Oh, I don't know! Michael's in the pit with a score of friends to cry me up. But I'm scared!"

"Nonsense. What are you scared of? Those high-born sluts and fop-doodles out there? Don't let them scare you—" He paused, as suddenly the fiddlers in the music-room above the stage struck up the first bars of a gay country air. "Listen! His Majesty's come!" And he drew back the curtains so that he and Amber could look out.

There was a scraping of benches and a low running murmur as they got to their feet, turning to face the King's box which was in the first balcony in the center just above the stage, gilded and draped with scarlet velvet and emblazoned with the royal coat-of-arms. And then, as the King appeared, the music swelled and the hats of the men swept off with a flourish. The tall and swarthy Charles, smiling easily, lifting one hand in greeting, dominated the group of men and women who surrounded him; but no one overlooked Barbara Palmer at his side, glittering with jewels, haughty and beautiful and a little sullen. They seemed very magnificent and awe-inspiring; and staring at them from behind the curtains Amber was suddenly overcome with an agonizing sense of her own insignificance,

"Oh," she breathed unhappily. "They look like gods!"

"Even gods, my dear, use a chamberpot," said Charles Hart, and then he walked away, back to the tiring-room to get his cloak, for he was to speak the prologue. Amber looked after him and laughed, somewhat relieved.

But her eyes returned immediately to Mrs. Palmer, who was leaning back in her chair, smiling and speaking to a man who sat behind her. As she looked Amber's face hardened with hate. Her fingers with their long nails curled involuntarily and she had a sharp satisfying image of clawing across the woman's face, tearing away her beauty and confident smile. The jealousy she felt was as violent and painful as on that far-away night when she had looked down into the street and seen Bruce Carlton's head bend to kiss a red-haired woman leaning out of her coach and laughing.

Soon, however, she was surrounded by the other actresses, who came trooping up behind her, giggling, elbowing her aside —until she gave one of them a sharp jab in the ribs—lifting back the curtain to wave at their admirers below. All of them seemed as merrily unconcerned as though this were nothing but another rehearsal. But Amber was wishing desperately that she might bolt and run, out of the theatre, back to the quiet and security of her own rooms, and hide there. She knew that she could never force herself to go out onto the stage and face those hard smart critical people whose eyes and tongues would go over her like rakes.

The prologue was done, the curtains had swung back, and Charles Hart and Michael Mohun had started to speak their lines. The theatre was settling down, quieting as much as it ever did, though the buzzing and murmuring went on and there were occasional laughs or loud-spoken comments. Amber, who knew most of the lines by heart, now discovered that she was not able even to follow the dialogue, and the ladies-in-waiting had already started out when Kynaston gave her a little shove.

"Go on!"

For an instant she hung back, unable to move, and then, with her heart pounding so hard she thought it would burst, she lifted her head high and walked out. During the rehearsals the other women had always maneuvered to keep her in the background, despite the fact that Killigrew said he wanted the audience to see her, but now because of her late entrance she stood in the front, closer to the audience than any of them.

She heard a man's voice from nearby, in the pit. "Who's that glorious creature, Orange Moll?"

Another one spoke up. "That must be the new wench. By Jesus, but she's handsome, I swear she is!"

And from the gallery the 'prentices sent up a low appreciative hum.

Amber felt her cheeks begin to burn and sweat start in her armpits, but at last she forced herself to sneak a glance out of the corner of one eye. She saw several upturned faces beneath her, grinning, and all at once she realized that these were only men like any other men. Just before the ladies-in-waiting went off the stage she threw them a dazzling smile, and heard another rising hum of approval. After that she stood in the wings and fretted because her part was done. By the time the play was over she was incurably stagestruck.

Beck Marshall spoke to her as they were going into the tiring-room. "Look here, Mrs. What-d'ye-call," she said, pretending to have forgotten Amber's name. "You needn't strut up and down like a crow in the gutter. Those gentlemen will have a swing at anything new—"

Amber smiled at her, superior, very well satisfied with herself. "Don't concern yourself for me, madame. I'll have a care of my own interests, I warrant you."

But she was more than a little disappointed when Michael and three of his friends appeared promptly, surrounding her and shutting her off from any possible outside interference, for several of the young men were watching her, asking about her, curious and interested and admiring.

Oh, well, she thought, I won't always be troubled with Michael.

Chapter Sixteen

THE NEXT day Amber was given the part of the first Court lady, and had four short lines to say. Not very long after that she was taking important roles, singing songs and, dressed in a tight pair of breeches and thin white blouse, performing the dance at the end of the play. It was her chief qualification as an actress that she could easily achieve an accurate and only piquantly exaggerated imitation of almost any kind of woman, whether great lady or serving-wench. And little more was expected, for the audience had no interest in the subtleties of character delineation. The taste was for crude gorgeous exciting effects, whether in women, scenery, or melodrama.

They liked the bloody noisy terrifying tragedies of Beaumont and Fletcher, considered Ben Jonson the greatest playwright of all time, thought Shakespeare too realistic and hence deficient in poetic justice. He required considerable altering before he could qualify for presentation. A great deal of singing and dancing, frequent changes of scenery and costume, battles and deaths and ghosts, profanity and smut and seminudity was what they liked and what they got. At every murder or suicide sheep's blood spurted from concealed bladders and covered the actor with gore; ghosts rose and sank on trapdoors; scenes of torture by rack, wheel and fire filled the theatre with anguished screams and groans. But through it all the fops in the pit kept up a stream of banter with the actors and prostitutes and orange-girls, and the ladies in the boxes waved their fans and cast lazy smiles at the gallants below.

Amber's popularity was considerable—because she was new, the women insisted—and every day after the performance she was surrounded by a flock of gallants who kissed her, tied her garters, watched her dress, and invited her to spend the night with one or all of them. She listened and laughed, flirted with everyone, but went home with Michael Godfrey.

She was afraid of arousing his jealousy, for he knew all her secrets and could ruin her if he chose. But even had she been free of him, she had not yet heard the offer which could interest her. She was looking for a man of both importance and wealth, who would keep her according to the manner in which she intended to live—clothes and jewels and a coach, a generous annual allowance, handsomely furnished lodgings, a serving-woman, and a footman. The man who could supply those things was not to be found every day, even among the tiring-room gallants, and when found he was not likely to be a ready dupe. Amber was impatient, eager to better her status, but determined to make no rash change which might precipitate her down the steep narrow road leading to common prostitution. Penelope Hill's advice meant more to her now than when she had first heard it—and she intended to turn some man's weakness to her own advantage.

More than a month went by and still Amber was on no better terms with the other actresses than she had been at first. They missed no opportunity to confuse or embarrass her, either on the stage or in the tiring-room, circulating rumours that she had the French-pox and that she was living incestuously with her brother—Michael—and were more annoyed than ever when she treated them all with cool, superior contempt. But nothing they said seemed to discourage the men, who brushed it all aside as mere jealous female slander.

"Well," said Beck Marshall to her one day, "they may poach after you here in the tiring-room, but I don't notice *one* of 'em's made you an offer of more than half-a-crown."

Amber sat on one of the tables, legs crossed and carefully drew a black line along the edge of her eyelid. "And what about you, madame? Who's your stallion? The Duke of York, I doubt not?"

Beck gave her a smug, complacent smile. "Not his Highness, perhaps. But then, Captain Morgan's a man of no mean consequence."

"And who the devil's Captain Morgan? That straight-haired nincompoop I saw you with at Chatelin's the other night?" She got up and turned her back, beckoning Scroggs to come help her into her gown.

"Captain Morgan, Mrs. Double-tripe, is an officer in his Majesty's Horse Guard—and a mighty handsome fellow into the bargain. And he's so mad in love with me he's going to make me a settlement and take me off the stage. I don't doubt he'd marry me quick enough—if I could make up my mind to endure matrimony," she added, examining her nails.

Amber stepped into her gown and stooped over to pull it up. "You'd better make up your mind to endure it before long," she said, "or you'll be leading apes in hell." Leading apes in hell was supposedly the destiny of an old maid, and Amber liked to taunt Beck with the fact that she was two or three years her senior. "But where d'you keep this wonder? Under lock and key?"

"He's been out of town these two months past—his family's got a great estate in Wales, and his father's just died. But he wrote me he expects to return within the week and then—"

"Oh, I don't doubt I'll be in a green-sickness of jealousy at the very sight of 'im."

At that moment a boy stuck his head in the door calling, "Third music, ladies! Third music!" and they all began to troop out, for the third music meant that it was time for the curtains to be drawn. Amber thought no more of Beck's Captain Morgan and several days went by. But late one afternoon as she was dressing after the performance, surrounded by her circle of impudent gallants, a man appeared in the doorway who instantly arrested her attention.

He was well over six feet tall with wide, square shoulders, lean hips, and magnificent legs. Powerful and virile, in his red and blue uniform he was an exciting contrast to the pale effeminate young fops who talked incessantly of their claps and poxes and carried a box of turpentine-pills wherever they went. His face was crudely handsome, with well-defined features; he had waving brown hair and skin tanned to a tawny-gold. Amber stared at him in surprise and admiration. wondering who he was, and then as he smiled slowly the corners of her eyes went up and she gave him a faint answering smile.

At that moment there was a scream from Beck.

"Rex!"

And she rushed over to throw herself into his arms, took his hand, and led him to the opposite side of the room. She dressed hastily then and hurried him out, but as he went he gave Amber a backward glance.

"Well!" said Beck the next morning, as they sat in the pit watching a rehearsal. "What d'ye make of him?" But her eyes were slightly narrowed and she was more defiant than triumphant.

Amber smiled innocently and gave a little shrug. "Oh, no doubt he's a very fine person. I don't wonder you rushed 'im out as fast as if you were going for a midwife." Her eyes took on a malicious sparkle. "It'd never do to let a fellow like that make the acquaintance of other ladies, would it?"

Beck flared. "I smoke your design, madame! But let me tell you this—if I find you spreading your nets for him I'll make you sorry for it! I'll carbonado you, I swear I will!"

"Pooh!" said Amber, and got up to leave her. "Your bellow-weathering doesn't scare me!"

Still, Captain Morgan did not appear backstage again for several days, and when Amber gibed at her for not daring to show her prize not only Beck but her older sister Anne flew into a rage and threatened her with the wrath of God, as well as their own. "Just you dare meddling with Captain Morgan!" cried Anne dramatically, for she was the tragedienne of the company. "You'll wish you hadn't!"

But Amber was so little impressed by their threats that whenever she saw him in the pit, as she often did, she flirted openly with him. It would have pleased her a great deal to steal Beck Marshall's admirer, even if he had been much less attractive than he was.

She was going into the theatre early one afternoon when a ragged little urchin came limping up, glanced hastily around, and thrust a wax-sealed paper into her hands. Curious, Amber tore it open. "For Madame St. Clare," she read. ("Madame" was the title applied to all actresses.) "I must confess I am hopelessly smitten by you, for all that a lady known to us both has warned me you're not to be trusted and already belong to another man. Still, I have made so bold as to reserve a table for us at the Fox-Under-the-Hill at Ivy Bridge. I shall hope to see you there tomorrow evening at seven. Your most humble obliged servant, madame, I am, Captain Rex Morgan." And he added a postcript: "May I ask you, madame, to have the kindness for me as not to mention this note to anyone?"

Amber smiled slyly to herself, and after a moment tore the paper into little bits, tossed them up over her head and went on into the theatre. She had no intention of telling Beck about the note. Not, at least, until she was sure that he was captured; but she could not resist giving her a fleeting little smile that annoyed the other girl even if it told her nothing.

She had no performance the next afternoon and spent the day washing her hair—in spite of the almanac, which said that the time was astrologically unfavourable—deciding what she would wear, and trying to think of an excuse to give Michael. She was still undecided when she took a hackney and rode to the Royal Exchange to buy some ribbons and gloves and a bottle of scent. Coming back with her arms full of parcels, her cloak and hood covered with raindrops, she opened the door and found Michael standing in conversation with another man.

He was much older than Michael and as he turned to look at her there was a stern scowl on his face. She knew instantly who he was: Michael's father. For some time past Michael had been getting letters from his father, demanding to know why he had been expelled from the Middle Temple, insisting that he return home at once. Michael had read each one to her, laughing, saying gaily that his father was a formal old coxcomb, and had thrown them into the fire without ever sending an answer. Now, however, he wore a hang-dog expression and a look of cowed helplessness.

"Amber," he said at last, "this is my father. Sir, may I present Mrs. St. Clare?"

Sir Michael Godfrey merely stared at her without speaking, and after a moment she crossed the room, laid down her packages, and spread her cloak on a chair before the fire. That done she turned to find both men still watching her, and Sir Michael's hostile eyes made her aware that her neckline was cut very low and her face obviously painted. He turned away.

"Is this the woman you kept in the Temple?" As he said it Amber had an uncomfortable feeling that she was the commonest kind of whore.

"Yes, sir."

Michael was not flippant with his father as he had been with Mr. Gripenstraw. The wild gay boy who had delighted in getting drunk every night and breaking the windows of sleeping citizens had quite disappeared in the chagrined, embarrassed dutiful son.

Sir Michael Godfrey turned to Amber. "Madame, I fear you shall have to cast about elsewhere for a young fool to meet your expenses. My son is returning with me into the country and you shall get not a farthing more by his misplaced generosity."

Amber merely stared at him coolly and curbed her impulse to give him a tart answer because she remembered all that Michael had done for her, and all that he could still do, if he chose, to injure her. With a gesture of his hand Sir Michael signalled his son from the room. And though he hesitated for a moment he went, turning back once to give Amber a wistful pleading look of goodbye, which Sir Michael cut short by thrusting him sharply out and banging the door after them. Amber was sorry for Michael; evidently his life would now be sadly changed, but her pity soon gave way to relief—and then to eagerness for the night.

My stars are lucky! she thought exuberantly. Just when I had no more use for 'im—he's gone!

Amber was only a little late, but as she was ushered upstairs to the private dining-room, Captain Morgan flung open the door and greeted her with happy enthusiasm. "At last you're here! How kind of you to come!" His eyes glistened with pleasure as they looked down at her and he took her muff and cloak, tossed them over a chair, and turned her about by one hand. "You look wonderful! By God, you're the most glorious creature I've ever seen!"

Amber laughed. "Come now, Captain Morgan! Beck Marshall tells me you've said kinder things to her by far."

But she luxuriated in his admiration, feeling a warm glow of pleasure go through all her body at the expression on his face. It had been a long while since she had seen a man so infatuated—not, in fact, since she had left Marygreen. And she was glad that he had the sense to appreciate a pretty gown, for she had worn her best and newest one; too many of the young fops were so concerned with their own "garnitures" and "petite-oie" they scarcely knew what a woman was wearing. The dress was made of bright green velvet, with the skirt slit down the front and draped up over a black-satin sequin-spattered petticoat, and she had one part black-satin bow tied at either temple.

He snapped his fingers. "The devil with Beck Marshall. She's nothing to me, I assure you."

"That's what every man says about his old doxy when he has a mind to a new one."

Rex Morgan laughed. "I see you have wit as well as beauty, madame. That makes you perfect."

At that moment there was a loud rap at the door. Morgan called out for them to enter, and in marched the host and three waiters, loaded down with covered pewter dishes, knives and spoons, napkins, glasses and salt-dishes, and two bottles of wine. They set the places, removed all covers with a flourish so that Captain Morgan might inspect the contents, and then marched out again. Amber and Rex sat down to eat.

There was a great steaming bowlful of crayfish bisque, a well-seasoned leg-of-mutton stuffed with oysters and chopped onion, a chicken-pie covered with a flaky golden crust, and a pudding made of thick pure cream and pounded chestnuts. They sat side by side, facing the fireplace where sea-coals burnt brightly, and as they ate they fell into easy comfortable talk, enjoying the good meal and admiring each other.

He told her that she had the most fascinating eyes in the

world, the loveliest hair he had ever seen, the most beautiful breasts, and the prettiest legs. His voice had an authentic sincerity she did not even care to question, and he looked at her with frank adoration and desire. Why, he's mad in love with me already! thought Amber delightedly, and had an image of herself parading him into the tiring-room tomorrow like a tame monkey on a chain.

"Is it true," he asked her at last as they were beginning to eat the hot baked chestnut pudding, "that you're in the keeping of someone from the Middle Temple?"

"Lord Almighty! Who told you that?"

"Everyone I asked about you. Is it true?"

"Certainly not! Lord, I swear a woman can be raped here in London without losing her maidenhead! I'll admit I was occupying lodgings with a gentleman for a time—but he was my cousin, and he's gone back to Yorkshire now. Heavens, I can't think what my father would say, to hear the bawdy talk that goes on here—about nothing at all!" She gave him a look of wide-eyed indignation.

"Lucky for him he's only your cousin. I'd have had to send him a challenge to get him out of my way. But I'm glad he's gone anyway. Tell me, who are you? Where'd you come from? Everyone told me a different story."

"I'm Mrs. St. Clare and I came from Essex. What else d'you want to know?"

"What are you doing on the stage? You don't look as though you belong there."

"Oh, don't I? I've been told different."

"That isn't what I mean. You look like a person of quality."

"Oh. Well—" She gave him a sidelong glance as he began to pour the champagne. "To tell you truly, I am."

She took the glass as he handed it to her leaned back in her chair and began to spin for him the story upon which she had been embroidering almost since she had first come to London, improving upon it whenever she got a new idea. "My family's old and honourable and they had a good estate in Essex—but they sold everything to help his Majesty in the Wars. So, when an old ugly earl wanted to marry me my father was going to insist, to help repair his loss. I wouldn't have the stinking old goat—my father said I should have him, and he locked me into the house. I broke out and came to London— Of course I changed my name—I'm not *really* Mrs. St. Clare." She smiled at him over the rim of her glass, pleased to see that he apparently believed her.

He got up then, moved their chairs closer to the dying fire, and they sat down side by side. Amber lifted her legs, bracing her feet on one side of the narrow fireplace so that her skirts fell back above her knees and showed her legs in black silk stockings and lacy garters. He reached over to take her hand in his and they sat for several moments, perfectly still and silent, but with the tension mounting between them.

What shall I do? she was thinking. If I do, he'll take me for a harlot—and if I don't, maybe he won't ever come back again.

At last she turned to face him and found his eyes on her, intense and serious, glowing with desire. One arm reached out and went around her waist, drawing her slowly toward him, and she slid over onto his lap. For a moment she hesitated, and then her face bent to his and she felt the pressure of his mouth, moist and warm and eager; his hand moved over her breasts, and she could feel the heavy beating of his heart against her own. Her blood began to rush, filling her with warmth and quick passion—she felt herself sliding to surrender and had no inclination to stop.

But as he would have knelt before her she jumped up suddenly and left him, crossing the room to stand before the black windows, her head buried in her hands. Instantly he was behind her, his fingers taking hold of her shoulders, pressing her back against him. His voice whispered to her, pleading, and as his lips touched the back of her neck a thrill ran along her spine.

"Please, darling—don't be angry. I'm in love with you, I swear I am. I want you, I've *got* to have you!" His fingers cut into her shoulders and his voice in her ear was hoarse with intensity. "Please—Amber, please! I won't hurt you—I won't let anything happen— Come here" He swung her around to face him.

Amber wrenched herself free; her own eyes were a little wild and her face was flushed. "You've got the wrong opinion of me, Captain Morgan! I may be on the stage, but I'm no whore! My poor father would die of shame if his daughter gave herself up to a sinful life! Now let me go—" She brushed past him, starting to get her cloak, and when he turned swiftly, catching her arm, his jaw set and hard, she cried warningly, "Have a care, sir! I'm not one of your willing rapes, either."

She jerked away and getting her cloak, flung it on, took up her muff and went to the door. "Good-night, Captain Morgan! If you'd told me why you brought me here I could've saved you the cost of a supper!" She looked at him haughtily, but the cold angry expression on his face alarmed her.

Now! she thought. If he doesn't really like me I've spoiled everything.

One eyebrow went up as he stared at her and his mouth twisted slightly, but as she took hold of the knob he crossed over and stopped her. "Don't go away like this, Mrs. Clare. I'm sorry if I've offended you. I'd heard— Well, never mind. But you're a damned desirable woman. A man must be gelt if he wouldn't want you—and to tell the truth, I'm not." He grinned down at her. "Let me see you home."

After that she saw him often, but not at the theatre, for she was not sure of him yet and did not care to give Beck the opportunity of jeering at her. Beck, meanwhile, continued to boast and brag of his attentions to her, showed Amber his gifts, and gave her the intimate details of his visits. Amber was receiving some gifts, too: A pair of exquisite black-lace stockings from France, garters with little diamond buckles, a muff made of wide bands of gold brocade hooped at either end with black fox—but she was very mysterious about the giver.

She used every trick she knew—and by now they were several—to heighten his desire for her. But each time he imagined himself about to succeed she pushed him off and insisted again that she was a woman of virtue. Fortunately for her, he did not suggest that such behaviour seemed quite the opposite of virtuous. Sometimes he bellowed that she was a jilting baggage and stormed off, swearing that he would never see her again. Other times he stayed and pleaded, doggedly, with real desperation, and then finally went away defeated. But each time he came back.

And then one evening, his face haggard and his cravat askew, he slumped down into a chair, demanding, "What the devil *do* you want, then? I can't go on like this. I'm fretting my bowels to fiddle-strings over you!"

She had a sense of quick poignant relief.At last! And though a moment before she had been feeling tired and discouraged and all too inclined to be virtuous no longer, now she laughed, got up, and went to the mirror to smooth her hair.

"That isn't what Beck says. She was telling me today how last night you came to see her, so hot you wouldn't be put off for an instant."

He scowled, like an embarrassed boy. "Beck prattles too much. Answer me! What are you holding me off for? What do you want? Marriage?" She knew that he had been dreading to ask that, that he was no more eager to get married than were any of the other young men, and that even though he believed or pretended to believe her story about her aristocratic family, he would not marry an actress.

"Marriage!" she repeated in mock astonishment, staring at him in the mirror. "That's enough to give one the vapours! What woman in her right senses wants to get married?"

"Any woman, it seems."

"Well, they wouldn't if they'd ever *been* married!" She turned around and stood looking at him, her hands easily on her hips.

"Ye gods! Are you married?"

"No, of course not! But I'm not blind. I've seen a thing or two. What's a wife, pray? The men use 'em worse than a dog nowadays. They think they're good for nothing but to breed up their brats—and serve as a foil to a mistress. A wife gets a full belly every year, but a mistress gets all the money and attention. Be a wife? Pooh! Not me! Not for a thousand pound!"

"Well!" he said, obviously much relieved. "You talk like a

woman of rare good sense. But you don't seem very anxious to be a mistress, either. Surely you don't expect to be that worthless object, a virgin, all your life? Not a woman like you."

"Have I said I did? If a man I liked made me a fair offer, I assure you I'd do him the kindness to think it over."

He smiled. "Well, now—we're getting somewhere at last. And what's your notion of a fair offer, pray?"

She leaned her elbow back on the mantelpiece and stood with her weight on one foot, the other bare knee sliding out of her satin dressing-gown; she began to count on her fingers. "I'd want a settlement of two hundred pounds a year. I'd want lodgings of my own choosing, and a maid, and a neat little coach-and-four—and of course a coachman and footman—and leave to keep on acting." She had no intention of quitting the stage, for she had met him there and hoped someday to meet another and more important man. As she saw what was possible for a young and beautiful and obliging woman, her ambitions soared.

"You set a damned high price on yourself."

"Do I?" She smiled a little and gave a faint shrug. "Well—a high price, you know, serves to keep off ill company."

"If I take you at that figure I'll expect it to keep off *all* company, but mine."

It took Amber several days to find the lodgings that suited her and she rattled all over town in a hackney, searching, whenever she could be free from the theatre. But at last she found a three-room suite on the third floor of the Blue Balcony, down at the fashionable Strand end of Drury Lane. The rent was high, forty pounds a year, but Captain Morgan paid it in advance.

Everything here was in the latest fashion, reflecting the light gay colourful taste of the new age. The parlour was hung in emerald-green damask. There were French tables and chairs of walnut, some of them gilt, and all very different from the heavy old oaken pieces she was accustomed to seeing in inns. A long walnut couch had thick green cushions, fringed with gold, and there were several green-and-gold lacquered mirrors. She decided immediately that she would have her portrait painted and sink it flush with the wall above the fireplace, like one she had seen in the apartments of another actress, who was in the keeping of a lord.

The walls of the dining-room were covered with hand-painted Chinese paper, flaunting peonies and chrysanthemums, all aswarm with brilliant-hued birds and butterflies. The chairs and stools had thick bright-green cushions tied to them. In the bedroom the hangings were also of damask, patterned in green and gold; there was a five-leaved screen, two leaves red and three green, and green-and-red-striped chair cushions.

"Oh!" cried Amber, when Captain Morgan went with her to

see it and agreed that she might have it. "Thank you, Rex! I can't wait to move in!"

"Neither can I," he said. But she gave him a quick pout and then a smile.

"Now, Rex—remember what you said! You promised you'd wait."

"And I will. But for God's sake—not much longer."

She insisted on having the whole of her allowance in advance and, when she got it, hunted out Shadrac Newbold—whose name she remembered, Bruce Carlton had told her—and put it with him as six percent interest. In Cow Lane they found a second-hand coach which, though small, was freshly painted and in good condition. It was glossy black with red wheels and red reins and harness, and he bought four handsome black-and-white horses to draw it. The coachman and footman were named, respectively, Tempest and Jeremiah, and she ordered red livery trimmed with silver braid for them.

She hired her maid from an old woman Mrs. Scroggs recommended with the absolute assurance that the girl was honest, demure, and well-bred, that she could carve and sew and clean, would not sleep late or gossip to the neighbours or run about in slovenly dress. She was a plain-faced girl whose teeth had wide spaces between them and whose face was entirely covered with little pale freckles. Prudence was her name, which Amber did not like, for she remembered simple harmless Honour Mills who had been in league with a pair of thieves to rob her. But still the girl seemed anxious to please and looked so pitiful at the prospect of not being hired that Amber took her.

The first night at her new apartments she and Rex had an elaborate supper sent in from the Rose Tavern nearby and opened a bottle of champagne, but they scarcely drank a glass, for he picked her up impetuously and carried her in to the bedroom. And yet for all his passionate fervour he was tender and considerate, as eager to give pleasure as to take it, and Amber thought that this was far more like a wedding-night than that wretched experience she had had with Luke Channell. For the first time in a year and a half she was wholly and completely satisfied, for Rex had the same combination of experience, energy, controlled violence, and instinctive understanding which Lord Carlton had also had.

There's a world of difference, she told herself, between being a man's mistress and his wife. And as far as she was concerned that difference was all for the better.

The next afternoon Amber found the women's tiring-room buzzing like a swarm of angry hornets, and Beck Marshall was the centre of their chattering indignation. She realized instantly that they had heard about her and Rex. And though they all turned at once to fix upon her their cold wrathful stares, she sauntered into the room and pulled off her gloves with a great show of unconcern. Scroggs waddled over to her immediately, a self-satisfied grin on her ugly old face.

"Damn me, Mrs. St. Clare!" she said now, and her deep hoarse rough voice carried above all the noise of the room. "But it pleased me mightily to hear of your good fortune!" She leaned close, smelling strongly of brandy and spoilt fish, and gave Amber a jab in the ribs. "When ye asked me t'other day where ye might hire a woman I says to m'self, 'Aha! Mrs. St. Clare's a-goin' into keepin', I'll warrant you!' But I'll swear I never guessed the gentleman'd be Captain Morgan!" She leered and nudged, and jerked her thumb in the direction of the glowering group across the room.

Scroggs had taken Amber's cloak and fan and muff and was helping her out of her gown. "Neither did anyone else, I see," murmured Amber, glancing toward them with a significant lift of one eyebrow. She bent over to step out of her petticoats.

"Foh! Ye should've seen the look on the face of Mrs. Snottynose when she heard the news!" She laughed heartily, showing the holes in her mouth where teeth had been, and slapped her great thigh. "Damn me! I thought she'd bust a gut!"

Amber smiled, taking the combs out of her side curls and giving her hair a shake. And then, as she looked at her, Beck's head turned and their eyes met directly. For a long moment they stared, Amber exultant, taunting, Beck seething with rage, and then all at once Beck turned away, raising her right hand to show Amber the stiff middle finger. Amber laughed out loud at that and picked up the black wig she was to wear for her part as Cleopatra in Shakespeare's tragedy, sliding it down over her own coarse bright silken hair.

She knew well enough herself that she was ill-suited to play the Egyptian queen—the part might much better have gone to Anne Marshall—but the idea had been Tom Killigrew's and in her black wig with her eyes elongated by black pencil, a sleeveless sequin-spotted vest which just covered her breasts and a thin scarlet silk skirt slit to the knees in front, she had attracted an overflowing house for the past week and a half. Most productions were limited to three or four days, because so small a part of the London population attended plays, but some of the young men had been back four or five times to see this Cleopatra. They were used to a woman's breasts being displayed in public, but not her hips and buttocks and legs. Every time she walked onto the stage there were whistles and murmurs and the most unabashed comments, but the boxes had been noticeably empty and the ladies were said to have protested they could not tolerate so lewd and immodest a display.

Amber more than half expected trouble and was prepared for it, but though the atmosphere was undoubtedly tense, everything went as usual until the last scene of the last act. Then, as she stood waiting at the side of the stage for her cue to go on, both Beck and Anne Marshall came to stand beside her, Beck on her right, Anne slightly in back. Amber gave Beck a careless glance but continued to watch the stage where the men—in their great plumed headdresses which told an audience that this was tragedy being performed—were deciding Cleopatra's fate.

"Well, madame," said Beck. "Let me offer my congratulations. You've progressed mightily, they tell me—to be kept by only one man now."

Amber looked at her sharply, and then said with an air of profound boredom: "Lord, madame, you should see your 'pothecary. I swear you're turned quite green."

At that instant a pin pricked her from behind and she gave an angry start, but before she had time to say anything Mohun came off the stage, scowled, and muttered at them to go on. With Beck on one side and Mary Knepp on the other Amber walked out, proclaiming in a loud clear voice:

"My desolation does begin to make
A better life. 'Tis paltry to be Caesar . . ."

But for the commotion in the audience, the last scene progressed smoothly—through Cleopatra's dialogue with Caesar, her decision to end her life, the trial suicide of Iras, and then Cleopatra's own seizure of the pâpier-maché asp, which she addressed in full dramatic tones:

"With thy sharp teeth this knot intrinsicate
Of life at once untie; poor venomous fool . . ."

While Beck, as the faithful serving-woman who could not bear her mistress's death, ran distractedly about the stage, Amber applied the asp beneath her vest and heard a young man down in Fop Corner remark, "I've seen this six times. That viper should be weaned by now."

She clenched her teeth and shut her eyes as in a sudden spasm of pain. But she did not take her tragic parts very seriously and had to resist the inclination to laugh.

After standing motionless for a long moment she began to turn slowly in her death agony. Halfway around, she was arrested by a sudden barking shout of laughter from nearby. And then the sound was repeated from hundreds of throats. It swept on up through the boxes to the galleries beneath the roof, growing ever louder and noisier as it rose, until it seemed to fill the theatre and to come from all sides at once, hammering against her with an almost physical force.

Instinctively conscious that the laughter was directed at her, Amber swung quickly about, putting her hand to the back of her skirt. And though she half expected to find it torn open, she felt there instead a piece of cardboard and ripped it off, sailing it furiously across the stage. Beneath and before and above her she saw a blur of faces, a seemingly endless vista of opened mouths, and at the same instant the apprentices began to beat their cudgels and stamp their feet and a roaring chant went up:

"My tail's
For sale.
Half-a-crown
Will lay me down!"

Half-crown pieces had begun to ring upon the stage and Amber felt them pelting her sharply, hitting her from every side. The men were climbing onto their benches, shouting at the top of their lungs; the ladies had put on their masks but were shaking with laughter; from top to bottom the theatre was a bedlam of noise and confusion—though not more than forty seconds had passed since Amber's unlucky turn.

"You lousy bitch!" Amber ground the words through her clenched teeth. "I'll break your head for this!"

With a h sterical titter Beck started off the stage at a run and, just as the curtains swished frantically together, Amber went after her as fast as she could go, yelling, "Come back here, you damned coward!'

Anne, waiting in the wings, stuck out a foot to trip her, but Amber jumped over it, gave Anne a backhand swipe that sent her staggering, and rushed on. Flying down the narrow dark hallway Beck turned to look back just as she reached the tiring-room, gave a shriek when she saw how close her pursuer was, and dashing in slammed the door. But before she could throw the bolt Amber had burst against it, shoved it open, and with a violent push was inside. In one movement she flung the bolt herself and turned to grapple with Beck.

Clawing and biting, screaming and kicking and pounding at each other with their fists, they rocked and swayed from one side of the room to the other. Their flimsy costumes were soon torn to shreds; their wigs came off and the black eye-paint smeared their faces; bloody scratches appeared on cheeks and arms and breasts. But for the time they were engrossed in rage, unfeeling, unhearing, unseeing.

Outside a crowd had gathered and was pounding at the door, clamouring to be let in. Scroggs moved straddlelegged after them, keeping just out of reach of thrashing arms and legs, cheering and shouting for Madame St. Clare. Once, when she came too close, Beck gave her a vicious kick in the belly that knocked her into a breathless groaning quivering heap on the floor.

At last Amber locked one leg behind Beck's knee and they went down together, clasped as tight as lovers, rolling over and over with first one on top and then the other. Amber's nose was streaming and her throat was beginning to feel raw from the blood she had swallowed, but at last she got astride Beck and pummelled her head and face with her fists while Beck fought her off with teeth and clawing nails. Thus they were when Scroggs opened the door and half-a-dozen men rushed in to drag them apart, hauling Amber off and pulling Beck away in another direction. Both women collapsed from sudden nervous exhaustion, and neither protested at the interference. Beck began to cry hysterically, babbling an incoherent stream of accusations and curses.

Amber lay stretched out flat on a couch, Hart's cloak flung over her, and now while Scroggs sopped at the blood and muttered her fierce congratulations she began to feel the sting and smart of her wounds. Her nose was numb and seemed to have swollen immensely and one eye was beginning to close.

Faintly she heard Killigrew's loud angry voice: "—the laughing stock of all the town, you damned jades! I'll never dare show this play again! Both of you are suspended for two weeks—no, three weeks, by God! I'll have some discipline among you impudent players or know the reason why! And you can pay the cost of replacing your costumes—"

The voice went on but Amber's eyes were closed and she refused to listen. She was only relieved that Rex, who held his commission in his Majesty's regiment of Horse Guards, had been on duty at the Palace that day.

Still, when she came back at the end of her enforced vacation she found that though the other women probably liked her no better and envied her no less, she had been accepted as one of them. There was tension and amusement in the tiring-room the first day that she and Beck met face to face, but they merely looked at each other for a moment, then nodded and exchanged cool greetings.

A few days later Scroggs slyly gave Amber a new blue-velvet miniver-lined hood which some countess had just presented to the wardrobe. Blue was not Amber's colour and she knew it. "Thanks a million, Scroggs," she said. "But I think Beck should have it. It matches her gown."

Beck, standing only a few feet away and pulling on a stocking, heard her. She glanced around in surprise. "Why should I have it? My part's but a small one." Killigrew persisted in his punishment, and neither of them had yet been put into the roles they had played before.

"It's as big as mine," insisted Amber. "And anyway I've got a new petticoat to wear."

Still skeptical, Beck took it and thanked her.

In the comedy that day they played two frivolous girls, close friends, and halfway through the first act each suddenly discovered toward the other a new warmth which grew quickly into liking. At the end of the act everyone was astonished to see them coming off the stage arm in arm, laughing gaily. After that they were as good friends as most women, and Beck even flirted sometimes with Captain Morgan when he came to the tiring-room—though she knew as well as Amber that nothing would ever come of it. It was merely a gesture of good will.

Chapter Seventeen

CHARLES II was married to the Infanta Catherine of Portugal two years after his Restoration.

She had been decided upon by Charles and Chancellor Hyde—now Earl of Clarendon—very shortly after his return; the delay in the wedding had been political, designed to coerce a larger dowry from desperate little Portugal, just recently free but still menaced by Spain. In the end the Portuguese paid a high price for marrying English sea-power: they gave 300,000 pounds; the right of trade with all Portuguese colonies; and two of their most prized possessions, Tangier and Bombay.

The Earl of Sandwich had been sent to Portugal with a fleet to escort the princess back to England, but Charles could not leave London until he had prorogued Parliament, and that was several days after she had arrived at Portsmouth. But once it was dismissed he set out immediately and rode through the night. He arrived there early the next afternoon and went first to his own apartments to change his clothes.

Charles sat down and his barber lathered his face, then began to swipe across it with swift clean strokes of a sharp-edged razor. There were black circles beneath his eyes but he looked happy and alert, and somewhat amused, for the room was full of courtiers and he knew that the same thought was in every head.

They were wondering what kind of husband he was going to make, how this marriage would affect the status of each of them, and whether or not he really would, as he had said, keep no mistresses once he was married. For his own part he was glad to be away from London and the melancholy Barbara, who had sulked and pouted and cried for weeks past, though she bragged to acquaintances that she was going to lie-in of her second child at Hampton Court, while the King was spending his honeymoon there.

Now Charles glanced up at Buckingham who stood beside him, stroking the head of a little brown-and-black spaniel. Buckingham had been there for some time and had already seen the Infanta.

"Well?"

"Well," said the Duke.

Charles laughed. "I think you're jealous, my lord." Buckingham's wife was a plain, plump little woman with odd, slanted eyes and a large turned-up nose. When the barber was finished the King got up and submitted to being dressed. "Well—for the honour of the nation I only hope I'm not put to the consummation tonight. I haven't had two hours rest in the past thirty-four, and I'm afraid matters would go off somewhat sleepily."

Dressed at last he slapped his hat onto his head and strode rapidly from the room, a pack of his spaniels running at his heels, a pack of courtiers following after them. The Infanta, he had been told, had caught a cold and been sent to bed; and that was where he found her, sitting propped against white silk pillows embroidered with the Stuart coat-of-arms, wearing a dressing-gown of pale pink satin with belled wrist-length sleeves. He paused in the doorway, bowing, and saw her eyes staring at him wide and half-frightened, her fingers twisting the counterpane nervously.

She was surrounded on all sides by her attendants, banked two or three deep about the bed as though for her protection. There were half-a-dozen long-robed priests, their tonsured heads shining, their eyes measuring and skeptical. There were the Countesses of Penalva and Ponteval, her Majesty's chaperons, two ugly, muddy-skinned, punctilious old women. And the six maids-of-honour, young but just as dark, sallow, and hideous to the eye of an Englishman. Instead of the sweeping, graceful low-cut gowns then in fashion, they were without exception dressed in stiff-bodiced, old-fashioned farthingales which had not been worn in England for thirty years. If they had breasts they were so tightly cased as to appear perfectly flat, and their skirts jutted out from the waist on either side like shelves that swung and teetered clumsily whenever they moved.

As the King appeared in the doorway, his gentlemen crowded behind him, peering over his shoulders; the women stood motionless and waiting, a look of alarm on their faces. Portuguese etiquette was as rigid as the clothes they wore and the girls, having seldom seen men who were not members of their own families, regarded the entire sex with suspicion and distrust. They had been creating a good deal of trouble by refusing to sleep in any bed which had ever been occupied by a man, and at the sight of one of the creatures approaching had covered their faces and run off in another direction, cackling and gabbling. Now, unable to run, they stood and stared—defensive, nervous, wretchedly ill-at-ease. They would have been more so if they had guessed what the men thought of them.

Charles's face did not change and immediately he came forward, taking her hand to kiss. "My apologies to you, madame," he said in soft Spanish, for she knew no English. "Business kept me until late last night. I hope you've been made comfortable?" He straightened then and looked down at her.

Catherine was twenty-three but she looked no more than eighteen. Her hair was beautiful, a cascading mass of dark brown waves, and her eyes which were also brown were large and bright, gentle and just a little wistful as she looked up at him. They seemed to beg for kindness and to ask apology for her own shortcomings. For her skin was inclined to sallowness; her front teeth protruded a little. And he had been told that she was scarcely five feet tall.

Still—he thought—for a princess, she's not bad.

Catherine had been bred in a convent, embroidering, praying, singing hymns, waiting for her mother to find her a husband. When she did, Catherine was already far beyond the age when most princesses married and still she knew nothing at all of men, was almost as ignorant of their natures as if they had been members of another species. She had expected to learn to love her husband because it was a woman's duty to do so; but now as she looked up at Charles she realized that she had already fallen in love with him. Everything about him seemed wonderful to her: his swarthy good-looks, the powerful grace of his body, the deep smooth gentle tones of his voice which lapped over her like a warm tide, stilling some of her terrors, echoing in her heart.

The next morning they were married, first by a secret Catholic ceremony in her bedchamber, again in the afternoon according to the rites of the Church of England. A few days later they set out for Hampton Court. And though there was much gossip to the effect that Charles was disappointed in his marriage and ready to accept Barbara Palmer back again as soon as she had recovered from her confinement, both their Majesties seemed perfectly happy and content and as much in love as though they had not married for reasons of political expediency.

But if Catherine was satisfied, there were others in her suite who were not.

Penalva, an ailing, near-sighted old virgin, disliked England the moment she set foot upon it. It was too different from Portugal to be good. The women, she decided immediately, were wanton and bold, the men unscrupulous and dishonourable, and she undertook to warn the naïve little Queen of these facts.

"The Court of England," she said sternly, "must needs be much remodelled before it is fit for the occupancy of your Majesty."

Catherine, who was still admiring her splendid crimson-and-silver-hung apartments, examining the massive toilet and mirror made out of pure beaten gold, looked at her in surprise, but with a happy little smile.

"Why, perhaps it should be. I've not heard what condition it's in, but I don't doubt his Majesty will be glad to make any repairs I ask—he's so kind to me." Her dark eyes went out the windows, looking across the stretches of green lawn, the blooming flower-plots, and something dreamy and thoughtful came into them that evidently annoyed Penalva.

"You misunderstand, your Majesty! I was not speaking of the *furnishings* of the Palace. Quite possibly it will be as barbarous as this—" She gestured quickly, for she did not like English taste either. "I was speaking of the manners and morals of the courtiers and ladies themselves."

"Why," said Catherine, "what's wrong with them?"

"Can it be your Majesty has not noticed how these women dress? All of them go half naked from morning till night."

"Well—" she admitted with some reluctance, for she did not want to be disloyal to her new land and husband. "They are—different—from what we're used to seeing at home."

"Different! My dear, they're indecent! No woman whose intentions were innocent would display herself before a man as these creatures do. Your Majesty, you have an opportunity to earn for yourself the gratitude of all England—by reforming the Court."

"I wouldn't know how to begin. Perhaps they wouldn't like to have an outsider—"

"Nonsense, your Majesty! What does it matter what they would like! You're not their subject! They are yours, and must be made to understand so immediately—or you will find yourself a mere hanger-on at your own Court."

Catherine smiled gently, thinking that the poor old lady was so concerned for her happiness that she saw a great deal of evil where none existed. "I think you've misjudged them, my lady. They all look so fine—I'm sure they must be good."

"Unfortunately, your Majesty, that is not the way of the world. The good are never ostentatious—these creatures are. Now, your Majesty, you must listen to the advice of an old woman who has lived a long while and seen a great deal. Be mistress in your own Court! Be a leader, not a follower, or they'll leave you alone for whoever does undertake to lead, and Heaven knows, in this abandoned place it could be no one of good character. Begin, your Majesty, by putting off those absurd English clothes his Majesty gave you. Return to your native costume, and others will be forced to follow."

Catherine looked down, somewhat dismayed, at her pink-and-blue taffeta gown with its full-gathered skirt, billowing sleeves the neckline cut more discreetly than were those of most ladies, but still quite daring, she had thought. She felt that in it she was prettier than she had ever been before in her life.

"But," she protested softly, "I like it."

"It doesn't become you, my dear, as your native costume does. Go back to your farthingales, or these English will think they've converted you to their ways already. They're an arrogant race, and will have scant pity or respect for whoever is easily tamed by them. And one thing more, your Majesty—*don't* learn the language. Let them speak to you in your own tongue—"

Catherine had listened to Penalva all her life, and she knew that the old lady had nothing but love and affection for her. She bowed to the wisdom of age and that night she appeared at a banquet in her bobbing, black-silk farthingale. She gave Charles a quick anxious glance, to see whether or not he disapproved of the change, but his face was inscrutable. He smiled, bowing, and offered her his arm.

The honeymoon was celebrated with endless entertainment and gaiety. There were banquets and balls and cock-fights, picnics, rides on the canal in the luxurious royal barges, plays performed by actors who came down from London. All day long the staircases, the chain of great rooms and galleries, were crowded with a brilliantly dressed throng of men and women. In plum-coloured velvet, blue satin, gold brocade, they clattered and swished from room to room, strolled down the cradlewalk of interlaced hornbeam, drifted lazily on the river. And the sound of their voices, calling to one another, laughing, chattering eternally, reached Catherine whether she was with them or—more often—when she was in her own apartments at prayer or talking to her ladies and priests. She liked to hear them, for though she felt shy and lonely when she was among them, from a distance it gave her a sense of being part of their gay, debonair, heedless world.

She did not guess what they thought of her.

"She's ugly as a bat," they told one another, after the first glimpse, and greatly magnified her defects because she did not look like an English-woman.

They dissected her among themselves, the women giggling and murmuring behind their fans even when she was in the room, for they knew she could understand nothing of what they said. And if by chance the Queen's brown eyes rested upon one of them and she smiled, they quickly composed their faces to smile back, curtsying faintly, and gave a wink and a nudge to the nearest lady.

"Gad! But she looks as demure as a dog in a halter!"

"I'll be damned if I can bring myself to admire a woman with such a dingy skin! Why the devil doesn't she give it a plastering of powder?"

"Oh, heavens, my lord! Her monster would never allow it! They say the old witch thinks we're a pack of infidels and counsel her Majesty to have a care we don't corrupt her."

"Look! how she gives the king the sheep's eye! Ugh! I swear it makes me queasy to see a woman who dotes so upon her husband—and in public in broad daylight!"

"I say it's a mark of his Majesty's good-breeding he can make such a tolerable show of seeming to endure her."

"Well—I'll wager he won't make such a tolerable show much longer. Castlemaine laid-in last week. She'll be here in another fortnight—and *then* we'll see—" Barbara Palmer had been created Countess of Castlemaine some six months before.

"It runs through the galleries the King promised long ago he'd make her a Lady of the Bedchamber when he married—"

"And she says he will or she'll know why!"

Much as they disliked Barbara for her insolence and airs, hot though jealousy of her flared among the other women, still she was one of them and they were united in her favour against this newcomer who outraged them with her modesty and reticence, her obstinate clinging to the fashions of her own country, her persistent devotion to her church. But it was not only the frivolous and cynical whom Catherine had offended. By seeming from the first to like Chancellor Clarendon she had unwittingly drawn upon herself the enmity of the most ambitious and able and influential men at Court.

But Catherine could know nothing of all this. And in spite of Penalva's repeated warnings she looked at her new subjects and saw only women dressed in beautiful gowns, with glossy golden hair and a look of sleek complacency—women she envied though she knew it was wicked to do so—and men with suave easy manners bowing over her hand, sweeping off their hats as she appeared, their closed faces telling her nothing. She was still a little frightened by England, but so much in love with her husband and so eager to please him that she tried to conceal her awe and uncertainty and thought that she was succeeding very well.

And then one evening, while she was being made ready for bed, Lady Suffolk, aunt of Lady Castlemaine, and the only English attendant thus far appointed, handed the Queen a sheet of paper with a list of names written upon it. "These are the persons proposed for your Majesty's attendants," she said. "Will your Majesty be pleased to sign?"

Catherine, now in her flowing nightgown of white silk, took it and went to her little writing-table. She picked up a pen and had bent to write her signature, when suddenly Penalva's hawknosed face appeared over her shoulder.

"Don't sign without reading it first, your Majesty!" she whispered.

Catherine gave her a glance of mild surprise, for she had assumed that if the King had chosen these ladies to attend her they could not be otherwise than acceptable. But already her old chaperon was mumbling them over.

"—Mrs. Price. Mrs. Wells. Mother of the Maids: Bridget Saunderson. Ladies of the Bedchamber: my Lady Castlemaine—" At the last name her voice became audible, suddenly sharp and indignant, and her face turned to Catherine's.

It was the only name which meant anything to her. For before she had sailed her mother—who had given her so little advice as to how to be happy, either as wife or queen—had warned her never to allow Lady Castlemaine to so much as come into her presence. She was, the old Dowager Queen had said, an infamous hussy for whom the King had shown a deplorable kindness during the days of his bachelorhood.

"Why!" said Catherine, horrified. Then quickly she glanced about to catch the cool eyes of Lady Suffolk upon her, and turned so that only her back was to be seen. "What shall I do?" she whispered, pretending to study the list.

"Scratch the creature's name *out*, of course!" With a quick motion she snatched up the pen which Catherine had dropped, dipped it into the inkwell and handed it to her. "Scratch it out, your Majesty!"

For a moment longer Catherine hesitated, her face troubled and hurt, and then resolutely she crossed her pen over the name with several dark broad strokes, until it was completely obliterated. She felt that by so doing she had also obliterated this menace to her happiness. She turned then and spoke to her interpreter.

"Tell my Lady Suffolk that I shall return the list to her in the morning."

Half an hour later Charles arrived to find her alone and, as usual, on her knees before the little shrine which had been set up next to the great scarlet-velvet bed-of-state. He waited quietly, but already his eye had caught sight of the paper on the writing-table and the black bar which marked out Lady Castlemaine. However, he said nothing, and when she turned and smiled at him he crossed over to help her to her feet; but as he stooped to kiss her he could feel her tiny body stiffen defensively.

For a few moments they talked, discussing the play they had seen that night—a performance of "Bartholomew Fair" done by the King's Company—but all the while Catherine was wondering nervously how she should broach the subject and wishing that he would mention it first. At last, in desperation, just as he excused himself to go into the dressing-room, she spoke quickly.

"Oh—and Sire—before I forget. My Lady Suffolk gave me the list tonight—it's over there—" She swallowed and took a deep breath. "I crossed out one name. I'm sure you know which one," she added hastily, a little note of defiance coming into her voice, for Penalva had warned her that she must let him know once and for all she was not to be treated like that again.

Charles stopped, glancing carelessly across his shoulder, for he was just passing the writing-table. He turned slowly to face her. "Have you an objection to a lady you've never seen?"

"I've heard of her."

Charles gave a shrug and one finger stroked his mustache, but he smiled. "Gossip," he said. "How people love to gossip."

"Gossip!" she cried, shocked now to see how crassly unconcerned he was at having been taken in this bold attempt. "It can't be just gossip! Why, my mother told me—"

"I'm sorry, my dear, that my personal affairs are known so far afield. And yet since you seem so well advised of my shortcomings, I hope you'll believe me when I tell you that that episode is past. I have not seen the lady since we were married, and I intend having nothing more to do with her. I only ask you to accept her so that she may not have to suffer the indignities sure to be otherwise imposed upon her by ladies and gentlemen who were her friends only a short while since."

"I don't understand you, Sire. What else does a woman of that kind deserve? Why, she was nothing but your—your concubine!"

"It's always been my opinion, madame, that the mistresses of kings are as honourable as the wives of other men. I don't ask you to make her your friend, Catherine, or even to have her about you—but only that she be allowed the title. It would make her life much easier—and could scarcely hurt you, my dear." He smiled, trying to convince her, but nevertheless he was surprised at her stubbornness, for he had never suspected that this quiet adoring little woman had so much spirit.

"I'm sorry, your Majesty, but I must refuse. I would gladly do anything else you ask—but I can't do this. Please, Sire—try to understand what it would mean to me, too."

A week later Charles, on the pretext of going hunting, went to see Barbara at her uncle's nearby estate. She had just arrived and had sent him a desperate, humble imploring letter which, however, touched him less than did the fragrance it carried—that heavy musky compelling odour with which she always surrounded herself.

Breathless from running, she met him just as he stepped into the great hallway where stag-horns decorated the walls and ancient armour and firearms hung in every corner. He looked at her and saw a woman more beautiful than the one he remembered—his memory was short for such things—with brilliant violet eyes, her hair in a lavish cluster of curls about her face, dressed in a becoming gown of deep-red silk.

"Your Majesty!"

She made him a sweeping curtsy and her head dropped gracefully. Her eyes closed and she gave a little sigh as he bent casually to kiss her upon the cheek. Then she took his arm and they walked on into the house and up the flight of stairs which led to the main apartments.

"You're looking very well," he said, determinedly ignoring her obvious efforts to enchant. "I hope your confinement was not difficult."

She laughed gaily and pressed his arm, as sweet and merry as she had ever been in the early weeks of their acquaintance before the Restoration. "Difficult! Heavens, Your Majesty,—you know how it is with me! I'd rather have a baby than a quartan ague! Oh, but wait till you see him! He's ever so handsome—and everyone says he's the image of you!" That was not what they had said about her first child.

In the chapel the bishop was waiting with Lord Oxford and Lady Suffolk and the baby. When the ceremony of baptism was over Charles admired his son, took it up into his arms with an air of knowing exactly what he was about. But presently it began to cry and was sent off back to the nursery. The others went into a small private room to have wine and cakes, and here Barbara maneuvered him off to one side, under the pretext of showing him a section of the garden.

But she soon turned from the roses and flowering lime.

"And now you're married," she breathed softly, looking up at him with her eyes sad and tender. "And I've heard you're deep in love."

He stood and stared at her moodily, his eyes flickering over her face and hair and down to her breasts and small-laced waist. He caught the faint lascivious odour of her perfume, and his eyes darkened. Practiced voluptuary as he was, Charles had begun to long for a woman whose senses he could arouse, and who could arouse his. Catherine loved him, but he was finding her innocence and instinctive reticence a bore.

He sucked a quick breath through his teeth and his jaw set, "I'm very happy, thank you."

A faint mocking smile crossed her face. "For your sake, Sire, I'm glad." Then she sighed again and looked wistfully out the window. "Oh, you can't think what a wretched time I had in London after you'd left! The very porters and 'prentices in the streets insulted me! If you hadn't promised to make me a Lady of the Bedchamber— Lord, I don't know how I'd shift!"

A scowl crossed his face, for this was what he had been expecting and dreading. Of course her aunt had told her the whole story. "I'm sure you exaggerate, Barbara. I think you'll get along very well, in spite of everything."

Her head turned swiftly, the black centers of her eyes enlarging. "What do you mean—in spite of everything?"

"Well—it's unfortunate, but my wife crossed out your name. She says she doesn't want you for an attendant."

"Doesn't want me! Why, that's ridiculous! Why doesn't she want me? My family's good enough, I hope! And what harm can *I* do her now?"

"None," he said, very definitely. "But all the same she doesn't want you. She doesn't understand the way we live here in England. I told her that I would—"

Barbara stared at him aghast. "You told her she needn't have me!" she repeated in a horrified whisper. "Why, how could you do such a thing!" Tears had swum into her eyes and already, in spite of Lady Suffolk's frantic signalling, her voice was rising and a quaver of hysteria had come into it. "How can you do such a thing to a woman who has sacrificed her reputation, been deserted by her husband, and left to the scorn of all the world—to give you happiness! Oh, ——!" She turned and leaned her forehead against the window, one closed fist pressed to her mouth. She took a deep sobbing gasp. "Oh, I wish I'd died when the baby was born! I'd never have wanted to live if I'd known you'd do a thing like this to me!"

Charles looked more annoyed than sympathetic or conscience-smitten. All he wanted was to have the matter settled one way or another—and whether Barbara won or Catherine did made little difference to him. There was something to be said for both sides of the question, he thought, but a woman could never see more than one.

"Very well," he said. "I'll speak to her again."

But instead he sent the Chancellor to do the delicate business for him, though the old man protested vehemently, for he thought that Castlemaine would be well served if she were sent into exile overseas. Clarendon came out of his interview wiping his red face and shaking his head, limping slightly to favour his gout-stricken right foot. Charles was waiting for him in his laboratory and that was where he went—but as the short, round, pompous little man passed through the galleries he was followed by a trail of smirks and whispers. The contest between their Majesties was giving amusement to the entire Court.

"Well?" said the King, getting up from where he had sat writing a letter to Minette—she was now Madame, Duchess of Orléans and third lady at the Court of France.

"She refuses, your Majesty." He sat down, ignoring ceremony, because he was tired and discouraged and his foot ached. "For a little woman who looks meek and obliging—" He mopped his wet face again.

"What did you tell her? Did you tell her that—"

"I told her *everything*. I told her that your Majesty no longer had commerce with the Lady—nor ever intends to. I told her that your Majesty has the greatest affection for her and will make her a very good husband if she would but agree to this one thing. Oh, I beg of your Majesty, don't send me again! I have no maw for this business—you know what my opinion is—"

"I don't care what your opinion is!" said Charles sharply, though usually he listened with a lazy patient smile to whatever criticism of his manners, morals or intellect the Chancellor cared to make. "What was her attitude when you left?"

"She was in such a passion of tears, I think she may be wholly dissolved by now."

Charles went to his wife's room that night in a mood defiant and determined. He had had a domineering mother; he had unwittingly chosen a domineering mistress; but he did not intend to be hen-pecked at home. He was less interested now in the fate of Barbara Palmer than he was in convincing his wife that he and not she would make the decisions. Catherine met him with an equally defiant air—though only an hour before they had been smiling politely at each other and listening to a choir of Italian eunuchs.

He bowed to her. "Madame, I hope that you are prepared to be reasonable."

"I am, Sire—if you are."

"I ask this one favour of you, Catherine. If you'll grant it, I promise it shall be the last hard thing I'll ever expect of you."

"But the one thing you ask is the hardest thing a man *could* ask of his wife! I can't do it! I won't do it!" Suddenly she stamped her tiny foot and cried in a flare of angry passion that astonished him, "And if you speak of it again I'll go home to Portugal!" She stared at him for a moment, and then bursting into tears turned her back and covered her face with her hands.

For a long moment both of them were silent, Catherine struggling to control her sobs but wondering miserably why he did not come to her, take her into his arms, and tell her that he realized how impossible it would be for her to accept his cast-off whore as an attendant. He had seemed so kind and gentle and tender, she could not understand what had happened to change him. Surely if he cared so much about the woman's having that place he must still love her.

But Charles, his stubbornness now thoroughly aroused, had a vision of himself going through life the meek, uxorious husband of a tyrannizing little despot. She could never learn earlier that he would rule his own household.

"Very well, madame," he said at last. "But before you go I think it would be wise to determine first if your mother will have you—and to find out, I'll send your attendants before you."

Catherine whirled around and stared at him with unbelieving astonishment. Those men and women of her own country were all she had to cling to in this strange terrifying land. Now, more than ever, when he was against her too, she needed them.

"Oh, please, Sire!" Her hands went out imploringly.

He bowed. "Good-night, madame."

To the amused relief of the Court most of Catherine's ugly train departed within a few days, for Charles allowed only Penalva, the priests, and a few kitchen attendants to remain. He did not trouble to send so much as a letter of explanation with them, but he hoped the Dowager Queen would know that he was displeased because she had paid most of the dowry—at the last moment—in sugar and spices instead of in gold.

For days the contest between them persisted.

Catherine remained most of the time in her own rooms and, when she did appear, she and Charles scarcely spoke. When the courtiers met in the garden or at the cockpit they asked each other: "Are you going to the Queen-baiting this afternoon?" The young and gay wanted to see Barbara Palmer triumphant because she represented their own way of living; the older and more circumspect sympathized with the Queen but wished that she understood men better and had been taught that tact could often accomplish what blustering and threats could not. As usual, Charles heard advice from both camps, but though he listened politely to everyone he was no more influenced than usual. In any matter which he considered to be of importance to his comfort he made his own decisions—and he did so now.

Queen Henrietta Maria was coming to pay her son another visit, and Charles did not intend that she should arrive to find his wife pouting and his house in a turmoil. Determined to settle the issue for once and all, he sent for Barbara to come to Hampton Court.

One warm late-July afternoon Catherine's drawing-room was crowded to capacity and many who could not force their way in stood in the anteroom. There was a sharp tension in the air which she felt but could not understand, unless it was because Charles had not yet appeared. In spite of herself she continued to look anxiously for him, over their heads toward the doorway. For he was always there, and even when he ignored her she could find some comfort in the mere fact of his presence. But now, feeling lonely and forsaken, she had to force herself to smile, bit the inside of her lower lip so that it would not tremble, swallowed hard over the lump in her throat.

Oh! she was thinking desperately, how I wish I'd never come to England! I wish I wasn't married! I wish I was back home again! I was happy then—

Her memory returned with longing to the lazy still afternoons in the convent garden, washed with the hot Portuguese sun, when she had sat with her brush and palette trying to catch the sharp contrast of white walls and blue shadows, or had worked her needle and listened to the murmurous chant of prayers in the chapel. What a quiet safe world that was! She envied that Catherine for the things she had not known.

And then suddenly she saw him and her back stiffened, a cold wave washed over her and the sadness and the dreamy languor was gone. Alert, glad to see him though she knew he would pay her no attention, a little smile touched her mouth. How tall he is, she thought, and how handsome! Oh, I do love him! She had scarcely noticed that a woman—dressed in white lace that sparkled with silver sequins—walked by his side.

As they came forward the room fell into a hushed waiting silence, every eye watching, every ear straining to hear. It was not until Charles, in a low but perfectly distinct tone, had spoken the lady's name that Catherine turned to look at her, holding out her hand to be kissed as the woman dropped to one knee.

At the same moment she felt a grasp on her shoulder and heard Penalva's hiss in her ear: "It's *Castlemaine!*"

Catherine's hand jerked involuntarily, and her eyes turned to Charles, surprised, incredulous, questioning. But he was merely watching her, his face hard and speculative, his whole manner coolly defiant, as though daring her to refuse him now. She looked then at Lady Castlemaine, who had risen, and had a quick unforgettable glimpse of a beautiful face—the lips curled faintly, the eyes shining with triumph and mockery.

She turned suddenly sick and weak. The world began to swim and rock dizzily, a ringing in her ears drowned out every other sound, and the room blackened before her eyes. She pitched forward out of her chair, but was kept from falling by the quick restraining hands of two pages and the Countess of Penalva, who glared at Charles with cold and unrelenting hatred. A sudden look of horror crossed his face and involuntarily one hand went out. But he quickly remembered himself, stepped back, and stood there silently while the Queen was carried from the room.

Chapter Eighteen

BECAUSE OF REX MORGAN'S place at Court, Amber was able to watch the King and Queen's state entry into London from the roof of one of the Palace buildings along the Thames.

For as far as it was possible to see in both directions the shores were packed; on the water the barges lay so thick a man could have walked from Westminster Hall to Charing Cross Stairs on them. Banners whipped out in the brisk breeze, and garlands of flowers trailed in the water. Music played, and as the first of the great gilded state-barges appeared cannon went off, roaring along the river-front, while shouts echoed back from shore to shore and every bell-tower in the city began to rock clamorously.

Amber, her hair blowing about her face, was standing over in one corner, very close to the edge and trying hard to see everything. With her were three young men who had just come from Hampton Court and who had been telling her the story of how the Queen had fainted when Castlemaine was presented to her, and how angry the King had been, thinking she had done it on purpose to embarrass him.

"And since then," one of them was saying, "the Lady's gone to all the balls and entertainments and they say his Majesty is sleeping with her again."

"Can you blame him?" demanded another. "She's a mighty delicate creature—but as for that olivader skinned—"

"Well, damn me!" interrupted the third. "If there isn't the Earl himself!"

Elbow-nudges and glances passed along the roof, but Roger Palmer ignored them all; and presently they turned their attention back to the pageant, for the great City barges were now moving by just below. A few minutes later, however, Barbara herself came up the stairway. She was followed by her handsome waiting-woman, Mrs. Wilson, and a nurse carrying her little son. She made a perfunctory curtsy to her husband, who bowed coldly, and immediatedy she was surrounded by the three young gallants who had left Amber with never a word of apology.

Angry and resentful, hot at the mere sight of this woman she despised, Amber gave her head a toss and turned away. At least *I'll* not stare like a country-bumpkin at a puppet show! she thought furiously. But no one else seemed to have any such compunctions.

Not very much later she was surprised by the sound of a strangely familiar masculine voice, a hand on her shoulder, and she looked swiftly about to see the Earl of Almsbury grinning down at her. "Well, I'll be damned!" he was saying. "If it isn't Mrs. St. Clare!" He bent then and kissed her, and she was so charmed by the warmth of his smile, the admiration she saw in his eyes, that she forgave him on the instant for having neglected her when she was in Newgate.

"Why, Almsbury!"

The questions rose immediately to her tongue: Where's Bruce? Have you seen him? Is he here? But her pride bit them down.

He stepped back now and his eyes went over her from head to toe. "You're looking mighty prosperous, sweetheart! Matters have gone swimmingly with you, I doubt not—"

Amber forgot Luke Channell and Newgate and Whitefriars. She gave him a little smile with the corners of her mouth and answered airily. "Oh, well enough. I'm an actress now—in the Theatre Royal."

"No! I'd heard they have females on the stage now—but you're the first I've seen. I've been in the country for two years past."

"Oh. Then maybe you never got my letter?"

"No—did you write me?"

She made a light gesture of dismissal. "Oh, it was a great while since. In December, a year and a half gone."

"I left town just after—at the end of August in '60. I tried to find you, but the host at the Royal Saracen said you'd packed and gone to parts unknown, and the next day I left myself for Herefordshire—his Majesty granted me my lands again."

At that moment the noise about them swelled deafeningly, for the Royal barge had reached the pier and the King and Queen were getting out, while the Queen Mother came forward to meet them.

"Good Lord!" shouted Amber. "What the devil is her Majesty wearing?" From the distance the Queen's propped-out skirts made her look almost as wide as she was tall, and as she moved they rocked and swayed precariously.

"It's a farthingale!" bellowed Almsbury. "They wear 'em in Portugal!"

When at last the crowds began to break up Almsbury took her arm, asking if he might carry her to her lodgings. They turned, to find Barbara with a man's wide-brimmed hat on her head, standing only a few feet away, and she gave Almsbury a wave and a smile, though her eyes slid with unmistakable hostility over Amber. Amber lifted her chin, lowered her lashes, and sailed by without a glance.

Her coach was waiting in King Street with a great many others, just outside the Palace Gate, and at sight of it Almsbury gave a low whistle. "Well! I didn't know acting was such a well-paid profession!"

Amber took the cloak which Jeremiah handed her and tossed it over her shoulders, for evening had set in and it was growing cool. Picking up her skirts she gave him a sly smile over her shoulder.

"Maybe acting isn't. But there's another that is." She climbed in, laughing as he sat down heavily beside her.

"So our innocent country-maid has listened to the Devil after all."

"What else could I do after—" She stopped quickly, colouring, and then hastily added, "There's only one way for a woman to get on in the world, I've found."

"There's only one way for a woman to get on very well—or very far. Who's your maintainer?"

"Captain Morgan, of his Majesty's Horse Guard. D'you know 'im?"

"No. I think I'm somewhat out of the fashion, in keepers and clothes alike. There's nothing will run a man out of the mode so quick as a wife and a home in the country."

"Oh! So now you're married!" Amber gave him a roguish grin, almost as though he had just admitted some indiscretion.

"Yes, now I'm married. Two years the 5th of next month. And I've got two boys—one a little over a year and another just two months. And—a—weren't you—" His eyes went down over her questioningly, but he hesitated.

"I have a boy, too!" cried Amber suddenly, unable to control herself any longer. "Oh, Almsbury, you should see him! He looks just like Bruce! Tell me, Almsbury: Where is he? Has he been back to London? Have you seen him?" She did not care any longer about seeming flippant and independent. She was happy with Rex and had almost thought that she was no longer in love with Bruce Carlton—but the mere sight of Almsbury had brought it all churning up again.

"I've heard that he's in Jamaica and sails from there to take Spanish ships. Lord, sweetheart, don't tell me you're still—"

"Well, what if I am!" cried Amber, tears in her voice, and she turned her head quickly to look out the window.

Almsbury's tone was soothing. He moved closer and put an arm about her. "Here—darling. Good Lord, I'm sorry."

She dropped her head onto his shoulder. "When do you think he'll come back? He's been gone two years—"

"I don't know. But I suppose one of these days when we least expect it he'll be putting into port."

"He'll stay here then, won't he? He won't go away again, will he?"

"I'm afraid he will, sweetheart. I've known Carlton for twenty years, and most of that time he's been just coming home or just going away. He doesn't stay long in one place. It must be his Scottish blood, I think, that sends him off adventuring."

"But it'll be different —now that the King's back. When he has money he can live at Court without having to crawl on his belly—that's what he said he didn't like."

"It was more than that. He doesn't like the Court."

"Doesn't like it! Why, that's ridiculous! That's where everybody would live—if they could!"

Almsbury shrugged. "Nevertheless he doesn't like it. No one does—but few of 'em have got the guts to leave."

Amber shook her shoulders, pouting, and leaned forward to get out as the coach drew up before her lodging-house. "That sounds like damned nonsense!" she muttered crossly.

Her maid, Gatty, was not in, for Amber had given her permission to see the pageant and then pay a visit to her father. Prudence she had long since dismissed when she had come home unexpectedly to find the girl parading about in her best and newest gown. And there had been two others before Gatty, one sent away for pilfering and the other for laziness. Amber sent Jeremiah to bring them some food from the Bear, an excellent nearby ordinary which sold French food cooked by Englishmen. Her meals were all sent in, from taverns or cookshops.

She showed him her rooms with great pride, pointing out every detail so that he should miss nothing. Rex was generous and gave her almost everything she asked for; consequently he spent much of his time when not on duty gambling in the Groom Porter's Lodge or at a tavern.

Among her recent acquirements was a chest of drawers from Holland made of Brazilian kingwood—chocolate brown with black veins, decorated with a great deal of florid Dutch carving. There was a lacquered black Chinese screen, and in one corner stood a what-not loaded with tiny figures: a tree of coral, a blown-glass stag, an old Chinese knife-grinder worked in silver filigree. And over the fireplace hung a three-quarter portrait of Amber.

"What d'you think of me?" she asked, gesturing toward the portrait, tossing her muff and fan aside.

Almsbury put his hands in his pockets and leaned back on his heels, examining it with his head to one side. "Well, sweetheart, I'm glad I saw you in the flesh first, or I should have been troubled to think you'd grown so plump. And who sat for the mouth? That isn't yours."

She laughed beckoning him into the bedroom where she

began to unpin her back hair. "Being in the country hasn't changed you so much, Almsbury. You're still as great a courtier as ever. But you should see the miniature Samuel Cooper did of me. I'm supposed to be Aphro—I forgot what he called it—Venus, anyway, rising from the sea. I stand like this—" she struck an easy graceful pose, "and haven't got a thing on."

Almsbury, sitting astride a low chair with his arms folded across the back, gave a low appreciative hum. "Sounds mighty pretty. Where is it?"

"Oh, Rex has it. I gave it to him for his birthday and he's carried it ever since—over his heart." She grinned mischievously and began untying the bows down the front of her gown. "He's mad in love with me. Lord, he even wants to marry me now."

"And are you going to?"

"No." She shook her head vigorously, indicating that she did not care to discuss the matter. "I don't want to get married."

Picking up her dressing-gown, she went behind the screen to put it on. Just her head and shoulders showed over the top of it, and as she took off her garments, tossing them out one by one, she kept up a merry chatter with the Earl.

Finally the waiter arrived and they went into the dining-room to eat. Rex had sent her a message that he would be on duty at the Palace until late, or she would never have dared eat her supper with a man, wearing only a satin dressing-gown. For she had discovered long ago that Rex was not joking when he said that if he took her into keeping he would expect a monopoly of her time and person. He kept the beaus from crowding her too closely or impudently at the theatre and discouraged them from visiting her—though all the actresses held their levées at home just as the Court ladies did and entertained numbers of gentlemen while they were dressing. The result was that during the last few months they had quite given up Mrs. St. Clare. Rex had a formidable reputation as a swordsman, and most of the tiring-room fops would rather see an apothecary for a clap, than a surgeon for a flesh-wound.

Throughout the meal Amber and the Earl talked with all the animation of old friends who have not met for a long while and who have a great deal to say to each other. She told him about her successes, but not her failures, her triumphs but not her defeats. He heard nothing of Luke Channell or of Newgate, Mother Red-Cap or Whitefriars. She pretended that she still had left a good deal of Lord Carlton's five hundred pounds, deposited with her goldsmith, and he admitted that she had been far more clever than most young country girls left to shift for themselves in London.

It was two hours later as they sat on her long green velvet-cushioned settle, empty wine-glasses in their hands and staring into the last glow of the sea-coal fire, that Almsbury drew her into his arms and kissed her. For a moment she hesitated, her body tense, thinking of Rex and how furious he would be if another man kissed her, and then—because she liked Almsbury and because he meant Bruce Carlton to her—she relaxed against him and made no protest until, at last, he asked her to go into the bedroom.

Then suddenly she shook back her hair and pulled the front of her gown together. "Oh, Lord Almsbury! I can't! I should never have even let you think I would!" She got up, feeling a little dizzy from the wine, and leaned her head against the mantelpiece.

"Good God, Amber, I thought you were grown up now!" He sounded exasperated and more than a little angry.

"Oh, it isn't that, Almsbury. It isn't because I'm still—" She was about to say "waiting for Bruce," but stopped. "It's Rex. You don't know him. He's jealous as an Italian uncle. He'd murder you in a trice—and turn me out of keeping."

"He wouldn't if he didn't know anything about it."

She smiled skeptically, turning her head to look at him, though her hair fell forward over her face. "Was there ever a man yet who could lie with a woman and not tell all his acquaintance within the hour? The gallants say that's half the pleasure of fornication—telling about it afterwards."

"Well, I'm no gallant, and you damned well know it. I'm just a man who's in love with you. Oh, maybe I shouldn't say that. I don't know whether I'm in love with you or not. But I've wanted you since the first day I saw you. You know now that what I told you that night is true, so don't put me off any longer. How much do you want? I'll give you two hundred pound—put it with your goldsmith, toward the day when you'll need it."

The money was a convincing argument, but the thought that someday Bruce Carlton might hear about it—and be hurt—was even more so.

It was true, as Amber had told Almsbury, that Rex Morgan wanted to marry her. During the past seven months they had been happy and content, leading a life of merry companionable domesticity. They took an instinctive pleasure in doing the same things, and it was heightened always by a warm suffusing glow of happiness at the mere fact of being together.

The summer just past they had been together most of the time, for with the King out of town Rex had no official duties and the theatres were always closed for a vacation period of several weeks—though twice Amber had gone down with the rest of the Company to perform before their Majesties at Hampton Court. With Prudence or Gatty or whomever she might have in service, they would pack a hamper and ride out Goswell Street on warm June evenings to eat a picnic supper at the lonely, pretty little village of Islington. Several times they found a quiet spot in the river and pulled off their clothes to go swimming, laughing and splashing in the cool clean water, and afterwards while she dried her hair Rex would catch a few fish for them to take home.

Or they rowed up the river in a hired scull, Amber with her shoes and stockings off and her ankles trailing in the water, screaming with delighted laughter to hear Rex bandy insults and curses with the watermen—caustic-tongued old ruffians who amused themselves by hooting and jeering obscenely at everyone who ventured upon the river, whether Quakeress or Parliament man. At Chelsea they would get out to lie dreamily in the thick meadow grass, watching the clouds as they formed and passed overhead, and Amber would fill her skirt with wild-flowers, yellow primroses, blue hyacinths, white dogwood. Then she would open the hamper and spread a clean white linen cloth, laying on it the potted neat's tongue, the salad which the celebrated French cook at Chatelin's had made for her with twenty different greens, fresh ripe fruits, and a dusty bottle of Burgundy.

They seldom quarrelled—only when, rightly or wrongly, Rex's jealousy was aroused, though before she had seen Almsbury she had never been unfaithful to him. But she did drive out to Kingsland to see the baby once a week. For a long while she contrived to keep her visits secret from him, but one day, to her astonishment, he accused her of having been with another man. During the violent quarrel which ensued she told him where she had been—and told him also that she was married.

For two or three days he was angry, but no matter what lies he caught her in he did not seem to love her less, and even after that he asked her again to marry him. She had refused before, pretending that she thought he was only joking, but now she objected that it was impossible. Bigamy was punishable by death.

"He'll never come back," said Rex. "But if he does—well, you let me alone for that. I'll see to it you're a widow, not a bigamist."

But Amber could not make up her mind to do it. She still had a lingering horror of matrimony, for it seemed to her a trap in which a woman, once caught, struggled helplessly and without hope. It gave a man every advantage over her body, mind and purse, for no jury in the land would interest itself in her distress. But neither that horror nor the greater one she had of being prosecuted for bigamy was the real reason behind her refusal. She hesitated because in her heart she still nursed an imp of ambition, and it would not let her rest.

If I marry Rex, she would think, what will my life be? He'd make me quit the stage and I'd have to start having babies. (Rex resented the child she had had—he thought by her first husband—even though he had never seen the little boy, and had a sentimental desire for her to bear him a son.) And then most likely he'd grow more jealous than ever and if I so much as came home a half-hour late from the 'Change or smiled at a gentleman in the Mall he'd tear himself to pieces.

He probably wouldn't be as generous as he is now, either, and if I spent thirty pound for a new gown there'd be trouble and he'd think last year's cloak could do me again. First thing you know I'd grow fat and pot-bellied and dwindle into a wife —and before I was twenty my life would be over. No, I like it better this way. I've got all the advantages of being a wife because he loves me and won't put me aside, and none of the disadvantages because I'm free and my own mistress and can leave him any time I like.

She had heard that King Charles had remarked more than once he considered her to be the finest woman on the stage, and that in particular after her last performance at Hampton Court he had told someone he envied the man who kept her.

A fortnight or so after Almsbury's return to town Amber got a new maid. She dismissed Gatty one day when the girl surprised her taking a bath and talking to his Lordship, sending her away with the warning that Almsbury had a great interest at Court and would order her tongue cut out if she spoke to anyone at all of what she had seen. She told Rex that she had turned the girl away because she was pregnant, and sent Jeremiah to post a notice for a serving-woman in St. Paul's Cathedral, where a good deal of such business was done.

But that same morning as she was riding from the New Exchange to a rehearsal, her coach stopped at the golden-crowned Maypole, and while Tempest was bellowing abuse at the driver and occupants of the coach that blocked his way, the door was flung open and a girl leaped in. Her hair was dishevelled and her eyes looked wild.

"Please, mam!" she cried. "Tell 'im I'm your maid!" Her pretty face was intense and pleading, her voice passionate. "Oh, Jesus! Here he comes! *Please,* mam!" She gave Amber a last imploring look and then retreated far back into one corner, pulling the hood of her cloak up over her red-blonde curls.

Amber stared at her in amazement and then, before she could speak a word, the door was thrown open and a blue-coated constable, carrying his staff of office, pushed his head in at them. At this Amber gave an involuntary backward start. But, remembering that a constable could mean nothing to her now, she quickly recovered herself.

He made her a half salute, evidently mistaking her for a lady of quality. "Sorry to trouble you, mam, but that wench just stole a loaf of bread. I arrest you," he shouted, "in the King's name!" And he lunged across Amber toward the girl, who cowered far into one corner, skirts drawn close about her. Even from where she sat, Amber could feel her tremble.

Suddenly furious, all her memories of Newgate rising like a tide, Amber brought her fan down with a hearty smack on the constable's wrist. "What are you about, sir? This girl is my serving-woman! Take your hands off her!"

He looked up at her in surprise. "Well, now, mam— I wouldn't care to be calling a lady a liar—but she just stole a loaf of bread from off that bulk over there. I seen 'er myself."

He leaned far in now, grabbing hold of the girl's ankle and dragging her toward him. A curious restless crowd was beginning to gather outside in the street—and as Amber gave him a kick in the chest with the toe of her shoe and a violent shove that sent him staggering, a loud joyous laugh went up. He lurched back; she leaned forward and slammed the door shut.

"Drive on, Tempest!" she shouted, and the coach rolled off, leaving justice to pick itself up from a swimming kennel of rain-washed filth.

For a moment both women were silent, the girl staring at Amber with gratitude, Amber breathing heavily from anger and the nervousness which the sight of a constable still roused in her.

"Oh—mam!" she cried at last. "How can I ever thank you? But for you, he'd have carried me off to Newgate! Lord, I didn't see 'im till he made a grab for me, and then I ran—I ran as fast as anything but the old fat pricklouse was right on my heels! Oh, *thank* you, mam, a million times! It was mighty kind for a great lady like yourself to care what happens to the likes of me. It wouldn't 've been any skin off your arse if I'd gone to Newgate—"

She rattled along in a quick light musical voice, the expressions playing vivaciously over her pretty face. She could have been no more than seventeen, fresh and dainty with clear blue eyes, light lashes and brows, and a golden sprinkle of freckles over her little scooped nose. Amber smiled at her, liking her immediately.

"These damned impertinent constables! The day's a loss to 'em that they don't throw a half-a-dozen honest citizens into jail!"

The girl lowered her lashes guiltily. "Well—to tell you truly, mam, I did steal that loaf of bread. I've got it here." She tapped her cloak, beneath which it was concealed. "But I couldn't help it, I swear I couldn't! I was so hungry—"

"Then go ahead and eat it."

Without an instant's hesitation she took out the crusty split-topped loaf, broke a piece off one end and crammed it into her mouth, chewing ravenously. Amber looked at her in surprise.

"How long since you've eaten?"

The girl swallowed, took another great bite and answered with her mouth full. "Two days, mam."

"Ye Gods! Here, take this and buy yourself a dinner."

From a little velvet bag inside her muff she emptied several shillings and dropped them into the girl's lap. By now they had drawn up before the theatre and the footman came to open the door. Amber gathered her skirts and prepared to get out and the girl leaned forward, staring through the glass windows with great interest.

"Lord, mam, are you goin' to the play?"

"I'm an actress."

"You are!" She seemed both pleased and shocked that her benefactress should be engaged in so exciting and disreputable a profession. But immediately she jumped out on her own side and ran around to make her curtsy to Amber. "Thank you, mam. You were mighty kind to me, and if ever I can do a good thing for you, I wish you'd be pleased to call on me. I'll not forget, you may be sure. Nan Britton's my name—serving-woman, though without a place just now."

Amber stopped, looking at her with interest. "You're a serving-woman? What happened to your last place?"

The girl lowered her eyes. "I was turned out, mam." Her voice dropped almost to a whisper and she added, "The lady said I was debauchin' her sons." But she looked up quickly then and added with great earnestness, "But I wasn't mam! I vow and swear I wasn't! 'Twas just the other way around!"

Amber laughed. "Well, my son's not old enough to be debauched. I'm looking for a woman myself, and if you want to wait in the coach after you've had your dinner we'll talk about this later."

She hired Nan Britton at four pounds a year and her clothes and lodging and food. Within three or four days they were good friends—Amber felt that Nan was the first real woman friend she had ever had—and Nan did her work quickly and well, taking the same delight in polishing a pewter pitcher or arranging Amber's hair that she did in riding to the 'Change or accompanying her and Rex on a visit to the Spring Gardens.

She was energetic, vivacious, and unfailingly good-natured, and as she became more sure of her place and accustomed to it, these qualities remained. Nan and Amber found much to discuss, exchanging the most unabashed feminine confidences, and while Nan learned almost all that there was to know about her mistress (except that she had been in Newgate and Whitefriars) Amber likewise heard the tale of Nan's adventures as a girl-servant in a household where there were four handsome boys. Her dismissal had come when one of them, deciding that he had fallen in love with Mrs. Nan, announced to his horrified parents that he intended to marry her.

When Rex was not there Nan shared the bed, but otherwise she slept on the trundle. As was customary, she was as much his personal servant as she was Amber's, helped him in and out of his clothes, was not embarrassed to be in the room when he was naked, and soon decided that Captain Morgan was the finest gentleman she had ever known. He enlisted her on his side and she urged Amber again and again to marry him.

"How Captain Morgan loves you, mam!" she would say in the mornings, while she brushed Amber's hair. "And he's the handsomest person, and the most genteel! I vow, he'd make any lady a mighty fine husband!"

But Amber, who merely laughed at first and teased Nan with having fallen in love with him herself, grew less and less interested in such advice. "Captain Morgan's well enough, I suppose," she said finally. "But after all, he's only an officer in the King's Guard."

"Well!" cried Nan, offended at such disloyalty. "And who will you have, mam? The King himself?"

Amber, smiling at this sarcasm, gave a superior lift of her eyebrows. She was just setting out for the theatre and now began pulling on her gloves. "I might at that," she drawled and, when Nan gasped, repeated, "Yes, I might at that." She strolled toward the door, leaving Nan staring pop-eyed after her, but just with her hand on the knob she turned suddenly. "But don't you dare breathe a word of this to Captain Morgan, d'ye hear me!"

After all, it might be only gossip that King Charles had told Buckingham who had told Berkeley who had told Kynaston who had told Amber that the King had a mind to lay with her.

Chapter Nineteen

AMBER UNLOCKED THE door and started up the steps two at a time. She was eager to look at herself in a mirror, for she was sure that she must be very much changed. She had almost reached the top when the door to her apartments was flung open, and Rex loomed there above her. The light was at his back and she could not see the expression of his face, but knew by his voice that he was angry.

"Where in hell have you been?" he demanded. "It's half after two!"

Amber paused for one astonished moment, staring at him almost as if he were some intruding stranger. And then, with, a haughty lift of her chin, she came on toward him and would have gone by without a word, but he grabbed her wrist and snatched her up close to him. His eyes had the dangerous glitter she had seen before when his ready jealousy was aroused.

"Answer me, you jilting little baggage! The plays at Whitehall are done by eleven! Who've you been with since then!"

For a long moment they stared at each other, and then at last Amber gave a pout and winced. "You're hurting me, Rex," she whimpered.

His face relaxed, and though he hesitated a moment he released her. But just as she moved away a heavy bag dropped out of her muff and fell clanking to the floor; by the sound it could only contain money. Both of them looked down at it, and then as Amber raised her eyes she saw that his were narrowed and gleaming with rage, and that the veins in his neck stood out.

"You God damned whoring little bitch," he said softly.

And then suddenly he grabbed her by the shoulders and began to shake her, harder and harder, until her head snapped back and forth so fast she felt that the top of it would come off.

"Who was it?" he shouted. "Who've you been laying with! Tell me, or by Jesus I'll break your neck!"

"Rex!" she cried imploringly. But the moment he let her go and she began to recover her senses her own rage mounted to heedless violence. "I was with the King!" she yelled at him. *"That's* where I was!" She began massaging her neck, and ended with a mutter, "Now what've you got to say!"

For a long moment he stared at her, incredulous at first, and then slowly, gradually, she saw the crumpling of his hopes and confidence. "You weren't," he said at last. "I don't believe it."

Her hands went up to arrange her hair where it had come loose, and she gave him a cruel superior little smile. "Oh, don't you?"

But he did and she knew it.

Then without another word he turned, took his cloak and sword and hat from the chair where he had left them, and started across the room. He gave her a last look of contempt and disgust before he went out, but she met it with merely a cool lift of the eyebrows. And as the door slammed behind him she gave a snap of her fingers, swirled about quickly and ran into the bedroom to a mirror.

For surely a woman who had been made love to by a king could not look like any common mortal. She half expected a glow, a luminous shimmer to her skin and hair, and was disappointed to see that she looked no different except that her hair was tumbled and there were tired shadows beneath her eyes.

But I'm not the same! she assured herself triumphantly. I'm somebody now! I've lain with the King!

When Nan tried to wake her the following morning she shooed her away, rolling over onto her stomach, saying she'd sleep as long as she liked and they could do without her at rehearsal. By the time she finally did wake up it was almost noon and the rehearsal long since over. She yawned and stretched, sliding back the heavy draperies which had made the bed so hot and sultry that she was wet all over, and then suddenly she reached beneath the feather mattress and brought out the bagful of coins, dumping them onto the pillow so that she could count them again.

There was fifty pounds. Only to think of it—fifty pounds as a gift for the greatest honour a woman could have.

Before going to the theatre she took the money to deposit

with Shadrac Newbold, and when she finally got there it was after two. As she had expected her appearance in the tiring-room created a considerable sensation; all the women began to babble and shriek at once. Beck ran to throw her arms about her.

"Amber! We thought you weren't coming at all! Quick! Tell us about it—we're a-dying to hear! What was it like?"

"How much money did he give you?"

"What did he say?"

"How long were you there?"

"What did he do?"

"Was it different than it is with ordinary men?"

It was the first time that King Charles had sent for a player and their feelings were divided between personal jealousy and occupational pride. But curiosity over-rode both.

Amber was not reticent; she answered all their questions. She described the rooms of Edward Progers where she had been received first, the appearance of the King in his brocade dressing-robe, the new-born puppies which had slept beside their mother on a velvet cushion near the fireplace. She told them that he had been as kind and easy, as courteous as though she were a lady of the highest rank. But she did not add that she had been so scared she thought she would faint, and she hinted that he had given her at least a thousand pounds.

"When are you going again?" Beck asked at last, as Scroggs began to help Amber out of her clothes.

"Oh," she said casually, "sometime soon, I suppose. Maybe next week."

She was very confident, for though she had not spent more than an hour with him she had come away feeling that of all the women he had known she had pleased him best. It did not occur to her that perhaps the others had thought the same.

"Well, madame!" It was Tom Killigrew's voice, sounding cold and sarcastic as he made his way through the crowded room toward her. "So at last you've come."

Amber looked up in surprise, and then gave him a friendly smile. She was prepared to be no different from usual, in spite of her changed status—at least until she was more secure in her new place. "I'm a little late," she admitted, ducking her head into her gown which Scroggs held for her.

"You were not at rehearsal this morning, I believe."

"No." She thrust her arms through the sleeves and as Scroggs pulled the dress down her head appeared once more. "But that's no matter. I've played the part a dozen times—I know it well enough without rehearsing." She took up a mirror and half turned to face the light, examining the paint on her face and wiping away a little smear of lip-rouge rubbed onto her chin as she had struggled into the gown.

"With your permission, Madame St. Clare, I shall decide who will rehearse and who will not. I've given your part to

Beck Marshall—I don't doubt you'll be able to play the strumpet well enough without rehearsal."

There was a concerted giggle at that. Amber shot Beck a quick glare and caught a smug look of mischief on her face. She was on the verge of bursting out that she would play her own part or none at all, when caution warned her. "But I know my lines! I know every one of 'em if I never rehearsed again! And the other's but a small part!"

"Perhaps it is, madame, but those who are too much occupied elsewhere must learn to be content with small parts—or with no part at all." He glanced around at the sparkling, smiling faces, on which malicious pleasure was but ill concealed. "And I advise all of you to keep that in mind—should another head be turned by attention from high places. Good-day." He swung about and left the room.

Amber was furious that he should have dared to treat her like that, and consoled herself with the promise that one day she would get even with him. I'll get his patent and run him out of the theatre, that's what I'll do! But for the benefit of the others she gave a shrug and a pout of her mouth.

"Pooh! Much I care! Who wants to be a player anyway?"

As the days began to pass, however, her disgrace was not alleviated by another request from the King. She continued to play small roles—and to wait for another invitation. No one let her forget that she had been sent for once and had expected to go again; the other women, even some of the actors, and the gallants who came back to the tiring-room, all knew about it and taunted her slyly. They seemed to have grown more insolent than ever. And Amber, though she tried to toss off the gibes with a laugh or counter them with some impertinence of her own, was sick at heart, disappointed and miserably unhappy. She felt that after all her bragging she would die of shame if he sent for her no more.

And though she had thought in her first high-flown confidence that she did not care whether or not she ever saw Rex again, she soon began to miss him. It was not quite a week after their quarrel that Beck told her he had given a diamond ring to Mrs. Norris of the rival playhouse and that she was saying he had offered to take her into keeping.

"Well, why tell me about it! It's nothing to me if he gives diamond rings to every tawdry little whore in Whetstone Park!"

But it was all bravado.

She was learning that Rex Morgan was more important to her happiness than she had ever suspected he could be. Though she had not realized it before, she knew now that he had protected her from much that would otherwise have been unpleasant. The tiring-room fops, for example, would never have dared patronize and bait her as they were doing. Without him she felt that she had been plunged suddenly into a hard and bleak world which hated her and wished her nothing but misfortune.

There was no kindness or sympathy in any of them—they enjoyed her failure, battened upon her humiliation, were amused by her not-well-concealed anger and frustration.

She began to wish again that she had never seen Lord Carlton and never come to London.

Nan, however, continued optimistic even when ten days had gone by. She could think of more reasons why the King had been too busy to see her than he could possibly have found himself. "Don't be downcast, mam," she would say. "Lord, it takes up one's time—being a king."

But Amber refused to be comforted. Slumped in a chair before the fireplace, she muttered petulantly: "Oh, nonsense, Nan! You know as well as I do if I'd pleased 'im he'd have sent long ago!"

Nan sat beside her on a stool, working on a piece of embroidered satin, pale green with a whole English gardenful of flowers on it, which she intended as a petticoat for Amber. Now she gave a little sigh and made no answer, for she was finally beginning to grow discouraged herself. But when, just a few minutes later, there was a knock at the door she leaped up and rushed across the room.

"There!" she cried triumphantly. "That must be him now!"

Amber, however, merely looked around over the back of her chair toward the door, expecting to see one of the gallants or perhaps Hart or Kynaston come to visit her. But as Nan threw open the door she saw that a young boy stood there, dressed in some unfamiliar livery, and she heard him ask:

"Madame St. Clare?"

"I'm Madame St. Clare!" She jumped up and ran across the room. "What is it?"

"I come from Mr. Progers, madame. My master presents his service to you and asks if you will wait upon him at his lodgings tonight at half-after eleven?"

It was the royal summons!

"Yes!" cried Amber. "Yes, of course I will!"

She picked up a coin off the table and gave it to him, and when he was gone she turned to throw her arms about Nan. "Oh, Nan! He did like me! He did remember! Only think! Tonight I'm going to the Palace!"

Suddenly she paused, made a stiff little bow and said: "Madame St. Clare? My master presents his service to you and asks if you will wait upon him tonight at his lodgings." And then she spun around and danced off across the room, laughing joyously. But in the midst of a whirl she stopped, her face serious again. "What shall I wear!" And chattering excitedly the two women ran into the bedroom. The clock on the mantel pointed to nine.

This time she was more sure than ever that he liked her.

Some of her earlier awe and self-consciousness was gone and they laughed and talked like old friends; she thought him the most fascinating man she had met since Lord Carlton. When she left he said, as he had the time before, "Good-night, my dear, and God bless you," gave her a playful slap on the buttocks, and another bagful of coins.

Tempest and Jeremiah were waiting for her at the Holbein Gate and they set off swiftly for home, rattling and clanging through the night.

But the coach had no sooner turned into the Strand than a party of horsemen rushed at them from out of the shadows. Before Amber knew what was happening Tempest had been hauled down from his perch and Jeremiah knocked to the ground. The horses began to rear and neigh with excitement. Amber was looking around her, wondering what she should do, when the door was flung open. A masked man leaned in, seized her by the wrist and began dragging her toward him. Amber screamed and started to struggle, though she knew well enough what little good that could do.

He gave her a rough shake. "Stop that! I won't hurt you—just hand me that bagful of coins his Majesty gave you! Quick!"

Amber was kicking at him and trying to tear his fingers loose from her wrist. But now as she leaned over to bite his hand he gave her a violent shove that knocked her across the coach and half onto the floor and she could seen the gleam of moonlight on his levelled pistol. "Give me that bag, madame, or I'll shoot you! I have no time for playful tricks!"

Amber continued to hesitate, expecting to be rescued somehow, but as she heard the sound of thc pistol cocking she took the bag from her muff and tossed it at him. He caught it, gave her a bow and backed away. But just before the door shut she heard a woman's triumphant laugh and a voice cried: "Many thanks, madame! Her Ladyship appreciates your charity! I promise you the money will be laid out in good cause!" The door slammed and there was a sound of prancing horses' hoofs as they wheeled about and then started off again at a gallop—riding back down King Street toward the Palace.

Amber lay for a moment without moving, dumfounded. That voice! she thought. I've heard it somewhere before! And then suddenly she remembered: It was the same laugh, the same aggressive, high-pitched feminine voice she had heard that night outside the Royal Saracen—it was Barbara Palmer!

That was the last of Amber's visits to Whitehall.

The King, it was well known, liked to live in peace and quiet, and a jealous woman's sharp venomous tongue could make that impossible. Fortunately for her though, gossip spread that Charles had said he liked Madame St. Clare well enough—but not to the point of sacrificing his ease for her. And that was all that saved her. As it was they kept at her for several days, stinging and biting like malicious insects, but at last they grew tired of baiting her and found another victim.

By the time a fortnight had passed her life had settled back to normal. Everyone but Amber had forgotten that the King had ever sent for her.

But she did not forget or intend to forget. She nursed her new grievance against Barbara Palmer as carefully as she had the old. Someday, she promised herself, I'll make her sorry she ever was born. I'll find a way to get even with her if it's the last thing I do on earth! She spent much time and found much pleasure in imagining her revenge, but those images, like everything else she could not see or touch, slid gradually into some back compartment of her mind to be saved and brought out again when she had a use for them.

She had been entertaining, one night, a dozen young men and women whom she had invited to supper and they had just gone home, leaving the tables littered with dishes, the floors covered with nut-shells and fruit-peelings and a torn deck of cards. There were wine-bottles and glasses, with only a sticky sediment in the bottoms, the air was thick with tobacco smoke, and the furniture had all been pushed out of place.

While Nan began to pile up dishes and pick up nut-shells Amber went to stand with her back to the fireplace, raising her skirts to warm her buttocks. It was mid-December and the ground was covered with snow, the first in three years, and even the Thames was frozen over. For a while they talked idly about who had said what, whether a certain lady was now having an affair with a certain gentleman or with another, or with both, and discussed at some length the gowns and coiffures and figures of the women who had been present, to the detriment of each.

Amber had taken off her gown and stood yawning and stretching in her puff-sleeved smock and frilly petticoats, when a low knock sounded at the door. Both of them started and then looked at each other, and Amber waited tensely as Nan crossed the room and flung back the bolt. Can it be—can it—

It was Captain Morgan who stood there, his long riding-cloak thrown across his shoulder, his hat pulled low. He looked in and his eyes met hers, pleading, his expression that of a small boy who has run away and now returns to his home. Instantly forgetting that she hoped it might be the King's messenger, Amber ran to him with her arms outstretched.

"Rex!"

"Amber!" He swung her up off the floor, kissing her face again and again, and at last he gave a kind of sobbing exultant laugh. "Oh, my God! I'm *glad* to see you!" He put her onto her feet again but kept her in his arms, stroking her head, running his hands eagerly over her back. "Jesus, darling! I couldn't stay away any longer! I love you—oh, God, I love you so much!"

There were tears in his eyes and from behind them came Nan's surreptitious sniffle as she stood and watched them, smiling and crying at the same time. They both turned to look at her and suddenly all three of them began to laugh.

"Come in, Rex darling! Close the door. Oh, how sweet of you to come back! Why— Have you been waiting outside for the others to leave?"

He smiled, gave a nod.

"But you knew them all! Why didn't you just come in! Lord, it's bitter-cold out there!"

He hesitated: "Well—I wasn't sure you'd—let me in."

"Oh, Rex!"

Suddenly and thoroughly ashamed of herself Amber stood staring at him, fully aware for the first time how kind and generous and good he had been to her, and great tears rolled down her cheeks.

"Here, darling! What are you crying for, you little minx? This is a night for celebrating! Look at this—" He reached into his pocket and drew out a jeweller's box, holding it toward her.

Slowly Amber took it from him and as she opened it Nan edged forward so that she could see too. As she lifted the lid both women gave a cry of astonished delight: there was a great topaz stone set in a golden heart, depending from a heavy golden chain. She looked up at him, doubtfully, for it must have cost a great deal. "Oh, Rex!" she said softly. "It's beautiful—but—"

He gave a wave of his hand, dismissing her objections. "I had a run of luck with the dice not long ago. And here, Mrs. Nan, is something for you."

Nan opened the box he handed her to find a pair of gold ear-rings set with tiny pearls. She gave a little scream of pleasure and jumped up to kiss him on the cheek—for he was at least a foot taller than she—and then quickly recovering herself she blushed and curtsied and turned in confusion to run into the bedroom.

"Hey!" called Rex. "Just a moment there, Mrs. Nan! Your mistress and I have a fancy to that place." He swung Amber up in his arms and started toward it. "You'll have to sleep out here tonight, sweetheart. This is a very special occasion."

The months began to go by swiftly, for she was happy and popular and thought herself very famous. The winter was unusually cold and through December, January and February there were hard frosts with much snow and ice, but at last the frost broke and there came the slush and mud and the new green buds of spring. Killigrew had put her into leading parts again, and she was very busy with her singing and dancing and guitar lessons.

When they played at Court or when he came to the Theatre Amber saw King Charles, and though he sometimes smiled at her, that was all. She heard the gossip that he was less interested in Castlemaine than he had been and was now engrossed in lovely Frances Stewart, though so far, they said, he had not succeeded in overcoming her scruples. Some thought that Mrs. Stewart was a fool and others that she was very clever, but there was no doubt she had captured the fickle heart of the King, and that was distinction enough in itself. Amber did not care whom he fell in love with if only Barbara Palmer lost by it.

In the middle of February Amber found herself pregnant again. And though she hesitated for some time, not telling Rex but arguing with herself as to whether or not she should marry him, in the end she went to Mrs. Fagg and had an abortion. This time it took more than a pot of herbs and a ride in a hackney and made her so sick that she had to spend most of a week in bed. Rex was wild with anger and fear when he found what she had done and begged her to marry him immediately.

"Why won't you, Amber? You say you love me—"

"I do love you, Rex, but—"

"But what?"

"Well, what if Luke—"

"He'll never come back and you know it as well as I do! Even if he did, it wouldn't matter. I could either kill him or get someone at Court to have the marriage annulled. What is it, Amber? Sometimes I think you put me off in hopes the King will send for you again. Is that it?"

She was sitting half-propped up in bed, pale and sick and discouraged, staring at nothing. "No, Rex, that's not it. You know it isn't."

She was lying, for she did still hope, but nevertheless she was almost convinced that if she did not marry Rex Morgan now she would regret it in the future. What did it matter if she left the stage? She had been playing for a year and a half and could not see that she had got anything by it. Her nineteenth birthday was less than a month away and she felt that the time was passing rapidly, leaving her in a backwash. And it was true, as she had said, that she loved him, though she could never quite force from her heart the memory of Lord Carlton or her ambitions for a more glorious and exciting life.

"Let me think about it, Rex—just a little longer."

Her son was to be two years old on the 5th day of April and, because she would not be free that day, Amber planned instead to go out on the 1st and take him the gifts she had bought. Rex left at seven while it was still dark outside, and the eaves dripped with rain that had fallen during the night.

He kissed her tenderly. "Twelve hours until I'll see you again. Have a good trip, darling, and give the little fellow a kiss for me."

"Why, Rex! Thank you!" Amber's eyes sparkled with pleasure, for usually Rex ignored her trips as he wanted to ignore the fact that she had a child; but since she had almost agreed to marry him he had evidently decided that he must reconcile himself to his step-son. "I'll bring one back from him to you!"

He kissed her again, gave a wave of his hand to Nan Britton, and was gone. Amber closed the door softly, leaning back against it for a moment, smiling. "I think I'll marry him, Nan," she said at last.

"Lord, mam, you should! A finer, kinder gentleman never lived—it makes my heart ache to see how he loves you. You'd be happy, mam, I know you would."

"Yes," she agreed. "I suppose I would be happy. But—"

"But what?"

"But that's all I'd be."

Nan stared at her, shocked and uncomprehending. "Good God, mam! What else d'ye want?"

It was not long before the singing-master arrived, and after him came the dancing-master to put her through the steps of the minuet—a new French dance which everyone was busily learning. Meanwhile Jeremiah trudged again and again through the parlour carrying buckets of hot water to pour into the wooden tub in the bedroom for her bath.

Nan washed her hair and rubbed it almost dry, piling it on top of her head where she secured it with half-a-dozen bodkins. It was now close to ten and at last the sun had come out, for the first time in many days, so that where she sat in her tub the warmth fell across her bare shoulders and filled her with pleasure. She felt, as she usually did, that it was a wonderful thing to be alive, and was urging herself to leave the soapy luxury of her bath when there was a knock at the door.

"I'm not home," called Amber after Nan. She had no intention of having her plans for this day disturbed, for anyone at all.

Nan returned a moment later. "It's my lord Almsbury, mam."

"Oh. Well, bring 'im in then." Almsbury had not stayed long in town the last autumn but had recently come again for the spring session of Parliament and he visited her frequently—though he had given her no more money. But Amber did not care, for she was very fond of him. "Is he alone?"

"No, there's another gentleman with him." Nan rolled her eyes, but Nan was easily impressed by men.

"Have 'em wait in the parlour—I'll be out in a trice."

She stood and began to dry herself with a towel. From the other room came the low sound of the men's voices; occasionally Nan giggled or burst into a peal of delightful laughter. Amber slipped into a green satin dressing-gown, took the bodkins out of her still slightly damp hair and ran a comb through it, stuck her feet into a pair of golden mules and started out. But she turned back again. After all—he might have someone of some consequence with him. She patted a little powder over her face, touched a perfume stopper to her wrists and throat, and smoothed some carmine into her lips. Then, pulling the neck-line apart to show her breasts, she went to the door and opened it.

Almsbury stood before the fireplace and leaning against the mantel, smiling down at Nan, was Bruce Carlton.

Chapter Twenty

HE RAISED HIS head quickly as she came in and their eyes met. Amber stood perfectly still, one arm braced against the door-jamb, staring at him. She felt her head begin to whirl and her heart to pound and she was suddenly paralyzed, unable to move or speak. He bowed to her then but Amber merely stood and trembled, cursing herself for a fool, but utterly helpless.

Almsbury came to her rescue. He crossed the room, kissed her casually, and slipped one arm about her waist. "What d'you think, sweetheart! The scoundrel put into town yesterday!"

"Did you?" said Amber weakly.

Bruce smiled, his eyes going swiftly down over her body. "The sailor's home from the sea."

"To stay?"

"No—at least not for long. Amber, may I go with you today?"

She glanced at Almsbury in surprise, for she had forgotten that she had told him her plans for the baby's birthday. "Yes, of course. Will you wait while I dress?"

With Nan she went back into the bedroom and when the door was shut she sank against it, her eyes closed, as exhausted as though she had just finished some tremendous physical labour. Nan looked at her in alarm.

"Lord, mam! What is it? You don't look well. Is *he* your husband?"

"No." She gave a shake of her head, and started for the dressing-table, but her legs felt as though every bone and muscle had dissolved. "Will you get out that new gown Madame Drelincourt just finished?"

"But it's raining again, mam. You might spoil it."

"Never mind!" snapped Amber. "Just do as you're told!" But she was instantly apologetic. "Oh, Nan, I'm sorry. I don't know what's the matter with me."

"Neither do I, mam. I suppose you'll not be wanting my company today?"

"No. Not today. I think you'd better stay here and polish the silver—I was noticing last night it's somewhat tarnished."

But as she painted her face and Nan dressed her hair she began to grow calmer, the blood seemed to flow in her veins again, and a passionate happiness replaced the first stunning sense of shock. She had thought him more handsome than ever, and the sight of him had filled her with the same intense irrational excitement she had felt the first time she had ever seen him. The past two years and a half had dissolved and vanished. Everything else in her life seemed suddenly unimportant, and dull.

Her new gown was made of chartreuse-coloured velvet and her shoes and stockings matched it exactly; her hooded cloak was topaz velvet, almost the same honey-rich colour as her eyes and hair, and she wore Rex Morgan's topaz heart around her neck. She picked up her great mink muff and started for the door, but Nan stopped her: "When will you be home, mam?"

Amber tried to answer casually, from over her shoulder. "Oh, I don't know. Maybe I'll be a little late."

She saw disapproval on Nan's face and knew that she was jealous for Rex, thinking that she ought not to go out there with another man, particularly a man who affected her as this one did.

"What about Captain Morgan?"

"The devil with Captain Morgan!" muttered Amber, and went back in to join Almsbury and Bruce.

When they were all in the coach, several gaily wrapped packages piled beside Amber, Almsbury gave a sudden snap of his fingers. "By God, I'm engaged to play at tennis with Sedley! Damned lucky thing I remembered!" With that he climbed out again, grinning back at them from the doorway. Bruce laughed and slapped him on the shoulder, Amber blew him a kiss, and the coach started off.

Behind them the Earl and Nan exchanged looks. "Well," said his Lordship, "there's no friend to love like a long voyage at sea," and he climbed into his own coach and rattled off in the opposite direction.

Amber turned instantly to Lord Carlton. "Bruce! Oh—is it really and truly you! It's been such a long time—oh, darling, it's been two years and a half!"

She was close beside him as she looked up, her eyes seeming to swim in some luminous light, and his arm went around her. He bent his head swiftly and his mouth came down hard upon hers. Amber returned his kiss with wild abandon, forgetting where they were, straining toward him with a longing to be crushed and enveloped. She had a sense of plunging disappointment when he released her, as if she had been cut off in the midst of a dream, but he smiled and his fingers passed over her face, lightly caressing.

"What a charming little witch you are," he said softly.

"Oh, Bruce, *am* I? Do you think so? Did you ever think about me—way over there?" She was intensely serious.

"I thought about you a great many times—more than I expected. And I worried about you too. I was afraid that someone might get that money away from you—"

"Oh, no!" protested Amber immediately. She would have died rather than let him know what had happened to her. "Don't I look well enough?" A wave of her hand indicated her expensive clothes, the coach they rode in, her own triumph over the great world. "I can shift for myself, I'll warrant you."

He grinned, and if he saw through her bluff he gave no indication of it. "So it seems. But I should have known you would. You've got the world's most marketable commodity—enough for ten women."

"What's that?" she asked him, putting on a demure face.

"You damned well know what it is, and I'me not going to flatter you any more. Tell me, Amber: What does he look like? How big is he?"

"Who?" She looked at him in sudden surprise, thinking that he meant Rex Morgan, and then they both burst into laughter. "Oh, the Baby! Oh, Bruce, wait till you see him! He's grown so big I can hardly lift him. And he's so handsome! He looks just like you—his eyes are the same colour and his hair is getting darker all the time. You'll adore him! But you should have seen 'im at first. Lord, he was a fright! I was almost glad you weren't there—"

Both their faces sobered at that. "I'm sorry, darling. I'm sorry you had to be alone. You must have hated me for leaving you."

She put her hand over his and her voice was low and tender. "I didn't hate you, Bruce. I love you and I'll always love you. And I was glad I had him—he was a part of you that you'd left with me, and while I carried him I wasn't as lonely as I'd have been otherwise. But I don't want any more babies—it takes too long. Maybe someday when I get old and don't care how I look I'll have some more then."

He smiled. "And when will that be?"

"Oh, when I'm about thirty." She said it as though she would never be about thirty. "But tell me what you've been doing. What's in America? Where did you live? I want to know everything."

"I lived in Jamaica. It's an island, but I went to the mainland too. It's a wonderful country, Amber—wild and empty and untouched, the way England hasn't been for a thousand years. And it's over there waiting—for whoever will come to take it." He sat staring ahead now, talking softly and almost as though to himself. "It's bigger than anyone knows. In Virginia the plantations are spreading back from the coast, hundreds of thousands of acres, and still there's more land. There are wild horses and herds of wild cattle, and they belong to whoever can catch them. The forests are full of deer and every year the wild pigeons come over in clouds that blot out the sky. There's more than enough food in Virginia alone to feed everyone in England better than he's ever been fed before. The soil is so rich that whatever you plant grows like weeds. It's something to catch your imagination—something you never dreamed of—" He looked at her suddenly, his eyes glittering with passionate enthusiasm.

"But it isn't England!"

He laughed, relaxed again, the tension gone. "No," he agreed. "It isn't England."

As far as Amber was concerned that settled the matter, and they began to talk, instead, of his adventures at sea. He told her that the life was unpleasant, that nothing could make a man uglier than being shut up for weeks at a time on a ship with other men, but that it was not very dangerous and was a sure road to riches. That was why so many seamen preferred sailing with the privateers to joining the British navy or the merchant fleets. At that moment the Thames was crowded with prizes just brought into port and more were arriving every day.

"I suppose you're a mighty rich man, now."

"My fortunes are considerably improved," he admitted.

It took an hour and a half to reach Kingsland, for the road was unpaved most of the way and the recent heavy rains had turned it into a slough. Tempest and Jeremiah had to pry the wheels free a dozen times.

But at last they arrived and went around to the kitchen-door of Mrs. Chiverton's pretty little thatched cottage, where they found her just cleaning the remains of the noon-day meal. Amber had given her frequent and generous gifts of money, for she wanted her son to live in a comfortable home, and the cottage now had an air of pleasant warmth and friendliness that it had not had at first.

The baby lay in his cradle, which he had now almost outgrown, flat on his back and sleeping soundly. Amber put up a cautioning finger as they came in and, walking softly, went over to look at him. His cheeks were flushed and there was a sheen of moisture on his eyelids, his breathing came quietly and regularly. For a long moment Bruce and Amber stood staring down at him, and then their eyes turned and met in a look of mutual pride and congratulation. Lord Carlton's slender, hard aristocratic hands reached down and closed under his son's armpits and he lifted him to his chest.

He woke up then, yawning, looked in some surprise at the man who held him, and then catching sight of Amber broke into a sudden smile and reached out for her.

"Mother!"

After a while, when they had eaten a bowl of hot pottage which Mrs. Chiverton insisted they have, they began to unwrap the baby's presents. There were numerous toys, including drums and soldiers and a Jack-in-the-Pulpit—a Puritan preacher which popped out of a box and swayed comically from one side to the other. And there was a doll with real blonde hair and an extensive wardrobe which Amber had bought for Mrs. Chiverton's four-year-old daughter. They stayed until mid-afternoon, but when finally they got ready to leave, the baby cried and wanted to go with them. While Amber tried to quiet him Bruce gave Mrs. Chiverton fifty pounds, telling her that he was grateful for the good care his son had received.

It was raining again as they started back, Amber chattering with the greatest enthusiasm and excitement about the baby. For she had been pleased and a little surprised to find that Bruce—who she had half expected would be an indifferent father—seemed to love the child as much as she did. But even while she talked she was conscious again of the rising surge of passion in both of them, temporarily calmed and forced back while they had been at the cottage. Now it was once more wild and violent, immediately demanding, determined to sweep away two years and a half in a few moments of savage union.

Stopping in the midst of a sentence she turned and looked up at him. Bruce gave a swift glance out the window, and as one arm went about her he leant forward to rap on the side of the coach. "We're coming to Hoxton," he said quickly to Amber. "I know a good inn there. Hey!" he raised his voice to a shout. "Stop up here at the Star and Garter!"

When Amber got home, after nine o'clock that night, she found Nan sitting beside the fireplace mending one of Rex's shirts while he stood next to her, his hands jammed into his pockets and a scowl on his face. Amber paused, looking at him with a sense of surprise, for he seemed almost unreal to her—and then he had crossed the room and had her hands in his.

"My God, darling! What happened! I was just going out to try to find you!"

She forced a smile. "Nothing happened, Rex. The baby didn't want me to go and I kept staying on—and then the coach got stuck and once it almost turned over." She reached up to caress his cheek, a little sorry to have cheated him as she had, for he looked at her with such adoration and not the faintest hint of doubt or suspicion. "You mustn't worry about me all the time, Rex."

"I can't help it, darling. I love you, you know."

Amber turned away to escape the expression in his eyes and as she did so she saw Nan's look of disapproval and resentment.

Early the next morning, when they were alone, Amber asked her if she had told Rex about the visit of Almsbury and Lord Carlton. Nan was making the bed, smoothing out the sheets with a bed-staff, and she answered without looking at Amber,

"No, mam, I did not," she said crisply. "Lord, I'm sure I don't know why you should think I'd meddle in your business. I never have before. What's more. I wouldn't tell Captain Morgan you were playing him false for a thousand pound. It would break his heart!" She turned around all at once and the two women stood staring at each other; there was a gleam of moisture in Nan's eyes.

"You weren't so finical when it was the King I was playing him false with!"

"That was different, mam. That was serving the Crown. But this—this is wicked. Captain Morgan loves you beyond his own life— It's—it's not kind!"

Amber gave a sigh. "No, Nan, it's not kind. But I can't help it. I'm in love with Lord Carlton, mad in love with him. Nan! He's Bruce's father! Not my husband—I married Luke after Lord Carlton had gone to America. Oh, you've got to help me, Nan; help me to keep Rex from finding out. While he's here I've got to see him—and I will see him!—but he'll be gone soon, in a month or two, and when he's gone Rex will be none the wiser. I'll marry him then—to make it up to him. *Will* you help me, Nan? Will you promise?"

As Amber talked Nan's flexible face changed, her expressions shifting like the play of sunlight over water, and at the end she ran to throw her arms about Amber. "Oh, I'm sorry, mam! I didn't know—I didn't guess—I thought he was just some gentleman you'd taken a fancy to." Suddenly she smiled broadly, holding onto Amber's arms. "And so he's little Bruce's father! Oh, of course! Why, they look alike!" She gave a gasp and put one hand to her mouth. "Lord, but it's mighty lucky the Captain would never go out with you to see 'im! If he ever saw his Lordship—"

Carlton was staying at Almsbury House and two days later Amber sent a note inviting him, with Almsbury and his countess, to see the play—she wheedled Killigrew into reserving four seats in the front row of the King's Box—and she asked them to have supper with her in her apartments afterward. Lord and Lady Almsbury were intended as decoys in the event that Captain Morgan should arrive unexpectedly.

They accepted, and for the next forty-eight hours Amber was in a flurry of excited preparation. She had Nan call in a woman to help her clean so that every speck of dust was brushed from the drapes and the walnut furniture oiled and polished until it gleamed. She went herself to the New Exchange to buy a great supply of artificial silk flowers, since the fresh ones were not yet in bloom, and she badgered Madame Drelincourt into finishing a new gown for her several days before it had been promised. She consulted the head-cook at Chatelin's about the supper and the wine, trying to remember everything that Bruce liked best, and just before she left for the theatre she repeated once more to Nan the multifarious instructions which covered each smallest detail.

Halfway down the stairs she stopped suddenly, turned about, and ran back again. "Don't forget to put a decanter of water on the tray with the brandy, Nan! Lord Carlton likes it that way!"

She got there very early and, once dressed and painted, went down into the pit to circulate about among the young men. She made a great show of all her charm and gaiety, hoping that Lord Carlton would see her and be impressed and perhaps a little jealous to find how popular she was with all the fops. But it was almost three-thirty and she was once more back behind the curtains when she saw him come in.

Lord and Lady Almsbury walked ahead, going to the seats which Amber had sent some boys to keep for them; but as one of the ladies leaned back and put out a hand to take hold of Bruce's wrist he stopped, smiling, and bowed. Amber watched with anxious alarm while he bent over to hear what she was saying and saw her languid-eyed stare, the lazy intimate grasp which her hand kept on his, as though they had been long and well acquainted.

"Hey!" She heard Beck's voice suddenly just beside her. "Who's the handsome fellow my Lady Southesk is giving an assignation to?" Carnegie's husband had recently succeeded to the earldom of Southesk.

"That's Lord Carlton and he's *not* making her an assignation!"

Beck looked at her in mild surprise and then smiled. "Well—" she drawled. "And if he is or isn't—what's that to you, pray?"

Quick anger at her own foolishness rushed over Amber, for she knew well enough that in spite of the half-hearted friendship which existed between them nothing would please Beck so much as an opportunity to create trouble between her and Rex Morgan. "It's nothing at all to me! But I happen to know he's laid his affections elsewhere."

"Oh? And where's that?" Beck's voice was a musical purr and her eyes gleamed with sly malice.

"On my Lady Castlemaine!" snapped Amber, though it burnt her tongue to say it, and she flounced off.

She wished then that she had not invited Bruce to come back to the tiring-room after the play—for she knew that Beck's sharp eyes would be upon them—and just before the last act she sent a boy to their box with a note asking him to meet her at Almsbury's coach instead. She was not on the stage at the end of the play, and she rushed through her dressing to be ready to go by the time the crowds began streaming out of the theatre.

She left before anyone had returned to the tiring-room and made her way over to Almsbury's coach, where Bruce stood waiting at the opened door. "Bruce! I'm so glad to see you!" She lowered her voice and glanced quickly around, for she did not want to be seen or overheard by anyone who might know Rex. "I sent you that note because I thought—"

He smiled. "Never mind, Amber. No excuses are necessary.

I believe I know what you thought. May I present you to Lady Almsbury?"

She gave him a quick glance of indignation—for she wished he would not understand her motives so readily, or would be more offended by them when he did. But he seemed not to notice the look, took hold of her arm and began to make the introductions.

As Amber saw at once, Emily, Lady Almsbury, was by no means a beauty. Her hair, her eyes, even the clothes she wore, seemed indefinite in colouring, though there was nothing otherwise amiss in her features, and her teeth were white and even. Paint and false curls, a few patches and a low-necked gown, as well as a little natural audacity, might have made quite another woman of her. And it was noticeable that she was pregnant again.

Lord! thought Amber. How unprofitable it is to be a man's wife!

Bruce and Amber went to ride in her coach and with them went a little Negro boy who could have been no more than five or six and who had much ado to keep his master's cloak, which he carried, from getting into the mud. He was perfectly black and shiny, so that the whites of his eyes gleamed in his face, and as Amber smiled at him he gave her a broad ingratiating grin.

"This is Tansy," Bruce explained. "I got him a year ago in Jamaica."

Some of the nobility owned black servants, but Amber had never seen one of them at close range before and she examined him as though he were some small inanimate object or a new dog, looking at the pale-coloured palms of his hands and admiring the dazzling whiteness of his teeth. He wore a splendid suit of sapphire-blue satin and his head was wound in a silver-cloth turban, stuck through with a large ruby pin. But his shoes were shoddy and much too large for him and he was then easing the heel of one down off his foot with the toe of the other, while his big solemn eyes stared up at her.

"Oh, Bruce, what a pretty little moppet he is!" cried Amber. "Can he talk?" And without waiting for an answer she immediately asked him, "Why do they call you Tansy?"

" 'Cause my mother ate a tansy puddin' before I was born." He had a soft liquid voice which it was difficult for her to understand. He stood up in the coach, leaning with one elbow on the seat beside Bruce, and he did not once glance out the window at the busy streets through which they were passing.

"What does he do? What's he for?"

"Oh, he's very useful. He plays the merry-wang—that's a kind of guitar the Negroes have—and makes coffee. And of course he sings and dances. I thought perhaps you'd like to have him."

"Oh, Bruce, is he for me! You brought him across the ocean

for me! Oh, thank you! Tansy—how would you like to stay here in London with me?"

He looked from Amber to Bruce, then shook his head. "No, sir, mam. I's goin' back to see Mis' Leah."

Amber looked questioningly at Bruce, and caught a quick passing smile on his face. "Who's Miss Leah?"

"She's my housekeeper."

Instant suspicion showed in her eyes. "Is she a blackamoor too?"

"She's a quadroon."

"What the devil's that?"

"It's one who has a quarter Negro blood and the rest white."

Amber gave a mock shudder. "They must be a scurvy lot!"

"Not at all. Some of them are very beautiful."

"And do they call 'em all 'mis'?" she demanded sarcastically. "Or only yours!"

He smiled. "That's the way Tansy pronounces 'Mrs.' "

She gave him a sidewise glance of jealousy and mistrust, and though she wanted to ask him point-blank if the woman had been his mistress he was still a little strange to her and she did not quite dare. I'll ask Tansy, she decided. I can find out from him some way.

At that moment they stopped before her lodging-house. Bruce helped her out and whatever she was about to say to him was cut short by the appearance of Almsbury's coach, which had followed close behind them. She and the countess walked upstairs together, chatting about the weather and the play and the audience, and Amber found herself liking her very well, for she seemed kind and generous and apparently had none of the envy or malice which Amber habitually expected in a woman.

The meal was everything that Amber had hoped it would be.

There was a hot thick pea soup, steamingly fragrant, with leeks and chopped bacon and small crusty meat-balls that floated on the surface. There was roast duck stuffed with oysters and onions and walnuts; fried mushrooms; sweet biscuits; and an orange pudding baked in a dish lined with a crisp flaky puff-paste and decorated with candied orange-blossoms. And she had ordered a potful of black coffee because she knew that Bruce liked it—it was becoming a fashionable, though still an expensive, drink. The men were enthusiastic and Amber was as pleased as though she had cooked it all herself.

When supper was done they went into the parlour to talk; Amber and Lady Almsbury sat on the couch before the fire while the men took chairs, one on either side of them. For a few minutes Amber and her Ladyship discussed the new fashions—gowns were now being made with trains three feet long—and Bruce and the Earl talked of the Dutch war, which both were sure would come soon. But Amber presently grew tired of that. She had not invited Bruce there to talk to Almsbury.

"You say you're not here to stay, my lord," she said now, turning to him. "What do you intend doing?"

Bruce, who sat with both elbows resting on his wide-spread legs, holding his brandy glass in his two hands, glanced across at Almsbury before he answered her.

"I'm going back to Jamaica."

"Why there, for Heaven's sake? I've heard it's a nasty place."

"Nasty or not, it's a very good place for my purpose."

"And what's your purpose, pray?" She was thinking of Mrs. Leah.

"To get some more money."

"Some more? Aren't you rich enough by now?"

"Is anyone ever rich enough any time?" Almsbury wanted to know.

Amber ignored him. "Well, now, sure you don't intend to be a pirate all the rest of your life!" She knew well enough what was the difference between a pirate and a privateer, but liked to make his profession sound as disreputable as she could.

Bruce smiled. "No. Another year or two, perhaps, depending on what luck I have—and then I'm through."

Her face brightened. "Then you'll come back here to stay?"

He drew a deep breath, drained his glass, and as he answered her he started to get up. "Then I think I'll go to America and plant tobacco."

Amber stared at him, nonplussed. "Go to America!" she cried, and then added, "To plant tobacco! Why, you must be out of your head!" Suddenly she sprang up and ran after him where he had gone to pour himself another glass of brandy. "Bruce! You're not serious!"

He looked down at her. "Why not? I don't intend to stay here and play at cross-or-pile with the Court politicians for the next thirty years."

"But why America! It's so far away! Why not plant your tobacco here—in England?"

"For one thing, there's a law against planting tobacco in England. And even if there were not it would still be impractical. The soil isn't suitable and tobacco culture requires a great deal of ground—it exhausts the land quickly and you've got to have room to spread out."

"But what will you get by it? You won't need money over there—money's no good if you're not where you can spend it!"

He did not answer her, for just then the door opened and Rex Morgan came in; and paused in surprise to find her staring up so intensely at a man he had never seen before. Amber was disappointed and a little troubled, wondering what her expression had been at the moment he had opened the door, but immediately she ran to take his hand, welcoming him gaily.

"Come in, darling! I wasn't expecting you and we've eaten

everything but the nut-shells! Here—let me present my guests—"

Rex had already met Almsbury but neither the Countess nor Bruce, and once the introductions were acknowledged Amber made a quick suggestion that they play cards. She did not want the men to begin talking. They sat down to a five-handed game of lanterloo and as Almsbury began to shuffle the cards Amber saw Rex and Lord Carlton exchange glances across the table that sent a chill down her spine.

Oh, Lord! she thought. If he guesses!

She played badly, unable to keep her mind on her cards, and the room seemed too hot and close. But Bruce paid her no particular attention and was as casual in his manner as though he were merely the friend who had come along because he happened to be staying at Almsbury's house. And in her turn Amber tried desperately to convince Rex of her undivided interest in him. She flirted with him as flagrantly as though they had just met, asked his opinion on several matters of no importance, called Nan to fill his wine-glass the moment it was empty, and scarcely looked at Bruce. For he had given her no reason as yet to think she would not continue to need Rex Morgan.

But she was uncomfortably nervous and the back muscles of her neck were beginning to ache when Almsbury, giving his wife's pregnancy as an excuse, suggested that it was time to go home. She threw him a look of grateful relief.

Nan brought out the men's cloaks and plumed hats and Amber walked into the bedroom with Lady Almsbury, telling her how pleased she was to have made her acquaintance. She held her cloak for her and took her fan while Emily adjusted her hood, then gave back her own instead. Emily did not notice the change and they went back into the parlour. The three men were having a last drink and all of them seemed to be on perfectly friendly terms; when they left Rex invited them to come again.

Nan went out with a candle to light them to the bottom of the stairs and Amber waited a minute or two. "Oh!" she cried then. "I've got her Ladyship's fan!" And before Rex, who had gone into the dining-room to pick up a cold biscuit, could offer to take it down for her she had run out of the room. She reached them when they had just gotten to the bottom of the stairs, for Emily had to move with care, and all of them laughed politely as they made the exchange.

But as she turned to go back up again she gave a swift glance around, and then whispered to Bruce, "I'll come to Almsbury House tomorrow morning at eight," and before he could reply or object she had picked up her skirts and was running up the stairs once more.

Bruce was busy most of the time.

The days he spent down at the wharves overseeing the cleaning and repairing and supplying of his ships, signing new men, and talking to the merchants from whom he ordered provisions, for many of them had a monetary share in his ships. Privateering was the greatest speculative business of the nation, and not only the King and courtiers but most of the great merchants and many of the lesser ones were engaged in it, usually through money invested in a venture such as his. At night he went to Whitehall, saw the plays there, gambled in the Groom Porter's Lodge, attended the never-ending succession of balls and supper-parties.

Consequently Amber saw him for only an hour or two in the morning when she visited his apartments at Almsbury House, and she did not go every day because, when he could, Rex waited until she was ready to start for the Theatre before he left. But as far as she knew he had no slightest suspicion that she had seen Lord Carlton either before or since that one night. And she intended to make sure that he never would suspect it.

But contending against her determination to be cautious and clever, to keep Rex Morgan's confidence and his love, was the violent infatuation which made her reckless in spite of herself.

She had begged Bruce again to take her with him when he went and again he had refused, nor would any amount of tears and imploring change his mind. She was accustomed to Rex, who could usually be coaxed, and his obdurate refusal filled her with frantic, impotent fury.

"I'll stow away on your ship then!" she told him one day, half-joking, but thinking nevertheless that if she did there would be nothing he could do about it. She would be there and he couldn't very well throw her overboard.

"And I'll send you back again when I find you, no matter how far out we are." His eyes had a warning glitter as he looked at her. "Privateering's no game of handy-dandy."

Amber worried because she knew that soon he would be gone and she would not see him at all—perhaps for years—but she worried even more because now, while he was here, the days were getting away from them one by one and they were able to be together only for a snatched hour or two at a time. She longed to spend whole days and nights with him, uninterrupted by either his obligations or hers. And at last she discovered the solution—a plan so simple and obvious it seemed incredible she had not thought of it weeks ago. They would go away together into the country.

"And what about Captain Morgan?" Bruce wanted to know. "Is he going along too?"

Amber laughed. "Of course he isn't! Don't you trouble yourself about Rex. I'll take care of him, I warrant you. I know just what I'm going to tell him—and he'll never suspect a thing. Oh, please, Bruce! You will go, won't you?"

"My dear—I'd like to, of course. But I think you'd be taking a very great risk for a very small reward. Suppose that he—"

But she interrupted him swiftly. "Oh, Bruce, he won't! I know Rex better than you do—he'll believe anything I tell 'im!"

He gave her a slow smile. "Darling, men aren't always as gullible as women think they are."

He finally agreed, though, to go away with her for five or six days, after he had settled his business. A Spanish merchant-fleet was known to be returning from Peru, heavily laden with gold and silver, and he hoped to intercept it sometime at the end of May, which meant that he must leave London in the middle of the month.

And, as when he had agreed to bring her to London, Amber thought that she had persuaded him. She still did not realize that selfishness and cynicism made him indifferent to what might happen to her. He had warned her, but he did not believe that he either could or should protect her from the risks of living and of her own headstrong temper.

They took the main road down through Surrey toward the sea-coast. As in London it was raining—and had been almost every day for a month and a half—so that they travelled slowly and had to make frequent stops to haul the coach out of mud-bogs, for the roads were now nothing more. But the country-side was beautiful. This was the rich agricultural heart of England and prosperous farms lay spread over the rolling hills; many of them were enclosed by hedges, though that practice was as yet an uncommon one. The cottages and manor-houses were made of cherry-coloured brick and silver oak and the luxuriant gardens were massed with purple-and-white violets, tulips, crimson ramblers.

Amber and Bruce sat side by side, hands tightly clasped, looking out the glass windows and talking softly. As always his presence gave her a sense of finality, a sureness that this was all she wanted from life and that it would last as it was forever.

"It makes me think of home," she said, gesturing to take in the village through which they were passing. "Marygreen, I mean."

" 'Home'? Does that mean you'd like to go back?"

"Go back—to Marygreen? I should say *not!* It gives me the vapours to so much as think of it!"

The first night they stopped at a little inn, and since the rain continued they decided to stay there. It was warm and comfortable and friendly and the food was good. The host was a veteran of the Civil Wars, a bluff old fellow who cornered Bruce every time he saw him and went into lengthy reminiscences of Prince Rupert and Marston Moor. They were the only guests there.

But the week which she had expected would pass so slowly seemed to pick up speed as it went and the precious minutes and hours rushed along, slipping out of her hands as she tried to catch at them and drag them back. So soon now it would be over—he would be gone—

"Oh, *why* does the time go by so fast, just when you want it to go slow!" she cried. "Someday I hope the clock will stand still and never move!"

"Haven't you learned yet to be careful of what you wish for?"

They spent the days idly, lay long in the mornings, and went to bed early at night. While the rain poured down outside they sat before the fire and played card games, costly-colours, putt, wit-and-reason; invariably he won and, though she thought that she had become very clever, he always seemed to know when she was cheating. If the evenings were nice, as two or three of them were, they bowled on the green beside the inn.

They had brought the baby with them—as well as Nan and Tansy—and Bruce told her that he had arranged with Almsbury to take him from Mrs. Chiverton and put him into the nursery with the Earl's two sons. Amber was delighted to see how intensely fond he was of the child she had borne him. It encouraged her to think that sooner or later he would give up his roving life, and marry her—or take her to America with him.

Until the last day she kept her resolution not to argue with him, and then she could not resist making one more effort to convert him. "I don't see why you want to live in America, Bruce," she said, pouting a little before he had even had time to answer. "What can you like about that country—full of nothing but wild Indians and blackamoors! Why, you said yourself there isn't a town the size of London in the whole of it. Lord, what can you find to do? Why don't you come back to England and live when you're done privateering?"

The rain had stopped and the sun came out hot. They had spread a blanket beneath a beech-tree, heavily laden with long drooping clusters of purple blossoms, and Amber sat cross-legged on it while Bruce lay stretched out on his stomach. As she talked she kept an eye on the baby who had wandered some yards away to watch a duck and several little tawny ducklings swimming on a shallow pond; from his hand trailed a neglected wooden doll tied to a cord. She had just cautioned him not to go too close, but he was absorbed in the ducks and paid her scant attention.

Bruce, with a stalk of green grass between his teeth and his eyes narrowed against the sun, looked up at her and grinned. "Because, my darling, the life I want for myself and my children doesn't exist in England any more."

"Your children! How many bastards have you, pray? Or are you married?" she asked suddenly.

"No, of course not." He gave a quick gesture as she started to open her mouth. "And let's not talk about that again."

"Oh, I wasn't going to! You have such a damned high opinion of yourself! I don't have to go begging for a husband, let me tell you!"

"No," he agreed. "I don't suppose you do. I'm only surprised that you aren't married already."

"If I'm not it's because I've been a silly fool and thought that you'd— Oh, I'm not going to say it! But *why* don't you like England? Lord, you could live at Court and have as fine a station as any man in Europe!"

"Perhaps. But the price is too high for my purse."

"But you'll be rich as anything—"

"It isn't money I mean. You don't know anything about the Court, Amber. You've only seen it from the outside. You've seen the handsome clothes and the jewels and the fine manners. That isn't Whitehall. Whitehall's like a rotten egg. It looks good enough until you break it open—and then it stinks to the heavens—"

She did not believe that and was about to tell him so, when there was a sudden splash and a loud howl from the baby as he tumbled into the pond. Bruce was on his feet at a bound and running, with Amber close behind, to pick his son out of the water. And when the little boy found himself unhurt and safe in his father's arms all three burst into laughter. Bruce set him up on one shoulder and they started for the inn to get him out of his wet clothes.

It was late the next night when she left Bruce at Almsbury House. A nurse he had already hired came out to get the baby and disappeared with him. But for a moment Bruce stood in the rain beside the opened door of the coach, while Amber struggled with her tears. This time she was determined that he should go away with a pleasant memory of her, but her throat ached painfully and she thought that she would never be able to bear the parting. For hours she had kept herself talking and thinking of other things, but now she could pretend no longer. This was goodbye.

"I'll see you when you come back, Bruce—" she whispered, for she could not trust her voice.

He stood looking at her, but for a moment did not answer. Then he said, "I've put a thousand pound with Shadrac Newbold in your name—you can have it on twenty days' notice. If you have any trouble with Morgan because of this, that will help take care of you." He leaned forward quickly, kissed her, and turned to walk away. She watched him go, fading from sight in the wet darkness, and then suddenly she could control herself no longer and she began to cry.

She was still crying when she reached the Blue Balcony. She felt as though she had been away for a great while, it was almost strange to her, and she climbed the stairs slowly. The door, as she tried it, was already unlocked and she went in. Rex was there.

His eyes were bloodshot and he looked as though he had not shaved for days, nor perhaps slept either, for his face was haggard and his clothes rumpled. Surprised to find him there and in that condition she stood perfectly still for a moment, sniffling unconsciously though the tears had stopped at sight of him, and one hand went up to wipe her streaked face.

"Well," he said quietly at last. "So your Aunt Sarah died. Nothing else, I suppose, could make you look like that."

Amber was wary, for she could not be sure if that was sarcasm in his voice. But she did not think—if he knew where she had been— that he would be so still and calm. "Yes," she said. "Poor Aunt Sarah. It was a mighty bad shock to me—she was the only mother I ever—"

"Don't trouble yourself to lie to me. I know where you've been and who you've been with." He spoke between his teeth, biting off each word with a savage snap, and though his voice did not rise she saw all at once that he was insanely, murderously angry. She opened her mouth to make some denial but he cut her off. "What kind of a fool do you take me for? Don't you suppose it ever occurred to me to wonder why that brat of yours had the same first name he has? But you'd made me so many promises— Oh, you'd never be unfaithful to the man who loved you, not you! I was determined to believe in you and trust you no matter what happened. And then both of you went out of town at the same time— You ungrateful jilting little slut—I've been here four days and nights, waiting for you to come back— Do you have any idea what I've been through since you went? Of course you don't! You've never thought about anyone but yourself in all your life— You've never cared who you hurt if you got what you wanted— You selfish, mercenary, whoring little bitch. I should kill you—I'd *like* to kill you—I'd like to watch the breath go out of you—"

His voice went on in a low monotonous tone that did not sound like him and his face was twisted with rage and sickness and jealousy into something she could scarcely recognize. This was a man she had never known existed beneath the quiet gentle Rex Morgan she had taken so casually for granted; this was some malevolent, savage stranger.

Amber stared at him in terror. She took a step or two backward, intending to turn and run if he made the slightest move. Slowly he started toward her. And like a frightened animal she whirled, but he was quicker; before she knew what was happening he had grabbed her arm and jerked her back again. She screamed, but he clapped one hand over her mouth and gave her head a vicious shake.

"Shut up, you lousy little coward! I'm not going to hurt you!" He was straining every nerve and muscle, exhausted by jealousy and sleeplessness, to hold his fury in leash. Amber's eyes looked up at him, big and glittering with fear, but the grasp he had on her was so tight she could not have moved if she had tried. "I want you to live—I want you to live long enough to know how I've felt—I want you to live and wish you were dead because he is—" Suddenly he let her go.

Relieved. Amber shook herself a little. She had scarcely realized what he was saying but now, as he started out, she looked up suddenly. "Where are you going?" All at once she understood what he had meant. "Rex! You're not going to fight him!"

"I'm going to fight him, and kill him."

Confident that her own life was no longer in danger, Amber gave him a scowl of contemptuous disgust. "You're crazy, Rex Morgan, if you do! He's a better swordsman than you are—"

He slammed his hat onto his head, picked up his cloak and went swiftly out of the room. At the door he knocked into Nan and Tansy and Jeremiah just coming in with their arms full of boxes, but he brushed on by without a word of apology.

Nan caught her balance and her blue eyes widened as she turned to watch him running down the stairs. "Where's he going in such a rage, mam?" She looked back anxiously at Amber. "He's not going to fight Lord Carlton!"

"He's a fool if he does!" muttered Amber, and turned away.

But Nan whirled about, and started down the stairs after him, crying, "Captain Morgan! Captain Morgan! Come back here!"

Chapter Twenty-one

AN HOUR LATER BRUCE came to her rooms.

He walked in swiftly when Nan opened the door, and there was a dark scowl on his face that did not clear when Amber came running out of the bedroom in her dressing-gown. Her eager expectant smile disappeared as she saw his angry expression.

"Why, Bruce! What is it? What's happened?"

He crossed to her and gave her a folded sheet of paper on which the seal had been broken. "Look at this! It was just brought to me at Almsbury House!"

She took it and began to read:

"Sir: You have done me an injury which one gentleman may not accept from another. I will see you tomorrow morning at five in Marrowbone Fields, where Tyburn Brook meets the road. Have your sword in your hand. Or I shall be at your service at the earliest time you shall appoint.

"Your servant, sir,

"CAPTAIN REX MORGAN."

The handwriting was scratchy and the pen had splattered several times, streaking the page with black ink.

In his rage, Rex had ignored half the formal appointments for a duel, for it was customary to let the challenged name the time and the place and the weapon. Nor had he said anything of seconds, either one or two of which were usually selected by each man, according to the French style of fighting imported into England and already responsible for many unnecessary deaths.

Amber looked up at him, giving back the note, "Well?"

"Well! Is that all you have to say! for the love of God, Amber, what's the matter with you! You know that he'll lose his rank and have to go into exile— He might never come back again! If you don't care what happens to him you should at least have the sense to consider your own future Get hold of him tonight and tell him there's no reason for this ridiculous meeting!"

Amber was astonished, and then offended, for he obviously did not consider her sufficient cause for a duel. Her pride hurt, she wanted to hurt him, and now a mocking smile curled the corners of her mouth.

"You surprise me, Lord Carlton," she said softly.

Bruce looked at her, his eyes narrowed. "What do you mean by that?"

She gave a little shrug. "I wouldn't expect to find you troubled about a meeting with swords. I should think a privateer could defend himself as well as any other man."

Nan gasped, one hand going to her mouth as though to stop the words her mistress had just spoken. But Bruce's face had a sort of angry contempt on it.

"I'm not afraid to meet him and you damned well know it! But I don't care to fight a man without a better reason than this!"

"If you mean me, Lord Carlton, Rex thinks I'm reason enough!"

"Tell him you've already had a son by me and see what he thinks about it then!"

"He knows it—and he still wants to fight you! Anyway, I don't know where he's gone! If you don't want to fight, you'll have to make your own excuses!"

She turned away from him, but as she did so she caught a glimpse of his face staring at her with an expression that was almost frightening, and without another word he wheeled and left the room, his long riding-cape swirling about him.

"Oh, mam!" cried Nan despairingly. "Now what 've you done!"

"I don't care! He needn't expect me to beg him off!"

"But it wasn't because he's afraid, mam! You know that!"

Irritably Amber gave a kick at a low stool and went back into the bedroom, slamming the door hard to ease her feelings. For a few minutes she paced back and forth, angry with Bruce and Rex and herself and all the world. A pox confound all men! she told herself furiously, and flung off her dressing-gown to get into bed, even though she knew she would not be able to sleep.

When Nan came in an hour or so later Amber was still awake and tossing restlessly, but the anger was beginning to wear off and worry was taking its place. The prospect of the duel did not trouble her, for in spite of the fact that duels were forbidden by law they took place every day and hot-tempered young men fought over the flimsiest pretexts: a quick thoughtless word, bad luck at the gaming-table, the giving or taking of the wall as they passed on the streets, a difference of opinion over religion or wine or a woman. Every gentleman learned to handle his sword almost as soon as he learned to walk, and he knew that the art was acquired to be used.

She was not afraid of having them fight. She was, in fact, flattered and almost pleased—or would have been had Bruce been less frankly insulting—for a duel was not often fatal and was usually stopped at the first drawing of blood. But she was afraid now of what would happen to her when it was over.

Suppose Rex would not forgive her this time? Suppose he did have to leave the country and never came back again? Then what would become of her? She had no illusions left about a woman's place in Restoration London—she knew that she had been lucky to find a man like Rex Morgan who had loved her. For love was not in fashion any more, and without it a man had no obligations, a woman no rights. She realized all at once that she had been a fool to take such a chance— Of course he was sure to know— Her lame story about Aunt Sarah falling sick! And yet, how else could she have done it? She was forced now to admit to herself that there was only one way she could have avoided this—she should never have left London with Bruce. She had wanted too much, she had been too greedy—and this was what she got for it.

What was the matter with me? she asked herself furiously. I had Rex—and I had Bruce, too—now what have I got! But swiftly her anger reverted to Bruce. Damn him! He's never been anything but trouble to me!

As she heard Nan tiptoeing about in the dark, she spoke to her.

"Light a candle if you want, Nan. I can't sleep."

Nan went back to the other room, returned with a wax candle, and lighted three or four others in wall-sconces while Amber sat with one arm across her knees and her hand clenched in her hair.

"Lord, Nan! What'll I do?"

Nan, who was beginning to undress, heaved a sigh. "To tell you truly, mam, I don't know. It's the devil's own mess we're in."

Both of them look worried and disconsolate. At last Nan blew out the candles and got into bed and they lay side by side, talking; neither one of them was able to sleep for a long while. Finally Nan fell asleep but Amber continued to toss and turn from one side to the other and she heard the bell-man go by, calling out each hour as it passed: one, two, three.

I'm not going to just lie here, she thought, and let my life be ruined! And when she heard, "God give you good morrow, my masters! Past three o'clock and a fair morning!" she flung back the covers and got out of bed, turning to shake Nan.

"Nan! Wake up! Get up! I'm going to Marrowbone Fields!"

"Good Lord, mam! I thought the house was afire—"

Amber dressed quickly but carefully, as though she was aware that this would be a dramatic moment in her life and wanted to look ready for it. She painted her face and stuck on a couple of patches, combed out her hair and let it fall in deep loose waves down over her shoulders. She wore a scarlet velvet suit, the coat of which was cut exactly like a man's. It fitted her snugly and the neck-line opened in a low V, and there were elaborate scrolls of gold braid decorating the deep cuffs and borders of the coat and skirt. The brim of her low-crowned Cavalier's riding-hat billowed with scarlet ostrich plumes and she had a pair of red-velvet boots lined with miniver. She had had a tailor make this suit and expected to set a new fashion, but she had not worn it before.

While Jeremiah went to hire four riding-horses Amber drank some hot coffee which Tansy had just made and, well laced with brandy, it tasted good to her for once. It was after four when Jeremiah returned and they set out for Marrowbone Fields, Amber and Nan, with Tempest and Jeremiah. It was just beginning to grow light but a heavy mist was falling which blurred the outlines of houses and trees and made it impossible to see more than a few feet ahead; Amber was annoyed, for the dampness would probably spoil her gown.

She soon forgot her appearance, however, and the closer they came the more her anxiety mounted.

It took them no longer than twenty minutes to reach the place in the road where Tyburn Brook ran under a little stone bridge—and looking off toward the east they could dimly see a party of men and several horses, half obscured by a spacious group of Lombardy poplars. Amber immediately turned her horse and started toward them. Presently she could distinguish Bruce and Rex, Almsbury, Colonel Dillon whom she knew slightly, and two others who were apparently the surgeons. But only Bruce and Rex had removed their outer coats to show that no armour had been worn.

At the sound of horses' hoofs pounding across the field they all turned; it was not uncommon for a party to be sent to stop such meetings. But as Amber pulled on her reins and they saw who it was Bruce looked quickly away—though not before she had seen the angry annoyance on his face. Rex, however, stood and stared at her.

"Oh, Rex, darling!" she cried, stopping only a few feet from him and holding out her hand. "Thank God I got here in time!

You mustn't fight this duel—you mustn't Rex! Please, darling, for my sake!" Her eyes turned swiftly to the corners and she saw Bruce look across at her; his expression was sombre and a cynical half-smile touched one side of his mouth. Sick with fury she wanted to hurt him, any way she could. "There's no reason for you to fight, Rex! Why, I don't care any more for him than the man in the moon!" There! she thought savagely, and flung him a vindictive glance; he met it with cold contempt, impervious as stone.

But as her eyes shifted across to Bruce and back again she missed altogether the look on Rex's face, and when she looked down at him it had gone. The wild unreasoning rage of despair had disappeared. Now he was quiet, self-possessed, and seemed cool. In her preoccupation with her own worries Amber did not realize that his seeming calm was a deadly determination and that his own tension quivered like the thin blade in his hand. Misunderstanding, she still thought that she could make him do what she wanted.

"You shouldn't have come out here, Amber," he said. "A duelling-ground is no place for a woman. Go on back." He turned away and walked toward the rest of the group.

"Rex!" she cried, really alarmed now, and as Jeremiah came to help her dismount she got down as quickly as she could and ran after him, grabbing him by the arm. "Rex! I don't want you to fight! I don't want you to, d'you hear me?"

He neither looked at her nor answered, but jerked his arm free and went on. Amber would not have stopped even then, but suddenly Almsbury caught hold of her. "Come back here. You'll be in the way up there."

"But I can't let them fight! I won't—"

"Amber, for the love of Christ!" he growled at her. "Now stay here! Don't move!"

Helplessly she stood where he had left her. Bruce and Rex both had unsheathed their swords, and with Almsbury and the officer they were talking in low tones. At last, giving a shrug of his shoulders, Almsbury moved back; Dillon took out a white handkerchief and indicated where each man was to stand. The Earl looked at her with a scowl.

"What is it?" she asked him anxiously. "What's the matter?"

"Carlton wants to consider it settled when blood has been drawn, but your noble champion won't be satisfied until one of them is dead."

"Dead! Why, he's out of his mind! He can't! I won't let him!"

She broke away from Almsbury and started forward at a run. "Rex!"

Almsbury caught her arm before she had gone three steps and brought her up with a jerk. "Stop it, you little fool! A duel's no game between children! Keep your mouth shut or go back home! You've got no business here in the first place!"

Surprised, she obeyed him, and stopped perfectly still. The

two men now stood facing each other, poised, sword-tips touching, and Colonel Dillon held the handkerchief over his head.

"All's ready!" called Bruce and Rex in the same voice.

"All's ready!" Dillon brought the handkerchief down with a sweep.

Both of them were quick, fierce, and graceful, expert swordsmen. But the English style of fencing was to cut rather than to thrust, as the French did, and as they were almost of a height neither had the advantage in that respect. Rex, however, was not fencing but fighting with reckless fury, and obviously intended to kill or be killed, while Bruce was on the defensive—protecting himself but making no effort to wound his antagonist.

Amber stood watching them, her eyes darting from one to the other; her throat was dry and she twisted her skirt in her fingers. But her fears were all for Bruce—she might not have even known the man he was fighting. And when Rex's sword pierced his right upper-arm, just below the shoulder, and drew a quick streak of blood she gave a scream and started forward. Almsbury threw one arm about her waist and dragged her back.

Bruce had lowered his sword and Rex, refusing to seize an unfair advantage, dropped his own to his side. The blood from the small gash was streaming down Bruce's right arm, staining his shirt and making red rivers along the exposed brown skin, and the sight of it filled Amber with terror and remorse.

"Oh, Bruce!" she wailed. "You're hurt!"

Rex's jaw set tensely, but Bruce ignored her.

"There," he said to Rex. "That should satisfy you."

More furious than ever since Amber's impulsive cry, Rex answered him through clenched teeth. "Nothing could satisfy me but to see you dead."

Amber gave a terrified scream that momentarily drew all eyes to her but Almsbury clapped his hand to her mouth and gave her a rough shake.

"If you don't shutup you'll distract him and he *will* get killed!"

Already the swords had begun to ring out and clash again; now there was no doubt that Bruce was fighting in earnest, no longer merely defending himself. For several minutes the men moved rapidly back and forth, slashing and hacking, without either one being able to touch the other.

And then all at once the swords met, engaged, and locked. For a long tense moment they strained to get free, both men pouring sweat, their faces contorted with the intensity of effort. Then, so swiftly that it was not possible to see it happen, Bruce forced his sword free and thrust it into Rex's chest until the tip showed through his shirt in back; and then he withdrew it, red with blood.

For an instant Rex stood as though stunned, and then he fell slowly, crumpling. The surgeons ran toward him and Amber rushed forward, dropping to her knees beside him where he lay on the grass. Her throat muscles were so stiff with horror that for a moment she could not even say his name, but she took his head into her arms, cradling it against her breast, and then suddenly a mournful frightened sob broke from her and her tears splashed onto his face.

"Oh, Rex! Rex!" she moaned. "Speak to me, darling! Speak to me—please!" Her mouth touched his forehead, his temples and eyelids, with frantic passionate kisses.

Behind her, Bruce took Almsbury's handkerchief and wiped the blood from his sword, jammed it back into its case and buckled the belt around his hips once more. By tradition the sword of the defeated man was forfeit, but he made no move to take it and Rex's fingers were still loosely clasped on the hilt. Bruce's surgeon was tearing open his shirt and binding the wound with a strip of white cloth while Bruce stood, hands on his hips and feet spread, looking down at Rex. His face was dark and grim, bitter but not triumphant.

Rex was moving restlessly, as if to escape the pain, and though he coughed and turned his head to spit out blood there was very little blood coming from the wound in his chest. Amber was sobbing hysterically, covering his face with kisses and stroking his head with her hands.

"Rex, darling! Look at me! Speak to me!"

He opened his eyes at last, very slowly, and as he saw her he tried to smile. "I'm ashamed, Amber," he said softly, "that you saw me—beaten."

"Oh, Rex! I don't care about that! You know I don't! All I care about is you— Are you in pain? Does it hurt you?"

A quick spasm crossed his face and the sweat started suddenly, but his features relaxed again as he looked up at her. "No—Amber. It doesn't hurt. I'll be—" But at that moment he coughed again and turned his head to spit out a great glob of clotted blood. His mouth was splattered with it; his eyes shut and one hand pressed hard against his chest in an effort to stop the gurgling cough.

Bruce slid his arms into the doublet Almsbury held for him, gave Rex a last look and then tossing his cloak over his arm started off, with the Earl and his surgeon, toward where a young page held their horses.

Amber looked around suddenly and saw him walking away. She glanced swiftly at Rex. He lay now quiet and with his eyes closed; she hesitated only an instant and then, very gently, she laid his head onto the grass. Hurriedly she got to her feet and ran after Bruce, calling his name in a soft voice so that Rex would not hear.

"Bruce!"

He swung around and looked at her, incredulity on his face and violent anger. When he spoke his teeth were clenched and the muscles at one side of his mouth twitched with nervous rage. "There's a man dying over there— Go back to him!"

Amber stared at him for a moment in stunned helplessness, unable to believe the contempt and loathing she saw on his face. As though from a distance she heard Rex's voice, calling her name. Blind fury raged in her and before she knew what she was doing she had drawn back her hand and slapped him squarely across the mouth with all the force in her body. She saw his eyes glitter as the blow struck but at the same moment she whirled, picking up her skirts, and was running back to kneel beside Rex. His eyes were open now but as she bent over him she saw that they stared without seeing, his face was expressionless—he was dead. And in his hand, held closely as though he had been trying to lift it high enough to see, was the miniature of herself which she had given him the year before.

PART III

Chapter Twenty-two

GROPING LANE was a narrow dirty disreputable little alley on Tower Hill. The houses were crazily built and old, and the overhanging stories leaned across the street, almost touching at the top and shutting light and air from the festering piles of refuse that lay against each wall. The great gilded coach tried to turn into the lane but, finding it too narrow, was forced to stop at the entrance. A woman, completely covered by a black hooded cloak and with a vizard over her face, got out and with two footmen on either side of her hurried several yards farther up the alley and disappeared into one of the houses. The footmen remained below, waiting.

Running swiftly up two flights of stairs she paused and knocked on the door just at the top. For a moment there was no reply and she knocked again, hammering impatiently, glancing around as though some unseen pair of eyes might be watching her there in the pitch-dark stairwell. Still the door did not open, but a man's voice spoke from behind it softly:

"Who is it?"

"Let me in! It's Lady Castlemaine, you logger-head!"

As though she had given the magic formula the door swung wide and he bowed from the waist, sweeping out one hand with a gesture of flourishing hospitality as Barbara sailed in.

The room was small and bare and dark, furnished with nothing but some worn, cane-bottomed stools and chairs and a large table littered with papers and piled with books; more books and a globe of the world beside it on the floor. Outside the night was frosty, and the meagre sea-coal fire which burnt in the fireplace warmed only a small area around it. An ugly mongrel dog came to reassure himself by a curious sniff at Barbara's velvet-booted feet, and then returned to gnaw at a bone.

The man who admitted her looked little better than his dog. He was so thin that his chamois breeches and soiled shirt hung upon him as though on a rack. But his pale blue eyes were quick and shrewd and his face for all its gauntness had a look of enthusiasm and intelligence, combined with a certain slyness that was revealed in the shifting of his eyes and the unctuous quality of his smile.

He was Dr. Heydon—the degree he had bestowed upon

himself—astrologer and general quack, and Barbara had been there once before to find out whom the King would marry.

"I apologize, your Ladyship," said Heydon now, "for not opening the door immediately. But to be honest with you I am so hounded by my creditors that I dare not open to anyone unless I first make certain of his identity. The truth of it is, your Ladyship," he added, heaving a sigh and flinging out his arms in a gesture of despair, "I scarcely dare leave my lodgings these days for fear I shall be seized upon by a bailiff and carried off to Newgate! Which God forbid!"

But if he hoped to interest Barbara in his problems he was very much mistaken. In the first place she knew well enough that there was no ribbon-seller or perfumer or dressmaker in London with a trade at Court who did not hope to enrich himself at the expense of the nobility. And in the second she had come there to tell him her troubles, not to listen to his.

"I want you to help me, Dr. Heydon, There's something I *must* know. It means everything to me!"

Heydon rubbed his dry hands together and picked up a pair of thick-lensed spectacles which he perched midway down his nose. "Of course, my lady! Pray be seated." He held a chair for her and then took one himself just across the table, picking up a pen made of a long goose quill and beginning to caress his chin with the tip of it. "Now, madame, what is it that troubles you?" His tone was sympathetic, inviting confidence, implying a willingness and ability to solve any problem.

Barbara had removed her mask and now she tossed back the hood and dropped the cloak down from her shoulders. As she did so the diamonds at her throat and in her ears and hair caught the light and struck off brilliant sparks; Dr. Heydon's eyes widened and began to glow, focusing upon them.

But Barbara did not notice. She frowned, stripping off her gloves, and for several moments she remained silent and thoughtful. If only there was some way she could get his advice without telling him! She felt like a young bride going to consult a physician, except that her scruples were those not of modesty but of angry and humiliated pride.

How can I tell him that the King's grown tired of me! she thought. Besides, it's not true! I know it isn't! No matter what anyone says! It's just that he's so pleased at the prospect of having a legitimate child—for once! I know he still loves me. He must! He's just as cold to Frances Stewart as he is to me—! Oh, it's all because of that damned woman—that damned Portuguese!

She raised her eyes and looked at him. "You've heard, perhaps," she said at last, "that her Majesty finally proves with child?" She accentuated the word "finally," giving it an inflection which suggested that the delay was due to Catherine's own malicious procrastination.

"Ah, madame! Of course! Haven't we all heard the happy

news by now? And high time it is—but then, better late than never, as they say. Eh, your Ladyship?" But at Barbara's quick disapproving scowl he sobered, cleared his throat, and bent over his papers. "Now, what were you saying, your Ladyship?"

"That her Majesty proves with child!" snapped Barbara. "Now, it seems that since it was learned the Queen is pregnant, his Majesty has fallen in love with her. That must be the reason since no one noticed that he paid her any undue attention before. He neglects his old friends and scarcely goes near some of them. I want you to tell me"—suddenly she leaned forward, staring at him intently—"what will happen once the child is born. Will he go back to his old habits then? Or what?"

Heydon nodded his head and bent to his work. For some time he was silent, poring over an extremely complicated map of the heavens which was spread before him, pursing his lips and frowning studiously. From time to time he sucked air through a space between his two front teeth and drummed his fingers on the table. Barbara sat and watched him, her excitement mounting and her hopes, as well, for she could not believe that he would give her any really bad news. Somehow, this would all work out to her satisfaction—as everything had always done.

"Faith, madame," he said at last, "you ask me a very difficult question."

"Why? Can't you see into the future? I thought that was your business!" She spoke to him as though he were a glovemaker who had just told her that he would be unable to get the kind of leather she wanted.

"My years of study have not been in vain, madame, I assure you. But such a question— You understand—" He shrugged, spreading his hands, and then made a gesture as of a knife being run across his throat. "If it should be known I had made a prognostication in a matter so important—" He glanced down at his charts again, frowning dubiously, and then he murmured softly, as though to himself: "It's incredible! I can't believe it—"

Barbara, in a froth of sudden excitement, sat far forward on the edge of her chair and her eyes blazed wildly. "What's incredible? What is it? You've got to tell me!"

He leaned back, putting his finger-tips lightly together and contemplating the bony joints. "Ah, madame—it is information of too much importance to be disposed of so casually. Give me a few days to think it over, I pray you."

"No! I can't wait! I've got to know now! I'll run mad if I don't! What do you want—? I'll give you anything! A hundred pound—"

"Have you a hundred pound with you?"

"Not with me. I'll send it tomorrow."

He shook his head. "I'm sorry, madame, but I can no longer do business on credit. It was that practice which brought me to the condition you now see. Perhaps it would be best if you returned tomorrow."

"No! Not tomorrow! I've got to know *now!* Here—take these ear-rings, and this necklace, and this ring—they're worth more than a hundred pound any day!" She took off her jewels swiftly, tossing them across the table to him as though they were glass baubles bought at a fair or from some street vendor. "Now— Tell me quick!"

He gathered up the jewellery and slipped it into his pocket. "According to the stars, madame, the Queen's child will be born dead."

Barbara gasped. One hand went to cover her mouth and she sank back into her chair, her face shocked and unbelieving. But presently there began to creep into her eyes a look of cunning and of malignant satisfaction.

"Born dead!" she whispered at last. "Are you sure?"

"If the stars are sure, madame, I am sure."

"Of course the stars are sure!" She got up swiftly. "Then he'll come back to me, won't he?" In her sudden joy and new confidence she spoke recklessly.

"It would seem likely, would it not—under the circumstances?" His voice had a soft purring sound and his face was smiling and subtle.

"Of course he will! Good-night, Dr. Heydon!" She lifted the hood up over her head once more as she walked to the door and he followed her, opening it and standing back to bow her out. The dog came too to see the visitor off. She took one step down, holding up her skirts so that she would not stumble in the darkness, and then all at once she glanced back over her shoulder and gave him a dazzling smile. "I hope the diamonds keep you out of Newgate, Doctor! *That* news was worth far more than a thousand pound to me!"

He bowed again, still smiling and nodding his head, and as she got to the landing and disappeared he closed the door and slowly fastened the bolt. Then he bent to stroke his dog and the animal went meekly down onto its back, its long rat-like tail thumping the floor.

"Towser," he said, "at least we'll eat for a while."

Barbara, however, took the Doctor absolutely at his word and from then on the Queen's health was her greatest concern. She went to her levée every morning, invited her to supper in her own rooms, bribed some of the pages to bring her immediate word if the Queen should fall sick—she kept a constant close but secret watch on everything she did. But Catherine seemed to thrive. She looked healthy and happy and prettier than she ever had.

"Your Majesty is not feeling well?" Barbara asked her at last in desperation. "You look so pale, and tired."

But Catherine laughed and answered in her heavy accented

English: "Of course I'm well, my lady! I've never been more well!"

Barbara began to grow discouraged and even considered demanding the return of her jewels from Dr. Heydon. And then, in mid-October, sometime in the fifth month of Catherine's pregnancy, a rumour swept through the Palace corridors: her Majesty had fallen ill, and had miscarried of the child.

Catherine lay flat on her back in bed, surrounded on all sides by her maids and waiting-women. Her eyes were closed tightly to keep back the tears, for she was desperately sick and afraid. But as she heard Penalva turn and tell one of the women in a whisper to call the King she looked up swiftly.

"No!" she cried. "Don't do that! Don't send for him! It's nothing— I'll be better presently—Wait until Mrs. Tanner comes."

Mrs. Tanner was the midwife who had been taking care of her Majesty, and the moment Catherine had begun to feel sick and faint they had sent for her. She arrived a few minutes later, and as she went toward the bed her cheerful vulgar face contrived to appear both alarmed and optimistic. Mrs. Tanner resembled nothing so much as a fish-wife masquerading as a great lady. Her hair was dyed the fashionable silver-blonde colour that was almost white, her cheeks were so brightly painted with Spanish paper that they looked like autumn apples, and her fingers and wrists and neck were loaded with expensive jewellery—tokens of appreciation from her patients and a convenient and portable form of advertising.

Catherine opened her eyes to find the woman bending over her. "Your Majesty is feeling unwell?"

"I've been having pains—here—and I feel as though—as though I'm bleeding—" She looked up at her with the great mournful eyes of a puppy who begs a favour.

Mrs. Tanner swiftly masked the horrified surprise that came to her face and immediately began to take off her rings and bracelets. "Will your Majesty permit me to make an examination?"

Catherine nodded and Mrs. Tanner gave a signal for the curtains to be pulled about the bed. Then oiling her hands thoroughly with sweet-butter which an assistant had brought, she disappeared for several moments behind the curtains. Once there was a tormented little cry and a soft drawn groan from the Queen, and the face of every woman there winced with sympathetic pain. Finally Mrs. Tanner parted the curtains, dipped her right hand into a basin of water, and whispered to another woman: "Her Majesty has miscarried. Send for the King." A wave of excited murmurs and significant glances rushed around the room.

A few minutes later Charles came in on the run and went immediately to Mrs. Tanner, who was now wiping her hands while two maids sponged blood from the floor. He had been called from the tennis-court and wore only his open-necked shirt and breeches; and his brown face—streaked with sweat—was drawn taut by anxiety.

"What happened? They told me her Majesty had fallen sick—"

Mrs. Tanner could not meet his eyes. "Her Majesty has miscarried, Sire."

A look of horror struck across his face. Swiftly he parted the curtains and knelt beside her bed, out of sight of the roomful of curious watching eyes. "Catherine! Catherine, darling!" His voice was urgent, but low, for she lay with her eyes closed and appeared to be unconscious.

But at last her lashes lifted slowly and she saw him. For a moment there was scarcely even recognition on her face, and then the tears came and she turned her head away with an agonized sob.

"Oh, Catherine! I'm sorry—I'm so sorry! Have they given you something to ease the pain?" His face looked tired and as haggard as hers, for above all things on earth he wanted a legitimate son; but pity made him yearn to protect her.

"It isn't the pain. I don't care about that. Pain doesn't matter— But, oh, I so wanted to give you a son!"

"You will, darling—you will someday. But you mustn't think about that now. Don't think about anything but getting well."

"Oh, I don't want to get well! What good am I on earth if I can't do the one thing I'm put here for? Oh, my dear—" Her voice now sank so low that he had to lean forward to hear it and she stared up at him, her eyes flooded with self-reproach. "Suppose it's true what they say—that I'm barren—"

Charles was shocked and his breath caught sharply. He had not known she had heard that gossip, though it had been circulated through the Court and even out in the town from the first month of their marriage, perhaps earlier.

"Oh, Catherine, my darling—" His long fingers stroked her hair, caressed her pale moist cheeks. "It isn't true; of course it isn't true. People will talk maliciously as long as they have tongues in their heads. These accidents happen so often, but they mean nothing. You must rest now and grow well and strong—for my sake." He smiled tenderly, and bent his head to kiss her.

"For your sake?" She looked up at him trustingly, and at last she gave him a grateful little smile. "You're so kind. You're so good to me. And I promise—this won't happen the next time."

"Of course it won't. Now go to sleep, my dear, and rest, and presently you'll be well again."

He remained kneeling beside her until her breathing was deep and regular and the little frown of pain had left her forehead, and then he got up and without a word walked from the room and back to his own apartments where he went into his closet alone.

Catherine was no better the next day and she grew steadily worse with each day that passed. They did everything they knew to cure her: They bled her until she was white as the sheets she lay on. They cut live pigeons in two and tied them to the bare soles of her feet to draw out the poison. They gave her purgatives and sneezing-powders, pearls and chloride of gold. Her priests were with her constantly, groaning and wailing and praying, and at every hour the room was filled with people. Royalty could neither be born nor die in quiet and privacy.

Hour after hour Charles sat there beside her, anxiously watching each move that she made. His grief and devotion amazed them all; but for that one episode regarding Castlemaine, he had been a kind but by no means adoring husband.

They were all convinced that she would die, most of them hoped she would, and the talk was not so much of the dying Queen as of the new one. Whom would he marry next? For of course he must and would marry, after a decent interval of mourning.

Frances Stewart was the bride they had selected. She had some royal blood in her veins, enough to make such a match possible, she was beautiful—and she was still a virgin. That, at least, was the opinion of the best-informed, even though his Majesty had been pursuing her for months, ever since she had come from France to take a place as one of Queen Catherine's Maids of Honour.

She was not quite seventeen but rather tall, and slender as a candleflame; she had about her an air of tranquil poise which could be suddenly broken by a bubbling merry laugh that gurgled up out of a happy well of youth and confidence. Her beauty was pure and perfect, flawless as a cut gem, delightful as the sight of a poplar glistening in the sun.

Charles had been first attracted by the irresistible lure of beauty, and then, discovering in her a modest shyness that was to him as incredible as it was genuine, he began a systematic program of seduction. So far, it had been unsuccessful. But her fresh youth and naïveté appealed to him strongly, sent him yearning toward the lost years as though in her he could catch again for a moment something of that perishable and precious charm.

During the past four months, since the discovery of her Majesty's pregnancy, Charles had seemed to lose interest in Frances; he had been as coolly polite as though he had never desired her at all—or as though he had already had her. But now he seemed to return to Frances again for comfort in his despair. They were so positive she would be the next Queen of

England that it was not even possible to find betting odds. Frances believed it herself.

But certainly not even the King's sorrow was more extravagant or more seemingly sincere than that of the least likely of all mourners, Lady Castlemaine. She kept a continuous stream of pages running from the Queen's apartments to her own at every hour of the day and night, went there frequently herself, and was reliably reported to pray for her Majesty's recovery five or six times a day. Barbara was alarmed.

It had never occurred to her, when Heydon had made his astounding prophecy, that the Queen would be as sick as she was. Certainly not that she would die. And she had not even considered the possibility that if she did she might be replaced by a woman like Frances Stewart, whose marriage to the King could mean nothing but Barbara's own ruin and, more than likely, her exile into France. She and Frances had not been friendly for some time, not, in fact, since Barbara had become convinced that his Majesty's infatuation for the girl was a serious one. She had always underestimated all women but herself, and it had taken her a long while to discover that Frances was really a formidable rival. Now she lived in terror that the Queen would die.

The gatherings in Barbara's rooms were sober affairs now, for though the King came almost every night at supper-time his mood was a morose and silent one, and discretion kept them from seeming to be as indifferent as they were.

On the tenth night after Catherine had fallen sick he stood in Barbara's drawing-room, over against the fireplace, thoughtfully swirling the red wine in his glass and talking in quiet tones which the most intent ears could not catch, to Frances Stewart. For Frances, though her own hopes of glory depended upon the Queen's death, was genuinely sympathetic and sorrowful for the quiet unhappy little woman who had befriended her.

"How was she when you left her, Sire?"

Charles scowled, a drawn and worried scowl which seldom left his face nowadays, and stared down into his glass. "I don't think she even knew me."

"Is she still delirious?"

"She hadn't spoken for more than two hours." He gave a quick shake of his head as though to drive away the painfully vivid image of her that dogged his memory. "She talked to me this morning." A strange, sad and cynical smile touched his mouth. "She asked me how the children were. She said that she was sorry the boy was not pretty. I told her that he was very handsome and she seemed pleased—and said that if I was satisfied then she was happy."

Frances gave a sudden hysterical sob, her fist pressed against her mouth, and Charles looked at her in quick surprise, as though he had forgotten that she was there. Just then a page entered the room, running in without ceremony, and went immediately to the King.

Charles whirled around. "What is it?"

"The Queen, Sire, is dying—"

Charles did not wait for the boy to finish his sentence but with a swift movement he flung the glass into the fireplace and ran out of the room. The Queen's bed-chamber was in the same miserable condition it had been in for days: All windows were closed and had been since she had first fallen sick, so that the air was heavy and hot and stinking; the darkness was complete, but for a few low-burning candles about the bed; and the priests hung over her like bald malefic ravens, their voices eternally wailing and moaning.

Catherine lay flat on her back. Her eyes were closed and sunken in dark pits, her skin was yellow as wax, and she breathed so faintly that at first he thought she was dead. But before he had even spoken she became aware of his presence beside her, her eyes opened slowly and she looked up at him. She tried to smile and then, painfully, she began to talk to him, falling back into Spanish.

"Charles—I'm glad you came. I wanted to see you just once more. I'm dying, Charles. They told me so, and I know it's true. Oh, yes it is." She smiled gently as he started to open his mouth to protest. "But it doesn't matter. It will be better for you when I'm dead. Then you can marry a woman who will give you sons—I want you to promise me that you won't wait. Get married soon—. It won't matter to me where I'll be—"

As she talked he stared at her, horrified and sick with shame. He had not realized before that she was dying because she had no wish to live. He had never wanted or tried to understand what this past year had been for her. The enormity of his selfish thoughtlessness, the guilty awareness that in his secret heart he had hoped for her death, struck him like a blow from a mighty fist. He had a moment of passionate regret, of devout promises for a better future.

Suddenly he leapt to his feet and turned to face the priest who was standing just beside him, interrupting the old man in the midst of his clamorous prayer.

"Get out of here." His voice was low and tense with fury. "Get out of here, I say! All of you!"

Priests and doctors stared at him in astonishment, but made no move to go.

"But, your Majesty!" protested one. "We must be here when her Majesty dies—"

"She's not going to die! Though God knows what you've put her through would kill a stronger woman! Now, get out, or by Jesus, I'll throw you out myself!" His voice rose to an enraged shout and one arm swept out in a violent gesture of dismissal. His face was dark as a devil's and his eyes glittered savagely; he hated them for his own errors as much as for theirs.

They began to straggle out, puzzlement on their faces as they looked back again and again, but he paid them no more attention and turning away dropped once more to his knees beside her. For a long minute her eyes remained closed and he watched her, his own breathing almost stopped; at last she looked up at him again.

"Oh—" she sighed. "It's so quiet now—so peaceful. For a moment I thought I must be—"

"Don't say it, Catherine! You're not going to die! You're going to live—for me, and for your son!"

But she shook her head, a vague almost imperceptible movement. "I have no son, Charles. I know I haven't. But, oh, I did so want to give you one—I wanted to be part of your life. But now, before very long, I'll be gone— And when you marry again you'll have sons— You'll be happier, and so I'm glad I'm going—"

Charles gave a sudden sob. The tears were streaming from his eyes and his two hands crushed her tiny one between them. "Catherine! Catherine! Don't talk that way! Don't say those things! You've got to want to live! If you want to you can— And you've got to—for me—"

She stared up at him, a new look in her eyes. "For *you,* Charles? You want me to?" she whispered.

"Yes, I do! Of course I do! My God, whatever made you think— Oh, Catherine, darling, I'm sorry—I'm *sorry!* But you've got to live—for me— Tell me that you'll try, that you will—"

"Why, Charles— I didn't know you— Oh, my darling, if you want me to— I can live— Of course I can—"

Chapter Twenty-three

It was not until after he was dead that Amber realized how much Rex Morgan had meant to her. She missed the sound of his key turning in the lock and the feeling of warmth and happiness he had always brought with him, as though a fire had just been lighted in a cold dark room. She missed waking up in the morning to find him half-dressed and shaving, screwing his face this way and that as he scraped the beard off. She missed the evenings when they had been alone and had played cribbage or crambo and he had listened to her strum her guitar and sing the popular bawdy street ballads. She missed his smile and the sound of his voice and the reassuring adoration in his blue eyes. She missed him in a thousand ways.

But most of all, though she scarcely knew it herself, she missed the comfortable sense of security with which he had surrounded her.

For now she found herself suddenly adrift, lost, and filled with a cold apprehension for the future. She had almost seventeen hundred pounds with Shadrac Newbold; so there was no immediate cause for concern on that score, and she could not be arrested for debt anyway. But even seventeen hundred pounds, she knew would not last very long if she continued to live on her present scale, and when it was gone she would be at the mercy of the tiring-room gallants.

The thought was not pleasant—for after a year and a half of association she saw them naked now and unvarnished with the guilt of a naïve young girl's illusions. To her they were no longer gallant and gay and valiant, fine gentlemen because they wore fine clothes and could trace their families to followers of William the Conqueror—but only a half-breed species of Frenchified Englishman, shallow, malicious, and absurd. They had all the trappings of cynicism, careless ill-breeding and light-hearted cruelty, which were now the marks of quality. There was not another man like Rex Morgan to be found among them.

"Oh, if I'd only known this would happen!" she thought, over and over again. "I'd never have gone away! And I wouldn't have gone to the King that time, either. Oh, Rex, if I'd known, I'd have been kinder to you—I'd have made you happy every minute—"

The first visitor she admitted after Rex's funeral—though many others had come—was Almsbury. He had been there before but she had been unfit to see anyone at all, and so Nan had sent him away. But one afternoon, ten days after the duel, he came again and this time she said that she would see him.

She was sitting on a couch before a burning fire, for the weather was cold and wet, and her head was bent in her arm. She did not even glance up until he sat down and reached over to put one arm about her, and then she looked at him with red and swollen eyes. Her dress was plain black and she wore not a ribbon or a jewel, her hair was tumbled and only carelessly combed, and her face was shiny with tears; her head ached and she looked thinner than she had.

"I'm sorry Amber," he said softly, tenderness and sympathy in his eyes and the tone of his voice. "I know how little it means to hear that when you've lost someone—but I mean it with all my heart, and please believe me when I say that Bruce—"

She gave him a venomous glare. "Don't you dare speak of him to me! Much I care how sorry *he* is. If it hadn't been for him Rex would still be alive!"

Almsbury looked at her in surprise and an expression of impatience crossed his features, but she had covered her face with her hands and was crying again, wiping at the tears with a wet wadded handkerchief.

"That isn't fair, Amber, and you know it. He asked you to stop the duel; he even let Captain Morgan cut his arm in the hope that that would satisfy him. There was nothing more to do unless he had let Morgan kill him—and surely even you couldn't have expected that."

"Oh, I don't care what he did! He killed Rex! He murdered him—and I loved him! I was going to marry him!"

"In that case," said the Earl, with unmistakable sarcasm, "it would have been better judgement not to go off on a honeymoon with another man—even if he was an old friend."

"Oh, mind your own business!" she muttered, and though he hesitated for a moment, Almsbury got to his feet, made her a polite bow and went out of the room. Amber neither spoke nor tried to stop him.

She did not feel able to go back to the theatre immediately, and then shortly after the first of June it closed for two months. But as soon as she began to admit visitors her own apartments became almost as crowded as the tiring-room. She found, somewhat to her surprise, that the duel had made her as much the fashion as red-heeled shoes or Chatelin's Ordinary. Lord Carlton was handsome, his family one of the oldest and most honourable, and his exploits as a privateer had made him a spectacular figure, not only at Court but throughout the city.

Amber knew how much such popularity meant, but she determined to take every advantage of it that she possibly could. Somewhere among those clamoring beaus, those beribboned fops and wit-imitators, there must be a man—a man who would fall in love with her as Rex had done; and if she could but single him out, this time she would know what to do. Marriage she did not expect, for the social position of an actress was no better than that of the vizard-masks in the pit, and with Rex dead her earlier opinion of matrimony had revived. But the brilliant lavish exciting life of an exclusive harlot seemed to her a most pleasant one.

She saw herself occupying a magnificent house in St. James's Field or Pall Mall, driving about town in her gilt coach-and-six, giving fabulous entertainments, setting the styles which would be taken up at Whitehall. She saw herself famous, admired, desired and—most of all—envied.

It was what she had wanted for a long time; and now that she had begun to reconcile herself to the fact of Rex Morgan's death, the wish opened once more into quick full blossom. Optimistically, she decided that he was all that had kept her from having those things.

But though she encouraged them all, flirted with them and laughed at their jokes, she never accepted their proposals. She knew that they held constancy in contempt, but also that they valued a woman more if she pretended concern for her virtue and made a great issue of surrender—just as they would rather win money from a man who hated to lose it. And so far no one had offered what she wanted.

"Phoo pox, Mrs. St. Clare!" said one of them to her. "A virtuous woman is a crime against nature!"

"Well," retorted Amber, "then there aren't many criminals nowadays."

But nevertheless she was growing uneasy and discouraged and in spite of her insistence that she intended never to err again, the other actresses taunted her because she had not found another keeper.

"I hear the young gentlemen are grown mighty shy of keeping these days," remarked Knepp one afternoon when she and Beck Marshall had come to call on Amber. Over her glass of clary—a potent drink made of brandy and clary-flowers flavoured with sugar and cinnamon and ambergris—she flipped Beck a sly wink. "They say three months is the limit a man will keep now, for fear of losing his reputation as a wit."

"Oh, gad, a man is as much laughed at for keeping as ever he was for taking a wife," said Beck. "More, I believe, for at least a wife brings a dowry to settle his debts, while a whore gives him nothing but a bastard and more debts."

"Especially," said Amber, "if she's being kept by three or four at once."

Beck looked at her sharply. "What d'you mean by that, madame?"

"Heavens, Beck." Amber opened her eyes wide in pretended innocence. "I'm sure it isn't my fault if your conscience troubles you."

"My conscience doesn't trouble me at all! Don't you agree it's better to be kept by three men at once—than by none at all?" She gave Amber a malicious tight-lipped smile, and then defiantly downed her drink at one gulp.

"Well," said Amber, "I'm glad I learnt my lesson on that score. I intend never to go into keeping again."

"Hah!" Knepp gave a sudden short barking laugh, and then she and Beck got up and prepared to leave.

As Amber closed the door after them she heard Knepp say, "She intends never to go into keeping again—until she can find the man who'll make her an indecent proposal at a high figure!" And the giggling voices of the two women faded away down the stairwell.

Amber turned back to Nan, who rolled her eyes and shook her head.

"Oh, Nan, maybe they're right! I half believe it's harder to find a man who'll keep than one who'll marry."

"Well, mam—"

"Now don't tell me again I should have married Captain Morgan!" she cried warningly. "I'm sick of hearing it!"

"Lord, mam, I wasn't going to say anything about that. But I have been thinking of a plan you might try."

"What?"

"If you quit the theatre, took lodgings in the City and set

yourself up for a rich widow, I'll warrant you'd find a husband with a good portion within the month."

"My God, Nan! Can you imagine me married to some stinking old alderman with nothing to do but breed his brats and visit his aunts and cousins and sisters and go to church twice on Sundays for my diversion? No thanks! I'm not that discouraged—yet!"

For three months it had rained, and then on the last day of June the sun came out brilliantly, the puddles in the streets began to dry, and the air was fresh and sparkling-clean. Children appeared, like a ragged legion sprung up overnight, in every alley and lane and courtyard in London, running and shouting joyously at their gutter games. Vendors and ballad-singers and housewives swarmed out-of-doors to feel the sun, and in St. James's Park and the Mall courtiers and ladies strolled again.

Since his Majesty's Restoration St. James's Park was open to the public and not only the nobility but other idlers were free to saunter through its broad tree-lined avenues and stop to watch the King playing pall mall, which he did with the same enthusiasm and skill he showed at every kind of athletic contest.

Amber went there that pleasant sunny afternoon with three young men—Jack Conway, Tom Trivet and Sir Humphrey Perepound—who had come to invite her to supper. It was scarcely four o'clock when they left her apartments and so they had some time to waste until the supper hour. At the Park entrance they got out of their hired coach and started off up Birdcage Walk, so called because the trees were full of cages containing singing and squawking birds from Peru, the East Indies, and China.

The three fops were all younger sons who lived far above their means and much in debt. Up at noon, they escaped by some back door or window to avoid their creditors. They strolled then to the nearest ordinary for dinner, went next to the playhouse where they got in free under the pretext of intending to stay for but one act, spent part of the evening in a tavern playing cards and the rest in a bawdy-house, and started for home at midnight, noisy and surly and drunken. Not one of them was over twenty, they would never inherit an estate, and the King probably was not even able to recognize them at sight. But Amber had been alone when they had called and she would rather be seen with anyone than no one—for obviously if a woman lay shut up in her house she could not bring herself to the attention of a great man.

She always hoped and expected that this day might be the day for which she had been waiting. But her hopes had been sorely buffeted these past six weeks and were beginning to show signs of wear.

They kept up an unceasing chatter, gossiping about everyone who passed, bowing obsequiously to the lords and ladies of higher rank but judging them vindictively once they had gone by. Amber scarcely listened to them, but her eyes saw every detail of a lady's gown and coiffure, compared it mentally with her own, and went on to the next. She smiled at the men she knew and was amused to see how much it annoyed the women they were attending.

"There's my Lady Bartley with her daughter fast in tow, as usual. Gad, she's exposed the girl at every public mart in town and still they haven't found a taker," Sir Humphrey informed them.

"Nor ever will, as far as I'm concerned. Curse my tripes, but they made a mighty play for me not long since. I vow and swear the old lady is hotter for a son-in-law than the daughter is for a husband—there's never a more eager bed-fellow than your wanton widow. It was her design I should marry her daughter but devote my manhood to her. She told me as much one day when— Now! What d'ye think! She went by like she'd never seen me before! Damn my diaphragm, but these old quality-bawds grow impertinent!"

"Who's that rare creature just coming? She looks as if she would dissolve like an anchovy in claret. Damn me, but she has the most languishing look—"

"She's the great fortune from Yorkshire. They say she hadn't been in town a week when she was discovered in bed with her page. Your country-wench may never learn the art of dressing her carcass, but it doesn't take her long to find out how to please it." Sir Humphrey, as he talked, had taken a bottle of scent from his inner pocket and was touching the stopper to his eyebrows and wrists and hair.

"For my part, gentlemen," said Jack Conway, who was lazily fanning himself with Amber's fan, a trick the beaus all had to show their gentility, "I consider every woman odious but the finest of her sex—" He made Amber a deferential bow. "Madame St. Clare."

"Oh, gad, and I too! I only spoke of the slut to give Sir Humphrey the opportunity of railing at her. I vow, there's no one has the art of wiping out a reputation almost in one breath as it were, like Sir Humphrey."

Jack Conway had begun to comb his hair with a great carved ivory comb and now Tom Trivet took a flagolet from his pocket and started to play a tune on it. Obviously, he had played in company more than he had practiced. Sir Humphrey took advantage of the noise to whisper in her ear.

"Dear madame, I'm most confoundedly your slave. What d'you think I've done with the ribbon you gave me from your smock?"

"I don't know. What did you do? Swallow it?"

"No, madame. Though if you'll give me another to take its

place I will. I've got it tied in a most pretty bow—I'd be most glad to show you. The effect is excellent, let me perish—"

Amber murmured "Hm—" in an absent-minded tone.

For advancing through the crowd with people bowing to him on every side sauntered the gorgeous figure of his Grace, Duke of Buckingham, an equipage of several pages following close in his wake. Everyone turned and stared as he passed, whispers ran along behind the raised fans of elegant ladies, ambitious mothers, eager young girls—all of them hoping for an extra moment's notice from the great Duke.

Oh, damn! thought Amber frantically. Why didn't I wear my new gold-and-black gown! He'll *never* see me in this!

The Duke was advancing steadily. The green plumes on his hat swayed with every nod of his head, the sun glittered on the diamond-buttons of his suit, his handsome, arrogant face and splendid physique gave every other man a look of drab insignificance. Amber had seen Buckingham in the pit and in the tiring-room, she had been presented to him casually once, and she had heard endless gossip about his amorous and political exploits—but he had never paid her any particular attention. Now, however, as he came closer she saw his eyes run over her swiftly and go on and then her heart gave a plunge as they returned again—and this time lingered. He was no more than four yards from her.

"Madame St. Clare?"

The Duke had stopped and was making her a flourishing bow while Amber quickly recovered herself and swept out her skirts in a deep curtsy. She was conscious that other men and women were watching them, turning their heads as they passed, and that her three gallants were stammering foolishly and making desperate efforts at nonchalance. The Duke's mouth was smiling beneath his blond mustache, and his eyes travelled down her body and back up again, as though measuring her by his own private yardstick.

"Your servant, madame."

"Your servant, sir," mumbled Amber, almost suffocated with excitement. She stabbed about wildly for something to say, something to arrest his attention—witty and amusing and different from what any other woman would have said, but she did not find it.

His Grace, however, was at no loss for words. "If I mistake not, you're the lady over whom Lord Carlton fought some officer, a month or so since?"

"Yes, your Grace. I am."

"I've always admired Lord Carlton's taste, madame, and I must say that you're so fine a person I can see no reason to differ from his judgement now."

"Thank you, your Grace."

"Oh, gad, your Grace!" interrupted Sir Humphrey, suddenly bold and swaggering. "Every man in town is adying to be the lady's servant. I vow and swear, her health is drunk as often as the King's—"

Buckingham gave him a brief glance, as though he had noticed him for the first time, and Sir Humphrey wilted instantly. Neither of the two others ventured to speak.

"My coach is at the north gate, madame. I stopped to take a turn in the Park as I was going to supper— It would please me mightily if you would be my guest."

"Oh, I'd like to, your Grace! But I—" She paused, her eyes indicating that she was obligated to the three fops who were now bridling and grinning in anticipation of being invited to sup with the Duke of Buckingham.

The Duke bowed to them, a bow which was at once polite and condescending, which showed his own breeding even while it contrived to belittle theirs. "Sure, now, gentlemen—you've enjoyed the lady's company all afternoon. I know you're all too much men of wit and understanding to wish to deprive others of that privilege. With your permission, gentlemen—"

He offered his arm to Amber, who could not conceal her delight and pride, and making a quick bobbing curtsy to the three beaus she sailed off. She had never been so stared at or felt so full of importance in her life as she did now, for wherever he went the Duke attracted as much attention as the King himself and more than his Highness ever had. On the way to the north gate they passed the Mall where Charles was playing before a gallery crowded with ladies and a packed row of courtiers and beggars and loitering tradesmen. The King—who had just struck the little wooden ball into a hoop suspended from a pole at the opposite end of the Mall—saw them going by and waved. Buckingham bowed.

"If the King would spend as much time in the council-room as he does at the tennis-court and Mall," murmured the Duke as they went on, "the country might be in a better state than it is."

"Than it is? Why, what's the matter with it? It seems well enough to me."

"Women, my dear, never understand such matters and should not—but you may believe me. England's in a most miserable condition. The Stuarts have never been good masters. Here's my coach—"

They circled around the Park and stopped at Long's, a fashionable ordinary in the Haymarket, which was a narrow little suburban lane lined with hedges and surrounded by green fields. The host led them upstairs to a private room and supper was served immediately, while below in the courtyard the Duke's fiddlers played and people gathered from neighbouring cottages to sing and dance to the music. From time to time a cheer went up for the Duke, who was popular with the Londoners because he was well known to be a violent anti-Catholic.

The food was excellent, well-cooked and seasoned, and

served hot by two quiet unobtrusive waiters. But Amber could not enjoy it. She was too much worried about what the Duke was thinking of her, what he would do when the meal was over and what she should do in her turn. He was such a great man, and so rich— If only she could please him enough it might be the making of her fortune.

But it did not seem likely the Duke would be an easy man to please.

He was thirty-six years old, and his life had left him nothing of either illusion or faith. He had raked and probed his emotions, experimented with his senses until they were deadened and dull and he was forced to whip them up by whatever voluptuous device occurred to him. Amber had heard all this and it was what made her uneasy. She was not afraid of what he would do—but that she would never be able to interest this bored and jaded libertine.

Now, once the table had been cleared and they were left alone, he merely took a pack of cards from his pocket and began to shuffle them idly; they flew through his fingers with a speed and sureness which proclaimed the accomplished gamester.

"You look uneasy, madame. Pray compose yourself. I hate to see a woman on edge—it always makes me feel that she expects to be raped, and to tell you truly I'm not in the mood for such strenuous sport tonight."

"Why, I didn't think the woman breathed who couldn't be persuaded by your Grace by an easier means than that." In spite of her awe and eagerness Amber could not keep a certain tartness from her voice; something in the personality of the Duke set her teeth on edge.

But if he noticed the sarcasm he ignored it. He dealt himself two putt hands, one from the top and the other from the bottom of the deck, inspected each with satisfaction and began to shuffle again.

"She doesn't," he said flatly. "Women are all inclined to make two mistakes in love. First, they surrender too easily; second, they can never be convinced that when a man says he is through with them he means it." As he talked he continued to watch the cards, but there had spread over his face a look of brooding discontent, a self-occupied bitterness. "It's long been my opinion the world would run far smoother if women would not insist on expecting love to be a close relation of desire. Your quality whore is always determined to make you fall in love with her—by that means she thinks she justifies the satisfaction of her own appetite. The truth of the matter is madame, that love is only a pretty word—like honour—which people use to cover what they really mean. But now the world has grown too old and too wise for such childish toys—thank God we're beyond needing to deceive ourselves."

He looked up at her now and tossed the cards away. "I take

it you're for hire on the open market. How much do you ask?"

Amber looked at him, her eyes narrowed slightly and slanting at the corners. His harangue, made obviously for the sole purpose of amusing himself, since it was plain he did not consider it necessary to convince her of anything, had made her angry. She had been listening to that kind of talk from the tiring-room gallants for a year and a half, but the Duke was the first man she had met who wholly believed what he said. She would have liked to get up, slap his face and walk out of the room—but he was George Villiers, Duke of Buckingham, and the richest man in England. And her morals were dictated rather by the expediency of the moment than by any abstract formula of honour.

"What am I bid?"

"Fifty pound."

Amber gave a short unpleasant laugh. "I thought you said you weren't in the mood for a rape! Two hundred and fifty!"

For a long moment he sat and stared at her, and then he got up and walked to the door. Amber turned, watched him apprehensively, but he merely spoke to a footman who was waiting just outside and who ran off down the steps. "I'll give you your two hundred and fifty, madame," he said. "But pray don't flatter yourself it's because I think you'll be worth it. I can give you that sum without missing it any more than you would miss a shilling flung to a whining Tom o' Bedlam. And when all's said and done, I doubt not you'll be more surprised by this night's business than I."

Amber was surprised; it was her first experience with perversion. And it would, she swore, be her last if she starved in the streets.

Shocked and disgusted, she conceived a violent loathing for the Duke which not even one thousand pounds could dispel. For days she thought of nothing but how she could contrive to pay him back. But in the end all she could do was put him in her list of enemies to be dealt with at some future date—when she should be powerful enough to ruin them all.

The theatre reopened late in July, and Amber found that she now had among her admirers the finest beaus in town. Buckingham had done that much for her, at any rate.

There was Lord Buckhurst and his plump black-eyed friend Sir Charles Sedley. The huge and handsome Dick Talbot, wild Harry Killigrew, Henry Sidney whom many thought to be the finest-looking man in England, and Colonel James Hamilton who was generally considered the best-dressed man at Whitehall. All of them were young, from Sidney who was twenty-two to Talbot who was thirty-three; all of them came of distinguished families and were allied through marriage or blood to the country's ruling houses; all of them frequented the innermost circles of the Court, associated on familiar terms with the

King and might have been men of more consequence if they had cared to spare the time from their amusements.

Almost every night she went to supper with one or more of them, sometimes in a crowd of young men and women—actresses and orange-girls and other professed whores—often it was an intimate group of only two or three. They drank toasts to her and strained wine through the hem of her smock, and anatomized her among themselves. She went to the bear-baitings and cockfights and spent three or four days at Banstead Downs with Buckhurst and Sedley, attending the horse-races—for the old passionate English love of field sports had returned three-fold since the Restoration.

She went several times to Bartholomew Fair during the three weeks it was in progress, saw every puppet-show and rope-dancer, gorged herself on roast pig and gingerbread and made a great collection of Bartholomew Babies—the pretty dolls which it was customary for a gentleman to buy and present to the lady he admired.

One Sunday afternoon she visited Bedlam, to see the insane hung up in cages, their hair matted and smeared with their own filth, raving and screaming at the sight-seers who jeered at and tormented them. At Bridewell, where they went to watch the prostitutes being beaten, Talbot recognized a woman he had known some time since and she began to yell at him, pointing her finger and accusing him of being the cause of her present shame and misery. But when they wanted to stop at Newgate to visit the great highwayman, Claude de Vall, who was holding his court there, Amber declined.

After the play she often drove in Hyde Park with four or five young men, and sometimes she saw a copy of her latest gown on one of the Court ladies. She slept short hours, neglected her dancing and singing and guitar lessons, and was so little interested in the theatre that Killigrew threatened to turn her out and would have done so but for the intervention of Buckhurst and Sedley and his own son. When he chided her for missing rehearsal or forgetting her lines—or not even troubling to learn them—she laughed and shrugged her shoulders or flew into a fit of anger and went home. The fops threatened to boycott the theatre if Madame St. Clare was not there, and so Hart and Lacy and Kynaston would be sent to coax her back again. Her popularity made her arrogant and saucy.

At first she had intended to be just as independent and unattainable as she had been at the beginning of her acquaintance with Rex Morgan. But the gentlemen were not subtle. They told her frankly that they would never spend the time courting an actress which they would lavish on a Maid of Honour. And Amber, faced with the alternative of abandoning either her resolutions or her popularity, did not hesitate long in her choice. When Sedley and Buckhurst offered her one hundred pounds to spend a week with them at Epsom Wells she went. But she was never offered so large a sum again.

To each of her lovers she gave a bracelet made from her abundant hair, and some who did not get them had imitations made which they swore were hers. Her name began to appear in the almanack records of half the young fops in town, many of whom she did not even know. Buckhurst gave her a painted fan with a dreamy sylvan scene on one side and on the other the loves of Jupiter which depicted the god in the guise of a swan, a bull, a ram, an eagle, with various women—all of whom looked like Amber. Within a week copies of it were hiding blushes and veiling smiles in the Queen's Drawing-room.

In December a filthy verse which was unmistakably about her—though the woman in it was called "Chloris" and the man "Philander," after the old pastoral tradition—began to circulate through the tiring-room and the taverns and bawdy-houses. Amber, who was becoming tired, resented it deeply though she knew many similar poems had been written with far less provocation than she had given, but she could never find out whose it was. She suspected either Buckhurst or Sedley, both poets and very creditable ones, but when she accused them they smiled blandly and protested their innocence. Harry Killigrew followed the insult by flipping her a half-crown piece one night when she tardily suggested a settlement.

Early in January she spent two nights in succession at home without a caller or an invitation, and she knew all at once that her vogue was passing. And only a few days later Mrs. Fagg confirmed her fears that she was again with child. She felt suddenly sick and discouraged and exhausted. It was all but impossible for her to force herself to get out of bed in the morning, her appetite was gone, she looked pallid and thin and there were dark smudges beneath her eyes. Almost anything could bring forth a passionate flood of tears or a hysterical tantrum.

"I wish I were dead!" she told Nan. For her future was only too clear.

Nan suggested that they go away from London for a few weeks and when Mrs. Fagg advised a long ride in a coach, to be taken with her own special medicine, she agreed. "If I never see another fop or another play as long as I live I'll be glad!" she cried violently. She hated London and the playhouse, all men and even herself.

Chapter Twenty-four

AMBER DECIDED to go to Tunbridge Wells in the hope that drinking the waters would make her feel better. She set out early the next morning in her coach with Nan and Tansy, Tempest and Jeremiah. As it was raining, they could travel at but little more than a foot-pace, and even then the coach almost turned over several times.

Amber rode along in sullen silence, eyes tight shut and teeth clenched, not even hearing the chattering of Nan and Tansy. She had taken Mrs. Fagg's evil-tasting medicine and her belly was full of grinding cramps which seemed worse than those of child-birth. She wished that the earth would open and swallow them all, that a thunderbolt from heaven would strike her, or merely that she would die and be relieved of her misery. She told herself that if a man ever dared make her an indecent proposal again, though for a thousand pound in gold, she would have him kicked like a common lackey.

They stopped at an inn late that afternoon and went on the next morning. The medicine had taken its effect but she felt even worse than she had the day before, and at each turn of the wheels she longed to open her mouth and scream as loud as she could. She scarcely noticed when the coach came to a stop and Nan began wiping at the steamy window with her sleeve, putting her face against it to look out.

"Lord, mam! I hope we're not set upon by highwaymen!" She had the same apprehension almost every time Tempest and Jeremiah had stopped to pry the wheels out of the mud.

Amber scowled crossly, but kept her eyes shut. "My God, Nan! You expect a highwayman behind every tree! I tell you they don't go abroad in weather like this!"

At that moment Jeremiah opened the door. "It's a gentleman, mam, who's been stopped by highwaymen and his horses taken."

Nan gave a little cry and turned to her with an accusing stare. Amber made a face. "Well, ask him if he wants to ride with us. But tell 'im we're only going to the Wells."

The man who returned with Jeremiah was perhaps sixty, though his skin was clear and smooth and fresh-coloured. His hair was white, cut much shorter than a Cavalier's, and was not curled but had merely a slight natural wave. He was handsome, somewhat above six feet, erect and broad-shouldered. The clothes he wore were old-fashioned but well made of fine materials, sober black and untrimmed with ribbon or gold braid.

He bowed to her politely, but his manner suggested nothing of the French-tutored courtier. This was some plain City-bred man, very likely a parliamentarian who thought the worst of Charles Stuart and all his beribboned cursing whoring sword-fighting crew—a substantial merchant, perhaps, or a jeweller or a goldsmith.

"Good afternoon, madame. It's very kind of you to invite me into your coach. Are you quite sure I won't be making you uncomfortable?"

"Not at all, sir. I'm glad to be of service. Pray get in, before the rain soaks you through."

He climbed in, Nan and Tansy moved over to make room for him, and the coach started off. "My name is Samuel Dangerfield, madame."

"Mine is Mrs. St. Clare."

Mrs. St. Clare obviously meant nothing to him, and for once she welcomed the anonymity. "Did my coachman tell you that I'm only going as far as Tunbridge? I don't doubt you can hire horses and another coach there."

"Thank you for the suggestion, madame. But as it happens I too am going to Tunbridge."

They talked little after that and Nan explained her mistress's silence by saying that she was suffering wretchedly from a quartan ague. Mr. Dangerfield was sympathetic, said he had had that ailment himself, and suggested bleeding as a sovereign remedy. Within three hours they arrived at the village.

Tunbridge Wells was a fashionable spa and the previous summer her Majesty and all the Court had paid it a visit; but now, in mid-January, it was a dreary deserted scattered little village. Not a person was in sight, the elms that lined the single main street were naked and forlorn, and only the smoke drifting from several chimneys gave evidence of life.

Amber and Samuel Dangerfield parted at the inn, where he had accommodations, and she promptly forgot him. She rented a neat little three-room cottage, furnished with very old polished oak, chintz curtains, and an array of shining brass and copper utensils. For four days she did not get out of bed but lay sleeping and resting, and by the end of that time her vitality and energy began to return. She started worrying again about what was to become of her.

"Well, I can't go back to London, that's sure as the smallpox," she told Nan as she sat morosely in bed, propped against pillows and plucking at her brows with a silver-plated tweezer.

"I'm sure I don't see why, mam."

"Don't see why! D'you think I'd ever go back to that scurvy theatre again, and have every town-fop laughing in his fist at me? I will not!"

"Well, after all, mam, you can go back to London without going back to the stage, can't you? It's a sorry mouse that has but one hole." Nan liked well-worn aphorisms.

"I don't know where else I'd go," muttered Amber.

Nan drew in a deep breath to prepare for her next speech, but kept her eyes on her deftly stitching needle. "I still think, mam, that if you'd take lodgings in the City and set yourself up for a rich widow you'd not be long a-catching a husband. Maybe you don't want to—but beggars should be no choosers."

Amber looked at her sharply. Then suddenly she flung the tweezers away, tossed the mirror aside and slumped back against the pillows with her arms folded. For several moments both women remained silent and Nan did not even glance at her glowering mistress. But at last Amber smoothed out her face and gave a sigh.

"I wonder," she said, "if Mr. What-d'ye-call—who had his horses stolen—is rich enough to bother with." Mr. Dangerfield had sent two days earlier to inquire if her ague was improving; she had returned a careless ungracious reply and had thought nothing of him since then.

"He might be, mam. He's got a mighty handsome young footman I could go talk to for a while."

Nan came back a couple of hours later flushed and excited—not altogether, Amber suspected, by the news she had heard. "Well?" asked Amber, who was lying out flat with her arms braced behind her head. She had spent the time since Nan's departure gloomily mulling over her past errors and disliking the men she considered to have been responsible for them. "What did you find out?"

Nan swept into the room, bringing with her a gust of cool fresh air from the outside and a buoyant energy. "I found out *everything!*" she declared triumphantly, untying the strings of her hood and throwing it into a chair. With her cloak still on she rushed to the bed and sat down beside Amber, who stubbornly refused to catch her enthusiasm. "I found out that Mr. Samuel Dangerfield is one of the richest men in England!"

"One of the richest men in—England!" repeated Amber slowly, still incredulous.

"Yes! He's got a fortune! Oh, I can't remember! Two hundred thousand pound or something like that! John says everybody knows how rich he is! He's a merchant and he's—"

"Two hundred thous— Is he married?" demanded Amber suddenly, as her wits began to revive.

"No, he isn't! He was but his wife died—six years ago I think John said. But he's got fourteen children; some other ones are dead—I forget how many. He comes up here every year to drink the waters for his health—he had a stroke. And he's just getting ready now to go down to the wells—Big John's going with 'im!"

Suddenly Amber flung back the covers and began to get out of bed. "I think I'll go drink some waters myself. Get out my green velvet gown with the gold braid and the green cloak. Is it muddy enough to wear chopins?"

"I think it is, mam." Nan was scurrying busily about, searching through unfamiliar drawers for smocks and petticoats, ransacking the still half-unpacked trunk for garters and ribbons, chattering all the while. "Only to think, mam! What luck we're in! I vow and swear you must have been born with a caul on your head!" Both women were gayer and in better spirits than they had been for some weeks past.

It had stopped raining the day before and the night had been cold, so that there was a crust on the mud. A pale sun sifted down through the grey-blue sky and there were whiffs of clouds overhead, too white and thin to threaten more immediate rain. Country girls in straw hats and short skirts, with baskets over their arms, appeared in the street crying their wares of poultry and fresh butter, milk and vegetables. And when Amber, with Nan and Tansy, strolled to the well two young men in ribboned suits and plumed hats, with long curling wigs and elaborate swords, bowed ceremoniously and begged leave to present themselves. It was the custom of such resort-places, where a man might with propriety introduce himself.

They were Frank Kifflin and Will Wigglesworth and they told her that they had come down from London to avoid a lady who was beginning to insist that Will marry her. Amber had never seen either of them at the theatre and decided that they were most likely a pair of rooks who posed as men of quality, or perhaps younger sons who had to live like gentlemen without being given the means to do so. Card-sharpers, pickpockets, forgers, they preyed upon the naïve ad unsuspecting—young country squires and heiresses were their easiest dupes. Luke Channell had been a crude specimen of the breed; Dick Robbins who had lived at Mother Red-Cap's a subtler and more clever one. Probably, since Tunbridge could not be a very fertile field for such activities at that time of the year, they had been run out of London or some other city and were in temporary retirement here.

To Amber's dismay they perked up immediately when she told them her name. "Mrs. St. Clare?" repeated Will Wigglesworth, an ugly pock-marked weasel-toothed young man. "I vow to gad the name's familiar, madame. What about you, Frank? Haven't we met Mrs. St. Clare somewhere before?"

"Why yes, I'm sure we have, madame. Where could it have been, I wonder? Were you at Banstead Downs last year, perhaps?"

Oh, damn! thought Amber. If these fools find out who I am and Mr. Dangerfield hears about it, I wouldn't have any more chance with him than the man in the moon!

But she smiled at them very sweetly. "No, gentlemen, I'm sure you've got some other lady in mind. Neither of you looks at all familiar to me—and I know I'd never have forgotten your faces if we'd ever met."

Both of them took that for a compliment, grinned and coughed and made simultaneous bows. "Your servant, madame." But even then they would not let the subject drop and, probably for lack of other conversation, galloped along in relentless pursuit. Frank asked Will if they hadn't seen her in the Mall, and Will assured Frank it must have been in the Drawing-room. Amber denied having been anywhere at all and was casting about for a means of escape when Mr. Dangerfield arrived and came to speak to her.

"You're looking very well, madame. I hope your ague is improved?"

She curtsied and smiled at him, and wished she could blow Kifflin and Wigglesworth away like two puffs of smoke. However, while Amber and Mr. Dangerfield talked of the weather, the taste of the well-water, and Tansy's scuffed shoes, they fiddled with their ribbons and combs and rolled their eyes about, obviously wishing that the old dotard would go away. But when Amber presented them to him she was amused to see the great change in their manners. She knew for sure then that she had guessed them for what they really were.

"Samuel Dangerfield, sir?" repeated Will Wigglesworth, as both of them jerked suddenly to attention. "I know a Bob Dangerfield. That is, we met once at the home of a mutual friend. He's a member of the great merchant family. Are you, by any chance, sir, a relative?"

"I'm Bob's father."

"Well, well. Only fancy, Frank. This is Bob's father."

"Hm, only fancy. Pray take our regards to Bob, sir, when you return to London."

"Thank you, gentlemen, I will."

Amber was growing nervous for she did not want them to begin talking and guessing at her identity again before Mr. Dangerfield. "If you'll excuse me, gentlemen, I must be getting back now. Your servant, sir." She curtsied again to Mr. Dangerfield, but as she would have left, the two young men insisted that they be allowed to see her home.

"Faith and troth, Will," said Frank Kifflin, as soon as they were out of Mr. Dangerfield's hearing. "Only think of meeting Bob's old father here. He seems a close acquaintance of yours, Mrs. St. Clare."

"Oh, no. I happened upon him just after his coach had been held up and his horses stolen, and carried him the rest of the way."

Will was indignant. "Lord, to see the effrontery of the highwaymen nowadays! I vow it's barbarous! They'll stop at nothing to gain their ends. And only to think of the scurvy rascals daring to attack a man of Mr. Dangerfield's consequence!"

"Barbarous!" agreed Frank.

As Amber stood in her doorway bidding them goodbye, Wigglesworth, who had been studying her face carefuly for some moments, suddenly gave a snap of his fingers. "I know who you are now, Mrs. St. Clare! You're the player from His Majesty's Theatre!"

"Of course! That's who she is, Will! I knew all along we'd seen you before, madame. But why so modest, pray? Most actresses are—"

"An actress!" protested Amber. "Lord, whatever put that unlucky notion into your heads! It may be I resemble one of the wretches, but then it's the practice of all of 'em to try to look like quality, they tell me. No, gentlemen, you've made a mistake. I assure you I've never been nearer the stage than the middle-box. And now, good-day."

But she knew by the sly looks they exchanged and the smiles on their faces when they bowed, that she had not convinced them. When the door was shut Amber leaned back against it with a low whistle.

"Whew! Blast those two paper-skulled nuisances! I've got to find a way to be rid of *them,* that's flat!"

When they came that night and invited her to go with them to the gaming-house Amber's first impulse was to refuse. But it occurred to her then that she might be able to catch them at something and scare them away from the Wells, and so she agreed. On the way Frank Kifflin suggested that they stop and ask Mr. Dangerfield to join them.

"Most likely the poor old gentleman's lonely, and though gad knows I hate to play with an old man I can't bear to think of Bob's old father being lonely."

But Amber did not intend to have Mr. Dangerfield told that she was an actress. "Mr. Dangerfield never plays cards, gentlemen. He hates the sight of 'em worse than a Quaker hates a parrot. You know these old Puritans."

The men, obviously disappointed, agreed that they did.

There were not a score of persons gathered about the tables in the gaming-house, and of those some were obviously natives of the town playing for only a few pence or shillings. Amber and the two men watched for a while and finally Frank Kifflin suggested that they try their luck at raffle—a dice game which they assured her was the most harmless in the world and depended upon nothing but a turn of the wrist. "Oh, heavens, gentlemen," said Amber with an air of surprised innocence. "I can't play. I only came along to watch and keep you company. I never carry money with me when I'm travelling."

That seemed to please Mr. Kifflin. "Very wise, Mrs. St. Clare. Travel is full of too many hazards these days. But pray let me lend you ten or twenty pound—it's but dull entertainment watching others play."

Amber pretended to hesitate. "Well—I don't know if I should or not—"

"Tush, madame! Why shouldn't you? And let's not speak a word of interest, I beg of you. Only a rook would accept interest from so fine a person as yourself."

"What a courtier you are, Mr. Kifflin!" said Amber, thinking that if they did not want interest for their money they must have some other game.

Between them Mr. Kifflin and Mr. Wigglesworth produced a great many shiny shillings from their pockets and put them on the table before her. There was not a guinea or a penny or another coin in the pile, nothing but shillings. It was not very difficult to guess that they must be hired by some counterfeiter to pass his false money and get back true. Amber obligingly lost several pounds and when she quit said that she would send a note to her goldsmith immediately so that they could collect next time they were in London.

"But remember, Mrs. St. Clare," said Wigglesworth the last thing before they parted. "We'll accept not a penny in interest. Not a penny."

Amber examined some of the coins and was sure that they were "blackdogs"—double-washed pewter discs; they looked and sounded exactly like those made by the counterfeiter who had lived on the third-floor at Mother Red-Cap's. She tossed one of them up and caught it, laughing and giving a wink to Nan.

"I'll take care of those two young fop-doodles, I warrant you. Send Jeremiah the first thing tomorrow morning to invite Mr. Dangerfield to take his dinner with me. Let's see—I believe I'll wear that black velvet gown with the white lace collar and cuffs—it gives me a maidenly air, don't you think?"

"If anything could, mam."

When Samuel Dangerfield arrived Amber met him at the door. Her gown was high-necked but the bodice fitted snugly. She had her hair combed into deep waves and held at each temple by a black velvet bow; and her face was painted so subtly that even a woman could not have been sure the colouring was not natural.

"It was kind of you to invite me to dinner, Mrs. St. Clare."

"I know it isn't proper," she said demurely, "but I sent such a barbarous reply to your note—pray forgive me, sir. It was the sickness made me churlish."

Amber knew that her invitation was unconventional but hoped she could affect sufficient modesty to fool him. He smiled at her now much as he might have smiled at a pretty little kitten.

They discussed her ague for a few moments, and then took their places at a table which Nan had set in the parlour next the fireplace. The footman had informed Nan that his master had a hearty appetite—though he was now under his physician's orders to eat sparingly—and the meal Amber had had sent down from the inn was an ample one. She thought it would be more to her interest to please Mr. Dangerfield than his doctor.

Without much difficulty Amber had soon maneuvered the conversation around to Mr. Kifflin and Mr. Wigglesworth. Off-handedly, she told him how they had come to her house last night to ask her to change some money for them. She said that she had only brought fifteen or twenty guineas to Tunbridge, but that she had given them to the young men to pay their gambling debts with, and was now wondering how she would ever pack all those shillings into her trunk.

Mr. Dangerfield, as she had hoped, seemed somewhat

alarmed by this innocent tale. "Are you well acquainted with Mr. Kifflin and his friends?"

"Heavens, no! I met them yesterday morning at the well. They introduced themselves. You know how little one goes upon ceremony in places like this."

"You're very young, Mrs. S. Clare, and I don't imagine you understand the ways of the world so well as an old man. If I may I'd like to give you some advice—and that is not to accept too much money from those gentlemen. They may be honest as they pretend, but when you've lived as long as I you'll know it's best to be cautious with a new acquaintance—particularly if you happen upon him at a public resort."

"Oh," said Amber, suddenly crestfallen. "But I thought that Tunbridge Wells was frequented by persons of the best quality! My physician who sent me here told me that her Majesty was here with all her ladies only last summer."

"Yes, I believe she was. But where there's quality there are sure to be rooks. And it's unworldly young persons like yourself of whom they'll take the greatest advantage."

While he talked Amber reached up to adjust the bow in her hair, as a signal for Nan who was waiting just outside and peeking in the window. "Oh!" she said, with a troubled frown, "how could I have been so foolish! I hope—"

At that moment Nan came in, out of breath, and stood in the doorway taking off her chopins. "Heavens, mam!" she cried excitedly. "The landlord at the inn refused the money! He says it's a false coin!"

"A false coin! Why, that was one Mr. Kifflin gave me last night!"

Samuel Dangerfield turned in his chair. "May I see it?" He took it from Nan, rung it upon the table and felt of the edges while both women watched him. "It is a false one," he said seriously. "So the young coxcombs are counterfeiters. That's a sorry business—and a dangerous one. I wonder how many others they've got to change money with them?"

"Everyone who looked simple enough, I suppose!" said Amber indignantly. "Well, I think we should call the constable and put 'em where they belong!"

Mr. Dangerfield, however, was less inclined to be vindictive. "The laws are too harsh—they'd be hanged, drawn, and quartered." That would not have troubled Amber but she thought it best not to say so. "I believe we can manage them some other way. Do you think, Mrs. St. Clare, that you could get them to come here on some pretext or other?"

"Why, they should be along any mintue—they asked me to walk to the well with them."

When they arrived, not much later, Nan opened the door. At sight of Mr. Dangerfield their mouths opened into broad grins—and then closed suddenly when he said: "Mrs. St. Clare and I have just been discussing the fact that there seem to be counterfeiters at Tunbridge."

Kifflin raised his eyebrows. "Counterfeiters? Gad! It's unthinkable! I swear the wretches grow bolder every day!"

While Wigglesworth exclaimed, as though he could not believe his own ears, "Counterfeiters at Tunbridge!"

"Yes," said Amber. "I have a shilling that was just refused at the inn and Mr. Dangerfield says it's not a true coin. Perhaps they'd like to see it, sir."

He gave it to Wigglesworth and both young men examined it closely, frowning, while Kifflin cleared his throat. Their faces were beginning to shine with sweat.

"It looks good enough to me," said Kifflin at last. "But then I'm such a simple fellow someone has always got me on the hip."

Wigglesworth laughed, not very enthusiastically. "That's exactly my case, to the letter." He returned the coin.

"The constable," said Mr. Dangerfield gravely, "will be along soon to look at this coin. If he finds it to be false I suppose he'll examine every person in the village."

At that moment a country girl went by outside carrying a basket over her arm and crying, "Fresh new eggs! Who'll buy my new fresh eggs?"

Kifflin turned about quickly. "There she is, Will. I hope you'll excuse us, Mrs. St. Clare, but we came to ask if we might wait upon you later in the day. We overslept and came out in search of some eggs for our dinner. Good-day, madame. Good-day, sir."

He and Wigglesworth bowed, backed their way out of the room, and once outside turned and started off in all haste. Their pace increased, they passed the girl without giving her so much as a glance, and when they had gone two hundred yards broke into an open run and at last cut off the main street and disappeared from sight. Amber and Mr. Dangerfield, who had gone out to watch, looked at each other and then burst into laughter.

"Look at 'em go!" cried Amber. "I vow they won't stop for breath till they've reached Paris!"

She shut the door again and gave a little sigh. "Well, I hope I've learnt my lesson. I vow I'll never put my trust in strangers again."

He was smiling down at her. "A young lady as pretty as you are should be suspicious of all strangers." He said it with the air of a man who intends to be very gallant, without ever having had much practice. And when she answered the compliment with a quick upward slanting glance he cleared his throat and his ruddy face darkened. "Hem—I wonder, Mrs. St. Clare, if you'd care to put your trust in this stranger long enough to walk to the well with him?"

Confidence was beginning to sweep through Amber, and the

intoxication she always felt when she knew a man was attracted to her. "Of course I would, sir. I think I know an *honest* man when I see him—even if I can't always tell one who isn't."

Amber had acted in numerous plays depicting the rigid austere hypocritical life of the City families, and, though all of them had been bitter and satirical and slanderously exaggerated, she had taken them for literal truth. Consequently, she thought she knew exactly what Samuel Dangerfield would admire in a woman; but she soon discovered that her own instinct was a surer guide.

For as she became better acquainted with him she began to realize that even though he was a City merchant and a Presbyterian he was nevertheless a man. And she found to her surprise that he bore no resemblance at all to the sanctimonious severe dour old humbugs who had occasioned such derisive laughter at His Majesty's Theatre.

If he was not frivolous, neither was he grimly sober; his disposition was a happy one and he laughed easily. He had worked hard all his life, for he had accumulated most of that vast fortune himself, but he was all the more susceptible to a young woman's gaiety now. His family life had been a close one, but that had given him perhaps a sense of loss, and of curiosity. Amber came into his life like a spring gale, fresh, invigorating, a challenge to whatever he had of dormant venturesomeness. She was everything he had never known before in a woman, and much he had scarcely suspected.

It was not long before they were spending hours out of every day together, and though Samuel insisted that she must grow bored with the company of an old man and urged her to become acquainted with the few young people who were there, Amber insisted that she hated young fellows who were always so silly and empty-headed and thought of nothing but dancing or gambling or going to the play. She kept in close and never went out when she could avoid it, for she was afraid that someone else might recognize her.

And she thought that she could guess pretty well what he would think of an actress, by his opinion of the Court in general. For one day, after some mention of King Charles, he said: "His Majesty could be the greatest ruler our nation has ever had but, unfortunately, not only for him but for all of us, the years of exile were his ruin. He learned a set of habits and a way of living during that time from which he can never escape—partly, I'm afraid, because he doesn't want to."

Amber, stitching on a piece of embroidery borrowed from Nan's work-basket, observed soberly that she had heard Whitehall had grown a most wicked place.

"It is wicked. Wicked and corrupt. Honour is a sham, virtue a laughing-stock, marriage the butt for vulgar jests. There are still decent and honest men aplenty at Whitehall, as everywhere else in England—but knaves and fools elbow them aside."

Most of their conversation, however, was less serious, and he seldom cared to discuss ethical or even political matters with her. Women were not interested in such things, and pretty ones least of all. Besides, she was his escape from them.

But Amber did often ask him to advise her about financial matters; and listened wide-eyed and with her head nodding every so often to his talk of interest and principal, mortgages, title-deeds, and revenue. She talked of her goldsmith and when she mentioned Shadrac Newbold's name was glad to see how favourably impressed he seemed. She said that it was a great responsibility for her to handle her husband's money—she represented herself as a rich young widow—and that she worried a great deal for fear someone would cheat her out of it. That was another reason, she said, why she was always suspicious of young men who wished to strike up an acquaintance. She almost talked frequently about her family and what terrible things they had suffered in the Wars—recounting, with elaboration, tales she had heard from Almsbury about his own or Lord Carton's difficulties. By these devices she hoped to discourage him, had he been so inclined, from taking her for a fortune-hunter.

They played dozens of games of wit-and-reason, and she always let him win. She made him laugh with her mimicry of the fat middle-aged women and gouty old men who were there taking the waters. She played for him on her guitar and sang songs—not ribald street-ballads, but gay country tunes or the old English folk-songs: "Chevy Chase," "Phillida Flouts Me," "Highland Mary." She pampered and flattered him and teased him, treated him at all times as though he was much younger than he was, and yet was as solicitous for his comfort as if he had been much older. She guessed his age one day at forty-five and when he told her that his eldest son was thirty-five, insisted he could never make her believe that Banbury-story. She gave a lively imitation of a woman most thoroughly infatuated.

But at the end of three weekes he had not tried to seduce her and she was growing worried.

She stood at the window one evening just after he had gone and traced idle patterns on the frosted pane with her finger-nail. Her lower lip stuck out and there was a scowl on her forehead.

Nan, who was lifting hot embers out of the fireplace with a pair of tongs and putting them into a silver warming-pan, glanced sideways at her. "Something amiss, mam?"

Amber swung around, giving a petulant switch to her skirt. "Yes, there is! Oh, Nan. I'm ready to run distracted! Three weeks I've been coursing this hare—and haven't caught 'im yet!"

Nan closed the warming-pan and started into the bedroom with it. "But he's getting winded, mam. I know he is."

Amber followed her in and began to undress, but her face was gloomy and from time to time she gave an impatient ill-tempered sigh. It seemed to her that she had been trying all her life to make Samuel Dangerfield propose to her. Nan came to help her undress and stood behind her, unlacing her busk.

"Lord, mam!" she protested now. "You've got no cause for such vapourings! I know these formal old Puritans—I've worked in their houses. They think fornication's a serious matter, let me tell you! Why, I'd bet my virginity he hasn't laid with any woman save his wife these twenty years past! Heavens, give the gentleman leave to overcome his modesty! And what's more, don't forget you've gone to the greatest pains to make him take you for a woman of virtue. But I've watched him like a witch and I know he's mighty uneasy—there's fire in the flax and it'll be quenched," she added with a sage nod. "Only give 'im the right opportunity and you'll have 'im—secure as a woodcock in a noose." She made her two hands into a trap and put them about her own neck.

While Amber stepped out of her smock Nan whisked the warming-pan over the sheets, held back the covers and Amber jumped in, pulling them up quickly about her chin. Then she lay there in luxurious warmth and considered her problem.

This was, and she knew it, her last chance to take the world by its ears and climb on top. If she failed now—but she could not fail. She did not dare. She had seen too much at first hand of what happened to the women who, like her, made a livelihood by their wits and physical attractions but who had somehow let the years and the opportunities pass without achieving security.

Somehow, somehow, she thought desperately. I've got to do it; I've *got* to make him marry me!

And as she lay there thinking, it occurred to her all at once that perhaps she had been wrong, trying to make him marry her out of remorse and a sense of guilt. Why, she thought, with a sudden feeling of discovery, that would never even enter his head! Of course he's not going to seduce me! He thinks I'm innocent and virtuous and he respects me! He'll never marry me any way at all but from his own free will. That's what I've got to do— I've got to get him to make me an *honest* proposal of marriage! Why didn't I think of that long ago? But how can I do it—how can I do it—?

Amber and Nan put their heads together over that problem, and at last they worked out a plan.

About a week later Amber and Samuel Dangerfield set out for London in his coach. He had told her several days before that he must return and she had said that since she was leaving soon they might as well travel together; she would feel much safer riding with him. Her own coach, carrying Nan and Tansy, followed them. They had had a breakfast together at her cottage that morning—a substantial meal to prepare them for the journey—and though Amber had been gay and playful while they ate, now she had subsided into wistful and pensive quietness. From time to time she gave a little sigh.

The day was grey and dark and the rain seeped steadily down through the leafless branches of the forest. The air had a wet and penetrating chill, but they had fortified themselves against it with fur-lined cloaks and a fur-lined robe spread across their laps. Beneath their feet each one of them had a little brazier, like the ones people took to church, full of burning coals. So it was warm and moist inside the great lurching and rocking coach, and the warmth with the steam on the windows gave it a strange intimacy, making it a private little island shut off from the world.

Perhaps it was that seclusion and aloneness which made him bold enough to reach for her hand beneath the robe and say, "A penny for your thoughts, Mrs. St. Clare?"

For a moment Amber said nothing, and then she looked at him with her tenderest and most appealing smile. She gave a faint shrug of her shoulders. "Oh," she said, "I was just thinking that I'm going to miss our card games and suppers and walking up to the well in the afternoons." She gave another soft little sigh. "It's going to seem mighty lonely now I've grown used to company." She had told him how retired she lived in London, where she had no relatives, only a few friends, and was wary of making new acquaintances.

"Oh, but, Mrs. St. Clare, I hope you won't think our friendship is over. I— Well, to be honest, I've been hoping we might meet sometimes in London."

"That's kind of you," said Amber sadly. "But I know how busy you'll be—and you have all your family about you." Most of the children, she knew, grown and small alike, still lived at the great family mansion in Blackfriars.

"No, I assure you I won't. My physician wants me to do less work and as for the matter of that, I find, I've a taste for idleness—if it's spent in pleasant company." She smiled, and lowered her eyes at the compliment. "And I'd like to have you meet my family. We're all very happy together and I think you'd like them—I *know* they'd like you."

"You're so kind, Mr. Dangerfield, to care about what— Oh! is something amiss?" she cried, as a sudden spasm of pain shot across his face.

For a moment he was silent, obviously embarrassed to be caught with an ailment at a moment so delicately romantic. But at last he shook his head. "No—" he said. "No, it was nothing."

But presently the look of agony came again and his face flushed dark. Amber, now greatly alarmed, seized hold of his arm.

"Mr. Dangerfield! Please! You must tell me—What is it!"

He now looked wretchedly uncomfortable and was finally

forced to admit that something, he could not imagine what, was causing him great abdominal discomfort. "But don't trouble yourself for me, Mrs. St. Clare," he pleaded. "It will pass presently, it's only—Oh!" A sudden uncontrollable grunt escaped him.

Amber's own face reflected sympathetic pain as she watched him. But instantly she was in practical charge of the situation. "There's a little inn not far up the road—I remember we passed it on the way down. We'll stop there. You must get into bed right away, and I'm sure I have some— Oh, now don't make any objections, sir!" she said as he began to protest, and though her tone would permit no argument it was tender as a mother's speaking to her sick child. "I know what's best for you. Here—I've got some hawkweed and camomile in this little bag, I always carry it with me. Wait till I get this waterflask open so you can wash it down—"

It was not long before they reached the inn, at which Amber called out to order the coachman to stop, and Mr. Dangerfield's gigantic footman, Big John Waterman, helped him to make his way inside. Big John offered to carry him, and no doubt could easily have done so, but he flatly refused and resented such assistance as he was forced to receive. Amber was as busy as a hen with chicks. She rushed ahead to bid the hostess get a chamber ready, directed Tempest and Jeremiah which trunks to unload, ran back a half-dozen times to make sure Mr. Dangerfield was all right. At last they had him upstairs and, against his will, lying down in the great testered bed.

"Now," said Amber to the hostess, "you must make a hot fire and bring me a kettle and crane so that I can heat water. Bring me all the hot-water bottles you have and some more blankets. Nan, open that trunk and get out the boxful of herbs—Jeremiah, go find my almanac—it's in the bottom of the green leather trunk, I think. Now get out of here, all of you, so Mr. Dangerfield can rest—"

Amber loosened his clothes, took off his cloak and hat, cravat and doublet, piled hot-water bottles around him and covered him with blankets. She was quick and gentle, cheerful but concerned; an outsider would have thought she was already his wife. He begged her not to trouble herself with him, but to go on to London and send back a doctor. And, apparently in some apprehension that this might be another and perhaps final stroke, he asked her to notify his family. Amber firmly refused.

"It's nothing serious, Mr. Dangerfield," she insisted. "You'll be hearty as ever in a few days, I know you will. It wouldn't be right to scare them that way—especially with Lettice about to lie-in." Lettice was his eldest daughter.

"No," he agreed meekly. "It wouldn't be right, would it?"

And in spite of his discomfort it soon became clear that he was enjoying his illness and the attentions it brought him. No doubt he had always felt obliged to be stoical before; now, far from home and those who knew him, he could luxuriate in the care and endless concern of a beautiful young woman who seemed to think of nothing at all but his comfort. She refused even to leave him alone at night, for fear the attack might recur, and slept there on the trundle only a few feet away.

The slightest sound from him and she was out of bed and beside him, her rich heavy hair falling about her face as she bent over him, the faint light from the candle throwing shadows across her arms and into her breasts. Her murmuring voice was like a caress; her flesh was warm whenever she happened to touch him; the heat in the room brought out an intoxicating fragrance of jasmine flowers and ambergris in her perfume. No illness had ever been so pleasant. And, half because she persuaded him he was pale and not strong enough to be removed, he remained in bed many days after all the pain had gone.

"Ye gods!" said Amber to Nan one day as she was dressing in the room which adjoined his chamber. "I think when I marry this old man I'll be a nursemaid and not a wife!"

"Heavens, mam, it's you've insisted he can't get out of bed! And it was your idea in the first place to feed 'im those toadstools—"

"Shhh!" cautioned Amber. "You've got no business remembering such things." She got up, gave herself a last glance in the mirror, and went toward the door into the next room; an expression of sweet tenderness spread over her face before she opened it.

Chapter Twenty-five

BARBARA'S HEAD LAY on James Hamilton's shoulder.

And both of them lay motionless, half between waking and sleeping, eyes closed, faces smooth and peaceful. But slowly Barbara began to grow uneasy. Her nose wrinkled a little and then the nostrils flared; she sniffed once or twice. What the devil's that smell? she thought irritably. And then all at once she realized.

Smoke!

The room was on fire!

She sat up with a start and saw that an entire velvet drapery was aflame, apparently having been ignited by a candle into which it had blown. She put her fists to her mouth and screamed.

"James! The room's on fire!"

The handsome colonel sat up and glared resentfully at the flaming drapery. "Good Lord!"

But Barbara was pushing him out of bed, sticking her feet into mules, reaching for her dressing-gown. And now, suddenly wide awake, Hamilton rushed across the room and with a swift movement jerked the hanging from its rod and started to stamp the flame out. But already it had spread to a chair and as he flung it onto the floor a Turkish rug caught fire.

Barbara ran to him with his clothes in her hand. "Here!" She thrust them at him: "Get into these! Quick—down that stairway before someone comes! Help! Help!" she screamed. "Fire! Help!"

James got out of the room just as Barbara admitted half-a-dozen servants from the other door. By now the flames were licking up the walls, the opposite drapery was afire and smoke was beginning to fill the room and make them cough.

"Do something, some of you!" yelled Barbara furiously, but though the room was filling with people—footmen, pages, blackamoors, serving-women, courtiers who had been passing by—no one had yet made a move to put out the fire. They all stood for several seconds, looking on in stupefied amazement, each waiting for someone else to decide what should be done.

And then a couple of footmen arrived carrying buckets full of water and pushed their way in; they gave a mighty sling and sent the water splashing over one burning chair and carpet. There was a hissing and the smoke rolled out and everyone retreated, squinting his eyes and coughing. Several now began to run for more water.

Dogs were barking. A scared monkey leaped chattering from one shoulder to another and in his terror bit the hand of a woman who tried to knock him aside. Men rushed in and out with buckets of water, most of the women ran around distractedly, doing nothing. Barbara was trying to give orders to everyone at once, though no one paid her much attention. And now she seized a page by the arm as he went hurrying by, huge buckets slopping with water in either hand.

"Boy! Wait a moment—I want a word with you!" The young man stopped and looked at her; his eyes were bloodshot and his face wet with sweat and smeared with soot. She lowered her voice. "There's a cabinet in there—a small one over in this corner—with a guitar atop it. Bring it out and I'll give you twenty pound."

His eyes flickered in surprise. Twenty pounds when his pay for the year was three! She must want it badly. "The whole side's aflame, your Ladyship!"

"Forty pound, then! But bring it out!" She gave him a shove.

Two or three minutes later he came back carrying the cabinet easily in one hand, for it was very small. One side had been charred and as she set it down it fell apart and several folded letters dropped to the floor. He stooped quickly to retrieve them but Barbara cried: "Leave them alone! *I'll* pick them up! Go back to your work!"

She knelt on one knee and began to gather them swiftly, when all at once a hand reached across and took one from beneath her very fingers. Looking up she saw the Duke of

Buckingham standing there smiling down at her. Her purple eyes narrowed and her teeth closed savagely.

"Give that to me!"

Buckingham continued to smile. "Certainly, my dear. When I've had a look at it. If it's so important to you, perhaps it's also important to me."

For a moment they continued to stare at each other, Barbara still half crouching, her tall cousin looming over her, both impervious to the noise and confusion all about them. And then suddenly she sprang at him, but he stepped lightly aside and warded her off with one raised arm, meanwhile sliding the letter into an inside pocket of his doublet.

"Don't be so hasty, Barbara. I'll return it to you in good time."

She gave him a sullen glare and muttered some impolite curse beneath her breath, but evidently realizing that she would have to wait until he was ready she went back to directing the workmen. The fire was almost out by now and they were carrying from the bedroom all the furniture which had not been scorched. But the entire apartment was black with smoke and the bedchamber a wet charred mess. The windows were flung open to air the rooms, though it was a gusty rainy night, and Wilson brought Barbara a mink-lined cloak to put over her dressing-gown.

When at last they had gone she turned back to Buckingham, who was strumming at a guitar. Barbara stared at him from across the room. "Now, George Villiers—give me that letter!"

The Duke made an airy gesture. "Tush, Barbara. You're always so brisk. Listen to this tune I pricked out the other morning. Rather pretty, don't you think?" He smiled at her and nodded his head in time to the gay little melody.

"A pox on you and your damned tunes! Give me that letter!"

Buckingham sighed, tossed the guitar into a chair and took the letter from his pocket; as he began to unfold it she started toward him. He held up a warning hand. "Stay where you are, or I'll go elsewhere to read it."

Barbara obeyed him and stood there, her arms folded and the toe of her mule tapping impatiently. The crisp parchment crackled in the quiet room, and then as his eyes went rapidly over the contents a smile of amusement and contempt stole onto his face.

"By God," he said softly, "Old Rowley writes as lewd a love-letter as Aretino himself." Old Rowley was his Majesty's nickname, after a pet goat that roamed the Privy Gardens.

"Now will you give me that letter!"

Buckingham slipped it once more into his own pocket. "Let's talk this over for a moment. I'd heard his Majesty wrote you some letters just after you'd met. What do you expect to do with 'em?"

"What business is that of yours!"

The Duke shrugged and started for the door. "None, I suppose, strictly speaking. Well—a very fine lady has made me an assignation and I should hate to disappoint her. Good-night, madame."

"Buckingham! Wait a minute! You know what I intend doing with them as well as I do."

"Publishing them some day perhaps?"

"Perhaps."

"I've heard you've threatened him with that once or twice already."

"Well, what if I have? He knows what a fool he'd look if the people were ever to read them. I can make him jump through my hoop like a tame monkey by the mere mention of 'em." She laughed, a gleam of reflective gloating cruelty in her eyes.

"A time or two, perhaps, but not for long. Not if he really decides to put you by."

"Why, what do you mean? Age won't stale these! Ten years will only give 'em a higher savour!"

"Barbara, my dear, for an intriguing woman you're sometimes uncommonly simple. Has it never occurred to you that if you really tried to publish those letters you wouldn't be able to find 'em?"

Barbara gasped. It had not, though she kept them under lock and key and until tonight no one but herself had known where they were. "He wouldn't do that! He wouldn't steal them! Anyway, I keep them well hidden!"

Buckingham laughed. "Oh, do you? I'm afraid you take Old Rowley for a greater fool than he is. The Palace swarms with men—and women too—who make it their business to find anything that will bring a good price. If he really decided that he wanted those they'd disappear from under your nose while you had your eye on 'em."

Barbara was suddenly distraught. "Oh, he wouldn't do that!" He wouldn't play me such a scurvy trick! You don't *really* think he would, do you, George?"

He smiled, very much amused at her distress. "I know he would. And why not? Publishing them wouldn't be exactly a gesture of good faith on your part, would it?"

"Oh, good faith be damned! Those letters are important to me! If he ever gets tired of me they'll be all I have to protect myself—and my children. You've got to help me, George! You're clever about these things. Tell me what I can do with them!"

Buckingham heaved himself away from the wall against which he had been leaning. "There's only one thing to do with them." But as she started eagerly toward him he made a gesture of one hand, and shook his head. "Oh, no, my dear. You'll have to puzzle this out for yourself. After all, madame, you've not been my best friend of late—unless I've heard amiss."

"*I've* not been *your* best friend! Hah! And what good turns have you done me, pray? Oh, don't think I don't know about you and your Committee for Getting Frances Stewart for the King!"

He shrugged. "Well, a man must serve his King—and pimping's often the high-road to power and riches. However, it all came to nothing. She's a cunning slut, if I've ever seen one."

"Well," said Barbara, beginning to pout. "If it had it might have undone me for good and all. I thought you and I were pledged to a common cause, Buckingham." She referred to their mutual hatred of Chancellor Clarendon

"We are, my dear. We are. It's my fondest wish to see that old man turned away in disgrace—or better yet to see his head on a pole over London Bridge. It's time the young men have a swing at governing the country." He smiled at her, a friendly ingratiating smile, all malice and scorn gone from his face. "I can't think why we're so often at odds, Barbara. Perhaps it's because we both have Villiers blood in our veins. But, come—let's be friends again—And if you'll do your part I'll try what luck I can have to bring you back into his Majesty's favour again."

"Oh, Buckingham, if only you would! I swear since her Majesty's recovery he's done nothing but trail after that simpering sugar-sop, Frances Stewart! I've been half-distracted with worry!"

"Have you? I'd understood there were several gentlemen who'd undertaken to console you—Colonel Hamilton and Berkeley and Henry Jermyn and—"

"Never mind! I thought we were going to be friends again—but that doesn't give you leave to slander my reputation to my face!"

He made her a bow. "My humblest apologies, madame. I assure you it was but an idle jest."

They had similarly quarrelled and made friends a dozen times or more, but both of them were too fickle, too mercurial, too determinedly selfish to make good partners in any venture. Now, however, because she wanted his help she gave him a flirtatious smile and was instantly forgiving.

"Gossip will travel here at Whitehall, be a woman never so innocent," she informed him.

"I'm sure that's your case to a cow's thumb."

"Buckingham—what about the letters? You know I'm but a simple creature, and you're so clever. Tell me what I shall do."

"Why, when you ask so prettily of course I'll tell you. And yet it's so simple I'm half ashamed to say it: Burn 'em up."

"Burn them! Oh, come now, d'you take me for a fool?"

"Not at all. What could be more logical? As long as they exist he can take them from you. But once they're burned he can turn the Palace upside down and never find 'em—and all the while you're laughing in your fist."

For a moment she continued to regard him skeptically, and then at last she smiled. "What a crafty knave you are, George Villiers." She took a candle from the table and going to the cold fireplace tossed into it those letters which she held in her hand. Then she turned to him. "Give me the other one."

He handed it to her and she tossed it too on the heap. The candle-flame touched one corner and in a moment the slow fire began to creep up the paper, making it curl as it turned black. And then suddenly they broke into a bright blaze which burned for a moment or two, the sealing-wax crackling and hissing, and began to die out. Barbara looked up over her shoulder at Buckingham and found him staring into the low fire, a thoughtful enigmatic smile on his handsome face. She had a quick moment of misgiving, wondering what he could be thinking; but it soon passed and she got to her feet again, relieved to have the troublesome letters safe at last.

About a week later most of the Court went to the opening performance of John Dryden's new play, "The Maiden Queen."

The house was full when the Court party arrived and there was a great buzzing and scraping as the fops in the pit climbed onto their benches to stare, while the women hung over the balconies above. One of them impudently dropped her fan as the King passed beneath and it landed squarely on top of his head. It began to slide off and Charles caught it and presented it with a smile to the giggling blushing girl above, as a spattering of handclaps ran over the theatre.

The King, York, and the young Duke of Monmouth were all in royal mourning—long purple cloaks—for the Duchess of Savoy.

Monmouth, the King's fourteen-year-old bastard by an early love affair, had come to England in the train of Queen Henrietta Maria a year and a half before. Some said he was not really the King's son, but at least he looked like a Stuart and there could be no doubt that Charles thought he was one. Almost since the day of the boy's arrival he had shown him the most conspicuous affection and as a result of the title conferred upon him by his father he took precedence over all but York and Prince Rupert. The year before, his Majesty had married him to Anne Scott, eleven years old and one of the richest heiresses in Britain. Now the boy was appearing publicly in royal mourning—to the scandal of all who reverenced the ancient proprieties or who believed that blood was not royal unless it was also legitimate.

Down in Fop Corner one of the sparks commented: "By God, if his Majesty isn't as fond of the boy as if he were of his own begetting."

"It runs through the galleries he intends to declare him legitimate and make him his heir now it's been proved the Queen's barren."

"Who proved it?"

"Gad, Tom, where d'ye keep yourself? My Lord Bristol sent a couple of priests to Lisbon to prove that Clarendon had something given her to make her barren just before she sailed for England."

"A pox on that Clarendon's old mouldy chops! And will you have a look at his mealy-mouthed daughter up there—as smug and formal as if she was *Queen* Anne!"

"And so she may be one day—if it's true what they say about her Majesty."

Another fop, catching the last phrase, perked up. "What's that? What about her Majesty?"

All over the theatre the gossip went on, hissing and murmuring, while the royal party found its seats. Charles took the one in the center, with Catherine on his right and York on his left. Anne Hyde was beside her husband, and Castlemaine at the opposite end of the row next the Queen. Around and all about them were the Maids of Honour, both her Highness's and the Queen's. They were a group of pretty, eager, laughing girls, white-skinned, blue-eyed, with shining golden curls, their satin and taffeta skirts making a rustle as they arranged the folds and fluttered their fans, whispering and giggling together over the men down in the pit. They had arrived at Court during the past year and almost all of them were lovely—as though nature herself had sought to please the King by creating a generation of beautiful women.

On Barbara's right sat one of the Queen's Maids, Mrs. Boynton, a lively little minx who liked to affect an air of great languor and grew faint three or four times a day when there were gentlemen about. Now Barbara spoke to her in an undertone which was nevertheless loud enough for Frances Stewart, just behind them, to overhear.

"Mrs. Stewart is looking wretchedly today, have you noticed? I would swear her complexion has a greenish cast."

It was a well-known fact that Frances had been suffering from jealousy over the sensation created by the recent arrival at Court of Mrs. Jennings, a fifteen-year-old blonde who was currently being admired by all gentlemen and criticized by all ladies. Barbara was delighted that someone had come to catch interest from Frances Stewart, since that was what had happened to her the year before when Frances appeared.

Boynton waved her fan lazily, lids half-closed, and drawled, "She doesn't look green to me. Perhaps it's something in your Ladyship's eye."

Barbara gave her a look that once might have troubled her and turned to talk to Monmouth who leant forward eagerly, obviously much smitten by his father's flamboyant mistress. He was tall and well-developed for his age, physically precocious as the King had been, and so extraordinarily handsome that grown women were falling in love with him. He had not only the Stuart beauty but also the Stuart charm—a merry gentle lovable disposition, and something in his personality so dazzling that he arrested attention wherever he went.

Boynton glanced around over her shoulder to exchange smiles with Frances, and Frances leaned forward, whispering behind her fan: "I just saw his Highness slip another note into Mrs. Jenning's hand. Wait a moment and I'll warrant you she tears it up."

Jennings had been amusing the Court for some weeks by refusing to become York's mistress, an office which was generally included in the appointment of Maid of Honour to his wife. She tore up his letters before everyone and scattered the pieces on the floor of her Highness's Drawing-Room. And now, as Boynton and Frances Stewart watched her, she tore his note into bits and tossed them high in the air so that they drifted onto the Duke's head and shoulders.

Boynton and Stewart burst into delighted laughter and York, glancing around, saw the scraps on his shoulder. Scowling, he brushed them off, while Mrs. Jennings sat very straight and prim-faced and looked down over his head at the stage, where the play was beginning.

"What!" said Charles, glancing at his brother as he brushed himself, and he laughed outright. "Another rebuff, James? Odsfish; I should think you'd have taken the hint by now."

"Your Majesty doesn't always take hints, if I may say so," muttered the Duke, but Charles merely smiled good-naturedly.

"We Stuarts are a stubborn race, I think." He leaned closer to James and murmured beneath his breath: "I'll wager my new Turkish pony against your Barbary mare that I break in that skittish filly before you do."

York raised a skeptical eyebrow. "It's a wager, Sire." The two brothers shook hands and Charles settled down to watch the play.

For two acts Barbara remained seated. She smiled at Buckingham and other gentlemen down in the pit. She twisted her pearls and fiddled her fan and put her hands to her hair. She took out a mirror to examine her face, stuck on another patch, and then tossed the mirror back to Wilson. She was, very ostentatiously, bored. And all the while Charles seemed unaware that she was nearby; he did not trouble to glance at her even once.

At last she thought she could bear this no longer, and fixing a determined smile on her face she leaned across Catherine and touched his arm. "It's a wretched performance, don't you think, Sire?"

He glanced at her coldly. "No, I don't think so. I'm enjoying it."

Barbara's eyes glittered and the blood rushed to her face, but in a moment she had recovered herself. All at once she stood up, smiling sweetly, and crossing behind the Queen went to force a place for herself between Charles and York. The two men gave her surprised and angry glances and turned instantly away while Barbara sat, her face impassive and motionless as stone, though humiliated rage was making her sweat. For a moment she thought that her heart would explode, so bursting-full of blood it seemed.

And then, out of the corners of her eyes, she looked at Charles and saw the ominous flicker of his jaw-muscles. She stared at him, longing violently to reach over and rake her nails across that dark smooth-shaven cheek until she drew blood—but at last with a determined effort she dragged her eyes away and forced them down to the stage once more. All she could see was a blur that shifted and rocked; there were faces, faces, faces, turned up and grinning, smirking, sneering at her—a whole sea of enemy faces. She felt that she hated each one of them, with a murderous savage hatred that turned her sick and trembling.

It seemed to her that the play went on for hours and that she would never be able to endure the next minute of sitting there—but at last it was over. She waited a moment, under the pretense of pulling on her gloves, still hoping that Charles would invite her to ride in his coach. But instead he went off with Harry Bennet to call on the Chancellor who was again sick in bed with his gout.

Barbara lifted her hood up over her head, put on her mask and with an impatient gesture to Wilson started out as fast as she could go—the people stepped back to make a path, for her name still had magic to part the waves. Outside she got into her coach, and though it blocked the traffic she kept it waiting while her coachman yelled and swore at whoever complained, telling them to be silent—my lady would go in her own good time. It was several minutes before Buckingham appeared.

But finally he came strolling out of the theatre with Sedley and Buckhurst, and she gestured her footman to open the door. Frantically she signalled to him, but he was talking to an orange-girl, a merry laughing young wench who chattered with the three great men, no more awed than if they had been porters and carmen. At last, completely exasperated, Barbara shouted at him:

"Buckingham!"

He glanced carelessly in her direction, waved, and turned back to continue his conversation. Barbara ripped her fan across. "Lightning blast him! I'll cut off his ears for this!" But finally he took an orange from the girl, kissed her, and dropping his coin into her low-necked bodice strolled toward the coach, tossing the orange to a tattered little ragamuffin who begged him for it.

"Get out and take a hackney," Barbara muttered hastily to Wilson, and as his Grace got in on one side the waiting-woman got out on the other.

"That little wench has the readiest wit in London," he said, sitting down beside her and waving out the window at the girl, while Barbara glared at him with a look so malignant he should have wilted. "She was put out into the streets at six to sell herring and was a slavey in Mother Ross's brothel at twelve. Hart keeps her now, but I say she belongs on the stage. Nell Gwynne's her name and I'd be willing to bet—"

Barbara had not listened to him but was yelling at her coachman to drive off, though now the traffic was so snarled on every side of them that it was impossible to move at all.

"A pox on you and your damned orange-girls!" she cried furiously, turning from the coachman back to her cousin. "A fine service you've done me! I've never been so humiliated—and in plain view of all the world! What 've you been about this past week?"

Buckingham stiffened, all his natural pride and arrogance rising in resentment at her hectoring tone and manner. "D'you expect miracles? Pray remember, madame, it's taken you some time to get so far out of his Majesty's favour. Even I can't put you back in all at once. You should have stayed in your own seat—you wouldn't have been humiliated there. And henceforward, madame, please don't shout at me on street-corners as though I were your footboy."

"Why, you impudent dog! I'll have you—"

"You'll what, madame?"

"I'll make you sorry for this!"

"I beg your pardon, madame—but you'll never make me sorry for anything again. Or have you forgotten already that I can undo you whenever I care to take the trouble? Don't forget, madame, that only you and I know that you burned his Majesty's letters."

Barbara's mouth fell open and for several seconds she sat staring at him with horror which turned slowly to writhing impotent rage. She was about to speak when he flung open the door and got out, gave her a careless wave of his gloved hand and climbed into the next coach. It was full of young women who sat in a billowing sea of silk and satin skirts, and they welcomed him with screams of delight and kisses as he sat down among them. While Barbara stared, her eyes burning purple in a white face, the coach started slowly and rolled off, but the Duke did not give her so much as a backward glance.

Chapter Twenty-six

DANGERFIELD HOUSE was in the aristocratic old quarter of Blackfriars and had been built twenty years before on the site of a great fourteenth-century mansion. It formed a broad sprawling H, with courtyards both in front and in back, and was four stories high with a fifth half-story; the ground floor and the basement served for offices and warehouse. Made of red brick it was perfectly symmetrical with innumerable large square-paned glass windows, several gables cutting into the roof-line and a forest of chimney-tops. It stood on the corner of Shoemaker Row, facing Greed Lane, and was surrounded on every side by a tall iron picket-fence, guarded by massive gates where servants waited at all hours of the day or night.

Climbing out of the coach before the twin staircases which led to the main entrance on the second floor, Amber looked up at it with wide wondering eyes.

This house was something bigger, more imposing, more formidable than she had expected. Two hundred thousand pounds was an even greater amount of money than she had realized. Until now she had thought of Samuel Dangerfield merely as a kind simple old gentleman whom she had contrived to hoodwink, but now he took on something of the awe-inspiring quality of his home, and she began to feel a little nervous at the prospect of meeting his family. She wished that she felt as convinced as he did that they were going to welcome her with open arms—love her at sight.

And now, as they stood for a moment in the February drizzle while he gave instructions to the footman regarding the disposal of their trunks and baggage, a third-story window was flung open and a woman appeared in it.

"Dad! At last you're back! We were so worried—you've been gone so long! But did it help you? Are you feeling better?" She did not, or pretended not to notice that there was a woman with her father.

But Amber looked up at her curiously. That, she thought, must be Lettice.

She had heard a great deal about Lettice—as she had heard a great deal about all his children—but more, perhaps, of Lettice than any of the others. Lettice had been married for several years, but at her mother's death she had returned to Dangerfield House with her husband and family to take charge of the housekeeping. Without intending to, Samuel had portrayed a prim energetic domineering woman, whom his wife was already prepared to dislike. And now Lettice was ignoring her, as though she were a lewd woman whom it was not necessary to notice.

"I'm feeling very well," said Samuel, obviously annoyed by his daughter's bad manners. "How is my new grandson?"

"Two weeks old yesterday and thriving! He's the image of John!"

"Come down into the front drawing-room, Lettice," Samuel said crisply. "I want to see you—immediately."

Lettice, after giving a quick stealthy glance at Amber, closed the window and disappeared and Amber and Samuel—with Nan and Tansy following—went up the staircase and into the house. The door was opened for them by a gigantic Negro in handsome blue livery and they stepped into a great entrance-hall out of which opened other rooms; a pair of broad curved staircases ran up either side of it to the railed-off hallway above.

Everywhere about them were the evidences of lush comfort and wealth: the beautifully laid floors, the carved oak furniture and tapestry-hung walls. And yet, somehow, the impression created was one of soberness, not frivolity. An almost ponderous conservatism marked each velvet footstool and carved cornice. It was possible to know at a glance that quiet and well-bred and moderate people lived in this house.

They walked off to the left into a drawing-room more than fifty feet long and Samuel saw immediately, to his regret, that he had made a careless mistake. For there, over the fireplace, hung a portrait of him and his first wife, painted some twenty years before; it had been there so long that he had forgotten it. But Amber, looking at the powerful prim unlovely face of the first Mrs. Dangerfield, understood immediately why it had been possible to induce Samuel to marry her—though she doubted whether his family would understand as well.

At that moment there were footsteps behind them and she turned to see a replica of the woman on the wall standing facing her. For an instant Lettice's eyes met hers in a quick fierce womanly stare, all-seeing, and condemning, and then she turned to her father. Amber gave her a sweeping glance which discovered that she knew nothing about clothes, was too tall, and looked older than her thirty-two years. The gown Lettice was wearing was like those Killigrew had put on the actresses when he wished to show a hypocritical Puritan, and against which they had always protested violently. It was perfectly plain black and fitted neither snugly nor too loosely, had a deep white-linen collar which covered her to the base of her throat, and broad linen cuffs. Her light-brown hair was almost entirely concealed beneath a starched little cap with shoulder-length lappets, and she wore no jewellery but a diamond-studded wedding-band. Against such simplicity Amber, who had thought herself very demure, felt suddenly gaudy and flamboyant.

"My dear," said Samuel to Amber, and he took her arm, "may I present my eldest daughter, Lettice? Lettice, this is my wife."

Lettice gasped and turned paste-white. Amber—once the ceremony was performed—had suggested to Samuel that they send a messenger ahead to notify the family. But he had insisted upon giving them what he was sure would be a most happy surprise.

Now Lettice stood and stared at her father for several stark quiet moments, and then as she turned to look at Amber there was an expression of frank horrified shock on her face. She seemed aware of it herself, but unable to help it, and this unexpected reaction on her part was making Samuel angry. Amber, who had prepared herself for it, smiled faintly and nodded.

At last Lettice managed to speak. "Your—wife? But, Dad—" She put one hand distractedly to her head. "You're married? But your letters never mentioned— We didn't— Oh, I—I'm sorry—I—"

She seemed so genuinely and painfully stunned that Samuel's rigid hauteur collapsed. He put one arm about her. "There, my dear, I know it's a surprise to you. But I was counting on you, Lettice, to help me tell the others. Look at me—And please smile. I'm very happy and I want my family to be happy with me."

For a long minute Lettice buried her head against her father's chest and Amber waited with a feeling of annoyance, expecting hysterics. But at last she stood erect, kissed Samuel's cheek and smiled. "I'm glad you're happy, Dad." She turned about quickly. "I'll make arrangements for dinner," and she ran out of the room.

Amber glanced at Samuel and saw a strange thoughtful look on his face as his eyes followed Lettice. She put her hand into his. "Oh, Samuel—she doesn't like me. She didn't want you to get married."

His eyes came back to her. "Well, perhaps she didn't," he agreed, though before he had never admitted such a possibility. "But then Lettice never likes anything new—no matter what it is. But wait until she knows you. She'll love you then—no one could help it."

"Oh, Samuel, I hope so! I hope they'll *all* like me. I'll try so hard to make them like me."

They went upstairs then to his apartments which were in the southwest wing of the building, overlooking the rear court and the garden. The suite consisted of a string of rooms opening one into another, all of them furnished in much the same style as the others she had seen. There were reminders of his first wife everywhere: another portrait of her above the fireplace, a wardrobe which must have held her clothes and perhaps still did; there was the impress of her personality on every rug and piece of furniture. Amber felt as though she had walked into a room which still belonged to the dead woman, and decided immediately that she would make some changes here.

Promptly at one o'clock Samuel and Amber entered the dining-room. They found every member of the family who was home and old enough to walk assembled there to meet her. Almost thirty persons stood about the huge table, several of them children who would ordinarily have been eating in the nursery. Such large families were common among the richer middleclasses, for their children did not die in as large proportion as did those of the poor and their women made no effort to prevent child-bearing as did the fashionable ladies of Whitehall and Covent Garden.

Now, as Amber and Samuel stood in the doorway, one little moppet inquired loudly: "Mother, is *that* the woman?" Her mother administered a hasty embarrassed slap and followed it with a shake to keep her from crying.

Samuel ignored this incident and began to make the introductions. Each person, when presented, came forward to bow, if a man, or to curtsy and give her a peck on the cheek if a woman. The children, staring round-eyed, likewise made their awkward bows and curtsies. It was obvious from their interest and awe that much had already been said among the grown-ups about the new Mrs. Dangerfield.

On the whole they were handsome people; Lettice's plain face was almost conspicuous. There was the eldest son, Samuel, with his wife and six children. Robert, the next son, whose wife was dead, and his two children. Lettice's husband, John Beckford, and their eight children. The third son, John, who also lived in the house with his wife and five children and was engaged as were the older sons in their father's business. A daughter who had come from her nearby home with her children for the occasion. James, with his wife and two children. And three younger children, girls fifteen and thirteen, and a twelve-year-old boy. There were others—one travelling abroad, one at Grey's Inn and one at Oxford, a girl who lived in the country and another whose first pregnancy had kept her from attending the great event.

Lord! thought Amber. So many people to divide a fortune between! Well, there's one more now.

They were all instructed to call her "Madame"—Samuel could not bring himself to tell them her first name—and a troop of footmen began to march into the room carrying great silver trays, porringers and tankards, steaming with the most deliciously fragrant food and brimful of good golden ale. The dining-room was as solemnly impressive as the rest of the house. The stools they sat on were covered with tapestry; a great carved-oak cupboard was loaded with silver plate that made Amber's eyes pop; they drank from fragile crystal glasses and ate from silver dishes. And yet in the midst of all that splendour they sat in their quiet unpretentious clothes, black and grey and dark green, with white collars and cuffs, drab as sparrows. Ribbons and lace, false curls and powder and patches were nowhere to be seen and Amber, even in her simple black velvet gown with the white lace collar, felt strangely conspicuous—and she was.

She had expected them to be hostile, and they were, for by law in the City of London one-third of a man's fortune must go to his widow, and if she bore him a child—as she hoped to do—she might get even more.

But that was not the only reason they disliked her. They disliked her first because their father had married her, and every grievance stemmed from that, though it was not probable they would have had a good opinion of her under any circumstances. She was, though she tried not to seem so, an alien, different from them in all the wrong ways.

Her beauty, even without obvious paint, was too vivid to be decent in their eyes. The women were convinced that she was neither as sweet nor as innocent as she seemed, for they recognized though they did not discuss her blatant quality of sexual allure. A woman's eyes should not have that wicked slant, nor her body an air of being unclothed even when thoroughly covered. They learned what her first name was and were shocked; their own names were the old-fashioned and trustworthy ones, Katherine, Lettice, Philadelphia, Susan.

And Amber, in spite of her protestations to Samuel that she wanted nothing on earth but the love of his family, did from the start many things which they could only resent and criticize.

She had already possessed an extensive wardrobe, but nevertheless she was constantly ordering and buying new things—elaborate gowns, fur-lined cloaks, dozens of pairs of silk stockings, fans and shoes and muffs and gloves by the score. For weeks at a time she never appeared twice in the same costume. And she wore her jewels, emeralds, diamonds, topazes, as carelessly as if they were glass beads. Her portrait, faintly smiling in a gold-lace gown, replaced that of Samuel and the first Mrs. Dangerfield in the drawing-room. The bedroom in which many of them had been born was refurnished and gold-flowered crimson-damask hangings went up at the windows and around the bed; the old fireplace was torn out and a new black Genoese marble mantel put in its stead; Venetian mirrors and lacquered East Indian cabinets and screens supplanted the respectable pieces of English oak.

But even those things they might have forgiven her had it not been for their father's obvious and shameless infatuation. For once married to him Amber was able to make use of a great many means for increasing his passion which she had not dared employ during the courtship. She knew that her chief hold over him was her youth and beauty and flagrant desirability—qualities his first wife had utterly lacked and would have scorned as more suitable to a man's whore than to his lawful wife. And, because she wanted a child to bind him even closer, she pandered in every way she could to his concupiscence. He neglected his work to be with her, lost weight, and —even though he made an effort to behave decorously before his family—his eyes betrayed him whenever he looked at her. They were aware of all this, aware in fact of more than any of them cared to mention, and their hatred grew.

At his age it seemed to them not only disgusting but actually treacherous, a desecration of the memory of their own mother. And it was incomprehensible, to the men as well as the women, for Samuel had lived so continently, had worked so hard and seemed so little interested in pretty women or any other form of divertissement, that they could not understand why he should now suddenly reverse all the habits of a lifetime.

But it was Lettice, more than any of the others, who resented her. She felt that Amber's presence in the house was a shameful thing, for she could not regard a wife of barely twenty as anything other than her sixty-year-old father's mistress, taken in his declining and apparently immoral years.

"That woman!" she whispered fiercely one day to Bob and the younger Sam as the three of them stood at the foot of the stairs and watched Amber run gaily up, curls tossing, skirts lifted to show the embroidered gold clocks on her green-silk stockings. "I vow she's no good! I'm sure she paints!" They always criticized her for the things they dared to say out loud to each other, though the rest was well if silently understood among them.

Twenty-year-old Henry, who was a student at Grey's Inn, had just sauntered up and stood watching her too. He was so much younger than the others that his share in the fortune would not be a large one and so he had no prejudice on that score. For the rest, he had a sly admiration for his step-mother which he often humoured in fanciful day-dreams.

"It wouldn't be so bad if she wasn't a raving beauty into the bargain, eh Lettice?" he said now.

Lettice gave her brother a look of scorn. "Raving beauty! Who wouldn't be a beauty with paint and curls and patches and ribbons and all the rest of it!"

Henry shrugged, looking back to his sister now that Amber had disappeared down the upper hallway. "It's a pity more women aren't then, since it's so easy."

"Faith and troth, Henry! You're getting all your ideas from the playhouse!"

Henry coloured. "I am not, Lettice I've never been inside a playhouse and you know it!"

Lettice looked skeptical, and the other two brothers threw back their heads and laughed. Henry, growing redder, turned hastily and walked off; and Lettice with a sigh went out toward the kitchens to resume her work. For Amber had made no attempt to take over the running of the household and though Lettice would have liked to force it upon her Samuel had asked her to continue in charge and she could not refuse him. But it was no easy task to organize and direct an establishment consisting of thirty-five children and adults and almost a hundred and fifty servants.

Upstairs Amber was getting into her cloak, putting the hood up over her hair, tucking a black-velvet vizard inside her muff. Her movements were quick and her eyes sparkled with excitement.

"I tell you, mam," said Nan, helping her but shaking her red-blonde curls, "it's a foolhardy thing to do."

"Nonsense, Nan!" She began pulling on a pair of embroidered, elbow-length gloves. "No one could recognize me in this!"

"But suppose they *do,* mam! You'll be undone—and for what?"

Amber wrinkled her nose and gave Nan's cheek a little pat. "If anyone wants me I've gone to the 'Change. And I'll be back by three."

She went out the door and down a narrow spiralling flight of stairs which led her into the back courtyard where one of the great coaches stood waiting. She got in quickly and the heavy vehicle lumbered about and drove out of the yard to turn up Carter Lane; she had kept Tempest and Jeremiah with her and they drove her wherever she went.

At last they stopped. She put on her mask and got out, crossed the street and turned into a lane which led through a teeming noisy courtyard and thence to the back of the King's Theatre. She glanced around, then went in and down to the door of the tiring-room which she found, as always, full of half-naked actresses and beribboned gallants, most of whom were wearing the brand-new fashion of periwigs.

For a moment she stood unnoticed in the doorway and then Beck Marshall spoke to her. "What d'you want, madame?"

With a triumphant laugh and a flourish Amber took off her mask and dropped back her hood. The women shrieked with surprise and Scroggs waddled forward to greet her, her ugly old face red and grinning, and Amber put an arm about her shoulders.

"By Jesus, Mrs. St. Clare! Where've ye been? See!" she crowed. "I told ye she'd be back!"

"And here I am. Here's a guinea for you to drink, Scroggs, you old swill-belly—that should keep you foxed for a week."

She came on into the room and was instantly surrounded on every side by the women who kissed her, asking a dozen questions at once, while the gallants hung close and insisted they had been adying for her company. There had been rumours that she had gone into the country to have a baby, had died of the ague, had sailed for America, but when she told them she had married a rich old merchant—whose name she did not disclose—they were much impressed. The actors heard that she was there and came in too, claiming a kiss each, examining her clothes and jewels, asking her how much money she would inherit and if she was pregnant yet.

Amber felt wholly at her ease for the first time in more than four months. At Dangerfield House she was constantly dogged by the feeling that she would inadvertently do or say something improper. And she was made more uncomfortable by a nagging mischievous desire to suddenly throw off her air of sweet naïveté, make a bawdy remark, wink at a footman, shock them all.

Then all at once she caught sight of a face which, for an instant, she did not recognize, seeing it in this unfamiliar environment. And suddenly she clapped her mask back on, turned up her hood and began to make her goodbyes. For there across the room, talking to one of the new actresses, was Henry Dangerfield. In less than a minute she was on her way down the dimly-lighted corridor, but she had not gone far when footsteps came up behind her.

"I beg your pardon, madame—"

Amber's heart jumped and she stopped perfectly still, but only for an instant and then immediately she went on again.

"I don't know you, sir!" she snapped, changing her voice to a higher pitch.

"But I'm Henry Dangerfield and you're—"

"Mrs. Ann St. Michel, sir, and travelling alone!"

"I beg your pardon, madame—"

To her intense relief Amber found that he had stopped and when she got outside and glanced back he was not in sight. Nevertheless she did not get into the coach but said softly to Tempest as she walked by, "Meet me at the Maypole corner."

Amber spent the rest of the afternoon in her room, nervous and restless. She paced back and forth, looked out the window dozens of times, wrung her hands and asked Nan over and over why Samuel was late. Nan had not said that she knew this would happen, but she looked it.

But when he came in, late in the afternoon, he greeted her with a smile and kiss, just as he always did. Amber, who had put on a dressing-gown and nothing else, laid her head against his chest.

"Oh, Samuel! Where 've you been! It's so late—I've been so worried about you!"

He smiled and, glancing around to make sure that Nan was not looking, he slipped one hand into her gown. "I'm sorry, sweetheart. A gentleman had come from out of town on business and we talked longer than I expected—" His head bent to kiss her again, and from behind his back Amber signalled at Nan to leave the room.

At first she thought she would stay there that night and not go down to supper, but finally she decided that it would do no good. If Henry had recognized her he could mention it tomorrow as well as today, and she could not hide in their apartments forever.

But the supper went exactly as it usually did and afterward, as was their custom, they all went into one of the small parlours to spend an hour or two before retiring. Again Amber thought of pleading a headache and getting Samuel to go upstairs with her, but again she decided against it. If Henry was suspicious and she stayed—perhaps he would think that he had been wrong.

Lettice, with Susan and Philadelphia and Katherine, sat

before the fireplace talking quietly and working on pieces of embroidery. The younger children started a game of blind-man's-buff. Samuel sat down to a chess game which had been going on for several nights between him and twelve-year-old Michael, and Henry pulled up a chair to watch. The older brothers smoked their pipes and discussed business and the Dutch and criticized the government. Amber, beginning to feel comfortable again, sat in a chair and talked to Jemima, prettiest of all the good-looking Dangerfield children.

Jemima, just fifteen, was the one friend Amber had made in her new home; and Jemima admired her wholeheartedly. She was too unsophisticated to understand much more regarding her father's recent marriage than that he had brought a new woman to live in the house. And this woman looked and dressed and behaved exactly as she would have liked to do herself. She could not understand the animosity felt toward Madame by her older brothers and sisters, and had often repeated to Amber the things she had heard them say about her. Once she told her that Lettice, upon hearing of how devotedly Madame had nursed him through his illness, had said that she would just as soon think she had made him sick herself to have the opportunity of making him well. Amber, somewhat uneasy to hear this, was relieved that the oldest brother had cautioned Lettice against being carried too far by her own jealousy. After all, he had said, the woman might be of dubious character—but she couldn't be *that* bad.

Amber—who usually got along well with girls too young or unattractive to compete with her—encouraged the friendship. She found Jemima's naïve admiration and talkativeness a convenient means of informing herself on the others—as well as a source of entertainment to help her pass the long dull days. Furthermore, she took malicious delight in annoying Lettice. For Lettice had warned Jemima repeatedly against the association, but Lettice was no longer head of the house and Jemima was spirited enough to enjoy disobeying her.

She was about the same height Amber was, but her figure was slight and less rounded. Her hair was rich dark brown with sparks of copper in it; her skin fine and white and she had blue eyes with a sweep of curling black lashes. She was eager, vivacious, spoiled by her father and elder brothers, independent, stubborn and lovable. Now she sat on a stool beside Amber, her fingers clasped over her knees, eyes shining in fascination while Amber told her a story she had heard at second-hand of the King begging my Lady Castlemaine's pardon on his knees.

Across the room Susan glanced at them and raised her eyebrows significantly. "How devoted Jemima is to Madame! They're all but inseparable. I should think you'd be more careful, Lettice. Jemima might learn to paint."

Lettice gave her a sharp glance but found her looking down

at her embroidery, taking tiny precise stitches. For several years, ever since Lettice had returned home and assumed management of the household, there had been a low-current feud going on between her and this wife of the eldest brother. The other two women smiled faintly, amused, for they were all secretly a little pleased that at last Lettice had found someone she could not dominate. But they were not so pleased it sweetened the bitter gall of lost money: the new wife was still the common enemy of them all, and their little personal animosities of but minor importance.

Lettice answered her quietly. "I'm going to be more careful in the future—for that isn't all the child might learn from her."

"Low-necked gowns without a scarf too, perhaps," said Susan.

"Much worse than that, I'm afraid."

"What could be worse?" mocked Susan.

But Katherine sensed that Lettice knew something she had not told them, and her eyes lighted with the prospect of scandal. "What've you heard, Lettice? What's she done?" At Katherine's tone the other two instantly leaned forward.

"What do you know, Lettice?"

"Has she done something *terrible?*" They could not even imagine what could be terrible enough.

Lettice threaded her needle. "We can't discuss it now with the children in the room."

Immediately Philadelphia rose. "Then I'll send them to bed."

"Philadelphia!" said Lettice sharply. "I'll handle this! Wait until she begins to sing."

For every night, after the children had gone to bed and just before they all retired, Amber sang to them. Samuel had instigated the custom, and now it was a firmly-established part of household routine.

The women fidgeted nervously for almost an hour, begging Lettice in whispers over and over again to send the children to bed, but she would not do so until exactly the time when they went every night. She returned from seeing them into the custody of their nurses to find Amber strumming her guitar and singing a mournful pretty little song:

"What if a day, or a month, or a year,
  Crown thy delights
With a thousand glad contentings?
Cannot the chance of a night or an hour
  Cross thy delights
With as many sad tormentings?"

When it was done the listeners applauded politely, all but Jemima and Samuel, who were enthusiastic. "Oh, if only I could sing like that!" cried Jemima.

And Samuel went to take her hand. "My dear, I think you have the prettiest voice I've ever heard."

Amber kissed Jemima on the cheek and slipped her arm through Samuel's, smiling up at him. She was still holding her guitar which had been a gift from Rex Morgan and was decorated with a streamer of multicoloured ribbons he had bought for her one day at the Royal Exchange. She was relieved to have the evening done and was eager to get upstairs where she could feel safe. Never again, she had promised herself a dozen times, will I be such a fool.

Lettice sat leaning forward in her chair, tense, her hands clasped hard, and now Katherine gave her an impatient nudge with her elbow. Suddenly Lettice's voice rang out, unnaturally clear and sharp: "It's not surprising that Madame's voice should be pleasant."

Henry, standing across the room, gave a visible start and his adolescent face turned red. Amber's heart and the very flowing of her blood seemed to stop still. But Samuel had not heard, and though she continued to smile up at him she was wishing desperately that she could stop up his ears, push him out of the room, somehow keep him from ever hearing.

"What do you mean, Lettice?" It was Susan.

"I mean that any woman who used her voice to earn her living should have a pleasant one."

"What are you talking about, Lettice?" demanded Jemima. "Madame has never earned her living and you know it!"

Lettice stood up, her cheeks bright, fists clenched nervously at her sides, and the lappets on her cap trembled. "I think that you had better go to your room, Jemima."

Jemimia was instantly on the defensive, looking to Amber for support. "Go to my room? Why should I? What have I done?"

"You've done nothing, dear," said Lettice patiently, determined that there should be no quarrel within the family itself. "But what I have to say is not altogether suitable for you to hear."

Jemima made a grimace. "Heavens, Lettice! How old do you think I am? If I'm old enough to get married to that Joseph Cuttle I'm old enough to stay here and listen to anything you might have to say!"

By now Samuel was aware of the quarrel going on between his daughters. "What is it, Lettice? Jemima's grown-up, I believe. If you have something to say, say it."

"Very well." She took a deep breath. "Henry saw Madame at the theatre this afternoon."

Samuel's expression did not change and the three women about the fireplace looked seriously disappointed, almost cheated. "Well?" he said. "Suppose he did? I understand the theatre is patronized nowadays by ladies of the best quality."

"You don't understand, Father. He saw her in the tiring-room." For a moment she paused, watching the change on her father's face, almost wishing that her hatred and jealousy had never led her to make this wretched accusation. She was beginning to realize that it would only hurt him, and do no one any good. And Henry stood looking as if he wished he might be suddenly stricken by the devil and disappear in a cloud of smoke. Her voice dropped, but Lettice finished what she had begun. "She was in the tiring-room because she was once an actress herself."

There was a gasp from everyone but Amber, who stood perfectly still and stared Lettice levelly in the eye. For an instant her face was naked, threatening savage hate showing on it, but so quickly it changed that no one could be certain the expression had been there at all. Her lashes dropped, and she looked no more dangerous than a penitent child, caught with jam on its hands.

But Susan pricked her finger. Katherine dropped her sewing. Jemima leaped involuntarily to her feet. And the brothers were jerked out of their lazy indifference to what they had thought was merely another female squabble. Samuel, who had been looking younger and happier these past weeks than he had in years, was suddenly an old man again; and Lettice wished that she had never been so great a fool as to tell him.

For a moment he stood staring ahead and then he looked down at Amber, who raised her eyes to meet his. "It isn't true, is it?"

She answered him so softly that though everyone else in the room strained to hear her words they could not. "Yes, Samuel, it's true. But if you'll let me talk to you—I can tell you why I had to do it. Please, Samuel?"

For a long minute they stood looking at each other, Amber's face pleading, Samuel's searching for what he had never tried before to find. And then his head came up proudly and with her arm still linked in his they walked from the room. There was a moment of perfect silence, before Lettice ran to her husband and burst into broken-hearted tears.

Chapter Twenty-seven

NO FURTHER MENTION was ever made, in the presence of Samuel Dangerfield, of his wife's acting.

The morning after Lettice had made her sensational disclosure, he called her into a private room and told her that the matter had been explained to his own satisfaction, that he did not consider an explanation due the family, and that he wanted no more talk of it among themselves, nor any mention to outsiders. Henry was told that he could either forgo visiting the theatre or leave home. And to all outward appearances everything went on exactly as it had before.

The first time Amber appeared at dinner after that she was as composed and natural as if none of them knew what she really was; her coolness on this occasion was considered to be the boldest thing she had yet done. They could never forgive her for not hanging her head and blushing.

But though Amber knew what they thought of her she did not care. Samuel, at least, was convinced that she was wholly innocent, the victim of bad luck which had forced her into the uncongenial surroundings of the theatre, and that she had been tainted neither physically nor morally by the months she had spent on the stage. His infatuation for her was so great, his loyalty so intense, that none of them dared criticize her to him, even by implication. And they were all forced by family pride and love of their father to protect her against outsiders. For though, inevitably, gossip spread among their numberless relatives and friends that old Samuel Dangerfield had married an actress—and one of no very good repute—they defended her so convincingly that Amber became acceptable to the most censorious and stiff-necked dowagers in London.

But if the rest of the family was shocked and ashamed to be related, even by marriage, to a former actress, there was one of them who thought it the most exciting thing that had ever happened. That was Jemima. She teased Amber by the hour to tell her all about the theatre, what the gentlemen said, how my Lady Castlemaine looked when she sat in the royal box, what it felt like to stand on the stage and have a thousand people stare at you. And she wanted to know if it was true—as Lettice had said—that actresses were lewd women. Jemima was somewhat puzzled as to exactly what a lewd woman was, but it did sound wickedly exciting.

Amber answered her questions, but only a part of each one. She told her step-daughter of all that was gay and colourful and amusing about the theatre and the Court—but omitted those other aspects which she knew too well herself. To Jemima fine gentlemen and ladies were fine because they wore magnificent clothes, had an elaborate set of mannerisms, and were called by titles. She would not have liked to be disillusioned.

And for all that Lettice could say or do she began to imitate her step-mother.

Her neck-lines went lower, her lips became redder, she began to smell of organe-flower-water and to wear her hair in thick lustrous curls with the back done up high and twisted with ribbons. Amber, motivated by pure mischief, encouraged her. She gave her a vial of her own perfume, a jar of lip-paste, a box of scented powder, combs to make her curls stand out and seem thicker. At last Jemima even stuck on two or three little black-taffeta patches.

"Faith and troth, Jemima!" said Lettice to her sister one day when she came down to dinner in a satin gown with huge puffed sleeves that left her shoulders and too much of her bosom bare. "You're beginning to look like a hussy!"

"Nonsense, Lettice!" said Jemima airily. "I'm beginning to look like a lady!"

"I never thought I'd see the day my own sister would paint!"

But Sam put his arm about Jemima's tiny laced-in waist. "Let the child be, Lettice. What if she does wear a patch or two? She's pretty as a picture."

Lettice gave Sam a look of scornful disgust. "You know where she learns all this, don't you?"

Jemima sprang hotly to the defense of her step-mother. "If you mean I learned it from Madame, I did! And you'd better not let Father hear you speak of her in that tone, either!"

Lettice gave a little sigh and shook her head. "What have we Dangerfields come to—when the feelings of a common actress are—"

"What do you mean a 'common actress,' Lettice?" cried Jemima. "She isn't common at all! She's a lady of quality! Of better quality than the Dangerfields are, let me tell you! But her father—who was a knight, I'll have you know—turned her out when she married a man he didn't like! And when her husband died she was left without a shilling. Tom Killigrew saw her on the street one day and asked her to go onto the stage, and so she did—to keep from starving! And as soon as her husband's father died and left her some money she quit and went to Tunbridge Wells where she could live quiet and retired! Well—what are you both smirking at?"

Sam sobered immediately, for it was his opinion that Jemima would be less injured by her association with the woman if she did not know what she really was. "Is that the story she told Father?"

"Yes, it is! You believe it, don't you, Sam? Oh, Lettice! You make me sick!"

Suddenly she swirled about and lifting up her skirts started off up the stairs and as she went Lettice saw that with everything else she had begun to wear green silk stockings. Sam and Lettice looked at each other.

"Do you suppose he really believed that wild tale?" he asked at last.

Lettice sighed. "I know he did. And if he thought that we didn't—well, he mustn't ever think it, that's all. I don't know what happened to him to make him change, but something did and we must hide our feelings and thoughts for his sake. We still love him even if—even if—" She turned about quickly and walked away, though Sam gave her arm a brief pressure as she went. And at that moment Samuel and Amber walked into the room, Jemima triumphantly beside them with one arm linked through her step-mother's.

. . .

By June Amber, who was not yet pregnant, was beginning

to worry frantically. For Samuel, she knew, was anxious to have a child—mostly, she suspected, to justify his marriage to her in his own and his family's eyes. And she wanted one herself. He had already redrawn his will to give her the legal one-third, but she thought that a baby might induce him to give her even more. He had grown almost comically sentimental about babies, considering that his first wife had borne him eighteen children. And perpetually aware as she was of the hostility they all felt toward her, she believed that a baby would protect her as nothing else could.

Enveloped in a cloak, her face covered with a vizard, she went to consult half the midwives and quacks and physicians in London, asking their advice. She had a chestful of oils and balsams and herbs and a routine of smearing and anointing which occupied a great deal of time. Samuel's diet included vast quantities of oysters, eggs, caviar, and sweetbreads—but still the maddening fact persisted, she was not pregnant. She finally went to an astrologer to have her stars read and was encouraged when he told her that she would soon conceive.

One very hot day in June she and Jemima returned from a visit to the Royal Exchange and came into her apartments to drink a syllabub cooled in ice. The streets had been dusty and the crowds bad-tempered. There were so many flies in the house that though Tansy was detailed with a swatter to kill them they zoomed and buzzed everywhere. Amber tossed aside her fan and gloves and the hood she had been wearing and dropped onto a couch, beginning immediately to unfasten the bodice of her gown.

Jemima was less interested in the heat than in the exciting adventure they had just had. For two very fine and good-looking gentlemen had stopped her step-mother in the Upper Walk of the 'Change and one of them had asked, with charming impudence, to be presented to "that pretty blue-eyed jilt"—meaning Jemima. And then he had kissed her on the cheek, bowed most graciously, and invited her to drive to Hyde Park with him and have a syllabub.

"Imagine!" cried Jemima delightedly. "Mr. Sidney saying that after meeting me the day seemed hotter than ever!" She giggled and sipped her drink. "I vow I've never seen such handsome men—at least not in a great while. And the other one, Colonel Hamilton, is my Lady Castlemaine's lover, isn't he?" She felt flattered to have been looked at admiringly by a gentleman her Ladyship loved. Barbara's notoriety was now so extensive that she had become a kind of myth, known even to innocent and sheltered girls like Jemima.

"That's the gossip," said Amber lazily.

"Of course I know you were right to tell them we couldn't go—and yet they seemed so fine, and so genteel and well-bred. I vow we'd all have been mighty merry."

Amber exchanged a sly glance with Nan, who was across the

room behind Jemima. "No doubt," she agreed and got up to begin undressing. The Dangerfields entertained a great deal—more than ever since Samuel was so eager to display his lovely young wife—and it was her chief diversion to change one beautiful gown for another.

"You know," said Jemima now, not watching her stepmother but staring reflectively down into her glass. "I think it would be a mighty fine thing to have a lover—if he was a gentleman, I mean. I hate common fellows! All the Court ladies have lovers, don't they?"

"Oh, some of 'em do, I suppose. But to tell you the truth, Jemima, I don't think Lettice would like to hear you talk that way."

"Much I care what Lettice would like! What does she know about things like that? The only man she ever knew was John Beckford—and she married him! But you're different. You know everything—and I can talk to you because you won't tell me I'm wanton. Husbands are always such dull fellows—the gentlemen never seem to get married, do they?"

"Not while they can get—not while they can help it," amended Amber.

"Why not?" Why don't they?"

"Oh," she shrugged into a dressing-gown, "they say they'll lose their reputations as men of wit. But come, Jemima, you don't really mean all this. I thought that you were going to marry Joseph Cuttle."

Jemima made a violent face. "Joseph Cuttle! You should see him! Don't you remember— He was here last Wednesday. He's got teeth that stick out and skinny legs and pimples all over his face! I hate him! I won't marry him! I don't care what they say! I won't!"

"Well—" said Amber soothingly. "I don't think your father will make you marry a man you hate."

"He says I have to marry him! They've been planning it for years. But, oh, I don't want to! Amber!" she cried suddenly, and rushed to kneel before her where she sat in her dressing-gown, stroking a great purring tortoise-shell cat. "Father will do anything you say! *You* make him promise I don't have to marry Joseph Cuttle, will you? *Will* you, Amber, please?"

"Oh, Jemima," protested Amber, "you mustn't say such things! Your father doesn't do what I tell him to, at all." She knew that even Samuel would not want his family to think he was hen-pecked. "But I'll speak to him about it for you—"

"Oh, if only you would! Because I won't marry him! I can't! I'm— Do you want to know something, Amber? I'm in love!"

Amber seemed duly impressed, and asked the expected question. "How fine. Is he handsome?"

"Oh," breathed Jemima fervently. "The handsomest man I've ever seen! He's tall and his hair's black and his eyes—I forget what colour they are, but when he looks at me I get such a queer feeling right here. Oh, Amber, he's wonderful! He's everything in the world that I admire!"

"Hey day!" said Amber. "Where's this wonder to be seen?"

Jemima grew wistful at that. "Not here—not in London. At least not now—but I hope he'll be back one day soon. I've been waiting for him for thirteen months and a week—and I'll never love another man till he returns."

Amber was amused, for Jemima's enthusiasm seemed quite childish to her, considering that the girl did not guess what the primary business of love was about. Naïve kisses and queer feelings were the limit of her experience. "Well, Jemima, I hope he comes back to you. Does he know you're waiting?"

"Oh, no. I suppose he scarce knows I'm alive. I've only seen him twice—he was here one night for supper and another time I went down with Sam and Bob to see his ships, just before he sailed for America."

"Sailed for America! Who is this man! What's his name!"

Jemima looked at her in surprise. "If I tell you will you promise not to tell a soul? They'd all laugh at me. He's a nobleman—Lord Carlton— Oh! What's the matter? Do *you* know him?"

It was like a smack in the face with cold water, rude and shocking, and it made her angry because it scared her. But why should it? she thought, annoyed by her own uneasy lack of confidence. This girl can't mean anything to him— Why, she's just a child. Besides, she's not half as pretty as I am— Or is she? Amber's eyes were going swiftly over her step-daughter's face—seeing there now a threat to her own happiness. Don't be such a fool! she told herself wrathfully. Do you want her to guess— Only seconds had passed before she managed to answer, with a show of casualness:

"Why, I think I met him once at the Theatre. But how d'you come to be entertaining a lord and visiting his ships?"

"He does some business with Father—I don't know just what."

Amber lifted her eyebrows. "Samuel doing business with a pirate?"

"But he's not a pirate! He's a privateer—and there's a world of difference between 'em. It's the privateers we have to thank for keeping England on the seas—his Majesty's navy won't do it!"

"You talk like a merchant yourself, Jemima," said Amber tartly, but brought herself up with another quick warning. "Well—" She contrived a smile. "So you're in love with a nobleman. Then I hope for your sake he'll come back to England soon."

"Oh, I hope so too! I'd give anything to see him again! D'you know—" she said with sudden confiding shyness, "last Hallowe'en Anne and Jane and I baked a dumb-cake. Anne dreamed that night about William Twopeny—and now she's married to him! And *I* dreamed about Lord Carlton! Oh, Amber, do you think he could ever fall in love with me? Do you think he'd ever marry me?"

"Why not!" snapped Amber. "You should have a big enough dowry!" The instant she heard the words she was furious with herself and quickly added, "That's what men always think about, you know."

In less than an hour she broke her promise to Jemima, for Samuel came in and she could not resist the temptation to speak to him of Bruce, though she began by saying innocently, "I heard today in the 'Change that the Dutch have told his Majesty their fleet is only to defend their fishing trade, and that he's angry they should think he's stupid enough to believe it."

Samuel, who was putting off his outer clothes, laughed at that. "What a ridiculous lie! The Dutch fleet is for just one purpose—to run England off the seas. They've captured our ships, beaten our men in the East Indies, hung the St. George under their own flag, granted letters-of-marque against us, and done everything but dare us to fight them."

"But we've been granting letters against them too, ever since the King came back, haven't we?"

"If we have it's not supposed to be known—the letters were mostly against the Spanish, though I don't doubt that Dutchmen have been stopped too. Which is no better than they deserve. But how does it happen you know so much of our politics, my dear?" He seemed tenderly amused to hear his wife discussing serious matters.

"I've been talking to Jemima."

"To Jemima? Well, I suppose she has the latest news at her finger-tips."

"When it concerns privateers she does. She says you do business with 'em."

"I do, with three or four. But I never knew Jemima to be very much interested in my business affairs." He smiled as he stood before her, hands in his pockets while his eyes ran over her admiringly.

"It isn't your business she's interested in so much as the privateers."

"Oh, so that's it, is it? The little minx. Well—I suppose she thinks she's in love with Lord Carlton."

"How did you guess?"

"It wasn't very difficult. He was here for supper once about a year ago. She could hardly eat a bite and talked about nothing else for days. Well, she'd better get him out of her head."

"She says she's waiting for him to come back."

"Nonsense! He doesn't know she's on earth! His family's one of the oldest in England and he's made himself enormously rich privateering. He's not interested in marrying some upstart merchant's daughter."

Samuel had no illusions about his social relationship to the aristocracy. His family was a new one, just come into power and wealth during the last two generations, and he had no snobbish ambition to buy his way into the peerage—as some men he knew were doing—at the price of his own self-respect.

"I wouldn't want her to marry Lord Carlton if he'd have her. As a man, I like and admire him, but as a husband for my daughter—I wouldn't consider it even if he wanted to marry her, which I know he dosen't. No, Jemima's going to marry Joseph Cuttle and she may as well get such ridiculous notions out of her head. The Cuttles and I have done business together for years and it's a suitable marriage for her in every respect. I'll speak to her directly about such nonsense."

"Oh, please, Samuel—don't do that! I promised her I wouldn't tell you. But of course I thought you should know. Why not let me talk to her?"

"I wish you would, my dear. She has more respect for your opinion than for anyone's." He smiled and offered her his arm. "I don't want to force her, and yet I know that it's best for her and for all of us. The boy is young, but he's very fond of her and is a quiet hard-working lad, exactly the kind of man she should marry."

"Of course she should! But young girls have such silly ideas about men—" They started out of the room and Amber asked casually, "By the way, Samuel, is Lord Carlton coming to London soon?"

"I don't know. Why?"

"Oh, I was only thinking that the contract should be signed before she sees him again—or heaven only knows what foolishness she might do."

"That's a very good idea, my dear. I'll see the lawyers tomorrow. It's kind of you to take an interest in my family."

Amber smiled modestly.

Joseph Cuttle was among the guests they had that night and though Amber had met him before she had not remembered him. He was a tall awkward boy, eighteen years old, with a face which looked unfinished. His manners were clumsy and embarrassed, as though he always wished that he might run away and hide. It was almost ridiculous to think of dainty effervescent little Jemima married to so gauche a creature.

But Amber sought him out and though at first he was desperately uncomfortable she succeeded so well in putting him at his ease that presently he was confiding his troubles to her and begging her to help him. She promised that she would and hinted that Jemima liked him much better than she seemed to but that shyness kept her from showing her feelings. Once she caught Jemima's eyes on her, surprised and hurt and accusing. It was not long before Jemima, pleading that she had a headache, left the company and went upstairs to her own apartments.

She rushed into Amber's room early the next morning, while Amber lay drowsily sunk in her feather-mattress, contemplating the tufted satin lining of the tester over her head. She was indulging, as she often did when not quite awake, in a sensual reverie, half memory, half wishful imagining, about herself and Bruce Carlton. She had long since forgiven him for Captain Morgan's death and did not doubt that he had likewise forgiven her. And, since Jemima had talked about him, she felt that he was closer than he had been, that perhaps she would see him again before so very long. Now Jemima's appearance jerked her rudely from her voluptuous musing.

"Heavens, Jemima! What's the matter?" She half sat up.

"Amber! How could you be so civil to that nasty Joseph Cuttle last night!"

"I don't think he's nasty at all, Jemima. He's a good kind-hearted young man, and he adores you."

"I don't care! He's ugly and he's a fool—and *I* hate *him!* And you promised you'd help me!" All at once she began to cry.

"Don't cry, Jemima," said Amber, rather crossly. "I'll help you if I can. But your father told me to talk to him, and I couldn't very well refuse."

"You could if you wanted to!" insisted Jemima, wiping the tears from her face. "Lettice says you make him do anything you want—like a tame monkey!"

Amber repressed a burst of laughter at this, but said severely, "Well, Lettice is wrong! And you'd better not say things like that, Jemima! But make yourself easy—I'll help you all I can."

Jemima smiled now, for her tears were sudden and light and left no traces. "Oh, thank you! I knew you wouldn't turn against me! And when Lord Carlton comes—you will help me then, won't you?"

"Yes, Jemima, of course. Every way I can."

Amber, crossing the front courtyard to get into her coach, stopped suddenly and stared at another coach which was standing there. It was Almsbury's. And since it was not likely the Earl could have any business with Samuel, it must mean that Bruce was back. He was there, at that very moment, inside with Samuel!

For an instant she stood, stunned, staring at the crest; and then without a word she whirled and ran back across the courtyard. She had been in Samuel's offices no more than three or four times and the various men working there looked at her in some surprise and curiosity as she rushed through the outer rooms toward his private office. Without stopping for an instant to decide what she would say or do, to try to gather her composure, she flung open the door.

The room was large and handsomely furnished with carved

oak tables and chairs and stools, dark rich velvet hangings, panelled walls, and numerous candles burning in brass sconces. Samuel and Lord Carlton stood before a great framed map of the New World, and though Samuel was facing her Bruce had his back turned. He had on one of the new cassock-coats, made of dark-green-and-gold brocade and reaching to his knees, with a broad twisted satin sash about the waist and a belt slung from one shoulder to hold his sword. A broad-brimmed hat was on his head and he wore a periwig which was not, however, much different in appearance from his own hair; only the fops wore the long extravagantly-curled wigs.

Even from the back he looked different to her from any other man, and her heart was beating so violently she was almost stifled. I'm going to faint! she thought desperately. I'm going to do something terrible and make a fool of myself!"

"Oh, I'm sorry, Samuel," she said, still standing in the opened doorway and holding to the knob. "I thought you were alone."

"Come in, my dear. This is Lord Carlton, of whom you've heard me speak. My lord, may I present my wife?"

Bruce turned and looked at her and his eyes showed first surprise and then amusement. You—he seemed to say—of all people. You, married to a respectable rich old merchant. And she saw too that he had not forgotten their last parting, made in anger and tragedy.

But he merely took off his hat and bowed to her gravely. "Your servant, madame."

"Lord Carlton is just returned from America with his ships —and several others, as well," Samuel added with a smile, for the merchants were proud of the privateers, and grateful to them.

"How fine," said Amber nervously, and she had a terrible feeling that she was going to fall apart, collapse in little pieces from head to toe. "I just came to tell you, Samuel"—she spoke rapidly—"that I won't be home in time for dinner. I've got a call to make." She gave Carlton a swift uncertain glance. "Why don't you come to supper this evening, Lord Carlton? I'm sure you must have a great many exciting tales to tell of your adventures at sea."

He bowed again, smiling. "I don't believe sea-going stories hold much interest for ladies, but I shall be very glad to come, Mrs. Dangerfield. Thank you."

Amber gave them both an abrupt smile, curtsied, and went out in a rush of taffeta petticoats; the door banged noisily behind her. She ran back across the courtyard as if afraid that her legs would not carry her all the way to the coach. She climbed in, dropped down onto the seat, and closed her eyes.

Excitedly Nan seized her hand. "Is he there, mam?"

"Yes," she whispered weakly. "He's there."

Half an hour later she was at Almsbury House and Emily was greeting her with eager enthusiasm. Together they started upstairs toward the nursery.

"How kind of you to call! We've been in town less than a fortnight and we tried to find you but at the Theatre they could only tell us you'd married, but didn't know where you were living. Lord Carlton is here with us—"

"Yes, I know. I just saw him at my husband's office. Do you think he'll come back here for dinner?"

"I don't know. I believe that he and John were to meet somewhere at one."

They had reached the nursery and found the children having their porridge. Amber's disappointment over the prospect of missing Bruce was partly eased by her reunion with her son, whom she had not seen since the previous September. He was an extraordinarily beautiful child, healthy and happy and friendly, with dark waving hair and green eyes. She picked him up in her arms, laughing gaily when he kissed her and got cream on her cheeks and mouth and tangled his spoon in her curls.

Daddy's here too, Mother!" he announced loudly. "Aunt Emily brought me all the way to London to see him!"

"Oh," said Amber, a little jealous resentment pricking at her. "You knew he was coming?"

"He wrote to John," explained Emily. "He wanted to see the baby."

"He isn't married, is he?"

It was the one question she dreaded to ask, each time he came back, though she could not imagine whom a man could find to marry in that barbarous empty land across the ocean.

"No," said Emily.

Amber sat down on the floor with Bruce and a fat barking spotted puppy which belonged to him, while Emily's two sons came to join them. Between playing with the puppy and talking to her son, she managed to ask Emily some questions.

"How long is he going to stay this time?"

"A month or so, I believe. He's going to volunteer his ships for the war."

"The war! It hasn't begun yet, has it?"

"Not yet, but soon, I believe. At least that's what they're saying at Court."

"But what's he going to do that for? He might lose them all—"

Emily looked faintly surprised. "Why, he wants to. England needs every ship and every experienced seaman she can get. Many privateers will do the same thing—"

At just that moment Bruce came through the opened doorway and walked toward them. While Amber sat speechless and helpless, the baby broke out of her arms and ran to his father, who swung him up onto one shoulder. He was standing above her now, looking down and smiling.

"I thought I might find you here."

Chapter Twenty-eight

JEMIMA CAME running into the bedroom that evening as Amber was getting dressed for supper. "Amber!" she cried joyously. "Oh, Amber, thank you!"

Amber turned and saw to her annoyance that Jemima, dressed in a gown of cornflower-blue satin, with the skirt caught up by artificial roses and real roses pinned into her glossy curls, was looking prettier than she ever had.

"Thank you for what?"

"For inviting Lord Carlton to supper, of course! Father told me he was coming and that you had asked him!"

"Joseph Cuttle's coming too, remember," said Amber crossly. "And if you're not nice to him your father will be mighty displeased."

"Oh, Joseph Cuttle! Who cares about him! Oh Amber, I'm so excited. What'll I do? What'll I say? Oh, I do want to make a great impression! Tell me what I shall do, Amber, please— You know about those things."

"Just be quiet and modest," advised Amber, somewhat tartly. "Remember, men never like a pert woman."

Jemima was instantly subdued, struggling to compose her face. "I know it! I've got to be very formal and languishing— if only I can! But, oh, I think I'll faint at the sight of him! Tell me—how do I look?"

"Oh, tearing fine," Amber assured her. She got up to put on her gown.

Amber was unhappy and worried and sickeningly jealous, desperately afraid of her step-daughter. She and Bruce had been together all afternoon, and the glow of those hours still lingered, throbbing and reverberating through every cord of her being. But now here was Jemina, young, lovely, audacious, who suddenly seemed to her a dangerous rival. For by her own marriage to a rich old merchant Amber had acquired a sort of counterfeit respectability which she felt made her less alluring. She was married but Jemima was not; and for all Samuel's certainty that Lord Carlton would not care to marry into the Dangerfield family, Amber was scared.

Don't be a fool! she had told herself a hundred times. He wouldn't marry a simpleton like Jemina for *all* the gold in England! Besides, he's rich enough himself now. Oh, why doesn't Jemima look like Lettice!

She did not look at Jemima as she got into her gown but she could feel the girl watching her, anxiously, and her own confidence began to return. The gown was made of champagne-coloured lace over champagne satin, and was spangled with thousands of golden stars. She turned, still avoiding Jemima's eyes, and walked back to the dressing-table to put on her emeralds.

"Oh!" cried Jemima at last. "How beautiful you are!" her eyes wistfully sought out her own reflection in a mirror. "He won't even see me!"

"Of course he will, sweetheart," said Amber, better-natured now. "You've never looked half so pretty."

At that moment Jemima's woman, Mrs. Carter, stuck her head in the door. "Mrs. Jemima!" she hissed. "His Lordship's here! He just came in!"

Amber's heart gave a bound, but she did not turn her head or move. Jemima, however, looked as distraught as a girl summoned to her execution. "He's here!" she breathed. "Oh, my God!" That alone was enough to show her mortal desperation, for blasphemy was no more allowable in Dangerfield House than was bawdry.

And then Jemima picked up her skirts and was gone.

Five minutes later Amber was ready to go downstairs herself. She was eager to see how he looked at Jemima, what he seemed to think of her—but most of all she wanted nothing but to see him again, to hear his voice and watch his face, to be in the same room with him.

"Take care, mam," cautioned Nan softly, as she gave her her fan.

Amber saw him the moment she entered the drawing-room. He was standing across from her talking to Samuel and two other men, and Jemima was there at his side, staring up at him like a flower with its face turned to the sun. She started toward them but had to stop a great many times on the way to greet her other guests, most of whom were familiar to her for they had been there often during the past five months.

They were merchants and lawyers and goldsmiths, part of that solid body of upper-middle-class rich which was rapidly becoming the greatest force in England. More and more they were able to control governmental policies both at home and overseas, because they now controlled the largest share of the country's money. Almost without exception they had been on the winning side in the Civil Wars, and their fortunes had continued to grow during the years that the defeated Royalists suffered imprisonment and ruinous taxes at home or lived in desperate poverty abroad. Even the Restoration had not been able to bring about a return of the old conditions; these were the rich strong men of the kingdom now.

It was the merchants who were loudest and most insistent in demanding a war against the Dutch, which was necessary to protect England's commerce and trade from the most formidable rival she had in that sphere. And Lord Carlton, as a privateer who had been sinking Dutch ships and capturing Dutch merchandise, was vastly respected and admired by them, in spite of the fact that he was an aristocrat.

At last Amber came up to the small group which stood framed by the new gold-embroidered velvet draperies she had put in the drawing-room. She made a deep curtsy and Bruce bowed to her. Jemima watched them both.

"I'm glad you were able to come, Lord Carlton." She could face him more calmly now, though her inner excitement was still intense.

"I'm extremely happy to be here, Mrs. Dangerfield."

No one could have guessed that only three hours ago they had lain together. Now they were cool and polite—strangers.

Supper was announced and the guests began to straggle into the dining-room where the meal was being served in French buffet style. There was food enough to feed three times the hundred people there were to eat it, and gallons of white and red wine. Wax candles cast a soft bright light on the women's hair and shoulders; music of fiddles drifted from the rooms beyond. Some of the women were dressed with as great splendour as the Court ladies; the men were for the most part in sober dark velvets or wool.

Amber and Bruce were immediately separated, for she had her duties as hostess and he was captured by a circle of merchants who wanted to know when the war would begin, how many ships he had taken, and if it was true that there was a plague in Holland which would lay her so low she would be an easy victim. They asked him why the King did not mend his ways, how long the idleness and corruption at Court would continue and, privately, whether it was a safe investment to loan his Majesty a large sum of money. "Our ships," "our trade," "our seas," were the words that sounded over and over. The women gathered in groups to talk of their children, their pregnancies and their servants. Almost everyone would remark, sometime during the course of the evening, that England had been far happier under Old Oliver; they forgot how they had grumbled about that same Old Oliver.

They drifted out of the dining-room and back to the drawing-room to seat themselves about little round tables or on chairs and benches. And Amber, whose eyes followed Bruce wherever he went, even when she seemed most occupied with something else, was furious when Jemima at last succeeded in maneuvering him away from his questioners and into a corner alone with her. They sat down, plates on their laps, and began to talk.

Jemima was chattering at him and smiling, her eyes ashine with happiness and passionate admiration as she plied on him all the pretty tricks of a natural flirt. Bruce sat and watched her and now and then he said something, but though he seemed only lazily amused Amber was in a state of anguished jealousy.

She made several starts to go over and interrupt them, but

each time someone stopped her. At last one old dowager with a bosom like a shelf and the face of a petulant spaniel said to her: "Jemima seems mightily smitten with his Lordship. She's been making sheep's-eyes at him all evening. Let me tell you, Mrs. Dangerfield, if Jemima was my daughter I'd find a way to get her out of his company—I admire his Lordship's exploits on the sea as much as anyone, but his reputation with women is none of the best, you can take my word for that."

Amber was horrified. "Oh, heaven! Thank you for telling me, Mrs. Humpage. I'll take a course with her this instant."

And immediately she was off across the room to where Joseph Cuttle stood in a corner talking to Henry and trying to pretend he did not know Jemima was with a man who was not only handsome and titled but a hero into the bargain.

"Why, Joseph!" she cried. "Where have you been all evening? Whatever are you doing over here? I'll wager you haven't spoke so much as a word to Jemima!"

Joseph blushed and shuffled one foot awkwardly, while Henry looked into his step-mother's neckline. "I'm having a fine time, Mrs. Dangerfield. Jemima's busy."

"Nonsense, Joseph! Why, she'll never forgive you if you serve her at this rate!" she took his wrist, kindness and encouragement in her eyes. "Come along, Joseph—you can't help your cause with her by standing over here."

They began to make their way across the room and Amber kept a firm hold on Joseph's hand, as though afraid that he would bolt and run. But Amber dragged him up to Bruce and Jemima, ignoring the reproachful accusing stare Jemima gave her, and presented him to Lord Carlton.

"I'm going to let you and Joseph start the dancing, Jemima," she said sweetly. "You can begin with coranto."

Reluctantly Jemima got to her feet, but her face began to sparkle again as she turned to Bruce. "Excuse me, your Lordship?"

Bruce bowed. "Certainly, madame. And I thank you for your company at supper."

Jemima gave him a long smile, one he was not intended to forget—ignoring the tormented boy by her side—and then with a brief curtsy to Amber she went off toward the ballroom, but she did not take Joseph's arm or seem aware that he was with her.

Amber waited until they were out of ear-shot and then she turned to Bruce, to find him smiling down at her. He seemed to know exactly what she was thinking. "Well!" she said, "And did you have a pleasant evening!"

"Very pleasant. Thank you for inviting me. And now—" He glanced across the room at a clock. "I must be going."

"Oh, you must be going!" she repeated sarcastically. "As soon as *I* come along you must be going!"

"I have business at Whitehall."

"I can imagine what *your* business is!"

"Smile a little, Amber," he said softly. "Some of your guests are beginning to wonder at your familiarity with me. A woman never quarrels with a man she doesn't know well."

His mocking tone made her furious, but what he said scared her even more. And now she forced a bright smile onto her mouth if not into her eyes, and gave a quick sweeping glance to see if they were being watched. I've *got* to be careful! she warned herself. If anyone guessed— Oh Lord, if they ever guessed!

She raised her voice a little, smiling. "I'm so glad you could come tonight, Lord Carlton. It isn't often we have the company of a man who's done so much for England."

Bruce bowed, bending with his careless, light feline grace. "Thank you, madame. Good-night."

He left her then and made his way across the room to speak to Samuel. Suddenly Amber, who had turned about to talk to a white-haired old gentleman, left him with the excuse that she must see about replenishing the wine. In the hallway she picked up her skirts and ran as fast as she could go, out the door and round to the front courtyard where she saw Bruce just getting into a coach.

"Lord Carlton!" she cried breathlessly, her high heels clicking as she ran across the brick pavement toward him.

He stopped, turning to look at her. "Did you call me, Mrs. Dangerfield?"

"I have a message from my husband, your Lordship." With that she climbed into the coach and beckoned him to follow her, motioning the footman then to close the door. "Bruce—when can I see you again?"

"Amber, you little fool! What are you thinking about?" His voice was impatient and there was an angry look in his eyes. "You've got to use more sense this time!"

She frowned a little as she glanced out the window, wishing that that stupid footman would go away with his torch, for it sent a flaring light in upon them. "I'll be careful! Only I've got to see you, Bruce! When? I can come any time."

"Come to the ships tomorrow, then. We'll be unloading and no one will be surprised if you're there."

"I'll be there in the morning."

She leaned a little toward him, longing for a kiss.

"Amber!"

Reluctantly she got out of the coach and ran back into the house again. To her horrified amazement she found the drawing-rooms in an uproar of excitement and turmoil, though she had left her guests talking and laughing and beginning to dance.

"What is it? What's happened?" She rushed up to the first person she saw.

"It's your husband, Mrs. Dangerfield. He's fainted."

"Fainted!"

The terrible thought went through her mind that he had somehow guessed or been told about her and Bruce and that the shock had brought on a stroke. She was more worried for herself than for Samuel, as she ran up the stairs.

She found the outer rooms full of people, servants and members of the family, but without stopping to speak to them she went directly into the bedroom. Samuel lay at full length on the bed and Lettice knelt beside him, while the four oldest brothers stood anxiously nearby. None of them glanced at her. Dr. de Forest, who was his physician and who had been at supper, was holding his wrist and taking the count of his pulse.

Instinctively Amber lowered her voice to whisper. "What happened? I went out to see about the wine and when I came back they said he had fainted."

"He *has,*" said Sam curtly.

Amber went to stand beside the bed, on the opposite side from Lettice. She did not dare look at her or at the others, but she sensed that none of them was paying her any attention; all interest was focused on their father. And though it seemed to her that she waited there for an endless time, it was actually but a few minutes. When he opened his lids he was looking up at Lettice; his eyes shifted, searching for Amber, and when he found her he smiled. She was watching him breathlessly, afraid that now he would say something that would tell her she was caught.

She bent across the bed and kissed him gently. "You're here, Samuel, with us. There's nothing to worry about."

"I don't remember what happened—I thought we were—"

"You fainted, sir," said Dr. de Forest.

Lettice was crying, very softly so that she would disturb no one, and her eldest brother reached down and took her by the shoulders to raise her to her feet. At the doctor's request they left the room, all but Amber. He began to talk to them both then, very seriously, of the necessity for Samuel to be perfectly quiet for a few days, to avoid exertion of any kind—and he particularly addressed himself to Amber who looked at him solemnly and nodded her head.

"You must help your husband, Mrs. Dangerfield," he said privately to Amber when she was showing him out. "His life's in jeopardy if you don't. You understand me?"

"Yes, Dr. de Forest. I will."

When she came back Samuel took her hand and smiled. "Dr. de Forest is full of ridiculous notions. We won't pay any attention to him, will we?"

But Amber answered him firmly. "Yes, we *will,* Samuel. He says it's for your good and we will. We must. Promise me, Samuel—promise you'll do as he says."

He was obviously embarrassed, but Amber was insistent. She would allow him to do no thing, not the smallest, which might be injurious to his health. And they would be just as happy as before—he must never think that it mattered to her in any way at all. Nothing mattered to her but his safety and well-being. Samuel, deeply touched by this manifestation of tender devotion, could not restrain a few tears. But while she sat beside him and talked and stroked his head Amber was thinking that if she became pregnant now the child would be Lord Carlton's —and if only it happened soon, Samuel would think it his own.

The next morning he was feeling somewhat better, but Amber insisted that he remain in bed as the doctor had said he should, and much against her will she stayed in the room with him. About one o'clock Jemima came in with her two oldest brothers to say that they were going down to watch Lord Carlton's ships being unloaded.

"Why don't you go with them, my dear?" Samuel asked Amber. "You've been shut up here with me all day."

Jemima looked at her anxiously, obviously hoping that she would not come, and though for a moment or two Amber insisted that she could not leave him she allowed herself to be persuaded. But the trip was a disappointment. They had not so much as a word alone together and Bruce was so busy he seemed scarcely aware of her presence. Her only consolation was that Jemima was as much disappointed as she was, and did not conceal it so well.

He did, however, make each of them a handsome present. To Jemima he gave a magnificent length of material which looked as though molten gold had been poured over a piece of silk, and a pattern etched in it by sensitive fingers holding a feather; to Amber he gave an elaborate necklace of topaz and gold. Both gifts had been captured from one of the Dutch ships returning from the East Indies.

But early the next morning she slipped out of the house in a black cloak and mask and took a hackney to Almsbury House. They spent half an hour in the nursery with the baby and Emily and Almsbury, and then they went back to his apartments.

"Suppose someone finds out about this," he said.

Amber was confident. "They won't. Samuel was asleep and Nan was to say I went to have a gown fitted, so I wouldn't have to trouble him with women about in the room." She smiled up at him. "Oh, I'm a marvellously devoted wife, I'll warrant you."

"You're a hard-hearted little bitch," he said. "I pity the men who love you."

But she was too happy to get angry about anything, and there was a light in his green eyes as he sat looking at her which would have made her forgive anything. She went over and sat on his lap, putting her arms about his neck and her mouth against his smooth-shaven cheek.

"But you love me, Bruce—and I've never hurt you. I don't think I could if I tried," she added with a pout.

He gave a lift of one eyebrow and smiled. He had never indulged in the extravagant compliments which were a fashion among the gallants, and she sometimes wondered jealously if he paid them to other women. Jemima perhaps.

"What do you think of Jemima?" she asked him now.

"Why, she's very pretty—and naïve as a Maid of Honour her first week at Court."

"She's mad in love with you."

"A hundred thousand pound or so, I've discovered, will make a man more attractive than he'd ever suspected himself of being."

"A hundred thousand! My God, Bruce! What a lot of money! When Samuel dies I'll have sixty-six thousand. Think what a fortune that would be if we put it together! We'd be the richest people in England!"

"You forget, darling. I won't be in England."

"Oh, but you—"

Suddenly he stood up and swung her into his arms; his mouth closed over hers. Amber sailed away dizzily, her arguments effectively stopped. But he had not heard, by any means, the last of it. For now she had contrived to get something which she knew he valued, money, and she hoped to bargain with it. If only he would marry her—if only she could have him forever. There was nothing else she wanted, really. All her other great ambitions would vanish like a piece of ice dropped on a red-hot stove.

She did not go back to Almsbury House the next two mornings, for Bruce had warned her that unless she was very careful she would be found out. "If you're sailing that ocean under false colours," he said, "and I suppose you must be—you'd better remember it won't take much to make them suspicious. And if they ever caught you—your sixty-six thousand might dwindle considerably." She knew that it was the truth and determined to be cautious.

But when Jemima asked her what she had thought of Lord Carlton the blood shot suddenly to her face and she had to bend over to retie her garter. "Why—he's mighty handsome, of course."

"I think he liked me—don't you?"

"What makes you think so!" Her voice was sharp in spite of herself, but she hastily changed its tone. "You mustn't be so bold, Jemima. I'm sure everyone thought you were flirting with him—and courtiers are all the same."

"All the same? In what way?"

Worried and annoyed by what seemed to be Jemima's stupidity she snapped: "Just remember this—take care he doesn't do you some harm!"

"Harm, pish!" said Jemima scornfully. "What harm *could* he do me when I love him?"

Amber had an impulse to run after her and grab her by the

hair and slap her face, but she restrained herself. It would certainly not be in keeping with the character she had built for herself, a structure put together at too much pain and cost to kick it over carelessly now because of a silly girl who meant nothing to him. Nevertheless, she and Jemima were henceforward somewhat cool when they met and Jemima—who was even now puzzled as to what had caused this change in their friendship—again began to call her "Madame."

The next afternoon she returned from visiting some of Samuel's innumerable relatives and found Jemima waiting in the entrance hall with Carter, both of them dressed to go out. Jemima was painted and patched and perfumed, her hair was curled and her buttercup-yellow satin gown cut so low that it seemed her small round breasts might escape at any moment. There were yellow roses in her hair and she wore her yellow-lined black-velvet cloak hung carelessly on her shoulders, to cover as little of her as possible. She looked for all the world like a Court beauty or the town's reigning harlot.

"Ye gods, Jemima!" said Amber, pausing in shocked amazement to look at her step-daughter. "Wherever are you going dressed like that?"

Jemima's eyes sparkled and her voice was triumphant, almost defiant. "Lord Carlton is coming to take me for a drive in Hyde Park."

"I suppose you asked him?"

"Well, maybe I did! You don't get what you want by sitting and waiting for it!"

Amber had told Jemina something like that once, but now Jemima said it without remembering its source. She thought it was her own idea. And Amber, who had meddled in a spirit of malicious mischief, encouraged Jemima's rebellion against family traditions, was faced with the prospect of having her own advice turned against her. Three months ago Jemima would never have dared ask a man to take her riding. Amber was not thinking of retributive justice, however, as she stood staring at Jemima with her hatred showing plain in her eyes. Oh! if only I wasn't married to her father! she thought, furious at her own impotence.

"Jemima, you're making a fool of yourself! You don't know the kind of man Lord Carlton is!"

Jemima lifted her chin. "I beg your pardon, Madame, but I know exactly. He's handsome and he's fascinating and he's a gentleman—and I love him."

Amber's lip curled and she repeated the words, mimicking her with cruel accuracy. "He's handsome and he's fascinating and he's a gentleman—and you love him! Hoity-toity! And if you're not mighty careful you'll find that your maidenhead is missing!"

"I don't believe you! Lord Carlton isn't like that at all! Besides, Carter is going along!"

"She'd better! And see that she stays along, too!"

She was now so angry that, in spite of Nan's frantic nudges and grimaces, she might have gone on to say much more, but the knocker clattered and the footman who answered it admitted Bruce. He swept off his hat to both of them, and his eyes glittered with amusement to find Amber and her stepdaughter so obviously engaged in a quarrel.

Damn him! thought Amber. Men always think they're so superior!

"This is a pleasant surprise, Mrs. Dangerfield," he said now. "I hadn't expected to have your company too."

"Oh, Madame isn't coming!" said Jemima hastily. "She's just returned from a drive!"

"Oh," said Bruce softly. "I'm sorry, Mrs. Dangerfield. I'd have enjoyed having you with us."

Amber's eyes stared at him, hard and shining and slanting like a cat's. "*Would* you, Lord Carlton?"

And she turned and ran up the stairs, but as she heard the door close behind them she stopped abruptly on the balcony above, swirling about to look down. They were gone. Suddenly she raised her arm and threw her fan as hard as she could at the floor below. She had not realized that anyone was about, but at that moment a footman appeared and looked up in some surprise; her eyes met his for an alarmed angry instant and then she rushed off.

She was still somewhat excited when Samuel came up from the office where he had gone to spend an hour or two. But she kissed him affectionately, made him sit down, and then took a stool beside him and put her hand into his. For a few moments they chatted of various small things and then she gave a troubled little frown, and stared off pensively into space.

He stroked the smooth crown of her head, where the hair lay in burnished satin waves. "What is it, my dear? Nothing's amiss?"

"No Samuel, nothing. Oh, Samuel—I must tell you! It's about Jemima! I'm worried about her!"

"You mean about Lord Carlton?"

"Yes. Why, only an hour ago I met her in the hall and she'd asked him to take her driving in Hyde Park!"

He gave a heavy tired sigh. "I can't understand her. She's been as carefully brought up as could be possible. Sometimes I think there's a taint in the air nowadays—the young people fall sick of it. Not all of them, of course," he added with a smile of fondness. "I don't think he's at all interested in her—Jemima isn't the kind of woman he can be used to associating with—and I think that if she had let him alone he'd never have given her a second thought."

"Of course he wouldn't!" agreed Amber, very positively.

"I don't know what's to be done—"

"I do, Samuel! You must make her marry Joseph Cuttle—right now! Before something much worse happens!"

Chapter Twenty-nine

THAT WAS THE end of Jemima's friendship with her stepmother. For by an unerring feminine instinct she knew immediately who was responsible for her father's sudden determination to marry her to Joseph Cuttle without more delay. It was the one thing Amber had done of which the family approved, for they had been worried too about Jemima's infatuation for a Cavalier—though they considered that it was Madame's fault Jemima had ever fallen in love with him. They did not believe it would have occurred to Jemima to admire such a man, but for the bad example of false values Amber had set. But Bruce seemed somewhat shocked when Amber told him the contract had been signed and the marriage date set for August 30th—forty days from the time of betrothal.

"Good Lord!" he said. "That awkward spindle-shanked boy! Why should a pretty little thing like Jemima have to marry him?"

"What difference does it make to you who she marries!"

"None at all. But don't you think you're meddling rather impertinently in the affairs of the Dangerfield family?"

"I am not! Samuel was going to make her marry him anyway. I just got the matter settled—for her own good."

"Well, if you think I intend seducing her, I don't. I took her driving because she asked me to and it would have been an affront to her father if I'd refused." He gave her a long narrow look. "I wonder if you have any idea what a very fine old gentleman Samuel Dangerfield is. Tell me—how the devil did you manage to marry him? The Dangerfields aren't people who would welcome an actress to the hearth-side."

She laughed. "Wouldn't you like to know!" But she never told him.

It was not long before Amber refused altogether to heed Bruce's admonitions—she went to Almsbury House three or four mornings in every week. Samuel left for his office at about seven and returned between eleven and noon; she was there when he left and there when he got back. But even if she had not been it would have occasioned no comment. He trusted her implicitly and when he asked her where she had been it was never from motives of suspicion, but only to make conversation or because he was interested in the little things which occupied her day. Whatever off-hand tale she told him, he believed.

And Jemima, meanwhile, turned sulky and bad-tempered, refused to take an interest in the elaborate preparations for her wedding. Dressmakers and mercers filled her rooms at all hours; she was to be married in cloth-of-gold and her wedding-ring was studded with thirty diamonds. The great ballroom in the south wing of the house where the wedding-feast and masque were to take place would be transformed into a blooming, green-leafed forest, with real grass on the floor. There would be five hundred guests for the ceremony and almost a thousand for the festivities afterward. Fifty of the finest musicians in London were being hired to play for the ball and a noted French chef was coming from Paris to oversee the preparation of the food. Samuel was eager to please his daughter and her persistent sullenness troubled him.

Amber magnanimously took Jemima's part. "There's nothing wrong with her, Samuel, but what's wrong with all girls old enough to be married who aren't. She's got the green-sickness, that's all. Wait till after the wedding, she'll be herself again then, I warrant you."

Samuel shook his head. "By heaven, I hope so! I hate to see her unhappy. Sometimes I wonder if we're not making a mistake to insist that she marry Joseph. After all, there are suitable matches enough for her in London if she—"

"Nonsense, Samuel! Who ever heard of a girl choosing her own husband! She's too young to know *what* she wants. And Joseph is a fine young man; he'll make her mighty happy." That settled it. And Amber thought that she had managed everything with great cleverness—Jemima was no source of worry to her now. Silly girl! she thought scornfully. She should have known better than to cross swords with me!

Scarcely six weeks had gone by since Bruce's arrival in London when she told him that she was sure she was pregnant, and explained why she believed the child must be his. "I hope it'll be a girl," she said. "Bruce is so handsome—I know she'd be a beauty. What do you think we should name her?"

"I think that's up to Samuel, don't you?"

"Pish—why should it be? Anyway, he'll ask me. So you tell me what name you'd like—please, Bruce, I want to know."

He seemed to give it a few moments' serious consideration—but the smile that lurked about his mouth showed what he was thinking. "Susanna's a pretty name," he said at last.

"You don't know anyone named Susanna, do you?"

"No. You asked me for a name that I liked, and I told you one. I had no ulterior motives."

"But you've named your share of bastards, I doubt not," she said. "What about that wench—Leah, or what d'ye call her? Almsbury said you'd had two brats by her."

By now Bruce had been back long enough and she had seen him so often that the jealousies and worries that beset her when he was away had begun to encroach upon the pleasure she found in being with him. She had begun to feel more discontented over what she was missing than grateful for what she had.

His voice answered her quietly. "Leah died a year ago, in childbirth."

She looked up at him swiftly, saw that he was serious and a little angry. "Oh, I'm sorry," she lied. But she turned to another subject. "I wonder where you'll be when Susanna's born?"

"Somewhere giving the Dutch hell, I hope. We'll declare war on them as soon as Parliament votes the money for it. While we're waiting I'll try what I can do to keep the peace the way his Majesty wants it kept." England and Holland had been at war everywhere but in the home seas for almost a year, and during the past two months the fight had blazed into the open; it needed only to be declared, but Charles had to wait on further preparation and Parliamentary grants.

They were lying on the bed, half-dressed. Bruce had his periwig off and his own hair had been cut short so that now it was no more than two or three inches long, and combed back from his forehead in a wave. Amber rolled over onto her stomach and reached for a bunch of purple Lisbon grapes in a bowl on the table.

"Heigh ho! I suppose it's a dull day for you when there isn't a town to burn or a dozen Dutchmen to kill!"

He laughed, pulled a small cluster of grapes from the bunch she held, and began to toss them into his mouth. "Your portrait's somewhat bloodthirsty."

She gave a sigh. "Oh, Bruce! If only you'd listen to me!" And then all at once she bounced up and knelt facing him, determined that he should listen to her. Somehow he had always managed to stop her before—but not this time. This time he was going to hear her out. "Go off to the wars if you must, Bruce! But when it's over sell your ships and stay here in London. With your hundred thousand and my sixty-six we'd be so rich we could buy the Royal Exchange for a summer pavilion. We could have the biggest finest house in London—and everyone who was anybody at all would come to our balls and suppers. We'd have a dozen coaches and a thousand servants and a yacht to sail to France in if we took the notion. We'd go to Court and you'd be a great man—Chancellor, or whatever you wanted, and I'd be a Lady of the Bedchamber. There wouldn't be anyone in England finer than us! Oh, Bruce, darling—don't you see? We'd be the happiest people in the world!"

She was so passionately convinced herself that she was positive she could convince him; and his answer was a painful disappointment.

"It would be fine," he said. "For a woman."

"Oh!" she cried furiously. "You men! What *do* you want then!"

"I'll tell you, Amber." He sat up and looked at her. "I want something more than spending the next twenty-five years standing on a ladder with one man's heels on my fingers and mine on the man's beneath. I want to do something besides plot and scheme and intrigue with knaves and fools to get a reputation with men I despise. I want a little more than going from the theatre to a cock-fight to Hyde Park to Pall Mall and back over the same round the next day. Playing cards and poaching after anything that goes by in petticoats and a mask and serving my turn as the King's pimp—" He made a gesture of disgust. "And finally dying of women and drink."

"I suppose you think living in America will keep you from dying of women and drink!"

"Maybe not. But one thing I know— When I die it won't be from boredom."

"Oh, won't it! I don't doubt it's mighty exciting over there with blackamoors and pirates and Newgate-birds and every other kind of ragamuffin!"

"It's more civilized than you imagine—there are also a great many men of good family who left England during the Commonwealth, remember. And who are still leaving—for the same reason I am. It isn't that I'm going there because I think the men and women in America are better or different from what they are in England; they're the same. It's because America is a country that's still young and full of promise, the way England hasn't been for a thousand years. It's a country that's waiting to be made by the men who'll dare to make it—and I intend getting there while I can help make it my way. In the Civil Wars my father lost everything that had belonged to our family for seven centuries. I want my children to have something they can't lose, ever."

"Well, then, why trouble yourself to fight for England—since you love her so little!"

"Amber, Amber," he said softly. "My dear, someday I hope you'll know a great many things you don't know now."

"And someday I hope you'll sink in your damned ocean!"

"No doubt I'm too great a villain to drown."

She jumped off the bed in a fury, but suddenly she stopped, turned and looked at him as he lay leaning on his elbow and watching her. And then she came back and sat down again, covering his hand with both of hers.

"Oh, Bruce, you know I don't mean that! But I love you so—I'd die for you—and you don't seem to need me at all, the way I need you! I'm nothing but your whore—I want to be your wife, *really* your wife! I want to go where you go, and share your troubles and plan with you for what you want, and bear your children—I want to be part of you! Oh, please, darling! Take me to America with you! I don't care what it's like, I swear I don't! I'll live in anything! I'll do anything! I'll help you cut down trees and plant tobacco and cook your meals— Oh, Bruce! I'll do *anything*, if only you'll take me with you!"

For a moment he continued to stare at her, his eyes glittering, but just when she thought she had convinced him he shook his head and got up. "It would never work out that way, Amber. It's not your kind of life and in a few weeks or months you'd get tired of it, and then you'd hate me for bringing you."

She ran after him, throwing herself before him, grabbing frantically at the happiness that seemed just to elude her fingers but which she was sure she could catch. "No, I wouldn't, Bruce! I swear it! I promise you! I'd love anything if you were there!"

"I can't do it, Amber. Let's not talk about it."

"Then you've got another reason! You have, haven't you? What is it?"

He was suddenly impatient and faintly angry. "For the love of God, Amber, let it go! I can't do it. That's all."

She looked at him for a long minute, her eyes narrowed. "I know why," she said slowly at last. "I know why you won't take me over there, and why you won't marry me. It's because I'm a farmer's niece and you're a nobleman. My father was only a yeoman, but *your* family was sitting in the House of Lords before there was one. My mother was just a plain simple woman, but *your* mother was a Bruce and descended from no one less than Holy Moses himself. My relatives are farmers—but *you've* got some Stuart blood in you, if you look hard enough to find it." Her voice was sarcastic and bitter, and as she talked her mouth twisted, giving an ugly expression to her face.

She turned angrily away and began to pull on the rest of her clothes, while he watched her. There was a kind of tenderness on his face now and he seemed to be trying to think of something to say to her that would help take away the painful sense of humiliation she felt. But she gave him no opportunity to speak. In only two or three minutes she was dressed and then as she picked up her cloak she cried: "That's why, isn't it!"

He stood facing her. "Oh, Amber, why must you always make things hard for yourself? You know as well as I do that I couldn't marry you if I wanted to. I can't marry just for myself. I'm not alone in the world, floating in space like a speck of dust. I've got relatives by the score—and I've got a responsibility to my parents who are dead and to their parents. The Bruces and Carltons mean nothing to you—and there's no reason why they should—but they're damned important to the Bruces and Carltons."

"That wheedle won't pass with me! You wouldn't marry me even if you could! *Would* you!"

They stared at each other; and then his answer cracked out, surprising as the sharp report of a pistol.

"No!"

For an instant Amber continued looking at him, but her face had turned beet-red and the blue cords throbbed in her throat and forehead. "Oh!" she screamed, almost hysterical with rage and pain. "I hate you, Bruce Carlton! I hate you—I—" She turned and rushed from the room, slamming the door after her. "I hope I never see you again!" she sobbed to herself as she dashed headlong down the stairs. And she told herself that this was the end—the last insult she would take from him—the last time he would ever—

Amber ran out of Almsbury House and straight to her coach. She jumped in. "Drive away!" she yelled at Tempest. "Home!" She flung herself back and began to cry distractedly, though with few tears, her teeth biting at the tips of her gloved hands.

She was so excited that she did not notice another coach waiting just outside the gates, with its wooden shutters closed, which started up and came rumbling along just behind her own. And it stayed there, just behind her, following every turn, halting when her coach halted, proceeding at exactly the same rate of speed and never letting another coach come between them. They were almost home before Amber noticed that two of her footmen, who were hanging on the side, kept looking back and gesturing, apparently both puzzled and amused. She turned and glanced through the back window, saw the hackney behind them, but was not much concerned.

And then, as they turned through the great south gate of Dangerfield House, the impertinent hackney turned in also. Amber got out, still scowling in spite of her struggles to compose her face, and confronted Jemima who had just stepped down from the hackney. Carter was paying the driver.

"Good morning, Madame," said Jemima.

Amber started off, and tossed Jemima what she hoped was a careless greeting. "Good morning, Jemima." But her heart was pounding and she had a sick feeling of despair. The damned girl had been spying! And, what was worse, had caught her!

"Just a moment, Madame. Haven't you time for a word with me? You were glad enough to be my friend—before Lord Carlton came."

Amber stopped still, and then she turned around to face her step-daughter. There was nothing to do but try to brazen it out with her. "What's Lord Carlton got to do with this?"

"Lord Carlton's staying at Almsbury House. That's why you were there just now—and day before yesterday and twenty other times this past month, for all I know!"

"Mind your own business, Jemima! I'm no prisoner here. I'll come and go as I like. As it happens Lady Almsbury is a dear friend of mine—I was visiting her."

"You didn't visit her before Lord Carlton came to town!"

"She wasn't here! She was in the country. Now look here, Jemima, I've a mighty good idea why you've been following me—and I've a mind to tell your father. He'll take a course with you, I warrant."

"*You'll* tell Father! Suppose *I* tell him a few things I know—about you and Lord Carlton!"

"You don't know a thing! And if you weren't as jealous as a barren wife you wouldn't have such suspicions, either!" Her eyes went swiftly from Jemima to Carter and back again. "Who puts these ideas in your head? This old screech-owl here?" Carter's guiltily shifted glance told her that her guess was right and Amber, with a great show of independent virtue, gave her a last warning and went off. "Don't let me hear any more of your bellow-weathering, Jemima, or we'll try which one of us your father will believe!"

Jemima evidently did not care to make the test, and Dangerfield House remained quiet. Amber pretended to have the ague so that her step-daughter could not ask why she had stopped going to visit Lady Almsbury. The time was drawing nearer for Jemima's wedding, though the date had been postponed a few days at her almost hysterical demand, and Amber was eager to have it over and the girl out of her way.

A week after her quarrel with Bruce, Samuel told her that Lord Carlton had been in his office that morning. "He's sailing tomorrow," he said, "if the wind serves. I hope that once he's gone Jemima will—"

But Amber was not listening. Tomorrow! she thought. My God—he's going tomorrow! Oh, I've got to see him—I've got to see him again—

His ships lay at Botolph Wharf and Amber waited inside her coach while Jeremiah went to find him. She was excited and anxious, afraid that he would still be angry, but when he returned and found who it was waiting there for him he smiled. The afternoon was hot and he wore no periwig but only his breeches and bell-sleeved white shirt, and his tanned face was wet with perspiration.

She leaned forward eagerly and put her hand on his as he stood in the door, and her voice spoke swiftly and softly. "I had to see you again, Bruce, before you went."

"We're busy loading, Amber. I can't leave."

"Can't we go on board? Just for a minute?"

He stepped back and took her hand to help her down.

Everywhere about them was activity. Tall-masted ships, elaborately carved and gilded, moved gently with the water, and the wharf was crowded. There were sailors who had been so many years at sea that they walked with a rolling gait which would distinguish them anywhere. Husky-shouldered porters were trundling casks or staggering along bent beneath great wooden boxes or iron-hooped bales. Well-dressed merchants strolled up and down, pestered by the beggars—broken old seamen who had given a leg or an arm or an eye for England.

There were wide-eyed boys, loitering old men and blatantly painted harlots—a noisy variegated crowd.

As they walked along the wharf every eye glanced at or followed them. For her clothes and her hair and her jewels glittered in the sunlight; she was beautiful and she had a look of breeding to which they were not very much accustomed. The prostitutes looked Bruce over with an interest not wholly professional.

"Why didn't you come to see me?" she asked him in an undertone, and then crossed over the wide roped-off plank which led to one of his ships.

Following her, he murmured, "I didn't think my company would be very welcome," and turned to talk for a moment or two to another man. Then he led her around the deck and down a flight of stairs to a small cabin. It looked comfortable, though not luxurious, and was fitted with a good-sized bunk, a writing-table and three chairs. Maps were nailed to the dark oak-panelled walls and on the floor were stacks of leather-bound books.

Inside she turned about swiftly to face him. "I'm not going to quarrel with you, Bruce. I don't want to talk—just kiss me—"

His arms had scarcely gone around her when there was a sharp knock. "Lord Carlton! A lady to see you, sir!"

Amber looked up accusingly at him, and as he released her he muttered a soft curse. But before he started for the door he gestured at her, and picking up her cloak and the muff she had dropped she hurried through the door he had indicated into the adjoining cabin. And then as Bruce opened the other door, she heard a pair of high heels coming down the stairway and Jemima Dangerfield's lilting young voice.

"Lord Carlton! Thank Heaven I found you! I've got a message from my father for you—"

Amber heard Jemima's feet walk into the cabin and the door swing shut. She stood close behind her own door, her ear against the wooden panels and her heart hammering violently as she listened. Her excitement was caused as much, just now, by fear of being caught as by jealousy.

"Oh, Bruce! I found out you're going tomorrow! I had to come!"

"You shouldn't have, Jemima. Someone might see you. And I'm so busy I haven't an extra moment. I came down here to get some papers—here they are. Come, and I'll walk back to your coach with you."

"Oh, but Bruce! You're going away tomorrow! I've *got* to see you again! I can meet you anywhere—I'll be at the Crown tonight at eight. In our same room."

"Forgive me, Jemima. I can't come. I swear I'm too busy—I've got to go to Whitehall, and we'll sail before sunup."

"Then *now!* Oh, Bruce, please! Just this once more—"

"Hush, Jemima! Sam and Robert will be here at any moment. You don't want them to find you here alone with me." There was a pause, during which she heard him turn and walk to the door and open it, and then he said: "Oh, I'm sorry. I didn't see you drop your glove." Jemima did not answer and they walked out.

Amber waited until she was sure that they were gone and then she went back into his cabin again.

Apprehension for her own safety, now that it was secured, dissolved instantly into a jealous fury against both Jemima and Bruce. So he *had* been making love to her! The dirty varlet! And the puling little milk-sop, Jemima! She'll smoke for this!

Bruce returned to find her sitting on the writing-table, her feet braced against the bunk and both hands on her hips. She looked at him as though expecting him to hang his head and blush.

"Well!" she said.

He gave a shrug, closing the door.

"So that's what you've been about this past week!" Suddenly she got up, walked across the room and turned her back on him. "So you didn't intend to seduce her!"

"I didn't."

She swung around. "You didn't! She just said—"

"I didn't intend to. Now look here, Amber. I haven't time for a quarrell. A fortnight or so ago Jemima came one morning to Almsbury House and sent up your name. You many think I should have indignantly ordered her out of my bedroom, but I didn't. The poor child was unhappy and disappointed over being made to marry Joseph Cuttle and she thinks, at least, that she's in love with me. That's all there is to it."

"Then what about the Crown—and our same room?" The last three words mocked Jemima's voice as she had said them.

"We met there three or four times afterwards. If you want to know anything else about it, ask Jemima. I haven't the time. Come on—I'm going back upon deck."

As he turned she ran forward and grabbed his arms. "Bruce! Please, darling— Don't go till we've said goodbye—"

Half an hour later they returned to her coach and he handed her in. "When will you come back to London again?" she asked.

"I don't know. It'll be several months anyway. I'll see you when I do."

"I'll be waiting for you, Bruce. And, oh, darling, be careful! Don't get hurt. And think of me sometimes—"

"I will."

He stepped back, swinging the door closed, and made a signal to the coachman to start. The coach began to move and he smiled back at her as she stuck her head out the opened window.

"Sink a thousand Dutchmen!" she called.

He laughed. "I'll try!" He gave her a wave and turned to go

back onto the ship. The coach moved on and the crowds closed between them; he disappeared from her sight.

Amber entered her apartments, still too full of the warm luxuriant afterglow of Bruce's love-making to have begun thinking of Jemima again. It was an unpleasant shock to find the girl there, waiting for her.

Jemima was tense and excited. "May I see you alone, Madame?"

Amber felt very superior; triumphant. "Why, of course, Jemima."

Nan herded the other servants out of the room, all but Tansy who stayed where he was, sitting cross-legged on the floor absorbed in working a Chinese puzzle which Samuel had brought him more than a week ago. A servant took Amber's muff and fan and gloves, one of which Amber had lost. She was careless with her belongings, they were so easily replaced; and if she lost something it gave her an excuse to buy another.

Amber turned and faced her step-daughter. "Now," she said casually, raising her hands to her hair. "What d'you want?"

The two women, both of them beautiful and expensively dressed, with well-bred features, presented a strange contrast. For one was obviously unsophisticated and essentially innocent, while the other was just as obviously the reverse. But it was not the way she looked, nor was it anything in her manner. It was rather a certain indefinable aura which hung about her, like a wickedly fascinating perfume, redolent of passion and recklessness and a greed for living.

Jemima was too overwrought, too disappointed and unhappy and angry to try to be subtle. "Where 've you been!" It was no question, but an accusation.

Amber gave her eyebrows a lift, and twisted around to straighten the seams in her stockings. "That's none of your business."

"Well, whether it's any of my business or not, I know! Look at this—it's yours, isn't it!" She held out a glove.

Amber glanced at it and then her eyes narrowed. She snatched it away. "Where'd you get that!"

"You know where I got it! It was lying on the floor in the master-cabin of the *Dragon!*"

"Well, what if it was? I hope I can visit a man who's gone to sea to fight the Dutch!"

"Visit him! Don't try to put that upon me! I know what kind of visiting you do! I know what *you* are! You're a harlot—! You've cuckolded my father!"

Amber stood and stared at Jemima and her flesh began to crawl with loathing and hatred. "You whining little bitch," she said slowly. "You're jealous, aren't you? You're jealous because I got what you wanted." She began to mimic her, repeating exactly the words and tone Jemima had used scarcely an hour before, but giving to them a savage twist that mocked and ridiculed. "Then *now!* Oh, Bruce, please! Just this once more—" She laughed, enjoying the horror and humiliation that came onto Jemima's face.

"Oh," said Jemima softly. "I never knew what you were like before—"

"Well, now you do but it won't do you any good." Amber was brisk and confident, thinking that she would settle Jemima's business for her now, once and forever. "Because if you're thinking to tell your father what you know about me, just stop long enough to consider what he'd say if he knew that his daughter had been sneaking out of the house to meet a man at public taverns! He'd be stark raving mad!"

"How do you know that!"

"Lord Carlton told me."

"You couldn't prove it—"

"Oh, couldn't I? I could call in a midwife and have you examined, remember!"

Amber had been about to order Jemima triumphantly from the room, when her next words came with the unexpected shock of a mid-summer thunderclap. "Call in anyone you like! I don't care what you do! But I can tell you this much—either you make Father stop my wedding to Joseph Cuttle or I'll tell him about you and Lord Carlton!"

"You wouldn't dare! Why it—it might kill him!"

"It might kill him! Much you'd care! That's what you want and you know it! Oh, the rest of them were right about you all along! What a fool I was not to see it! But I know what you are now—you're nothing but a whore."

"And so are you. The only difference between us is that I got what I went for—and you didn't."

Jemima gasped and the next instant lashed out with the palm of her right hand and smacked Amber on the cheek. So swiftly that it seemed to be part of the same movement Amber returned the slap, and with her other hand grabbed a fistful of hair and gave a jerk that snapped Jemima's head back like a chicken's. Jemima screamed in sudden fright and viciously Amber slapped her again. Her self-control had slipped away and she was not even wholly conscious of what she was doing. Jemima began to struggle to free herself, now genuinely terrified and screeching for help. The sight of her scared eyes and the sound of her cries infuriated Amber; she had a sudden savage determination to kill her. It was Nan, who rushed into the room and threw herself between them, who saved Jemima from a serious mauling.

"Mam!" she was shouting. "Mam! For God's sake! Are you mad!"

Amber's hands dropped to her sides and she gave an angry shake of her head to toss the hair back from her face. "Get out of here!" she cried. "Get out and don't trouble me again, d'ye hear?" The last words were a hysterical shriek, but Jemima had already fled, sobbing.

It was not easy to convince Samuel that Jemima's wedding must be postponed. But she did, at last, succeed in making him agree to put it off for a few more weeks to let the poor child recover from her grief at Lord Carlton's departure. Amber, nervous and worried and lonely for Bruce, was made even more morose and irritable by pregnancy. But she had to conceal her ill-humour from everyone but Nan, who listened patiently and with sympathetic concern to her mistress's perpetual grumbling and sighing.

"I'm so damned sick and tired of being virtuous," she said wearily one day as she came in from having paid several afternoon calls.

She spent a great deal of time visiting the wives and daughters of Samuel's friends, sitting about and discussing babies and servants and sickness with them until she wanted to yell. She worked hard at being a respectable woman. Now all at once she arranged her mouth into a smug smile and began to mimic the elderly aunt upon whom she had just called. No one—not even the immediate family—had yet been told that she was pregnant, though Samuel knew it and was almost absurdly delighted.

"My dear, I do hope you'll soon prove with child. Believe me, no woman can know what it is to be truly happy until she holds her first little one in her arms and feels its tiny mouth at her breast." Amber screwed up her face and gave a noisy rattle with her tongue: "I'll be damned if I can see where the pleasure is to throw-up every morning and look like a stuffed pig and blow and puff like an old nag going up Snow Hill!" She slammed her fan onto the floor. "Crimini! I'm sick of this business!"

To make matters worse, when Bruce had been gone four weeks Samuel firmly announced that the wedding-date was definitely set for October 15th. Nothing at all, he assured her, would induce him to change his mind again. The Cuttles were growing impatient, people were beginning to wonder at the delay, and it was high time Jemima stop her foolishness and behave like a grown woman. Amber was frantic with worry and though she mulled over her problem most of the day and half the night she could discover no solution. Jemima warned her again that if she did not do something to stop it she would tell her father, even though he threw both of them into the streets.

"Oh, Lord, Nan! After everything I've been through to get that money I'm going to lose it! I'll never get a shilling! Oh, I always knew *something* would happen! I knew I'd never *really* be that rich!"

"Something 'll save you, mam," insisted Nan cheerfully. "I know it will. Your stars are lucky."

"Something?" demanded Amber, her voice sliding up an octave. "But what! And when?"

By the tenth Amber was half-wild with worry and remorse. She wished that she had never seen Bruce Carlton. She wished that she was back home in Marygreen and married to Jack Clarke or Bob Starling. She paced the floor and beat her hands together and bit her knuckles.

Oh, my God, my God, my God, what am I to do!

Thus she was one morning, still in her dressing-gown and walking distractedly about the bedroom, when Nan came rushing in. Her cheeks were pink and her blue eyes sparkled triumphantly. "Mam! What d'ye think? I just saw one of Mrs. Jemima's women and she told me Mrs. Jemima's been in a green-sickness all this past fortnight—but no one's supposed to know it!"

Amber stared at her. "Why, Nan!" she said softly.

And then all at once she ran out of the bedroom, down the long hallway toward the opposite wing of the house, and into Jemima's chamber. She found it crowded with dressmakers, maids, several mercers and other tradesmen. Amber had told her that if she would go ahead and pretend she was going to be married, she would somehow find another excuse at the last moment—if she had to throw herself out the window. And Jemima, not because she wished to oblige her step-mother, but because she really was confused and helpless, had done so.

There were gowns heaped on every chair and stool, lengths of brocade and satin and sheer tiffany ran like rivers over the floor, fur-skins lay in soft shining piles. Jemima stood in the midst of the crowded, noisy room, her back turned to the door, having her wedding-gown fitted; it was made of the gold cloth Lord Carlton had given her.

Amber came in breezily. "Oh, Jemima!" she cried. "Such a marvellous gown! How I envy you—getting married in that!"

Jemima gave her a sullen, warning glance from over her shoulder. But Amber saw to her satisfaction that the girl was pale and seemed tired.

"Are you almost done now?"

Jemima spoke wearily to two of the dressmakers who were kneeling about her on the floor, pins in their mouths, arranging each smallest fold and crease with the most meticulous care.

"In a moment, madame. Can't you bear it just a little longer?"

Jemima sighed. "Very well. But hurry—please."

Amber went to stand before Jemima her head cocked to one side as she examined the dress, and her eyes ran tauntingly up and down the girl's figure. She saw Jemima begin to fidget nervously, a faint shine of sweat came to her forehead; and then all at once her arms dropped and she sank to the floor, her head falling back, her eyes rolling. The dressmakers and maids gave excited squeaks and the men stepped aside in alarm.

Amber took charge. "Pick her up and lay her on the bed. Carter, bring some cold water. You—run for some brandy."

With the help of two of the maids she got Jemima out of her gown, took the pillow from under her head and began to unlace her busk. When Carter brought the cold water she sent them all out of the room—though Carter was obviously reluctant to leave Jemima in the care of her step-mother—and wrung out a cloth to lay on Jemima's forehead.

It was not more than a minute before Jemima regained consciousness and looked up at Amber, who leaned above her. "What did I do?" she asked softly, her eyes going uncertainly about the empty room.

"You fainted. Take a sip of this brandy and you'll feel better." Amber put her hand behind Jemima's head and tipped it forward. Both of them were silent for a moment, and Jemima made a face as she tasted the brandy.

"The dizzy feeling's gone," she said at last. "You can call the others back in now." She started to sit up.

"Oh, no, Jemima. Not yet. I want to talk to you first."

Jemima glanced at her swiftly, her eyes guarded. "What about?"

"You know what about. There's no use trying to pretend. You're pregnant—aren't you?"

"No! Of course I'm not! I can't be! It's just that— Well, I've had the vapours, that's all."

"If you thought it was only the vapours why didn't you tell anyone? Don't try to fool me, Jemima. Tell me the truth and maybe I can help you."

"Help me? How could *you* help me?"

"How long has it been since your last flux?"

"Why—almost two months. But that doesn't mean anything! Oh, I know I'm not pregnant! I can't be! I'd die if that happened!"

"Don't be a fool, Jemima! What the devil did you think when you laid with him? That you had a charm of some kind—it couldn't happen to you? Well, it has, and the sooner you admit it the better for you."

Suddenly Jemima began to cry, scared and distracted now that she was finally forced to confront the fact from which she had been fleeing for weeks. "I don't believe you! I'll be well again in a few days, I know I will! You're just rying to scare me, that's all! Oh—go away and leave me alone!"

Amber gave her an angry shake. "Jemima, stop it! Most likely some of the servants are listening! D'you want everyone to know what's happened? If you'll keep your mouth shut and be sensible you can save yourself and your family too. Don't forget what a disgrace this will be for them if it's ever found out—"

"Oh, that's what I'm afraid of! They'll hate me! They'll—Oh—I wish I were dead!"

"Stop talking like an idiot! If you marry Joseph Cuttle on the 15th—"

Jemima snapped out of her hysteria as if she had been dashed with cold water. "Marry Joseph Cuttle! Why, I won't marry Joseph Cuttle and you know it! I wouldn't marry him for—"

"You've got to marry him! There's nothing else you can do now! It's the only way you can keep the Dangerfields from being disgraced."

"I don't care! I don't care about them! I won't marry him! I'm going to run away from home and take lodgings somewhere and wait till Lord Carlton comes back. He'll marry me then, when he knows what happened."

Amber gave a short brutal laugh. "Oh, Jemima, you silly green foolish girl. Lord Carlton marry you! Are you cracked in the head? He wouldn't marry you if you had triplets. If he'd married every woman he's ever laid with I don't doubt he'd have as many wives as King Solomon. Besides, if you ran away from home you wouldn't even have a dowry to offer him! Marry Joseph Cuttle while you've still got time—it's the only thing you can do now."

For a long moment Jemima lay perfectly still and stared up at her.

"So at last you're going to get your way," she said softly. Her eyes glittered, but her next words merely formed on her mouth:

"Oh, how I *despise* you—"

Chapter Thirty

JEMIMA'S WEDDING was a social event of considerable importance.

Between them the Dangerfields and the Cuttles had friends or relatives in almost every one of the great City families. Gifts for the bride and groom had been pouring into the house for weeks past, and had almost filled one large room set aside to receive them. The bride walked on a golden tapestry to the improvised altar which had been set up in the south drawing-room, while her aunts and female cousins sniffled and the mighty music of three great organs made the walls tremble. She wore her dark coppery hair flowing over her shoulders—symbol of virginity—and a garland of myrtle and olive and rosemary leaves; she was sober-faced and dry-eyed, which was unfortunate, for it was believed to be bad-luck if the bride did not weep. But she seemed preoccupied and almost unaware of what she was doing or saying, and when the ceremony was over she accepted the kisses of her eager happy groom and her friends and relatives with an air of absent-minded indifference.

The newly married couple opened the ball, and when the first dance was over they retired, as was customary, to the decorated bridal-chamber above. She began to cry when the women were undressing her, and everyone was pleased at this happy omen. When the two young people sat side by side in the great bed, Jemima's eyes now wide and troubled like those of a frightened animal which has been trapped, the spouted posset-pot was handed ceremoniously from one to another, all around the room.

There was no unseemly laughter, no bawdy jests or boisterous singing as was common at many weddings, but an atmosphere of quiet good-natured but serious responsibility. They went out then, leaving Jemima and her groom alone—and Amber heaved a grateful sigh of relief. There! she thought. It's done at last! And I'm safe.

But once she knew that she was secure, boredom began to settle on her like the gloomy fogs that hung over the river. She had bought too many gowns and too much jewellery to be satisfied by that any longer, particularly since she felt contemptuous of the opinion of those who saw them. Consequently she moped over her pregnancy, worried about the colour of her skin and the circles beneath her eyes, wept when her belly began to enlarge, and was sure that she was hideous and would always be so. For amusement she spent a great deal of time wishing for out-of-the-season foods—it was now winter—and since everyone knew that when a pregnant woman "longed" she must be satisfied or the child might be lost, it kept Samuel and all the household in a pother to supply her with the things she wanted. Usually by the time she got them the longing was gone, or another had taken its place.

She slept ten or eleven hours every night, no longer getting up at six with Samuel, but often drowsing till ten; and then she lay in bed another half-hour thinking discontentedly of the day before her. By the time she had dressed it was noon and dinner-time. If he stayed home after that she did too; otherwise she went to visit some of the dozens of Dangerfield relatives or the hundreds of Dangerfield friends, and sat talking talking talking of babies and servants, servants and babies.

"When do you reckon, Mrs. Dangerfield?" they asked her everywhere she went, and time after time. And then came the discussion of Cousin Janet and the frightful labour she had had—fifty-four hours of it—or of Aunt Ruth who had been brought to bed of triplets twice in succession. And all the while they sat and munched on rich cakes, thick pastries, cream and curds, plump good-natured happy satisfied women whom Amber thought the most absurd creatures in the world.

Weeks went by very quickly this way.

Ye gods! thought Amber dismally. I'll be twenty-one in

March! I'll most likely be too old to enjoy it when I finally get that damned money.

Christmas was a welcome diversion to her. The house swarmed with children, more of them than ever: Deborah who lived in the country had come to spend the holidays, bringing with her a husband and six children. Alice and Anne, though they both lived in London, followed the Dangerfield tradition and came home with their families. William returned from abroad and George came down from Oxford. Only Jemima preferred to stay at her husband's home, but even she paid them a visit almost every day, with Joseph always beside her—full of pride for his pretty wife and so happy at the prospect of parenthood he must tell everyone he saw the wonderful news. And Jemima seemed, if not in love with Joseph, at least tolerant of his adoration—which she had not been before; pregnancy had given her a kind of serene contentment. Her rebellion against the manners and morals of her class was over, and she was beginning to accept and settle into her place in that life.

Laurel and cypress and red-berried holly decorated every room and filled them with a spicy winter fragrance. An enormous silver bowl of hot-spiced wine, garlanded with ivy and ribbons and floating roast apples, stood ever ready in the entrance hall. And there was food in all the glorious ancient tradition: plum-porridge and mince-meat pies, roast suckling pig, a boar's head with gilded tusks, fat geese and capons and pheasants roasted to a crusty golden brown. Every dinner was a feast, and whatever was left was distributed to the poor who crowded at the back gates in vast numbers, baskets over their arms, for the Dangerfield generosity was well-known.

Gambling for money was traditionally permitted in all but the strictest households at Christmas-time, and from early morning till late at night cards were shuffled and dice rolled and silver coins clinked merrily across the tables. The children played hot-cockles and blind-man's-buff and hunt-the-slipper, shouting and laughing and chasing each other from one room to another, from garret to basement. And for more than two weeks a stream of guests poured continuously through the house.

Amber gave Samuel a heart-shaped miniature of herself (fully clothed) set in a frame of pearls and rubies and diamonds. She gave gifts almost as expensive to every other member of the family, and her generosity to the servants convinced them that she was the best-natured woman in the world. She received as much as she gave, not because the family liked her any better than before, but to keep up appearances for their father and for outsiders. Amber knew this but she did not care, for nothing could have dislodged her now that he thought she carried his child. He gave her a beautiful little gilt coach, upholstered in padded scarlet velvet trimmed with swags of gold rope and numerous tassels, and six fine black horses to draw it. She was not, however, allowed to ride in it but must go everywhere in a sedan-chair—Samuel would take no chances with her health or the baby's.

Twelfth Night marked the end of the celebrations. It was late in the evening that Samuel suffered another severe stroke, his first since the previous July.

Dr. de Forest, who was sent for immediately, asked Amber in private if Samuel had obeyed his earlier advice and she reluctantly admitted that for some time past he had not. But she defended herself, insisting that she had tried to persuade him but that he had refused to listen and had said it was ridiculous to think a man of sixty-one too old for love, and swore he felt more vigorous than he had in years.

"I don't know what else I can do, Dr. de Forest," she finished, giving the responsibility back to him.

"Then, madame," he said gravely, "I doubt that your husband will live out the year."

Amber turned about wearily and left the room. If she was ever to get rich Samuel must die, and yet she shrank from the thought of being his murderess, even indirectly. She had developed a genuine, if superficial, love for the handsome, kind and generous-spirited old man she had tricked into marriage.

In the anteroom to the bedchamber she came upon Lettice and Sam, and Lettice was in her brother's arms, crying mournfully. "Oh, Sam! If only it had happened any night but this one! Twelfth Night—that mean's he'll die before the year is out, I know it does!" Twelfth Night was the night of prophecy.

Sam patted her shoulders and talked to her quietly. "You mustn't think that, Lettice. It's only a foolish superstition. Don't you remember that last year Aunt Ellen had the ague on Twelfth Day? And she's been merry as a grig all year." He caught sight of Amber, pausing in the doorway, but Lettice did not.

"Oh, but it's different with Dad! It's that terrible woman! She's killing him!"

Sam tried to shush her beneath his breath, as Amber came on into the room. Lettice spun around, stared at her for a moment as though undecided whether to apologize or speak her mind. And then suddenly she cried out:

"Yes, *you're* the one I meant! It's all your fault! He's been worse since you came!"

"Hush, Lettice!" whispered Sam.

"I won't hush! He's my father and I love him and we're going to see him die before his time because this brazen creature makes him think he's five-and-twenty again!" Her eyes swept over Amber with loathing and contempt; Samuel's announcement of his wife's pregnancy had been a serious shock to her, as though it were the final proof of her father's infidelity to their dead mother. "What kind of a woman are you? Have you no heart in you at all? To hurry an old man into his grave so that you can inherit his money!"

"Lettice—" pleaded Sam.

Amber's own sense of guilt stopped her tongue. She had no stomach for a quarrel with his daughter when Samuel lay in the room beyond, perhaps dying. She answered with unwonted gentleness.

"That isn't true, Lettice. There's a great difference in our ages, I know. But I've tried to make him happy, and I think I have. He was sick before I came, you know that."

Lettice, avoiding her eyes, made a gesture with one hand. Nothing could ever make her like this woman whom she distrusted for a hundred reasons, but she could still try to show her at least a surface respect for her father's sake. "I'm sorry. I said too much. I'm half distracted with worry."

Amber walked by, toward the bedroom, and as she passed gave Lettice's hand a quick grasp with her own. "I am too, Lettice." Lettice looked at her swiftly, a questioning puzzled look, but she could not help herself; the woman's smallest gesture would always seem false-hearted to her.

Samuel refused to make his annual trip to Tunbridge Wells that January because his wife's advanced pregnancy would not allow her to accompany him. But he did rest a great deal. More and more he stayed in his own apartments with her, while the eldest sons took over the business. She read to him and sang songs and played her guitar, and with gaiety and affection tried to soothe her own conscience.

It was customary for men with financial responsibilities to check over and settle their accounts at the end of the year, but because of his stroke Samuel postponed doing so until early in February. And then he worked on them for several days. He had his wealth in goldsmiths' bills, stock in the East India Company—of which he was one of the directors—assignments upon rents, mortgages, shares in privateering fleets and other similar ventures, cargoes in Cadiz and Lisbon and Venice, jewels and gold-bullion and cash.

"Why don't you let Sam and Bob do that?" Amber asked him one day, as she sat on the floor playing a game of cat's-cradle with Tansy.

Samuel was at his writing-table, dressed in an East Indian robe which Bruce had given him, and there was a many-branched candlestick lighted above his head, for though mid-day it was dark as twilight. "I want to be sure myself that my affairs are in order—then if anything should happen to me—"

"You mustn't talk like that, Samuel." Amber got to her feet, dropping the cradle, and with a pat on the head for Tansy, she walked over to where he sat. "You're the picture of good health." She gave him a light kiss and bent over, one arm about his shoulders. "Heavens! What's all that? I couldn't puzzle it out to save my bacon. My senses seem to run a-wool-gathering at the sight of a number!" She could, in fact, not do much more than read them.

"I'm arranging everything so that you won't need to worry about it. If the baby's a boy I'm going to leave him ten thousand pound to start in a business for himself—I think that's better than for him to try to go in with his half-brothers—and if it's a girl I'll leave her five thousand for a marriage portion. How do you want your share? In money or property?"

"Oh, Samuel, I don't know! Let's not even think about it!"

He smiled at her fondly. "Nonsense, my dear. Of course we shall think about it. A man with any money at all must have a will, no matter what his age. Tell me—which would you prefer?"

"Well—then I suppose it would be best for me to have it in gold—so I won't get cheated by some sharp rook."

"I haven't that much cash on hand, but in a few week's time I think it can be arranged. I'll put it with Shadrac Newbold."

He died very quietly one evening early in April, just after he had gone upstairs to rest from a somewhat strenuous day.

In a great black mourning-bed, Samuel Dangerfield's body lay at home in state. Two thousand doles of three farthings each were distributed to the poor, with biscuits and burnt ale. His young widow—much pitied because it was so near the time of her confinement—received visitors in her own room; she was pale and wore the plainest black gown, with a heavy black veil trailing from her head almost to the floor. Every chair, every table and mirror and picture in the entire apartment had been shrouded in black crape, every window was shut and covered, and only a few dim candles burned— Death was in the house.

The guests were served cold meats, biscuits and wine, and at last the funeral procession set out. The night was dark and cold and windy and the torches streamed out like banners. They moved very slowly, with a solemn stumping tread. A man ringing a bell led them through the streets and he was followed by the hearse, drawn by six black horses with black plumes on their heads. Men in black mounted on black horses rode beside it, and there followed a train of almost thirty closed black coaches carrying all members of the immediate family. After that there came on foot and in their official livery the members of the guilds to which he had belonged and other mourners in a straggling line almost two miles long.

Amber could not go to sleep that night in her black room alone but insisted that Nan sleep with her and that a torchère be left burning beside the bed. She was not as glad to be a rich woman as she had expected she would be, and she was not as sorrowful at Samuel's death as she thought she should be. She was merely apathetic. Her sole wish now was that her pains would begin so that she could bear this child and be freed of the burden which grew more intolerable with each hour.

Chapter Thirty-one

THE ANTEROOM was crowded. Young men stood about in groups of two and three and four, leaning on the window-sills to look down into the courtyard where a violent mid-March wind racked the trees, bending them almost double. They wore feather-loaded hats and thigh-length cloaks, with their swords tilting out an an angle in back; lace ruffles fell over their fingers and flared out from their knees and clusters of ribbon loops hung at their shoulders and elbows and hips. Several of them were yawning and sleepy-eyed.

"Oh, my God," groaned one, with a weary sigh. "To bed at three and up at six! If only Old Rowley would find the woman could keep him abed in the mornings—"

"Never mind. When we're at sea we can sleep as long as we like. Have you got your commission yet? I'm all but promised a captaincy."

The other laughed. "If you're a captain I should be rear-admiral. At least I know port from starboard."

"Do you? Which is which?"

"Port's right, and starboard's left."

"You're wrong. It's the other way around."

"Well—it won't make much difference, this way or that. There never was a man so plagued by sea-sickness as I. If I so much as take a pair of oars from Charing Cross to the Privy Stairs I'm sure to puke twice on the way."

"I'm a fresh-water sailor myself. But for all of that I'm mighty damned glad the war's begun. A man can live just so long on actresses and orange-girls, and then the diet begins to pall. Curse my tripes, but I'll welcome the change—salt air and waves and fast gun-fire. By God, there's the life for a man! Besides, my last whore begins to grow troublesome."

"That reminds me—I forgot to take my turpentine pills this morning." He brought a delicate gem-studded box out of one pocket and snapped it open, extending it first to his friend who declined the offer. Then he tossed two of the large boluses into his mouth and gave a hard swallow to get them down, shaking his head mournfully. "I'm damnably peppered-off, Jack."

At that moment there was a stir in the room. The door was flung open and Chancellor Clarendon entered. Frowning and preoccupied as usual, his right foot wrapped in a thick bandage to ease his gout, he spoke to no one, but walked straight across and through the other door which led into his Majesty's bed-chamber.

Eyebrows went up, mouths twisted, and sly secret smiles were exchanged as the old man passed.

Clarendon was rapidly becoming the most hated man in England—not only at Court but everywhere. He had been in power too long and the people blamed him for whatever went amiss, no matter how little he might have had to do with it. He would accept no advice, allow no opposition; whatever he did was right. Even those faults might have been overlooked but that he had others which were unforgivable. He was inflexibly honest and would neither take nor give bribes, and not even his friends profited by his favour. Though he had lived most of his life at courts he was contemptuous of courtiers and scorned to become one.

And so they watched, and waited. If his hold on Parliament should once slip they would be at his throat like a pack of starving jackals.

"Have you been out Piccadilly to see the Chancellor's new house?" asked someone, when he had gone.

"Judging by the foundations I'd say he'll have to sell England to finish it. What he got from Dunkirk won't build the stables."

"How many more times does the old devil think he *can* sell England? Our value won't hold up much longer at the present rate of exchange."

The door into the King's private chambers opened again and Buckhurst strolled out with another young man. Two or three others crossed over to speak to them.

"What's the delay? I've been waiting here half-an-hour. Nothing but the hope of speaking to his Majesty about a place for my cousin could have induced me to get out of bed on a morning like this one. Now I suppose he's gone by way of the Privy Stairs and left us all to shift for ourselves."

"He'll be along presently. He's dickering with a Jesuit priest over the price of a recipe for Spirit of Human Skull. Have you got a tailor's bill in your pocket, Tom? If it's illegible enough sell it to Old Rowley for a universal panacea and your fortune's made. He's giving that mangy old Jesuit five thousand pound for his scrap of paper."

"Five thousand! Good God! What can an old man have to spend five thousand on?"

"What do you think? On a remedy for impotence, of course."

"The best remedy for impotence is a pretty wench—"

The voices grew temporarily quiet as the King appeared, strolling through the door with his dogs and sycophants behind him. He was freshly shaved and his smooth brown skin had a healthy glow; he gave them a smile and a nod of his head and started on out. The jostling for place began immediately as they streamed along in his wake, but Buckingham already had one elbow and Lauderdale the other.

"I suppose," said Charles to the Duke, "that by tomorrow it

will be running up the galleries and through the town I'm a confirmed Catholic."

"I've heard those rumours already, Sire."

"Well—" Charles shrugged. "If that's the worst rumour that goes abroad about me I think it's no great matter for concern." Charles was not inclined to worry about what anyone said of him, and he knew his people well enough to know that grumbling was a national sport, not much more subversive than football or wrestling. He had been home almost five years now, and the honeymoon with his subjects was over.

Leaving his own apartments he crossed the Stone Gallery and started down a maze of narrow hallways which led along the Privy Garden, over the Holbein Gateway and into St. James's Park. He walked so rapidly that the shorter men had to half run, or be left behind, and since most of them had a favour to ask they did not intend to let that happen.

"I think there's time," said Charles, "for a turn through the Park before Chapel. I hope the air's cold enough to make me sleepy."

They had reached the old stairway which led down into the Park when suddenly one of the doors up the corridor to the left burst open and Monmouth came out in a rush. The men stopped and while his father laughed heartily the Duke ran toward them; he arrived breathless, swept off his hat and made a low bow. Charles dropped an arm about the boy's shoulders and gave him an affectionate pat.

"I overslept, Sire! I was just going to attend you to Chapel."

"Come along, James. I've been wanting to talk to you."

James, who was now walking between the King and Lauderdale, gave his father an apprehensive glance. "What about, Sire?"

"You must know, or you wouldn't have such a guilty face. Everyone's been telling me about you. Your behaviour's a favorite subject of conversation." James hung his head and Charles, with a smile he could not wholly conceal lurking at the corners of his mouth, went on. "They say you've taken to keeping a wench—at fifteen, James—that you've run deep into debt, that you scour about the streets at night disturbing peaceful citizens and breaking their windows. In short, son, they say you lead a very gay life."

Monmouth looked swiftly up at his father, and his handsome face broke into an appealing smile. "If I'm gay, Sire, it's only to help me forget my troubles."

Several of the others burst into laughter but Charles looked at the boy solemnly, his black eyes shining. "You must have a great many troubles, James. Come along—and tell me about them."

The morning was cold and frosty and the wind blew their periwigs about, as it did the spaniels' ears. Charles clamped his hat firmly onto his head, but the others had to hold to their wigs—for they carried their hats beneath their arms—or lose them. The grass was hard-matted and slippery, and there was a thin sheet of ice over the canal; it had been an unusually cold dry winter, and there had been no thaw since before Christmas. The other men looked at one another sourly, annoyed that they must go walking in such weather, but the King strode along as unconcernedly as if it were a fine summer day.

Charles walked in the Park because he liked the exercise and the fresh-air. He enjoyed strolling along the canal to see how his birds, in cages hung in the trees on either side, were standing the cold weather. Some of the smaller ones he had had removed indoors until the frost should break. He wanted to know if the cold had hurt the row of new elms he had had set out the year before and whether his pet crane was learning to walk with the wooden leg he had had made for it when its own had been lost in an accident.

But he did not walk only for amusement and exercise; it was a part of the morning's business. Charles had always preferred that his unpleasant tasks be done under pleasant conditions—and there were few duties he disliked more than hearing petitions and begging for favours. If it had been possible he would gladly have granted every request that was made him, not so much from the boundless generosity of his nature as to buy his own peace from whining voices and pleading eyes. He hated the sound and the sight of them, but it was the one thing from which there never could be escape.

Some of them wanted a place at Court for a friend or relative, and there were always a hundred askers for each place that fell vacant. However he chose he left many disgruntled and jealous and the one who got it was seldom as well pleased as he had expected to be. Another would want a grant for a Plate Lottery—royal permission to sell tickets at whatever price he could command for a lottery of some crown plate. Others were there to beg an estate: it was common practice to bear the expense of arrest and prosecution of other persons in the hope that a cash-fine or confiscated property could be begged from the King. Another man wanted to go to sea to fight the Dutch, and he wanted to go as a captain or a commander, though his sea experience had been limited to a crossing from France in one of the packet-boats.

Charles listened to them patiently, tried when he could to refer the supplicant to someone else, and when he could not usually granted the request, though well aware that it might be impossible of fulfillment. And as he walked and listened to the petitions of his courtiers he was often approached by a sick old man or woman, sometimes a young mother with her child, who begged him to touch and heal them. The courtiers resented the intrusion, but Charles did not.

He liked his people and, though he had lived so long out of the country, he understood them. They grumbled about his mistresses and the extravagance of the Court, but when he smiled and stopped to talk to them and laughed with them in his deep booming voice they loved him in spite of everything. His charm and accessibility were potent political weapons and he knew it.

They walked along the Canal that crossed the Park from one end to another and back along Pall Mall, turning down King Street into the Palace grounds. The chapel bells began to ring and Charles increased his rapid pace, relieved that soon he would be where they could pester him no longer. Monmouth was far ahead of them. All along the way he had been running and leaping, calling the spaniels to follow him until now their long ears were soggy and wet and their paws clotted with mud.

Ah! thought Charles, and drew a deep breath as they came into the courtyard which led to the chapel. Another hundred yards and I'm safe!

At that moment Buckingham, who had given his place to others, caught up with him again. "Sire," he began. "May I present—"

Charles threw a quick comical glance at Lauderdale. "How is it," he murmured, "that every one of my friends keeps a tame knave?"

But he turned back with a smile to hear the man out, and stopped just at the chapel doors with the courtiers clustered around him. But the ladies were going in, and his eyes wandered. Frances Stewart came along with her waiting-woman and gave him a wave of her hand. Charles grinned broadly and made a quick move to follow her, but remembered that he was listening to a petition and checked himself.

"Yes," he interrupted. "I appreciate your position, sir. Believe me, I'll give it serious thought."

"But, Sire—" protested the man, holding out his hands. "As I told you, it's most urgent! I must know soon or—"

"Oh, yes," said Charles, who had not been listening at all. "So it is. Very well, then. I think you may."

Gratefully the man started to drop to his knees, but the King gave him an impatient signal not to, for he was eager to get away. And then, just before he entered the great carved oak doors he turned and said over his shoulder, "As far as I'm concerned, you may have your wish. But you'd best make sure the Chancellor has no other plans on that score."

The man opened his mouth again, the smile disappearing in a sudden look of dismay, but it was too late. The King was gone. "Catch him as he comes out," whispered Buckingham, and went on himself.

The chapel was already well filled and the music of the great organ thundered in the walls. Charles did not like going to church and sermons bored him, but he did contrive to please himself while there with some of the finest music to be had. And, much to the scandal of the conservative, he had introduced violins, which he loved better than any other instrument.

He sat alone in the Royal Closet in the gallery—Catherine attended her own Catholic mass—looking down over the chapel. Curtains at either side closed off the portion of the gallery where the ladies sat, though he knew that Frances was there just beside him, so close that he could whisper to her. The young clergyman who was to speak for the day had taken his place and was mopping his perspiring cheeks and forehead with his black-gloved hands, until as the dye came off he looked more like a chimney-sweep than a divine. Titters went up here and there and the young man looked more wretchedly uncomfortable than ever, wondering why they had begun to laugh before he had spoken so much as one word.

It was almost as difficult to preach to the Court as it was to act to it. The King invariably went to sleep, sitting bolt upright and facing the pulpit, as soon as the subject of the sermon had been announced. The Maids of Honor whispered among themselves, waved their fans at the men below, giggled and tried on one another's jewellery and ribbons. The gallants craned their necks back up at the ladies' gallery and compared notes on the previous night's activities or pointed out the pretty women present. The politicians leaned their heads together and murmured in undertones, keeping their eyes ahead as though no one could guess what they were doing. Most of the older ladies and gentlemen, relics of the Court of the first Charles, sat soberly in their pews and listened with satisfaction to the warnings repeatedly given by the pulpit to a careless age; but even their good intentions often ended in noisy snores.

At last the young chaplain, newly preferred to his place by an influential relative, proclaimed the subject of his first sermon before the King and Court. "Behold!" he announced, giving another swipe of his black glove along his cheek, "I am fearfully and wonderfully made!"

Instantly the chapel was filled with laughter, and while the bewildered frightened young man looked out over his congregation, tears starting into his eyes, even the King had to clear his throat and bend over to examine his shoe-lace to conceal a smile. A finger poked him gleefully through the curtains, and Charles knew that it was Frances whom he could hear gasping with laughter. But the chapel finally grew quiet again, the terrified clergyman forced himself to go on, and Charles composed himself to sleep.

Frances Stewart had replaced Barbara Palmer as the most popular and successful hostess at Whitehall. The suppers she gave in her apartments overlooking the river were crowded with all the powerful and clever men and pretty women of the Court. Both Buckingham and Arlington were trying to enlist her support for their own projects, for they were convinced as was everyone else that the King could be led through a woman.

Buckingham strummed his guitar for her and sang songs, mimicked Clarendon and Arlington, played with her at her favourite game of building card-castles, and flattered himself that she was falling in love with him. The Baron had no such social tricks at his command, but he did unbend enough to talk to her with a certain air of gracious condescension which was the best he could do toward charming a woman. And when Louis XIV sent his new minister, Courtin, to try to persuade Charles to call off the Dutch War, the merry little Frenchman immediately applied himself to Mrs. Stewart.

"Oh, heavens!" she said one evening to Charles, when he had finally maneuvered her into a corner alone. "My head's awhirl with all this talk of politics! One tells me this and another that and a third something else—" She stopped, looked up at him and then gave a sudden mischievous little burst of laughter. "And I don't remember any of it! If they only guessed how little I listen to their prittle-prattle I warrant you they'd all be mightily out of sorts with me."

Charles watched her, his eyes glowing with passionate admiration, for he still thought that she was the most perfectly lovely thing he had ever seen. "Thank God you don't listen," he said. "A woman has no business meddling in politics. I think perhaps that's one reason why I love you, Frances. You never trouble me with petitions—your own or anyone else's. I see asking faces everywhere I look—and I'm glad yours doesn't ask." His voice dropped lower. "But I'd give you anything you want, Frances—anything you *could* ask for. You know that, don't you?"

(Across the room one young man, watching them, said to another: "His Majesty's been in love with her for two years and she's still a virgin. I tell you, it's beyond credence!")

Frances smiled, a gentle wistful smile so young and artless that it clutched at his heart. "I know that you're very generous, Sire. But truly, there's nothing I want but to live an honourable life."

A look of quick impatience crossed his face and his eyebrows twisted with a kind of whimsical anger. But then he smiled. "Frances, my dear, an honourable life is exactly what he who lives it thinks it to be. After all, honour is only a word."

"I don't know what you mean, Sire. To me, I assure you, honour is much more than a word."

"But nevertheless it must be one or several qualities you associate with a certain word. His Grace of Buckingham, for instance, over there at the card-table, has quite another definition from your own."

Frances laughed at that, somewhat relieved that she could, for she did not like serious conversations and felt uneasy in the presence of an abstraction. "I don't doubt that, your Majesty. I think that's one subject where his Grace and I think no more alike than you and I do."

"Oh?" said the King, with an air of mild and amused interest. "And has Buckingham been trying to persuade you over to his interpretation?"

Frances blushed and tapped her fan on her knee. "Oh, that wasn't what I meant!"

"Wasn't it? I think it was. But don't trouble yourself about it, my dear. It's an old habit of the Duke's—falling in love along with me."

Frances looked offended. "Falling in love along with you! Heavens, Sire! You sound as if you've been in love mighty often!"

"If I tried to pretend I'd never noticed a woman until you came along—well, Frances, after all—"

"Just the same you needn't speak as though it's a common everyday occurrence!" She tilted her chin and turned a haughty profile to him.

Charles laughed. "I almost think you're prettiest when you're just a little—just ever so little—angry with me. You have the loveliest nose in the world—"

"Oh, have I, Sire?" She turned eagerly and smiled at him, unable to resist the compliment.

But suddenly the King glanced across the room and muttered in annoyance, "Good Lord! Here comes Courtin to lecture me about the war again! Quick! Let's go in here!"

He took her arm and though she started to protest he swiftly ushered her through the door and closed it. The room was dark but for the moonlight reflecting off the water, but he led her across it and into another beyond.

"There!" he said, closing the second door. "He'll never dare follow us in here!"

"But he's such a nice little man. Why don't you want to talk to him?"

"What's the use? I've told him a thousand times, England and Holland are at war and that's all there is to it. The fleet's at sea—I can't very well call it back for all the nice little men in France. Come here—"

Frances glanced at him dubiously, for each time they were alone the same thing happened. But after a moment of hesitation she walked to the window and stood beside him. White swans were floating there close to shore in the early spring dusk, and the reeds grew so tall the tips of them touched the glass. The water looked dark and cold and a brisk wind had whipped up the waves. He slipped one arm about her waist and for a minute or more they stood silently, looking out. And then slowly he turned, drew her close against him, and kissed her mouth.

Frances submitted, but she was unresponsive. Her hands rested lightly on his shoulders, her body held taut and her lips were cool and passive. His arms tightened and his mouth forced her lips apart; the blood seemed to vibrate through his veins with the intensity of his passion. He felt sure that this time he could bring her to life, make her desire him as violently as he did her.

"Frances, Frances," he murmured, a kind of pleading rage in his voice. "Kiss me. Stop thinking—stop telling yourself that this is wicked. Forget yourself—forget everything and let me show you what happiness can be—"

"Sire!"

She was beginning to push at him now, a little frightened, arching her back and trying to bend away from him, but his body curved over hers, his hands and his mouth seeking. "Oh, Frances, you can't put me off any longer—I've waited two years—I can't wait forever—I love you, Frances, I swear I do! I won't hurt you, darling, please—please—"

It was true that he was in love with her. He was in love with her beauty and her femininity, the promise of complete fulfillment which she seemed to offer. But he did not really love her any more than he had ever loved any other woman; and he believed furthermore that her show of virtue was a stubborn pretense, designed to get something she wanted. In his relations with women as in all other phases of his life, his selfishness took refuge in cynicism.

"Sire!" she cried again, really alarmed now, for she had never realized before how powerful was his strength, how easy it would be for him to force her.

But he did not hear. His hands had pushed the low-cut gown far off her shoulders, and he held her hard against him, as though determined to absorb her body into his own. She had never seen him so blindly excited and it terrified her, for her emotions did not answer his but fled to the opposite extreme—she was scared and disgusted. And all at once she hated him.

Now she put her crossed arms against his shoulders and pushed, and at the same time she gave a sobbing desperate cry. "Your Majesty, let me go!" She burst into tears.

Instantly he paused, his body stiffening, and then he released her, so swiftly that she almost lost her balance. While he stood there in the darkness beside her, so quiet she would have thought she was alone but for the sound of his breathing, she turned away and continued to cry—not softly but with whimpering sobs so that he would hear her and regret what he had done. And also so that he would realize she was even more offended than he could possibly be. For she was afraid now that he might be angry.

It seemed a long time, but at last he spoke. "I'm sorry, Frances. I didn't realize that I was repulsive to you."

Frances whirled around. "Oh, Sire! Don't think that! Of course you're not! But if I once give myself up to you I'll have lost the only thing I have that's any value to me. A woman can no more be excused because she gives herself to a king than if he were any other man. You know that your own mother says that."

"My mother and I do not always think alike—and certainly not on that point. Answer me honestly, Frances. What is it you want? I've told you before and I tell you again—I'll give you anything I have. I'll give you anything but marriage—and I'd give that if I could."

Frances's voice answered him crisply. "Then, Sire, you will never have me at all. For I shall never give myself to a man under any other conditions than marriage."

He stood with his back to the windows and his face in darkness, and she could not see the expression of savage anger that brushed across it. "Someday," he said, in a soft voice, "I hope I'll find you ugly and willing." He went past her swiftly and out the door.

Chapter Thirty-two

AMBER DID NOT like being shut up in a black room; it made her melancholy. But at least the fact that she was supposed to be in mourning secured her from what would otherwise have been an intolerable number of visits from every friend, acquaintance and remote relative of the entire family. Her child, a girl, had been born just a few days after Samuel's death. And she would have been expected to give a gossips-feast, a child-bed feast, and a great reception following the christening.

As it was she received calls only from close relatives and friends of the family, though many others sent gifts. During these she sat half propped in bed, looking very pale and fragile against all that sombre black. She smiled wistfully at her visitors, sometimes squeezed out a tear or two or at least a long sigh, and looked fondly at the baby when someone said that she was as much Samuel's image as if she had been spit out of his mouth. She was polite and patient and as decorous as ever, for she felt that she owed Samuel that much at least in return for the great fortune he had left her.

She scarcely saw the immediate family at all. Each of them came just once to her room, but Amber knew that it was only out of a persistent sense of duty to their father. She realized that now he was dead they expected and wanted her to leave as soon as she could get out of bed. And she did not intend to linger there any longer than necessary.

But it was only Jemima who said what the others were thinking. "Well—now that you've got Father's money I suppose you expect to buy a title with it and set yourself up for a person of quality?"

Amber gave her an impudent mocking smile. "I might," she agreed.

"You may be able to buy a title," said Jemima, "but you

can't buy the breeding that goes with it." That sounded to Amber like something she had heard one of the others say, but the next words were Jemima's own: "And there's something else you can't buy, either, not if you had all the money there is. You never *can* buy Lord Carlton."

Amber's jealousy of Jemima had faded, since she knew her to be securely trapped in marriage, to lazy contempt. There was nothing she had to fear from her now. And she gave her a slow, sweeping insolent glance. "I'm very sensible of your concern, Jemima. But I'll shift for myself, I warrant you. So if that's all you came for, you may as well go."

Jemima answered her in a low tense voice, for Amber's smugness and indifference made her furious. "I *am* going—and I hope I never see you again as long as I live. But let me tell you one thing—someday you're going to get the fate you deserve. God won't let your wickedness thrive forever—"

Amber's superiority dissolved into a cynical laugh. "I vow and swear, Jemima, you've grown as great a fanatic as the rest of them. If you had better sense you'd have learned by now that nothing thrives so well as wickedness. Now get out of here, you malapert slut, and don't trouble me again!"

Jemima did not trouble her again, and neither did anyone else in the family. She was left as strictly alone as if she were not in the house at all.

She sent Nan about the town searching for lodgings—not in the City but out in the fashionable western suburbs that lay between Temple Bar and Charing Cross. And about three weeks after the baby's birth she went herself to look at one Nan had found.

It was a handsome new building in St. Martin's Lane, between Holborn, Drury Lane, and Lincoln's Inn Fields, where she would be surrounded by persons of the best quality. The house was four stories high with one apartment on each floor and there was a top half-story for the servants. Amber's apartment was on the second floor; a pretty young girl just in from the country with her aunt to find a husband was above her, and a rich middle-aged widow occupied the fourth. The landlady, Mrs. de Lacy, lived below Amber. She was a frail creature who sighed frequently and complained of the vapours, and who talked of nothing but her former wealth and position, lost in the Wars along with a husband whom she had never been able to replace.

The house was called the Plume of Feathers and a large wooden sign swung out over the street just below Amber's parlour windows—it depicted a great swirling blue plume painted on a gilt background and was supported by a very ornate wrought-iron frame, also gilded. The coach-house and stables were up the street only a short distance. And the narrow little lane was packed with the homes and lodgings of gallants, noblemen, titled ladies and many others who frequented Whitehall. Red heels and silver swords, satin gowns and half masks, periwigs and feathered hats, painted coaches and dainty high-bred horses made a continuous parade beneath her window.

The apartments were the most splendid she had ever seen.

There was an anteroom hung in purple-and-gold-striped satin, furnished with two or three gilt chairs and a Venetian mirror. It opened into one end of a long parlour which had massed diamond-paned windows overlooking the street on one side and the courtyard on another. The marble fireplace had a plaster overmantel reaching to the ceiling, lavishly decorated with flowers, beasts, swags, geometrical figures and nude women. The chimney-shelf was lined with Chinese and Persian vases, there was a silver chandelier, and the furniture was either gilded or inlaid with ivory and mother-of-pearl. Nothing, Mrs. de Lacy explained proudly, had been made in England. The emerald-and-yellow satin draperies were loomed in France, the mirrors came from Florence, the marble in the fireplace from Genoa, the cabinets from Naples, the violet-wood for two tables from New Guinea.

The bedroom was even more sybaritic. The bedstead was covered with cloth-of-silver and all hangings were green taffeta; even the chairs were covered with silver cloth. Several wardrobes were built into the walls and there was a small separate bench-bed with a canopy and tight-rolled bolster for lounging, surely the most elegant little thing Amber had ever seen. And there were three other rooms, nursery, dining-parlour and kitchen, which last she did not expect to use.

The rent was exorbitant—one hundred and twenty-five pounds a year—but Amber had the merest contempt for such small change and paid it without a word of protest, though she hoped and expected that she would not be there even half that long. For Bruce should be back soon; he had been gone now more than eight months and the Pool was crowded again with captured merchant-shipping.

She moved her belongings from Dangerfield House before she herself left, and though the process took three or four days no one came near or commented on what she was taking, not all of which strictly belonged to her. She had hired a wet-nurse and a dry-nurse for the baby, and now she hired three maids, which completed the equipage necessary to a woman of fashion living alone. The day she left, the great house was perfectly silent; she scarcely saw a servant and not even one of the children appeared in the hallways. Nothing could have told her more plainly than this silent contempt how they hated her.

But Amber did not care at all. They were nothing to her now—those stiff precise formal people who lived in a world she despised. She sank back onto the seat of her coach with a sigh of relief.

"Drive away! Well—" she turned to Nan. "That's over—thank God."

"Aye," agreed Nan, softly but with real feeling. "Thank God."

They sat quietly, looking out the windows as the coach jogged along, enjoying everything they saw. It was a dirty foggy day and the moisture in the air made stronger than ever the heterogeneous and evil smells of London. Along one side of the street swaggered a young beau with his arm in a sling from a recent duel. Across the way a couple of men, obviously French, had been caught by a group of little boys who were screaming insults at them and throwing refuse picked up out of the kennels. The English hated all foreigners, but Frenchmen most of all. A ragged one-eyed old fish-woman lurched drunkenly along, holding by its tail a mouldering mackerel and bawling out her unintelligible chant.

All at once Nan gave a little gasp, one hand pressed to her mouth and the other pointing. "Look! There's another one!"

"Another what?"

"Another cross!"

Amber leaned forward and saw a great red cross chalked on the doorway of a house before which they were stalled. Beneath it had been printed the words, in great sprawling letters: LORD HAVE MERCY UPON US! A guard lounged against the house, his halberd planted beside him.

She leaned back again, giving a careless wave of her gloved hand. "Pish. What of it? Plague's the poor man's disease. Haven't you heard that?" Barricaded behind her sixty-six thousand pounds she felt safe from anything.

For the next few weeks Amber lived quietly in her apartments at the Plume of Feathers. Her arrival in the neighbourhood, she knew, created a considerable excitement and she was aware that every time she stepped out of the house she was much stared at from behind cautiously drawn curtains. A widow as rich as she was would have aroused interest even if she were not also young and lovely. But she was not so eager to make friends now as she had been when she had first come to London, and her fortune made her suspicious of the motives of any young man who so much as stepped aside to let her pass in the street.

The courtiers were all out at sea with the fleet and—though she would have enjoyed flaunting to them her triumph over the conditions which had once put her at their mercy—she had no real interest in anyone but Bruce. She was content waiting for him to return.

Most of the time she stayed at home, absorbed in being a mother. Her son had been taken away from her so soon, and she had seen him so infrequently since, that this baby was as much a novelty to her as if it were her first. She helped the dry-nurse bathe her, watched her while she fed and slept, rocked her cradle and sang songs and was fascinated by the smallest change she could discover in her size and weight and appearance. She was glad that she had had the baby, even if it had temporarily increased her waist-line by an inch or so, for it gave her something of Bruce's which she could never lose. This child had a name, a dowry already secure and waiting, an enviable place of her own in the world.

Nan was almost as interested as her mistress. "I vow she's the prettiest baby in London."

Amber was insulted. "In London! What d'you mean? She's the prettiest baby in England!"

One day she went to the New Exchange to do some unnecessary shopping, and happened to see Barbara Palmer. She was just leaving when a great gilt coach drove up in front and Castlemaine stepped out. Barbara's eyes went over her clothes with interest, for though Amber was still dressed in mourning her cloak was lined with leopard-skins—which Samuel had bought for her from some African slave-trader—and she carried a leopard muff. But when her eyes got as far as Amber's face and she saw who was wearing the costume she glanced quickly and haughtily away.

Amber gave a little laugh. So she remembers me! she thought. Well madame, I doubt not you and I may be better acquainted one day.

As the days went by red crosses were seen, more and more frequently, chalked on the doors. There was plague in London every year and when a few cases had appeared in January and February no one had been alarmed. But now, as the weather grew warmer, the plague seemed to increase and terror spread slowly through the city: it passed from neighbour to neighbour, from apprentice to customer, from vendor to housewife.

Long funeral processions wound through the streets, and already people had begun to take notice of a man or a woman in mourning. They recalled the evil portents which had been seen only a few months before. In December a comet had appeared, rising night after night, tracing a slow ominous path across the sky. Others had seen flaming-swords held over the city, hearses and coffins and heaps of dead bodies in the clouds. Crowds collected on the steps of St. Paul's to hear the half-naked old man who held a blazing torch in his hand and called upon them to repent of their sins. The tolling of the passing-bell began to have a new significance for each of them: Tomorrow, perhaps, it tolls for me or for someone I love.

Every day Nan came home with a new preventive. She bought pomander-balls to breathe into when out of doors, toad amulets, a unicorn's horn, quills filled with arsenic and quicksilver, mercury in a walnut shell, gold coins minted in Queen Elizabeth's time. Each time someone told her of a new preservative she bought it immediately, one for each member of the household, and she insisted that they be worn. She even put quicksilver-quills around the necks of their horses.

But she was not content merely with preventing the plague. For she realized sensibly, that in spite of all precautions one sometimes got it, and she began to stock the cupboards with remedies for curing the sickness. She bought James Angier's famous fumigant of brimstone and saltpetre, as well as gunpowder, nitre, tar and resin to disinfect the air. She bought all the recommended herbs, angelica, rue, pimpernel, gentian, juniper berries, and dozens more. She had a chestful of medicines which included Venice treacle, dragon water, and a bottle of cow-dung mixed with vinegar.

Amber was inclined to be amused by all these frantic preparations. An astrologer had told her that 1665 would be a lucky year for her, and her almanac did not warn her of plague or any other disease. Anyway it was true, for the most part, that only the poor were dying in their crowded dirty slums.

"Mrs. de Lacy's leaving town tomorrow," said Nan one morning as she brushed Amber's hair.

"Well, what if she is? Mrs. de Lacy's a chicken-hearted old simpleton who'd squeak at the sight of a mouse."

"She's not the only one, mam, you know that. Plenty of others are leaving too."

"The King isn't leaving, is he?" They had had this same argument every day for the past two weeks, and Amber was growing tired of it.

"No, but he's the King and couldn't catch the sickness if he tried. I tell you, mam, it's mighty dangerous to stay. Not five minutes' walk away—just at the top of Drury Lane—there's a house been shut up. I'm getting scared, mam! Lord, I don't want to die—and I shouldn't think you would either!"

Amber laughed. "Well, then, Nan—if it gets any worse we'll leave. But there's no use fretting your bowels to fiddle-strings." She had no intention at all of leaving before Bruce arrived.

On the 3rd of June the English and Dutch fleets engaged just off Lowestoft, and the sound of their guns carried back to London. They could be heard, very faintly, like swallows fluttering in a chimney.

By the 8th it was known that the English had been victorious—twenty-four Dutch ships had been sunk or captured and almost 10,000 Dutchmen killed or taken prisoner, while no more than 700 English seamen had been lost. The rejoicing was hysterical. Bonfires blazed along every street and a mob of merrymakers broke the French Ambassador's windows because there was no fire in front of his house. King Charles was the greatest king, the Duke of York the greatest admiral England had ever known—and everyone was eager to continue the fight, wipe out the Dutch and rule all the seas on earth.

The red crosses had now entered the gates of the City.

Nan came in a few days later with a bill-of-mortality in her hand. "Mam!" she cried. "Mam! There was 112 died last week of the sickness!"

Amber was entertaining Lord Buckhurst and Sir Charles Sedley who—along with the other gentlemen—had just returned from sea, all of them sunburnt heroes. Nan stopped on the threshold in surprise to find them there.

"Oh," she said. "I'm sorry, gentlemen." She made a curtsy.

"Never mind, Mrs. Nan. Damn me, Sedley! She's as pretty as ever, isn't she? But what's this? Sure *you're* not worried about the plague?"

"Oh, but I *am,* sir! I'm scared out of my wits! And all these other things they've got marked! I'll warrant you at least *half* of 'em died of the plague!" She began to read from the fresh-printed bill, for they were scarcely off the press before Nan had one. "Griping of the guts—3! Worms—5! Fits—2! How do we know those weren't all the plague too and not reported by the searcher because somebody greased 'em in the fist to give another cause of the death!"

Amber and the two men laughed but Nan was so excited she began to choke on the gold-piece she had in her mouth and ran out of the room. Only nine days later, however, the Queen and her ladies set out for Hampton Court, and the gentlemen intended to follow very shortly. Buckhurst and some of the others who had heard of her inheritance tried to persuade Amber to go along, but she refused.

Then at last, very much to Nan's relief, she began to make preparations for leaving town herself. She had the maids begin packing her clothes, and most of her jewellery she took to Shadrac Newbold, for she did not want to carry it about the countryside with her and had no idea as to where she would go. She found the street before his house crowded with carts and wagons and all the household in a turmoil.

"It's fortunate you came today, Mrs. Dangerfield," he told her. "I'm leaving town tomorrow myself. But I had assumed you were in the country with the rest of the family. They left at least a fortnight ago." The Dangerfields had a country home in Dorsetshire.

"I don't live at Dangerfield House any more. I think I'll take just a hundred pounds. That should be enough, don't you think?"

"I think so. The ways will be more crowded than ever with highwaymen. And the plague must be near spent by now. Excuse me a moment, madame."

While he was gone Amber sat fanning herself. The day was hot and she could feel her high-necked black-satin gown sticking to her skin; her silk stockings, moist with perspiration, clung tight to her legs Presently he returned and sat down to count out the pieces of gold and silver for her, stacking them in piles on the table while she watched him drowsily.

"That was a fine boy little Mrs. Jemima had, wasn't it?" he said conversationally.

Amber had not known that Jemima's child was born, but

now she said sarcastically: "So soon? She was only married last October."

He gave her a glance of surprise, and then smiled, shrugging his shoulders. "Well, yes, perhaps it is a little early. But you know how young people are—and a contract is as binding as the ceremony, they say."

He scooped the money into a purse and handed it to her as she got up to go. At the door she turned. "Any word of Lord Carlton?"

"Why, yes, as it happens, I have. Some ten days ago one of his ships put into port and a man came to tell me that his Lordship would be here soon. I've waited for him now longer than I'd intended, but I can't wait any longer. Perhaps he's heard of the sickness and decided not to come. Good-day, madame, and the best of luck to you."

"Thank you, sir. And to you."

Everyone was wishing everyone else good luck these days.

She drove immediately down to the wharves and sent Jeremiah to inquire for Lord Carlton. After half-an-hour or so he returned to say that he had found a man who had been on the ship which had come in and that he was expected at any time. The men who had manned the first ship were all waiting impatiently, for they wanted their shares of the venture.

Back home she saw that several carts piled with her own gilt leather trunks and boxes stood before the house, and Nan came running down the stairs to meet her. "A man died this morning only four doors up the street!" she cried. "I've got everything ready! We can leave this instant, mam! Can't we, please?"

Amber was annoyed: "No, we can't! I've just heard that Lord Carlton is expected in port any day and I'm not going till I've seen him! Then we'll all go together."

Suddenly Nan began to cry. "Oh, we're all going to catch it and die! I know we are! That's what happened to a family in Little Clement's Lane—every one of 'em died! Why can't you meet his Lordship in the country? Leave 'im a message!"

"No. He might not come at all then. Oh, Nan! For Heaven's sake! Stop your blubbering then. You can go tomorrow."

Nan set out very early the next morning with the baby, her nurses, Tansy, two of the maids, and Big John Waterman—who had come with them from Dangerfield House because he was in love with Nan. She was to go to Dunstable and wait there or, if there was plague in the town, to continue on until she found a safe place and sent back a message. Amber gave them a great many instructions and admonitions regarding the care of the baby and protection of her belongings and they rattled off, waving back at her. Then she sent Jeremiah back to the wharves—but Bruce had not come.

London was emptying rapidly now.

Trains of coaches and carts started out early every morning:

twenty-five hundred had died the week before. The sad faces of the plague prisoners—shut in with the sick—appeared at many windows, and bells tolled from almost every parish church in the city. People held their noses when they passed a cross-marked house. Some families were storing their cellars with great supplies of food and then sealing the house, stuffing every crack and keyhole, boarding the doors and windows to keep out the plague.

The weather continued hot and there was no fog; it had not rained for almost a month. The flowers down in the courtyard, roses and stocks and honeysuckle, were wilting and the meadows about the town were beginning to dry up and turn brown. Street vendors hawked cherries and apples and early pears, though oranges were scarce since the war had begun, and everyone who could afford it bought ice—cut off the lakes and rivers in the winter and stored underground packed in straw—to cool their wine and ale. They talked almost as much about the heat as they did about the war or the plague.

Amber was finally beginning to feel nervous herself. The long funeral processions, the red crosses on every hand, the tolling bells, the people passing with their noses buried in a pomander or bottle of scent had at last made her uneasy. She wanted to get away, but she was sure that if she left, Bruce would arrive the same day. And so she waited.

Tempest and Jeremiah were complaining about being kept so long in town and did not like being sent to the wharves. Jane—the serving-girl who had stayed with Amber—whined and wanted to go to her father's home in Kent and so Amber let her. When Nan had been gone four days she asked Tempest and Jeremiah to look for Lord Carlton once more and told them that if they found him she would give them each a guinea. But for the money, she knew, they would merely drive around or go to a tavern for a couple of hours and then come back. By noon they were home again. Lord Carlton had come in the night before and they had just seen him down at the wharves, unloading his ships.

END OF VOLUME ONE